Journey to Terreldor
A Tale of Growth and Adventure

Chris M. Hibbard

Journey to Terreldor
A Tale of Growth and Adventure
1st Print Edition

Terreldor Press
Houston, Texas
http://www.terreldor.com
publishing@terreldor.com
ISBN 10: 0-61564-382-5 (tpo.)
ISBN 978-0-61564-382-3
Published by Terreldor Press

Printed in the United States of America
First Edition

Acknowledgements

I would like to thank my wonderful wife and children for their patience, understanding, suggestions, interest in this series, and for their outstanding support.

Thank you.

Terreldor Press   http://Terreldor.com

Contents

Part V

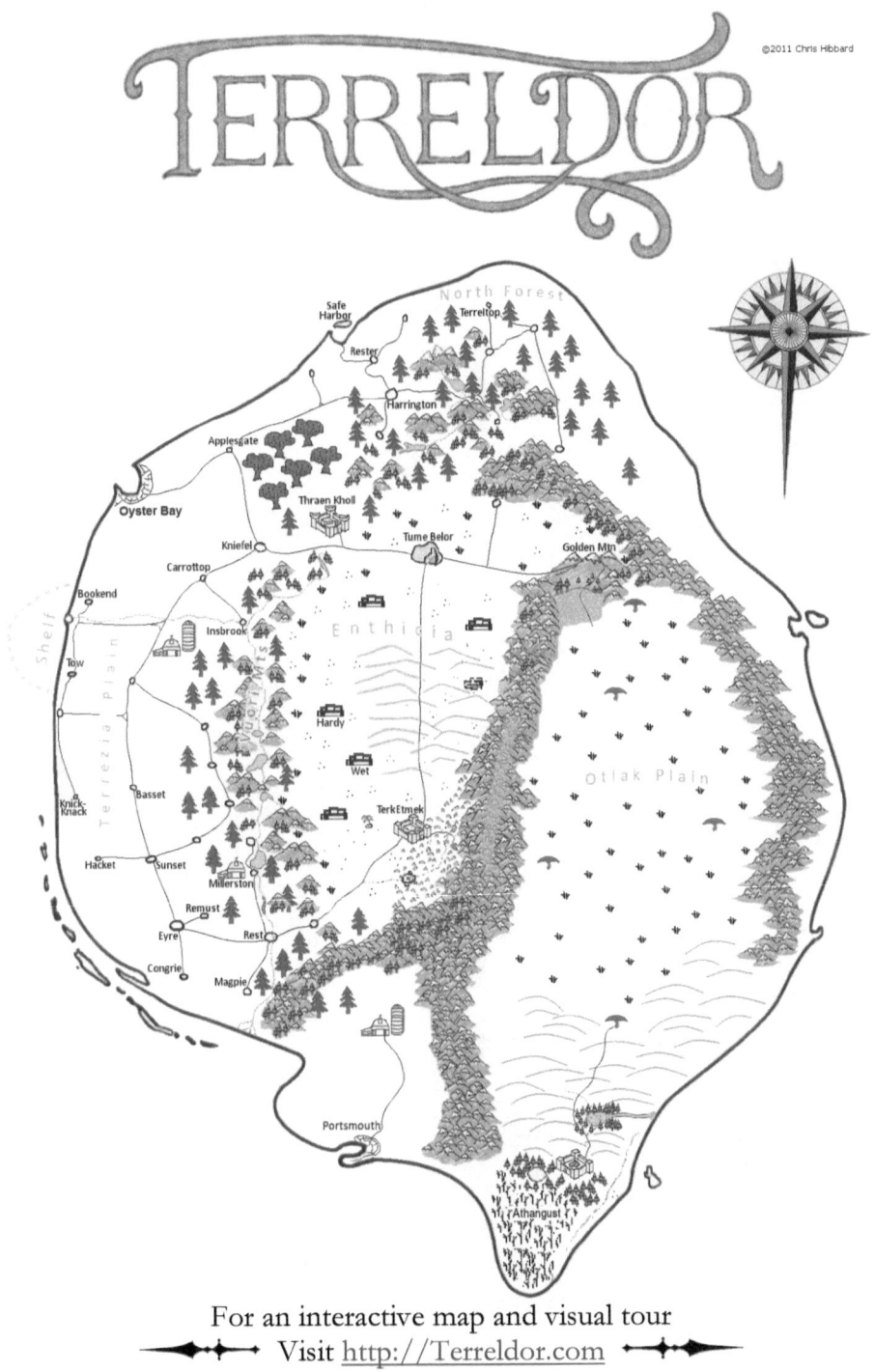

For an interactive map and visual tour
Visit http://Terreldor.com

Prologue

I've come to the point in my life when I've begun to think of my legacy. Now that I have few years left on this earth, I mean to tell a story I've never told before.

It began when my eldest son encouraged me to write down my memoirs...*My Life's Story*. It sounded so final—as if I'd never again do anything significant. No matter how likely that is, I didn't like the sound of it. Foolish you think? Well, pride has never been wise. I'll have to be content in accomplishing one last noteworthy act—preserving this story—and then hope it may inspire the hearts of others when I'm gone.

Until now, every attempt to arrange my memoirs felt like a sham. It was a falsehood by omission, but covered truth is still a lie. My most memorable experiences were each time abandoned. The tone and the message were clear and true, but incomplete nonetheless. My brother who's already gone knew these secrets, and it once seemed our father understood only too well, but that is another story altogether.

Instead of a dry record of my entire life, I'll tell of a single year—the missing year I've kept secret for so long. These remarkable months came to me when I was barely fifteen, and my brother a mere eighteen months older. How could I have survived it without him? Now I'm without him again in my old age—life plays its cruelest tricks on us more than once, it seems.

I should explain first, there's a reason I've never told this story; it's unbelievable. I don't mean it's extraordinary or remarkable—it's simply beyond belief. If there was ever a chance someone might have accepted this story, I would have shared it then. For so long I had to be content to take only the lessons I'd learned from these experiences and share them with whomever I could. It should have been enough, but it wasn't. This story is rich with the ingredients that shaped me into the man I became. The flavor of the story was lost when stripped down to the lessons it taught. Not that the lessons are unimportant—they are the lessons I lived by, and worked hard to pass on to my children. They are the same lessons I made sure were passed to *their* children, and lessons I taught to many others along the way.

After we first tried to share our experiences, it was clear further attempts would only serve to label us as insane or as liars. Later in life I didn't want this to detract from the training I'd passed on to others. If I'm completely honest with myself, I was worried I'd be labeled with some piteous dementia. By now, those whom I've taught have lived enough to test the steel of these lessons against their own experiences. No, I have nothing to lose now, and so I'll share my story.

Be patient, I ask of the reader. At the beginning of this story I was convinced I had lost my mind. I found myself in a strange land with no idea where I was or how I'd arrived there. Worse yet, I was confronted by enough impossibilities for even the most stable of us to question their minds. To go back to my earliest recollections would be as useful as describing the scrambled impressions of a half-forgotten nightmare. Instead, I'll begin my tale with the first day I can recall from morning to night—and in that order. I hope my account entertains you, but more than this, I hope it changes you—in fact, I expect it shall. Let me welcome you to the strange world where I spent the better part of my sixteenth year.

Part I

1.0 A Rude Awakening–Day Seven

I woke lying on my back and shivering. I saw rays of sunlight and patches of blue through pine boughs weighed down by snow. Though I was cold and stiff, I felt better than I had in days.

Why am I outside? I remembered and my heart sank. *It's only a dream,* I tried to convince myself. Yet that morning something seemed clearer, more real than the jumble of hallucinations and doubtful memories of the previous six days.

Focus, Mark, I told myself, *focus on today. The past will sort itself out soon enough.*

I couldn't have been more wrong.

Lying there, I heard the sounds of my older brother stirring. *At least we're together,* I thought. My mind reeled as I again failed to sort out the foggy memories of the day before I'd found him.

Without warning, my mind latched onto a more recent memory. I lay back on a bed of pine needles and let my mind sink into the dream I'd had just before waking. I saw it so clearly, and yet I fought its sense of reality.

My brother David shook me gently, holding a cold hand over my mouth. I sputtered before I realized he meant to keep me quiet.

"Shhhh," he whispered, removing his hand. "More trolls—they're coming toward us."

Trolls? My mind staggered as I fought growing panic. I held my breath and crawled on my knees to peer through prickly branches, trying not to disturb the snow weighing them down. I saw a nightmare's collection of ghouls marching toward us—monsters too horrible to consider real, and yet too fearsome to ignore. They were eerily familiar, as if I recognized them from a dream. My breath caught in my chest as they approached.

None of them were shorter than a man, and some were much taller. Where their skin showed, I saw some were covered in splotches of green, and the others had skin in tones of mud and sand. They were shaped like men, but short, squattish men who had no business being so tall. Their jaws seemed to project from their skulls, and they gave me the unlikely impression their teeth were trying to escape from their lips. I could imagine them capable of nothing but violence.

My panic didn't last long. Before they took a dozen steps, they veered left and headed downhill, away from us. Still and breathless, my mind shouted silent wishes after them. *Don't hear me breathing. Don't turn around.*

"That was the second group," David whispered. "I think they're on patrol."

"They're *organized?*" I didn't know what it might mean, but it certainly didn't sound good. "What *are* they?"

"*Trolls.*" David sounded a little shocked, but also scared. He added with a little contempt, "And yes, they're *organized*. Didn't you see the one with the outer vest? He was bossing the others around. I didn't understand what he said, but it sounded...*threatening.*"

I wondered how David had noticed more than I had. Could he have imagined it? Bitter fear settled in my stomach once again as I remembered the mental chaos of the previous days, and again I refused to deal with the surreal situation confronting me. I diverted my thoughts from the trolls. *How long have we been here?* I wondered. *How long have we been lost?* Three days by my own account, but no less than six by my brother's. My thoughts returned to the moment I woke.

"I had a dream—" I started.

"Me too," he interrupted. "We were running down the mountain. It was steep as the path we climbed the other day, and an avalanche was chasing us."

"How can an avalanche chase you?" I asked, frustrated he should interrupt me.

"Well, *it did*," he replied, in his older-brother-knows-best voice. "And there was a cloud of snow in front of it." "*And,*" he continued, after the briefest of pauses, "There was a long white tiger running in and out of the avalanche, looking for people to eat."

I thought on his words long enough to question their meaning, but thought better of interrupting him. He continued, confident I was listening intently.

"The avalanche was getting closer, and *I knew* the tiger would eat us. It jumped at us, but you—*no*, it was *me*—I punched it right in the nose."

"That's one dream I hope doesn't come true."

"Why not?" he asked, "After all, I scared it away."

"And what about the avalanche?"

"Well, I woke up before it got to us. That's *something*, isn't it?" He seemed bothered by my lack of gratitude for his imagined heroics. I sat down in the pine bedding beneath us, tired of kneeling. I hijacked the silence David left as he waited for my response.

"I had a dream too." I paused just long enough to make sure he wouldn't interrupt. "It was all dark, and terribly cold." I went on to tell him my dream. It felt like a nightmare, as if something horrible would snatch me up at any moment.

I was lost in a snowstorm, and bitterly cold. Low on the horizon behind me, the moon cast its dim light now and then, shining under the clouds trying to bury me with snow. I could make out ominous shapes around me, tall and threatening. I thought them to be giant ice boulders, or some kind of monoliths covered in ice and snow. Small crevasses caught at my boots, slowing me. The wind howled and stung at my face. The ground rose and fell, sometimes giving way beneath me. The crusted snow shoved at my pantlegs and scraped my shins raw. Then I felt a hot pain in my face, much sharper than the wind.

"That's all I can remember of it," I told him, with a hand on my cheek and my eyes still cast downward, looking for the forgotten ending to my dream. I looked up to David, wondering why he hadn't spoken yet.

"Are you serious?" His face tried to hide concern when he finally spoke—he was *worried* for me.

"Of course I'm serious. Why?"

"That's not a dream—it's what happened *last night*." He paused, but my face showed no reaction. "It was too cold to stop, and we had no place to rest. Don't you remember?" I shook my head, wishing my memories would start acting responsibly. "You were in front of me, and you walked right into these trees," he continued, grabbing a branch beside him. "*That's* what stung your face."

Looking around, I knew he was right. The hazy memories flooded back. I'd been surprised how tightly together the bushy pines had grown. After scraping our way into the cluster, we found no snow on the ground—the branches overhead had grown tightly together. We'd called it a *pine lodge*, as we pawed numbly to fish a little bread from our packs. The wind hardly reached us in the midst of those tightly woven branches. It was a comfort we'd paid for dearly with the scrapes and tiny cuts on our faces, and at our wrists between our mittens and jackets.

"I remember," I answered solemnly. Everything seemed to point back to the mystery of our previous days. It is disturbing indeed, not to know where you are, *or* how you got there. Each of our memories seemed to disagree with the next. Trolls were only the latest additions to our list of impossible memories; we'd seen much stranger already. I put them out of mind to coax some feeling of sanity to return to me. Once again, I set my mind on the present and told my brother we'd better get started. David peered out from our cozy pine nest.

"I guess it's safe—there's nothing as far as I can see in either direction."

When we'd wrestled free of the prickly branches, we looked back down the long winding path we'd taken from the foot of the mountain the previous day. Other than a well-packed trail in the snow, there was little else to see. It wound between tall boulders until it disappeared on its way down the mountain behind us. Before us, the ground rose in all directions, less so in the way of the fresh tracks. We followed the trolls' footprints up the gently sloping valley ahead. It was a mountain pass, and we hoped to get down the other side before we froze.

We kept our eyes on the trail in both directions, looking for any movement.

"Why do you think we didn't see any trolls yesterday," David started, "then saw two groups just when the trail wasn't so steep anymore?"

"How should I know? Maybe there are avalanches where it's steeper, and they want to stay clear of them."

"I'm glad there weren't any yesterday then," David chuckled, "Half the time, I felt like I was scaling a wall."

As we walked, I wondered just how lucky we'd been. We didn't see sign of avalanches on our way, but I doubt we would've recognized the signs if we had.

We marched through the snow with a goal set before us, but my thoughts wandered when I tried to recall what it was. My mind moved sluggishly when I called on it for memories of the past few days.

We were tired and hungry. Though I was alert at first, I soon fell into the slow rhythm of a long march—one I hoped wasn't too long for us to survive. David may have kept watch along the worn trail as we were funneled up the climbing valley, but I'd given up. I noticed as the valley grew steeper uphill, the snowy mountaintops flanking us climbed even higher.

David mentioned we wouldn't last another night out in the snow, and I knew he was right. We needed shelter or we would freeze. When he mentioned the *Winter Palace*, I shook my head to wipe away the thoughts his words brought. Again I concentrated on the path in front of us.

Despite my best efforts, my mind wandered as we plodded onward. I felt like I was dreaming. The things I realized seemed to hold no consequence for me. The slow rhythm of our trek began to play with my sense of balance. The bright sunlight reflected off the snow before us and washed all detail from the valley trail. Soon I could not discern forward motion, only the up and down of my own stride. With no conscious thoughts, my mind slipped into a strange daydream and I imagined myself on a raft, rocking on a calm ocean.

I wondered absently if I was remembering another dream, but it didn't match how I felt. It seemed more like recalling a dream I'd had *within* a dream, if such a thing were possible. Then a sudden revelation: it was a dream I'd had two nights ago, after a very long day. I remembered the dream first, and then, everything we'd done the day *before* the dream.

"David," I started, "what do you remember about the day before yesterday?"

When he didn't answer immediately, I knew he didn't trust his memory any more than I trusted my own. This shouldn't have made me feel better, but it did. When he spoke, his voice was cautious.

"We hiked up the mountain. We stopped just short of the snowline, and slept under a thick mat of moss."

It wasn't like him to give such a frank answer. My memories began to fall into place for a blessed moment. The day I'd just recalled was *three* days ago. I'd forgotten a whole day, and if David hadn't brought it up, I never would have known.

"All right, then what happened the day before *that*?" I asked. He sighed heavily before answering.

"We hiked all day across the dry, grassy plain. What's it called...Otlak? We thought we'd die of thirst, remember?"

It wasn't *at all* how I'd remembered it. I recognized the plain he mentioned, but I knew we hadn't crossed it on our own. I wondered if he'd edited out all the unbelievable parts. His version was easier to accept, but my memory seemed too real to ignore. Cautiously, David asked me to tell him everything I remembered from that day, and I sorted out the memories as best I could. It felt good to know something of our past for certain—even something as simple as *we crossed a large plain three days ago.* I would have to wait longer still, to discover it was on our fourth day since we'd arrived in this strange land, when we made our crossing.

I looked up at my brother with a confused look on my face. He caught my gaze, and stopped for a moment.

"Mark," he began, in an authoritative tone, "you're making this too hard. Yesterday we hiked up the mountain. The day before, we crossed the grassy plain. The day before *that,* you fell in the swamp..." David started walking as he spoke, and I followed, lost to his words.

When he finished his tirade, I was ready to counter him. We argued quietly as we hiked through the snow. While I welcomed the distraction, my brother only grew angrier.

"Just tell it how *you* remember it then," he challenged. So, as detailed possible, I recounted for him what we came to call our *third day in.*

1.1 Day Three: Treacherous Swamp

My third day in Terreldor began with my brother shaking me, violently tearing me from peaceful sleep.

"*Hurry up*," he started, "I want to talk to the *duke* again before we leave."

I sat on the edge of the simple wooden cot I'd slept on. I fought the urge again, to sort between recent memory and dreams. Already there were things I remembered, and yet didn't comprehend.

A man who called himself a *duke* owned the shack where we'd slept. He'd given us provisions and backpacks, drawn us a map, told us to make use of his guest cabin, and sent us on our way. *Who was he? Why did he help us?* David seemed to remember so much more than I did.

Before we left the tiny cottage, we opened our packs. We searched through the items our mysterious benefactor had packed in them the previous night. *Why don't we know what's in them already?* I asked myself. *Did I know last night, but forgot already?*

Each of our packs held a light coat, neither of them a good fit. I also found a pair of mittens, a long coil of rope, old leather boots—which fit surprisingly well, a thick pair of socks, a canteen, a wool blanket, and several loaves of hard bread, wrapped in waxed paper. David's pack also held a tarp and flint. We put the light jackets over the ones we already wore and set out.

Looking back on the weathered cabin, it was a wonder it didn't collapse on us. Its walls were made of weathered planks, green with rot near the ground. The sagging roof was covered with earth, topped with a carpet of grass and moss. The sun was low but bright, and the air was cold but hopeful, like an early morning in spring.

Beyond the shack, I could make out an overgrown orchard, surrounded on two sides by a high stone wall. A large mansion lay beyond that, and it seemed familiar to me. I had only the faintest memory of being inside it the night before. Turning directly opposite the shack, I faced a large door in the stone wall. I tried its latch, wondering if it was locked. It wasn't, but the door was so heavy I could barely move it. Beyond the gate lay a green pasture, dotted with low-sprawling trees. A trail led from the gate through the field.

"Where are you going?" my brother asked. "Are you so eager to get home, you don't have time to ask for better directions? All we have are some scratchings on an old page."

I remembered the map the old man had drawn for us—it was no work of art. Still, I didn't relish going back into the duke's manor.

"What will you ask him?" I replied, trying to hide my resistance.

"*Everything*," David replied, excitedly. "Where are we? How did we get here? What's wrong with our memories?"

I thought of what answers we might find, and I didn't reply. I had a paranoid idea someone was *doing this* to us. Had we been drugged, or part of some sinister experiment? These ideas felt so possible—even likely—though they were entirely wrong. Nonetheless, I was suspicious of anyone we met, and knew I would remain so until my head was clear once again. My brother must have read my expression and shared my thoughts.

"I see your point," he said with a sigh. He stepped past me and added, "We might as well get on our way."

He unlatched the gate and pried it open enough for the two of us to squeeze past it. The door closed on its own weight and latched shut. I noticed there was no handle or latch on the outside of the gate; we were locked out.

David pulled the freshly drawn map from his pack and showed it to me. My finger traced the dotted line of a trail from the cabin to a large empty area marked *Otlak Plain*. There the dotted line stopped, only to start again at the opposite end of the plain. From there, it continued up a long mountain trail, then ended at the words *mountain pass*, near the northern end of a long mountain range.

As we hiked along the trail, I hoped the sun would soon warm us. It grew sparse in parts, but every fifty paces or so, we found a square stone marker. The sky was clear, but the air was cold enough to show our breath in foggy puffs. The sun was slowly rising over the field and trees to our right.

While the sun was still low in the sky, we came to a fork in the trail, just as the map showed. There was no sign to show us which way to go. The path to the right was level and led into a dense forest. The other path led up a steep grassy hill, then turned toward the forest before disappearing from sight. The map showed both paths joining again after what we thought to be a few hours' walk. On the map, there were a few trees drawn clumsily around the path to the right, which we took to represent the forest ahead of us. There appeared to be a few words scribbled near the trees, but neither of us could make out a single letter of it. I found myself wishing we'd gotten more information from our strange host before leaving. At the time, I could hardly recall meeting him.

The sun had warmed us enough to remove our new, ill-fitting jackets, and even the warmer coats we wore under them. Realizing the map offered no help, we chose the more shaded path into the dense woods.

The trees were soon dense enough to tame the sunlight as it found its way through their leaves. What light we saw, was tinted green by the tall canopy above us. It was a fine day and the forest path was scenic and relaxing. The trail wound around a still, clear pond. We could hear frogs croaking and the buzz of many insects, but none bit us. Farther on, the trail became muddy. The pond began to look more like a bog, and in several places, it swallowed the trail entirely. At one point, the trail disappeared into the swamp for a long way. We were able to pass by hopping between low stumps, though they led us far from where we guessed our path led, under stagnant water.

Finally, the trail disappeared completely; no markers could be found. We were able to press on for a short while, though I nearly drenched myself when I landed with one foot on a stump and the other in the swamp. My foot sunk into the thick murk well past my knee, and still didn't touch bottom.

Soon we were far from solid ground, surrounded by dark water with no way around. We looked into the distance for a hint of the trail, but found none. The swamp flowed slowly past us, from left to right. There was no trace of the clean pond we'd first seen—only a foul-smelling bog of brackish water. I turned to David, hoping he wanted to turn back. He was looking to our left, into the swampy forest where the trail probably led.

"Should we go back?" I asked.

"It's getting late, and I want to get out of this forest while there's still daylight. See how dark it is over there?"

He pointed in the direction the swamp water seemed to flow from—the darkest part of the forest we'd seen yet. To our right, the water seemed to funnel into a large stream, maybe forty feet wide. Farther down, the trees were less dense, and I saw the hint of sunlight falling on a grassy hill. The distant rays looked warm and welcoming, but I had no intention of swimming through the smelly murk. The thought of sleeping outdoors in wet clothes worried me. In the end, we had little choice. David finalized the decision by jumping right into the swamp, holding his jackets and knapsack high over his head. He sunk right up to his waist. His face grew sour, as if he'd tasted spoiled milk.

"It's cold—and smells *foul*," he complained.

"I know that much," I replied. "Couldn't you tell before you jumped in?"

He only smiled back. I followed his example, and though it was frigid, I was shocked even more by the odor, far worse then I'd expected. David flashed a knowing smile my way, and led the way toward the far bank of the stream.

Soon we were out of the darkest part of the forest, and the water began to clear—both in appearance and odor. Once again we could see patches of blue sky overhead. The stream's current was gentle, and we easily waded toward its far side, aiming for the grassy hill. As the stream widened into a calm pond, an unexpected motion stole my attention. Something very large shifted beneath the surface, though I hoped it was only a beam of light falling through the gently swaying canopy above us. Before I could be sure, David let out a shout. When I turned toward him, his face had gone pale. I followed his gaze to the clearer water near the shore.

"*David*," I whispered, pointing where I last saw motion.

"Probably just a sunken log," he replied, though he didn't sound at all convincing.

My insides froze as I watched another massive shape turn toward me. I stood still as stone, by no effort of my own. The dark shape slid right by me, brushing my leg. *It's only a log*, I cried inwardly, but I did not convince myself. Time crawled by as I stood my ground. It didn't topple me, but my leg burned with hot pain as it slid by me. Without thinking, I reached down to feel my leg—it stung horribly. I brought my hand to my eyes and found pond scum, spotted with blood.

"*David*," I yelled, "It *cut* me."

He looked from my hand to my face, and his eyes grew wide with fear. I jumped nearly out of the water, and thrashed my way toward the shore. I might have been able to clear the distance faster by swimming, but the idea of being submerged in that water was unthinkable. Not for the first time, I nearly dropped my gear into the water.

David was already ahead of me. I thrashed wildly in the water, still a few yards from shore, when David leapt onto the bank and rolled over, onto the muddy sand. I threw my gear toward him, but he let it fall into the water at his feet. He raised his hand, pointing at me, his mouth gaping wide.

"It's *coming*," he shouted when he found his voice. Too horrified to look, I struggled even more frantically. David ran farther up the bank and grabbed a large branch lying in the mud. He jumped into the water and threw it to me, yelling all the while. I looked up just before it would have hit me in the face. David screamed, "*Now!*"

Catching the branch mid-air, I turned, swinging it with all my might. Nothing could have prepared me for what I saw.

It was the foulest, most frightening thing I'd ever heard of, in truth or fiction. It was smooth and slippery-looking, and black as night. It had dead eyes, which glowed yellow, above a gaping mouth. By all appearance, the creature seemed to be *nothing but mouth*. It had thin, hard white lips, almost like they were made of bone. Black, wiry tentacles hung thick as cables below its mouth. Its gaping jaws held a wide row of teeth on top and bottom, closing to fasten around my body. Its stiff black tongue stuck straight out at me.

My arms moved as through molasses, and my ears heard only the dull thrum of terror. I swung the thick branch into its gaping mouth, striking it in the teeth with every ounce of strength I could muster.

By my next recollection, I was underwater and out of breath. The beast had bitten down on the branch, saving me for the moment. Mouth closed, it rammed me, knocking me over and sending me sprawling. The beast thrashed wildly, pulling me along by the branch I still clung to. I was lifted out of the water and slammed back down into it. Then I was free, floating near the bank with the branch in my hands. David pulled me over the bank and dragged me from the shallow water. I jumped back up, screaming like a madman and shaking as if to fling the panic from me. David stepped back with a strange look in his eye. I still held the branch, and probably seemed to him ready to swing again.

"*Put down the branch*—you're safe now."

When I finally understood, I dropped the branch—but not before running far from the shore. David called after me.

"Where are you going?"

"*Come on*," I yelled, "before it jumps out of the water and swallows you whole!"

"What are you talking about?"

I searched David's expression, standing there so calmly on the bank. Then slowly, I walked cautiously back to him.

"How do you know it won't come after us?" I whispered.

"Since when do catfish swim on land?" David's face turned serious as he added, "Are you all right?"

Catfish? I thought. *I was attacked by a giant sea monster, and he's talking about catfish?*

It took a while before I was convinced. He picked up a twig and threw it far into the water, and one of several dark shapes jumped to grab it. I'd nearly been eaten by the largest catfish I'd even seen. Each of them was larger than the two of us together. David laughed.

"What did you *think* they were, aliens?"

It didn't seem humorous to me. Head-on, the giant catfish looked like a giant flying mouth with only eyes on top and tentacles below. Looking down at the branch, I saw something jagged near its end—the short root of a long tooth. I wiggled it back and forth and freed it from the wood. It felt almost like a dagger in my hand. I felt my leg where it stung from the water and mud, still trickling blood. It might have given me a gash and nearly swallowed me, but I was leaving with its tooth as a souvenir, and a story I wouldn't soon forget. I showed it to David and he congratulated me on my strange trophy.

We climbed back farther from the bank and sat in the sunlit grass, facing the murky stream. To our back was a steep grassy hillside, with only blue sky above. I rolled up my pantleg and David poured some water from his canteen onto my cut, washing away the mud and slime. Wincing, I squeezed skin around the cut to bleed it clean. David pulled his extra pair of socks from his dry pack and tied one around my leg to keep the cut clean and dry. I pulled the bread from my pack, hoping the wax paper it was rolled in might have saved it. Half of it was ruined. The other half went into David's pack.

We talked about following the water as it flowed away from the swamp. The trees were much thinner in this direction than in the swamp, but still not enough to give us a clear view of what lay farther downstream. Instead, we decided to try and find the trail we'd lost. If the strange map was trustworthy, we'd find it by angling up the hill where it turned to flank the swampy forest.

We rested only long enough to repack our knapsacks. The sunlight and the climb warmed us as we started up the steep hillside. It was so steep, it obscured all else from view as we gazed ahead. It had no features at all, other than the tall grass covering it. We soon realized it was much farther to the top than we could have guessed. Several times we were certain the crest was just ahead of us, only to find the slope of the hill grew less steep.

Since leaving the swamp, we'd climbed mostly northwest, with the sun on our backs. Eventually, we approached the top of the hill and were able to see what lay past it. The sun was almost setting over tall mountains in the distance before us, with only grassy foothills between us. Long evening rays shone past us, over uninterrupted ocean to the east; we were finally high enough to see past the dark forest we'd gladly left behind. We could see no beach nor any trace of a coast, as the forest to the south and east, and swelling hills to the northeast hid it from view. Further north and northwest, a wide expanse of grassland and hills lie ahead of us, dotted with wide-growing oaks.

We could see no sign of the trail ahead, and so we continued in the direction we thought we were most likely to find it. It was the same direction, more or less, as the closest tree in our view. The sprawling oak seemed to grow before our eyes as we neared it. It was midevening before we reached the massive tree. To say it was huge doesn't capture its size; many of its limbs would have made sizeable trees on their own. They bent low, parallel to the ground, some touching the ground again and again, like a weighed-down bird, failing to take flight. It seemed more like a *tree colony* than a single oak, and we stopped to wander under its large boughs.

"We'd better set camp for the night," David finally suggested. "Let's hang our wet clothes to dry."

I wrung out the contents of my pack, and hung each of them from snags on the low branches, along with my own two jackets. David lent me one of his in the meanwhile. He only had to worry about his wet socks, shoes and pants. He wore his blanket wrapped around his waist while he hung his own wet clothes.

We gathered dead sticks and fallen branches until nearly dark. By then, my hanging clothes were dry enough to wear. I pulled them on, shivering, and wrapped my blanket around me. Still shaking, I hung the rest of the wet items I'd been wearing, but too cold to take off earlier. We stretched the tarp from David's pack over a low branch broken off at its end. We found stones to weigh the corners of the tarp down for the night. It wasn't quite a tent, but it was all we had.

Near the end of the limb, we used a flint on the driest leaves we could find and started a fire—something much harder than we'd expected. By the time we got the fire built enough to enjoy it, we were too tired to stay awake. We sat in front of it long enough to feel a little warmer than was comfortable, then scattered the burning coals and scooped dirt over the largest of them. As fast as we worked, I was still cold by the time I dove under the tarp. I wore every spare piece of dry clothing we had, and still wished for more. We lay under the hung tarp, listening to wet clothes dripping nearby.

As we lay there half-asleep, we began to remember things from the day before. We talked about them on our way to sleep, consciousness ebbing quickly. I wasn't bothered by the impossibility of our memories just then.

"Last night in the cabin," I mumbled, "I was so afraid the hill troll would come back—and take his revenge on us for robbing him."

"But we didn't *rob* him," David objected lazily, "all that stuff was stolen."

"I doubt he saw it that way."

David went on, "I hope he tripped on a log and broke his leg." His words were cruel, and my mind floated back to the kind old man who'd done so much to help us.

"The duke was so forgiving," I said. "He was willing to let the troll rob him and cause him harm just to give him the *chance* to do right…again and again."

"I think he should set a trap and do away with him once and for all," he replied. He lifted his head from his sack and turned toward me, barely lucid. "Did you see the orchard and gardens? There were places where the plants and trees were broken and trampled. I bet the troll did it, and the duke didn't even mind."

"Oh, I think he minds," I answered, "But it hurts him more, when he expects the troll to change and he doesn't." The old man's image came once again to my mind. "He looked like he could use some extra food, don't you think?"

"Yeah," David replied, "and his friend too. I wish we could help them somehow."

"Me too," I said, and fell directly asleep.

I passed the fine line of consciousness, remembering the way the duke treated the troll, and the way the troll treated the duke. I wanted to understand it better, but I couldn't yet fathom their relationship.

As I completed my recounting, I saw my brother's expression was anything but agreeable.

"*That's* not the day we crossed the plains," David hissed in a stage whisper.

His words pulled me from my memories, into the frigid present. My feet hurt, and I could hardly feel my toes. The sifting noise of the light powder we'd tread over had turned into the *crunch, crunch* of crusted snow.

"It isn't?"

"*No,* it's the day *before.* Don't you remember *crossing* the plains?" he asked.

His last words brought a flood of memories to me. *Yes, of course,* I thought. I'd completely missed the day I'd *tried* to recall, and described instead the previous day—our third in Terreldor. Once again, I'd asked my mind for one memory, and it returned another. I went through these newer memories, tasting each one cautiously, as I might sip milk I suspected had gone sour.

"What did you say before, about the *Winter Palace*?" I asked. I dared to recall one of the stranger memories of our past few days. David answered, but I was already lost in thought, recalling *day number four* in this strange world. When he noticed my empty gaze, he yielded. "*Fine.* You tell it to me, just as you remember it."

I did, happy for the chance to have him confirm any details at all.

1.2 Day Four: The Antelope King

Even though we'd had only a tarp over our heads, I'd enjoyed a fairly restful night's sleep. Waking was a rude interruption. I woke *on our fourth day in Terreldor* at dawn, shivering. When I found I couldn't fall back asleep, I got up and changed clothes yet again. The clothes I wore were dry, but terribly cold—much colder than they'd been the previous morning.

I woke David and got my pack ready. He dressed while I ate some of our bread, then he packed his things as I waited.

David mentioned his worries of finding a safe place to sleep that night. I tried to ignore him, finding my own worries on the subject quite enough. If temperatures continued to drop as we climbed, it would grow colder yet on our way to the Winter Palace, where the duke had implied we might find help on our way home.

When we finally got moving, we angled further back westward, hoping above all to find the trail we'd lost in the swamp. Before long, we found a squared stone post, this time with iron rings bolted to it; a sure sign of the trail. When we looked down another grassy hillside below us, we saw several, showing the trail switched back and forth on its way up the steep hill. Though I had little reason to, I felt much better, finding our way along the path on our crude map.

When the morning began to warm us, we crossed a small stream. It seemed a waste for its clean water to be lost in the murky swamp below us. We tasted the water, then drank and filled our canteens. As they were empty, we had little choice.

The trail curved northward and continued to climb. Just over a small rise, we found our path was joined by another. Looking far down the other path, we saw it was the higher trail we chose not to take. We could see all the way down to the fork we'd passed the day before. Farther in the same direction, we saw the duke's manor. It seemed far too close, for all the trouble we'd seen since leaving it. David realized what I had; the higher path looked simple and easy, and he said as much.

I wasn't convinced. Who knew what dangers might lurk along the other trail, unseen from our distant view? The giant catfish might have been the lesser threat.

The trail ahead wound over hill after hill, each steeper than the last. The view below us grew wider as we climbed. Finally, I could see much of the island's east coast. My ears popped as we climbed. Hiking up the steep terrain was a lot of work, and soon we packed our ill-fitting outer coats into our canvas sacks, and slung them once again over our shoulders.

When it seemed the hills might go on forever, we found ourselves at the top of the last one. As we approached its peak, the horizon jumped away from us, revealing spacious plains and purple-tinged mountains far in the distance. The grass shifted almost immediately, where two species fought for space. The grass of the plain was a duller shade, and failed to reach our knees.

There was one last stone marker, nearly at the border of the two types of grass. We hiked in growing half-circles, in all directions leading onto the plain, but found no sign of the trail or any further markers. The map showed no trail there—only a large blank area we understood to be the plain before us. On the far side, the dotted line of the trail resumed, leading us over a carefully drawn pass, curiously labeled *Golden Mountain*. It seemed more a valley *between* two mountains, but we would have to wait for any explanation.

We argued for a while about the direction we would take. We were more cautions after our last attempt to interpret the map, when we chose the swamp path.

There was a tall wide tree in the distance. With nothing else to aim for, we eventually headed toward it. As we approached, David saw a pack of animals approaching from the opposite direction, and pointed them out.

"What are they?" I asked him.

"I think they're antelopes."

They *did* look like antelopes—just like ones we'd seen at the zoo. They were a little stouter, which made them seem smaller. The tree seemed to grow no closer to us as we walked toward it, and I mentioned the illusion.

"It must be a lot taller than it looks," David offered. I remembered the giant oak we'd left, only hours ago.

"The antelopes, too," I added thoughtfully.

The closer we walked, the larger I realized the tree and the antelopes were. I'd never heard of antelopes attacking people, but their unexpected size imposed more fear than anything else.

"Let's go back," I suggested, quietly.

"Go back *where?*"

I hurried to catch up to him and tugged on his shoulder.

"*Anywhere.* Those aren't antelopes. They're *huge.*"

"Never mind their size; they're *plant eaters.* They have a natural fear of us. Besides, I want to see them up close." He added with an air of indifference, "*You* can wait here, if you like."

I questioned his assertion any herbivore should fear us, but held my tongue. David left his pack beside me, and crawled army-style through the grass ahead. I felt exposed, standing alone in the grassland, so I lay down and tried to disappear completely. Before long, I left my pack near my brother's, and crawled after him.

I couldn't see him yet, though the grass wasn't tall enough to hide us completely. His trail of bent stalks wasn't hard to follow. After crawling a dozen yards, I heard a deafening bellow. At first, I thought I might jump straight into the air, but by the time the sound trailed off to silence, I found myself flat on my belly, holding my breath. I forced my head up and slithered forward in search of David. He hugged the earth so well, I nearly crawled right over him. Again the strange noise sounded, not more than a few feet in front of us.

I laid flat and covered my ears with my hands, unable to move. When the sound ended, I held my breath and dared to look up. Would the giant beast trample us? I tugged at David's pantleg.

I watched my brother as his gaze slowly followed the sound until he was staring up at the giant antelope's throat, which was nearly on top of him. He crawled backward until he was beside me, but stopped when a huge trunk of a leg pounded the ground before us. The third time the animal sounded was quieter than before, though not as quiet as I wished.

My fear faded enough to allow me to notice something; there was a rhythm to the animal's cry. The last time he sounded, it nearly seemed like separate *words*. By his fourth and final bellow, I had enough sense to listen.

"Who goes there? Who dares *approach the king?*" The words had been there all along. Apparently, David also noticed.

"We only want to pass," David replied. "Can you tell us the way to Golden Mountain?"

"Let them come," said a dark voice, far behind the threatening creature standing over us.

"Stand and follow," the closer beast rumbled, as he and another flanked us. They began to move forward, but stopped and turned back when we didn't move. I wouldn't say they *glared at us*, though they remained motionless, eyes fixed. We jumped to our feet and followed.

The herd before us opened a path to the largest of them all, resting in the shade of the massive tree. As we neared him, I saw he was nearly as tall as we were, while still lying in the grass. Amazed and fearful, I found curiosity enough to steal glances at the strange, gnarled trunk beside him. As two antelopes beside us came to a halt, I saw the king's mane had gold and jewels braided into it. They were strangely familiar to me.

"Look," I whispered to David as I recognized them, "just like the jewels from the hill troll." I silently wished *something* sane would happen soon. For a moment I mentally searched through my pack, wondering if it truly held proof of yet another impossible memory. If my memory was correct, it did: a finely woven web of gold chain and jewels—taken from the troll we'd encountered when we first entered the duke's manor.

David nodded, but remained silent. Two more antelopes dropped our packs beside us, startling us from behind. The guards we'd followed made a show of reaching one leg out straight toward the seated antelope, and bending the other. They lowered their heads until their horns touched the ground. One growled, "Hail to the *King of Otlak Plain.*"

An awkward silence hung about us and threatened to remain indefinitely. I felt the eyes of the entire herd burning into the back of my head. I looked to David, but he was plainly just as confused. Nervously, I bent one leg and set my opposite knee on the ground. David did the same.

"What do you ask of us, little men?" the antelope king asked in his strange voice. Wary of the uneasy silence between us, I spoke first.

"We only want to learn the way to Golden Mountain. We lost the path."

"You cannot pass Otlak Plain." He declared. David decided to speak up.

"Why not?" I glared at him. Many of the beasts stirred and made low noises.

"You may die trying if you like. Men can no longer pass the plain; you will die of thirst before you get halfway."

"But we have canteens," I offered. I opened my pack to show him.

"You couldn't carry enough water to last your journey—not since the *drinking trees* were lost." I sensed the beasts all around us stirring once again, more so than previously. "Forgive my subjects. They still hold anger for *another* two-legged people."

I returned my canteen and saw the jewels in my pack. I sighed, realizing I'd been hoping the memory was false. I held out the braided gold and jewels.

"Are these yours...uh, *sir?*"

Surprised sounds erupted from the herd. A strange murmur circulated, more excitedly than the angry noises they'd made before.

"How did you get them?" bellowed one.

"We were robbed by a brown troll—a real bully," I offered. I realized too late, the term *bully* might have a different meaning to a people who are half of them *bulls*. I stopped a moment when I realized I accepted these strange animals as *people*. They weren't *human*, but they were self-aware, and this somehow made them *people* in my mind.

"We stood up to the troll," I started again, "and took our belongings back. We took all he had, certain it was *all* stolen from *someone*. Some things we returned to the duke."

A short grunt came from the antelope king, and it sounded almost musical.

"I have an old friend who is a *duke*, far down the slopes you climbed. When I was younger, I carried him across this, our *Otlak Plain*. The treasure you hold is mine, lost in an old battle, against an army of savage trolls." I held it out toward him.

"Take it then. We only meant to return it to its owner." At this, the entire herd stirred even louder.

"Would you return it to my mane?" he asked.

It sounded like an odd request, with all the deference and reverence the others obviously held for him. Then I realized with embarrassment, hands were needed for this work.

"I would be proud to return it to you." It sounded odd even as I said it, but they seemed so serious, I felt the urge to mimic them.

I walked up to the massive beast, and leaned against his neck to reach his mane. I braided the jewelry as best as I could into his coarse hair, then noticed the jewelry he already wore had tiny clips on it. I attached loops of the braided gold into these clips. When I was sure it would not easily be removed, I retreated to where David still kneeled. When I stepped back, one of the guards inspected my work. He let out a soft bellow, which sounded approving, and the king thanked me.

"Share water with us. You must fill your canteens." He tossed his head in the direction of another antelope standing beside the tree, near a strange knot protruding from the wide, gnarled trunk. Curious, we walked nearer. The antelope bent low and *bit* the stubby knot. To our surprise, water began to flow from it. At first, I hesitated. After all, it was water from a *tree*, and it had just been bitten by a strange animal. I looked to David, who glared at me, and then stared at the dripping knot. I took a sip. It was cool and clear, and had none of the sappy flavor I'd expected.

I filled my canteen just as it dribbled to a stop. An antelope leaned forward, but David stepped in quickly and hit the knot with his canteen. He may not have thought it poisonous, but by the look he gave, I knew he didn't want to risk tasting antelope saliva. The knot started flowing again, and David drank and filled his canteen. We stepped away, and other antelopes stepped up to the knot and began to drink.

"How does it do that?" I asked in near-disbelief.

The king answered, "The drinking trees are a gift to our people. Their roots run deep. They drink from the deep and share their water with us. The plains were once dotted with these trees, and there was water enough for everyone. The trolls brought a curse on us when they killed our trees. This is why men and trolls can no longer pass the plains."

The herd murmured and grunted. They didn't seem as amiable as when I'd first returned the braided gold and jewels.

"I offer you safe and swift passage across the plains," the king went on, "to the foot of Golden Mountain. My son, the prince will carry you. Two of my guards will take you to him."

The king seemed pleased with us, even if the rest of his herd didn't. We quickly accepted his offer. When two antelopes kneeled before us, we took it as our cue to leave. Without hesitation, we climbed onto their backs.

They rose slowly, began to walk, and finally, to trot. Soon they were running at a terrifying speed. We flew over the plains and I held on for fear of death. David seemed to enjoy our ride as he bobbed up and down, over the grassy plain.

Perhaps two hours after we left, we came across another herd. This one was mostly females. They were a little smaller and thinner, and their long horns were missing.

The guards walked up to the largest male and knelt. David and I took it as our cue, and climbed down from them. There was another awkward silence. I felt foolish when I turned to see the guards—they were still kneeling. We knelt again, just as we had before, and one of the guards spoke.

"Prince, your father sends us to you."

"What word does he send?"

"Blessings—and a message."

"And what is his message?" Their speech seemed painfully slow to my ears. I faked patience as best I could.

"The king has promised safe and swift passage across the plain for these two *men*," one guard said gruffly.

The other added, perhaps hopefully, "They have returned to us a treasure. They defeated a brown troll and regained your father's braids."

The prince cocked his head to one side, and showed me an expression I guessed was either surprise or suspicion. He turned back to the guard who had spoken.

"Thank you. You will take up my charge until I return." He walked away from the herd and called back, "With *me,* little men, and I will carry you."

Will they all call us little? I wondered, somewhat offended.

We followed him away from the others. Only then did I realize the guards had been standing between us and the rest of the herd. I wondered if the prince could carry both of us. He called back to the herd, and one of the males followed. The prince paid him no attention just yet.

"Greetings, little men. I am sorry if our guards did not show you patience. You may think you look nothing like a troll, but to a people with four legs, everyone with two looks somewhat alike. My father teaches them, but he can only lead as far as they are willing to follow."

Something was wrong with the prince. He favored his hind leg on one side. The hair near his hoof was stained dark red. The prince turned to me and followed my gaze. "Yes, there is that. My father did not know I received an injury when he made his promise."

"Sir, are you all right?" my brother asked. "We can wait, or someone else can carry us."

"No, my father gave you his word." He paused, curiously. Just before I meant to break the silence, he continued, "I am the fastest. Your passage will be swift—though not as swift, perhaps, or quite as safe, as my father planned. There is a chance my injury could keep us from reaching the other side."

"Sir, then why risk it?" I asked. "We don't want to see you hurt worse." I contemplated the fate of a horse when it breaks a leg. There could be no doctor in a herd of antelopes.

"Don't worry for me, little one. My father made a promise and I will honor it. Stretch out your legs, and ready yourselves for a long ride. We will leave soon."

I looked back the way we'd come. I had no idea how fast they ran. It seemed at least as fast as a car, but I knew my guess could be far from accurate. I sniffed at the air—it was dry. I didn't think we could walk back even as far as we'd come already. Wherever we traveled from there, it would be on the back of an antelope.

David and I walked around a bit, taking the prince's advice. We talked nervously about the chances we'd take either way we went. Soon, I was tired of talking, and told the prince we were ready. I knew he was risking his life for us, but thought it was only out of foolish pride. I felt sorry for him in a way, but also grateful. I reached into my pack and pulled out another item we'd taken from the troll's loot: a giant gold ring. It was heavy, and at once I wondered how I'd carried it so far without giving it more thought. It was twice as thick as my thumb, and large enough around to wear as a bracelet. With effort, I held it out to the prince in one hand and said, "Would you accept this from us, in thanks? You could wear it on your...horn." The prince smiled, almost knowingly. His expression took a full second to register in my mind, then seemed to me an entirely reasonable expression for a giant antelope.

"I would be honored." He knelt down and lowered his head until I could reach the tip of his horns. He tilted his right horn toward me, and I slipped the giant ring over its tip. When he raised his head, it slid down almost to its base. I smiled over at David, only to find him glowering back at me. Perhaps he thought me overgenerous.

As it turned out, all their talk of the prince carrying both of us had only been a formality. I rode on the prince's back, and David rode on the back of a second antelope.

They ran even faster than the first two. It was like nothing I'd experienced before. I'd ridden horses a few times, and the two experiences had nothing in common. For one, riding bareback on a giant antelope is very *painful*. The prince's spine was a jagged ridge of vertebrae, seemingly bent on dividing me in half. Not long after we left the second herd, I found I could ride less painfully if I sat lopsided over his spine, leaning against his neck. I rode the giant beast in this way, shifting from side to side, holding onto his long horns.

Not long after, I realized the prince had been talking to me. Every once in a while he'd mutter some bit of history of the grassland flying speedily by us. It was interesting at the time, but thinking back I can't remember much of what he'd said. His comments were short and self-contained, such as, "where my mother brought my youngest brother onto the plain," or, "where I first saw my wife". These places held great importance to the prince, though they were identical to me. I kept silent, not knowing what to say.

When I thought I could ride no more, it began to grow dark. Though I could see the mountains at the far end of the plain, they didn't seem to grow closer since the sun sank low in the sky. I fell asleep a few times, only to be torn awake by the prince's spine digging into me, or by one of my hands slipping off his great horns.

I fell asleep one last time, and dreamed I was in the top of a tall leafless tree, hanging by the upper branches. A winter wind was blowing, trying to knock me out of the tree. It bucked and shook, but I would not let go. Finally an ugly troll came and chopped at the tree's base with an axe. Each blow shook me violently. The tree came down hard, jarring me loose, and leaving me face-down in coarse grass. I woke up and lifted my head from the prince's coarse mane. We had stopped. The prince lowered his head for me to dismount.

"Are you going to let the prince rest, or do you plan to sleep on him like a couch?" David asked wryly.

The sun was completely set. If not for the clear sky and full moon, I'm sure we would have been lost. Not far ahead was another tree in the same wide shape as the peculiar *drinking tree* we'd seen earlier. The two antelopes walked to it directly, taking turns at the same knotty limb, although several were within easy reach. When they had their fill, David and I drank, then filled our canteens. It was odd enough to drink from a tree, but doing so in the dark was even more troubling. I drank quickly, and hoped no small insects crawled helplessly into the trickle of water the tree gave us.

The antelopes lay down, though David and I were not ready to sit. They pulled at what grass they could reach, their legs folded somewhat under their bellies. Moonlight and a charred twig from the previous night's fire proved enough to update our map with whatever details we could remember since leaving the duke's manor.

Eventually, the antelopes moved under the drinking tree. We made a hasty camp, spreading our tarp and blankets on a soft patch of ground, not far from the great knobby trunk. The prince pointed his nose toward the mountain.

"There is a tall tree in that direction. The trail to the human herds you seek begins with this tree."

We looked in the same direction—there was only one tree in sight. Too tired to search in the dark, I hoped we would easily find a stone marker in the morning. I turned to the prince and his companion.

"Thank you, prince. We never could've crossed the plain without you."

"This is why we helped you."

He left an uncomfortable silence. I thought he misunderstood, but wasn't sure how to fix it. "I just meant we're very grateful."

"As well you should be. Yet we are in your debt, not the reverse. You restored a great treasure to my people, and I greatly anticipate seeing it in my father's mane."

"What happened to the missing drinking trees?" David asked suddenly. "Your father said trolls cursed your people and killed them."

"They did—but they condemned themselves at the same time." The prince seemed about to say something more, but remained silent. I wanted to hear more about his story.

"What trolls?" I asked, "Where did they come from?"

"A horde of brown trolls came to this plain many years ago. They were reckless and selfish. They destroyed the drinking trees wherever they went. They could have drunk from those trees for centuries, but instead they hacked great holes in them whenever they desired water. Each tree they came upon, they killed."

"Were they ignorant? Didn't they know they were killing them?" David prompted.

"They had plenty of evidence. After so many had been killed, any sane species would have realized the cause. We sent messengers to tell them to stop. They killed our messengers and burned them with fire. Then they hacked them into pieces and *ate* them."

"They *did?*" David asked. "How *could* they? I mean—did they know you can *talk?*"

"Have you met a troll yet? Their voice is not so different from our own. They were a foul group."

He was right; the troll at the duke's manor understood us easily, and we understood him. "What happened to them?" I asked.

"They don't cross the plains anymore. After they killed our trees, they couldn't cross the plains."

"Yes," I replied, "I know. But what happened to them? Did they go back to the forest? Did they all die of thirst?"

"They did not come from the forest, they came down this mountain." Again, the prince turned his head. His news didn't calm my worries on what the mountains might hold in store for us. I remained silent, waiting for the tired prince to answer my question.

"They did not return to their mountain. They were trapped near the center of the plain. The drinking trees had grown scarce, and the ones near to them were dying. Some carried huge loads of water to try and escape, but the more they carried, the slower they moved. None escaped the dry snare they made for themselves. They can't walk as far as even you could, I would say. Their bodies were not made for travelling long distances."

"It sounds like they did you a great deal of harm," I said sympathetically. The other antelope answered while the prince remained silent.

"They were *our enemies.* We are less now because of them."

"What do think he meant?" I whispered to David, but their hearing was better than I could have guessed. The prince turned one ear toward me and answered.

"There are fewer antelopes now than there have been in millennia. There are no other species for us to share the plain with. Worst of all, we now know the bitter taste of hate. All this lessens us *as a people*, not only our number."

"Who lived on the plain with you, before?" David asked. I glared at him; it certainly wasn't our host's favorite topic.

The prince replied wearing a sad frown. "Humans, like you. And more four-legged peoples: prairie dogs, rabbits, possums…little ones we miss dearly. Now only large birds visit us on the plains." An awkward silence settled once again over our party.

Wearing both my jackets, I pulled my wool blanket over me, silently thanking the duke once again. With my head lying on my pack, I thought of the day ahead of us, and what I might need to ask the antelopes while we had the chance. "Prince, what can you tell us of our journey ahead?"

He sounded sleepy. "If I could persuade you, I would urge you not to go. It is too cold for anyone but birds and trolls up there. We could try and take you further, but we would freeze and die. The pass over Golden Mountain is not a pass for us."

"What about humans?" David asked, "Is it too cold for humans to pass?"

"The duke and his people came down from the mountain. Some returned." He paused for a while, then went on, his words lazy and quiet. "If I had hands like you, I might use tools to survive the cold." He snorted. I couldn't guess what it might have meant. Disgust? Jealousy? I felt it was time to change the subject.

"Do you know what lies up the mountain?"

"Snow and wind. The path leads almost straight up in places. There you will have to grasp the mountain with your hands, and kick your feet into the ground. Then you will pass between the Glowing Mountains and find the human King's ice palace. Beware; it is rumored among the Sentinels an ice troll has reached this frozen place."

So little of what he said made sense to me, I hardly knew where to start.

"What are the *glowing mountains*?" I asked, foolishly avoiding all mention of the *ice troll*. Starting a frightening discussion late at night went against my natural desire to sleep.

"They are the two taller mountains surrounding the smaller mountain between them: the one you will climb tomorrow. It is called Golden Mountain, and the mountains on both sides, we call the Glowing Mountains. At morning and night, their tops glowed many years ago. My father never saw it, nor his father." His speech was becoming slow, and his head lowered. His head rose temporarily as he added, "Do not be tempted to take the steep valleys on either side of Golden Mountain. You must cross over its top. We know this from the humans who have traveled over it; the valleys are *dangerous*: to humans, or to trolls."

"Why weren't the *glowing* mountains called golden?" I asked, wondering if I'd misunderstood the prince. The antelopes were falling asleep and would answer no more questions, and I dared not object. They had carried us all day, running at high speeds. No sooner did I reflect on this, than I too was asleep.

I dreamt of riding the antelopes again. In my dream, it seemed I was sailing over rolling waves of grassland. Up and down, up and down, I looked around and suddenly I was on a ship. The water was bent up high on either side, giant hills of water surrounding me. The water didn't fall; it just rocked the ship back and forth. I saw an eagle overhead, and it dropped a rock on my head.

"*Ouch.*" I woke, looking up to find the antelope prince's colossal mouth looming over me, his breath steamy in the frigid morning air. I shivered.

"Sorry, I didn't mean to harm you. We need to leave, and I wanted to bid you farewell."

"Did you..." I hesitated as I sat up. "...did you drop a rock on my head?"

"*Excuse me?* What exactly do you mean?" The prince looked offended.

"Sorry, I was dreaming..." I stood and stretched. David was still sleeping happily with half the contents of his pack arranged on top of him. I started to arrange my pack, but as my head began to clear I turned back to the prince.

"Thank you again for your kindness and help. Please tell your father we were honored by it."

"I will," said the prince, "And if you meet representatives of the human King in his frozen palace, please send them our regards, and tell them their King still has our allegiance."

I stood and reached to shake one of his great horns. I didn't know if this was the correct farewell, but he lowered his head and seemed to understand.

"I will miss you," I told him.

"And I you." As he turned to leave, he added loudly over his shoulder, "May you always find sweet grasses." Then suddenly they sprang, running away from us, back over the plain.

"*That's not right,*" David said, as soon as I finished speaking.

His words pulled me back to the frigid present. He was clearly annoyed. I hushed him with a finger held over my lips, reminding him there might be trolls nearby. "We walked *all day long* to cross the plains," he went on, slightly more quietly. "We almost didn't make it. Don't you *remember?*"

"I remember the antelopes and their story of trolls."

"You even got the antelopes wrong. We never met their *king*," David trailed off, sounding confused.

"Well, *were* there giant antelopes, or not?"

"There weren't." He paused, clearly frustrated. When he spoke again, he sounded much less certain. "At least, I *thought* there weren't—I was sure they were only a dream."

I shared his frustration—a memory of two explanations, one believable, and the other impossible. If we remembered the same *impossible* stories, maybe our *rational* memories were only confabulations—attempts by our subconscious to help us cope with the shock of our impossible memories. I made a mental note to compare our rational memories later, to see if they matched. For one, I certainly had no recollection of *walking* across the plain.

"Think back," I started cautiously, "What do you remember of yesterday?"

"We woke up, and finished climbing the mountain," he replied confidently.

"And what else?" I asked. "How cold was it? Where did we wake up? Did we *see* anyone?"

"It was cold enough—we almost froze to death the night before. We woke under a pile of moss we made, then hiked to the pine trees where we slept last night."

"Is that all?" I asked incredulously. I had troublesome memories from the previous few days, and I wished he would confirm them.

"I don't know what else you'd like to hear," he said, growing angry.

I want to hear something to make me remember, I thought, *something to make it all better.* I envied his clear memory of the previous day, while it was only a blank page in my mind. I held my tongue, and for a while, we marched along the trail in silence. I wondered about *all* the memories—true and false—we'd made in the past few days. *Which of them will help us, and which will fool us?* I asked of myself, wishing I had an answer.

1.3 The Winter Palace

As high as we'd climbed, it was colder than I'd expected. Thankfully, the sun shone down on us from a clear sky, and our clothes and packs together with our swift pace, warmed us comfortably. The snow turned light and fluffy, and though we could tell where the trail led, we couldn't see the fresh tracks clearly. Neither of us was excited about following tracks made by vicious-looking trolls. I shuddered to remember them passing, as I watched fearfully from the cluster of pines where we'd slept. For all we knew, the tracks would lead us to an entire village of hungry trolls. If they'd eaten talking antelopes when they could, would they eat humans?

We kept our eyes on the trail in both directions. Close to noon, the trail crested, and it did my spirits well. *It's all downhill from here*, I thought hopefully.

We were surrounded on two sides by the taller mountains the antelope prince claimed had once *glowed*. For a while we could see a great distance in front and in back of us. In one direction, it was the same wondrous view we'd enjoyed the day before, appearing as a summary for us, having grown smaller with distance. In front, a new view unfolded down the longer, gentle slope of Golden Mountain. We saw more pines in clusters here and there, though we watched them more suspiciously than the previous day.

As we walked down the gentle sloping trail, I noticed the terrain changing again. It became just a little hilly. There were level areas here and there, where I would have expected ponds, if it were much warmer. David finally admitted recalling newfound memories of antelopes, and shared some of them with me. The beast he'd ridden told him the mountain pass was *always* frozen. He explained to David, the Winter Palace could not have been built otherwise. The explanation made more sense when it finally appeared, glimmering in the distance.

The Palace first appeared as a crystal sparkling brilliantly in the snow. It looked beautiful, though very strange. There was something peculiar about its walls. We weren't certain until we were much closer, but the Winter Palace seemed to be made *entirely of ice*. We crept slowly and cautiously toward it, drawn to such a mysterious sight.

It was much farther than we first thought. By the time we were truly close, clouds had blown in until the sky was overcast. The wind grew stronger, and darkness gathered around us more quickly than I expected. As we grew colder, we picked up our pace. Close to the Palace, we passed many tall ice sculptures on both sides of the trail, most of them broken. Some must have been twenty feet tall while they were whole. The pieces lay scattered on the sides of the trail. The trail became cluttered with bits of rubbish and an occasional broken board jutting out from the hard packed snow. We passed a wooden wheel from an old cart, half-buried. An eerie feeling crept over me as the moon rose in the sky.

"Remember how clean the duke's manor was, and how well-kept the grounds were?" David asked.

"Maybe the people in the Winter Palace are sloppier. Though it's hard to believe they'd be *this* messy..."

"Do you remember the only truly messy part of his whole manor?" he pressed his point further.

"Where the troll had moved in..."

"*Exactly.*" I saw his expression clearly, and recognized the same fear I shared.

"Do you think we should turn back?" I asked, trying to hide my concern, "Or skip the Palace altogether?"

"No." David stopped completely and spoke in hushed tones. "This way down the mountain isn't nearly as steep, so we're going to be in the snow a *lot* longer than on our way up. We won't survive a single night out in the open—and last night we were *lucky*. Don't forget, we're nearly out of bread and water. We don't have anything to melt snow in, even if we *could* start a decent fire. We *have* to stop at the palace."

I knew he was right, and all my hopes sank. We crept on, past the garbage in the snow and past the last of the ice sculptures in the growing darkness. Only a dozen yards from the palace walls, we came to an icy bridge over a deep moat. The biting wind blew across the face of the water and made tiny waves. I could taste salt in the air...*the moat was filled with salt water.* Even in the dim light I could tell it wasn't deep, but it didn't need to be. Falling into ankle-deep water at those temperatures meant a doom worse than drowning.

The entrance to the bridge was a tall tower, built of ice, and open on the front and back. When we walked through it, I noticed two alcoves in the tower's inner walls, their recesses veiled in darkness. When I peered farther into one of these openings, I nearly slid down into a very steep and slippery chute. David caught me by the back of my jacket, but not before I was able to see where the slide led. It curved at a right angle to the bridge, and led directly into the frigid moat below.

By then I was shaking considerably—and not only from the cold. We walked carefully through the tower to the edge of the bridge, and stood peering over the gap the wooden drawbridge would fill. We saw it had been hauled up for the night. It was too great a distance to jump. We glanced down at the deadly moat, dotted with patches of wet slush. There was a bell to ring, surely to ask for the drawbridge to be lowered.

We understood the gravity of the decision before us. If we rung the bell and there were trolls inside, we would surely be captured. Even if the King's men were inside, they might not trust us enough to lower the bridge after dark. The wind lashed at our faces and bit through our clothes, as if to force a decision from us. David looked around, to see if the moat went all the way around the strange palace.

Nervously, I stroked the bell, wishing it would ring itself and be done with it. I heard David *yelp* and turned fast enough to see him go over the edge, into the moat. I went quickly as I could to the slippery edge, to the very spot I last saw him.

"David, *where are you?*" I couldn't see him in the water. Could it be so much deeper than it looked? Some of the slush patches looked as if they might be floating chunks of ice. My eyes played tricks on me as my heart pounded and my ears hummed.

Should I jump in? Could I use the rope to climb down to the moat to find him? I stood frozen with indecision and despair, until I heard a stage-whisper from far below.

"*Down here!*" I turned to follow his voice, and found my brother standing on a narrow ledge under the draw bridge, against large blocks of ice I guessed were the mansion's foundation.

"Are you out of your mind? How did you get there?"

"*I slipped.* I made it to this ledge by luck. I didn't even see it until I was already halfway off the bridge. I just pushed off—and landed here. Look, there's a little door inside." I had no idea what he was talking about—there was no door in view. "There's a little room inside—*come on down.*"

David tied a bit of his rope to something I couldn't see, and leaned out over the moat ready to catch me and help me onto the ledge. I looked back at the bell one last time, and heard a low rumbling sound from higher up in the palace. I turned my ear into the wind, straining to hear more. The thought of trolls peering down on us overpowered any further hesitation.

"*Here I come.*" I pushed off with all my might, fearful of falling short of the ledge. I flew past my brother, and through the little door I couldn't see before I jumped. He rushed in to make sure I didn't hit anything on my headlong flight, then shut the wooden door, hiding us from the bitter wind outside.

Inside, it was completely dark. The small room was nearly full with dry hay—a fact pressed painfully upon me as I slid inside. With our mittens off, we felt wooden benches on two sides, a wooden floor, and walls all around us made of ice. The wall on the far end—furthest inside—held another wooden door. Beyond this was an opening—a foreboding hall neither of us desired to enter in the darkness. My eyes adjusted enough to show the slightest hints of what lay beyond, though I had no hope of discerning them in the darkness. I was happy to close the door to that eerie hallway, and tried unsuccessfully to use the giant fish tooth to wedge it shut.

We were cold, but not nearly as much as we'd been on the bridge. We jumped up and down quietly for a minute to warm ourselves, and piled all the hay in the center of the wooden floor. In the darkness, we clumsily wrapped ourselves in wool blankets, and dug our way into the hay. Our clothes, our blankets, and the hay worked together to slowly gather our body heat, and finally return it to us. I fell asleep as soon as I stopped shivering. While I slept, I dreamt of our second day in Terreldor—five days back.

1.4 Day Two: Silent Old Man

My dream began midafternoon. We followed a well-worn path, winding past high bushes and trees with low-hung branches. The dense woods we left behind felt ominous, though I could remember nothing about it yet. I felt the sun on my back; we were headed roughly north.

My dream skipped something, as many do, and I had the vague idea it was something dangerous, as if our lives had just been threatened. After this omission, I found we were just inside a large open gate, set in a tall stone wall. Cautiously, we continued up a well kempt garden path. I felt the thrill of anticipation as we walked. The path led us to a large stone building with smoke curling from a chimney near its peak.

David and I paused at a pair of tall wooden doors, a grand entrance to the massive structure. A foreboding doorknocker stood before us. It was large and heavy; a giant iron ring, clutched in the teeth of a hideous man with large fig leaves for ears. I lifted the oversized ring, and let it fall to its metal plate on the door. It was so deep a sound, it startled me. I was curious at what new impossibility might greet us, what adventure may lie ahead. And yet—most of me wanted the strangeness to go away. Above all else, I wanted to go home.

The great wooden door creaked slowly open, and I wondered how long ago it had last been used. For the briefest of moments, I thought a strange white bird had flown through the doorway and stopped at the threshold, just over our heads. I recovered soon enough, and saw it was the head of a wild-haired old man, peering at us around the door. My heart raced when I realized there was only an old man before us— though he *did* have an eccentric look about him. These were the thoughts running through my mind when I should have been saying *hello*, or *help*, or *where are we?* None of us spoke, and I began to feel uncomfortable.

"Hello," David started, as cheerily as if he were selling fund-raisers. "We're very lost, and were wondering if you could help us."

The man looked stunned, as if it were the last thing someone might say to him. When he didn't reply, I tried to explain further. When I opened my mouth, some foggy memory of the danger we'd faced at the beginning of the dream returned to me.

"We were attacked by some large creature—it tried to rob us."

The man's eyes opened wide, and he pulled us quickly inside. I surveyed the entranceway while he busied himself bolting the door, mumbling in a breathy sort of way.

We stood in the anteroom of a great mansion. There were paintings and tapestries and ornate decorations in every direction. Everything we saw looked terribly *old*. The items weren't worn or faded—though there were signs of disrepair—but archaic, as if they belonged in a museum.

The old man looked closely at us, as if he suspected we might be a hallucination. His hair was long and white, and stuck out in all directions, as if he'd gotten it wet and taken a nap immediately afterward. He wore an old robe of a cloth I'd never seen before. It was a deep burgundy, with a complex pattern I saw was woven, not printed. It looked very heavy as though he wore it for warmth more than convenience.

He opened his mouth to speak, and *strained*, but nothing more than a hoarse gurgling sound came. His bony hands flew rapidly in the air in a strange manner long enough for me to question our safety, and glance at the door's large bolt. Then suddenly—and not in a comforting way—he turned on his heels and walked briskly away from us, farther into his house. I began to wonder if he suffered from mental illness. David only shrugged, and followed.

We found him in a cluttered library, sitting at a large desk. He was scribbling on a large pale-brown sheet of paper. Through many poorly written notes and gestures, he conveyed he was a *duke*. He was mute, and he had arthritis, which limited his ability to write.

Many of our questions were returned only by quizzical shrugs. It seemed he couldn't understand some very basic questions about our location, and some of the impossible things we'd seen not far from his home.

I noticed suddenly, as happens often in dreams, I had a sack with me, and it was filled with stolen goods. At some point the duke pointed to the sack and gave me a questioning look. As I opened the bag in my dream, memory flooded into me and I immediately understood where I'd come upon its contents. It was the omission from the beginning of my dream.

As we'd entered the gate through the stone wall around the duke's manor, we were threatened by a strange beast with a shriveled hand and limp, who called himself the *hill troll*. He wanted to charge us for crossing his land, but in the end, he proved to be only a bully who was trespassing in the duke's manor. He fled from us when we refused to pay him. There was a disheveled guardhouse near the gate, which smelled of rotten food, and it was inside this tiny structure where we found the sack of loot.

Without notice, the duke was analyzing the contents of the sack, sorting them in two piles. He reacted to the first item, his expression seeming to say, *ah…that's what became of it*. He removed item after item with alternating expressions of disappointment, grave sadness and surprise. He replaced perhaps a third of the items into the sack, and returned it to me. Then he mimicked something—handing the items out to others, I guessed aloud, and he happily nodded his confirmation.

The duke answered our many questions with hand gestures and poorly-written scribbles. While we plied on, it grew dark and he lit a candelabra at his desk. Through hours of writing and gesturing—and nodding to our correct guesses, he taught us something of his troubled history.

He was a distant relative to a King who ruled *the whole world*, as best I could tell. Long ago, the duke had a modest estate on the other side of the kingdom, near their capital. He had little direct contact with the King, though it mattered little to the duke. One day, a traveling member of the court became angry with the duke, and brought his complaint to the King. The King was troubled by what he heard, and called for the duke to make an account of his actions.

The duke's *crime* was a long record of being lenient and generous to the subjects of his estate. For instance, the poorest of them had turned part of the duke's land into a shanty town, and paid him no rent. Also, a merchant regularly cheated him, and the duke did nothing to retaliate. In the duke's words, these people took nothing he had earned. They were stealing, in fact, that which had come to the duke by his noble birth.

It angered the King to hear such a notion, and he declared any representative of the Royal Family—including the generous duke—was bound to uphold the King's law. The King ruled if the duke chose to live outside the King's law, he must also live outside the boundary where the King's law was enforced.

Rather than sentence any of his subjects to prison or worse, the duke chose banishment. Moving outside the King's reign meant isolation and utter lack of protection on the far coast, or *Animal Coast* as he referred to it.

When the duke prepared to leave, he gave his maids and servants the choice to stay behind with a generous severance. All abandoned him but his most faithful servant. He hired a merchant caravan to bring them to the Animal Coast, and repair an ancient manor, a remnant of an earlier age.

This had happened 40 years ago. It seemed his servant had not aged as well as the duke. They were both frail, the arthritic duke and his bedridden servant he waited on. Instead of begrudging the turnabout, he seemed happy to serve his lifelong friend.

When his tale was done, I asked why he hadn't punished the crooked merchant, or much more recently, stopped the hill troll from sleeping in his guardhouse. At first he only smiled. *Must give chance to choose right*, he wrote on his cluttered page. When I suggested the hill troll might endanger him, or even kill him, he wrote only, *What if? Old man!* He tried his best to show me—if he didn't give the troll a chance to choose right, no one would.

Then it was our turn to explain. Though he smiled while we talked, his eyes betrayed his expression; he thought we were lying, or perhaps insane. He urged us to seek the King's help, beginning with a dangerous journey to a place he called the Winter Palace. I objected, complaining of the King's apparent lack of justice, but the duke softly rebuked me. He explained it wasn't right to speak ill of the King, no matter what coast we found ourselves in. He went on, gently explaining the King who had banished him was quite a bit older than himself, and had no heir. The throne had surely passed to the *rightful line*, to use his words. Then he quickly drew us a sketchy map to the Winter Palace, though it was clear his hand gave him considerable pain.

Finally, we had exhausted his arthritic hands and he could do no more than nod or shake his head. Though it was late, he sprang to his feet and bid us to follow him to his storeroom—which had obviously seen better days. He chose two handmade sacks with shoulder straps, and filled them with provisions he could hardly spare, before showing us to his guesthouse. Though it seemed it had never been used, it looked as if it might not last the night.

I woke from this dream with this one thought on my mind; sleeping in a pile of hay felt more like sleeping in a pile of needles after a very short time. Whenever I let a hand, or knee, or foot slip from my wool blanket, it was scratched and stabbed until I woke and withdrew it. Still, I woke feeling grateful for the clarity my dream had brought to my doubtful memories.

I realized—still half-asleep—if a foot slipping out from my blanket brought me itchy pain, it was far preferable to the bitter cold felt when I ventured from my pile of grassy insulation. Lying there half-conscious, parts of my dream played over and over in my mind. As it did, I was overwhelmed with another set of memories arranging themselves in my head.

The duke had described the kingdom as a vast island divided by a treacherous mountain range—the very range he told us we must pass, if we were to meet another human. As strange as it sounded, he believed the island was alone in an infinite sea—he believed it was the *whole world*. I wasn't entirely sure the duke was sane.

Nonetheless, he'd described the grassy plain we'd crossed, and the climb up Golden Mountain, nestled between taller mountains of the same range, and an ice palace just over its gentle peak. I don't know whether it reassured me or caused me further worry when I realized his tale had so far proved true.

Eventually my senses began to return, and my thoughts turned to the present. I worried about the ice palace—or rather, I feared those who might inhabit it. I climbed out of the hay, and saw the outside wall of the room glowing around the wooden door. The rising sun was glowing right through the wall. Tiny sunlit bubbles and specs of dust throughout the ice gave it the appearance of a mysterious crystal.

When we'd entered the room the previous night, I couldn't have known the wall was so transparent. I had a quick scare before I looked up at the ceiling. I'd worried the ice floor above us might be so clear, we could be seen right through it. It was thick, I could easily see. To my relief, however, its top was so scratched and scuffed, it was impossible to see through it. I rolled over to tell David, but saw in a panic he was gone.

I rolled out from the hay and ran down the hallway too dark to explore the previous night. I slowed as the light waned, and the walls seemed to close around me. I stretched my arms out and barely touched both sides of the tunnel—there was no change. The ceiling was close over my head, but it had been just so when I'd first entered the tunnel. Before long, the hall turned to the right and disappeared into the darkness. I sat down, cold and afraid. Had someone taken David away? Why wouldn't they have taken me? Could it have been so dark they missed me, buried in the hay?

Before long, my eyes began adjusting to the darkness. Straining to see new detail, I crept fearfully along the corridor. I heard a low noise, something of a *bump, bump, thump…bump, bump, thump.* I remained still and held my breath—the noise was definitely ahead of me. Soon I discerned a dark lump farther down the tunnel, with movement above it. My mind played tricks on me, imagining a thousand horrible scenes. I continued on, as quietly as I could.

It was David, standing in the middle of the tunnel and waving something over his head. When I crept closer still, he spun to face me and let out a little gasp before he recognized me.

"*Finally.* I thought you were going to sleep all day," he whispered. "Help me with this."

He held in his mittens a large chunk of ice, shaped like a club. He hefted it over his head, and stuck a part of the ceiling darker than the rest. It looked like a small wooden door.

"Thanks for waiting for me," I replied, letting irritation replace my earlier fears. When I came to my senses, I nearly yelled at him. "*Wait*—what's on the other side?"

"There's only one way to find out." There was a reckless determination in his voice.

"How far have you gone down this tunnel? Who knows what we'll find? Maybe some food…and something to start a fire with." I trailed off, realizing just how wishful I must have sounded. Perhaps I should've hoped for a tea kettle as well.

"This is as far as I've gone. It's too dark to see anything past here—we could walk off a ledge and fall to our deaths."

"Well," I said, hoping to dissuade him, "maybe your eyes have adjusted more by now. I can't see any farther, but let's walk a little more and see if *you* can."

David agreed and we walked onward at a cautious pace. To our surprise, we made out the bluish hint of the walls at our sides.

"This isn't our eyes adjusting," he started. "Something is lighting up the tunnel."

"The sun?" I offered hopefully.

"If it's only rising now, we'll be able to see *everything* in a few hours."

We walked onward, silently as we could. I was relieved David had abandoned his risky plan. I began to notice details we hadn't seen before. We found places where intricate scenes had been carved into the walls of the tunnel, and large alcoves with life-sized sculptures carved from ice. They were beautiful even in the near-darkness. Some looked like parts of nativity scenes, while others I could only guess were scenes of some unknowable history, stored in the eternal ice of the bizarre palace. We were torn from admiring an especially large scene carved in the wall, when we heard a muffled sound above us: *clink, clink*. We whispered back and forth.

"What do you think?" I asked. *Clink...clink, clink.*

"It could be a trap." *Clink.*

"What about a machine?"

"It might be. Or maybe it's someone trapped, trying to chip his way out."

At that, David kicked hard at the leg of a nearby ice figure, and snapped it off at the knee. Without a word, he struck hard at the ice above us. We heard a faint noise, perhaps a muffled shriek.

"That's no monster," David whispered, "it sounded like a woman—or a girl." I pulled the oversized fish tooth from my pack, and joined David in striking the ice over our heads.

We struck the ice faster—I took care to stay clear of David's wild blows—until a great chuck of ice, and quite a lot of chips and shards fell to the floor between us. A young teen-aged girl tumbled down through the hole and landed on all fours, sprawling over the ice chips at our feet.

She met our gaze with surprised horror, and sprinted down the tunnel in the direction we'd been walking. We looked at each other, then back at the girl, and started after her.

"*Wait*, we're—" "*...here to help*," "*Come back*," we called after her, as loudly as we dared. She slowed, then turned back, regarding us carefully.

"Who *are you?*" She asked.

"I'm Mark—"

"And I'm his older brother, David. We're here to help." I glared at David, frustrated by his interruption.

"Well..." she began, but fell silent. Her expression had changed from terror to a conflicted distress. She looked up at the hole in the ice we'd just made, and stared. She didn't say anything for a long while, and her face grew painfully contorted. Finally, she turned her gaze back at us, and blinked tears from her eyes. "Well, my troll guard won't sleep forever. Let's get moving."

She grabbed the sleeve of my jacket, and led me through the tunnel as fast as I let her. I wanted to stop to question her, but she moved so urgently, I expected death was somehow on our heels.

For a short while, I held my tongue while David hurried to follow. Her winding path led us through several hidden doors made of pivoting ice slabs concealed in the tunnel's walls. At each spinning door, she'd changed the pathway in a labyrinth she surely knew from memory.

"We should be safe for now," she whispered, finally slowing to a halt. "I don't think they know the tunnels yet." It was the first moment I caught more than a glimpse of her.

She was very pretty, and dressed in fine clothes, thick for warmth, but worn and rumpled. Through a thick fur hood I saw she wore diamonds in her hair. "Who *are you?*" David and I asked, nearly in unison.

"I am Princess Schelli. My father will be grateful to you for rescuing me."

"From the trolls?" David asked.

"Of *course.* Don't you know they captured us all? They turned the Winter Palace into a dungeon. My friends are locked up throughout the palace. I was going to chip through my floor and free them, but they watch me too closely—nearly all the time."

"Are you really *a princess?*" I asked.

"Yes. Now let's hurry, we need to free my friends. Wait," she said, suspiciously, "*why are you alone?* Weren't you sent with other soldiers? With...*older* soldiers? Did they have to shove you through a small hole to get into the tunnels? Are you *scouts?*"

"Soldiers? Scouts?" David responded. "*No.* No one *sent* us. Are you *really* a princess?"

"*Yes.* What you do mean you weren't *sent*? What are your positions?"

"*Positions?*" I asked, frustrated with her questions. "I don't hold any, other than a strong position on getting out of here alive." Doubting her every word, I asked yet again, "Are you *sure* you're a princess?"

"*What?* Look, my father *has* no other daughters. I am the *only* princess…and my father wouldn't have sent you without help." Where she'd spoken as forcefully as a king, desperation crept into her voice. "Doesn't he know you're *here*? He *has* sent you to set us free…*hasn't* he?"

David and I could only stare in astonishment. All uncertainty left her face, and she looked on us as she might a pair of fools who didn't quite know how to talk.

Her voice rose until I was afraid we'd be overheard by her guards. "We *can't* leave without Sally and the Captain. How do you expect to make it down the mountain—or *across Enthicia* for that matter?"

"Let's worry about the hike *later*," I seethed, "and get out of this troll-ridden ice-hole." I wasn't certain she understood me, though my words surely earned an interesting look in response. Her eyes turned hard, and her voice dropped low and raspy.

"Fine. If you don't want to help me, then leave. I'll get the Captain myself, and he'll take care of *everything*."

We wanted to take her back to the door by the moat, and I even thought of dragging her. I reminded myself we had no other plan or possibility of continuing down the mountain. We were far more likely to meet her captors than find our way out of the ice maze she'd led us through. We could either let her leave us, and face certain recapture, or try to free her friends. I turned to my brother, who merely shrugged.

In dizzy unbelief, we followed her. We needed a plan for freeing them, but David and I knew nothing about the strange building, or who needed to be freed. She ignored our chattering and led on defiantly.

The Princess knew the tunnels well. Eventually, she stopped at a rope ladder draped against the wall. It hung from a hole in the ceiling large enough to easily climb through.

"This is a hidden entrance into the main floor," she told us, as calmly as if she were lecturing us on grammar. "There's a thin tile of ice at the top of the ladder. We need only to remove it to climb through and find where the others are being held."

"Where does it lead?" I asked. "Will we find ourselves surrounded by giant trolls the second we break through the tile?" Her icy glare seemed to hurl unspoken insults at me.

"*Of course not.* You'll find yourself in small alcove set into a thick wall. There should be a table there, sculpted from ice, with a heavy crystal vase on it."

"*I* will?" I asked, insulted she should order me around so soon after we'd freed her. Not that she was free *yet*, but it seemed *somehow* inappropriate.

"Think about it," David interjected. "Did you expect we'd send her up first? *I'll* go up and see what I can find. You stay here until I see what's going on up there. Then—"

"We aren't far from the store room," Princess Schelli interrupted. "I think that's where they'd keep the Captain."

"Who's the Captain?" I asked, growing tired of her presumptuous tone.

"The Captain of the Royal Guard. *He'll* know how to free the others. And he's far more capable of fighting a green troll, should we meet up with one. Most of the guards are *browns*..." Her words were drowned out by my sudden recollection of the brown troll we'd met at the duke's manor, and also the green trolls who had passed us on the snowy trail the previous day. Comparing a frightened memory with a dream might not be the best of proofs, but the green trolls were by far larger, as best as I could tell.

I realized the Princess's voice had turned to a gentle caution as she continued. She asked if we had a knife or sharp stick. I handed her the giant fish tooth, which she gave an almost imperceptible pause to consider. Shortly, the strange girl began to scratch lines in the dimly lit ice floor.

"*This* is the alcove in the wall. *This* is where the store room is. Crouch low in the alcove until you're sure there's no one around, then cross the hall, open the door, and see what's inside."

"Right," David said, and turned to the rope ladder.

"*Wait*—why not me?" I asked, feeling offended only slightly less than I felt relieved.

"Mark, I'm taller, and have twenty pounds on you. I stand the best chance if a there's a green troll waiting for us." To this, I had no response—and I hated this fact.

"Wait a minute," I cautioned, then turned to the Princess, "How many trolls are up there?"

"I think about twenty, spread around the palace. I heard a lot of what my guard said to the others. As I said, most of the trolls inside are brown, but there are a few greens also."

"What do we do *then?*" I asked, turning back to David. He was already halfway up the ladder.

"Wait," he whispered over his shoulder, "I'll let you know what I find in a minute."

I took one last look at the Princess—equal parts furious and desperate—and followed my brother through the hole.

1.5 Royalty Freed

David didn't expect me to follow, and tried to shove me back down the hole. I shimmied my way up, nearly crowding him out of the alcove. It was just as the Princess had explained it, down to the crystal vase we nearly knocked off the small table in the alcove. We saw the wooden door to the storeroom right away, and after waiting a few breaths to listen for anyone nearby, David crossed the short hallway, opened the door, and slipped inside, closing the door behind him.

I waited impatiently. Countless thoughts flew through my head, each explaining why David was delayed, none of them favorable. I resolved to count to twenty, then to forty, before I finally surrendered to my impulses and ran across the hallway. I slipped through the door, wincing from some unknown pain I half-expected to receive.

I had to shove my brother aside to enter, he was so close to the door. He was pale and something less than happy to see me. I couldn't yet see what was beyond him, or I wouldn't have shoved him so. He lost his balance, and slid right onto a pile of furs and blankets. What chaos ensued is one of the most terrifying moments I care to recall.

David entered the storeroom and found someone sleeping on a stack of crates. The slumberer faced away from the door, covered from head to toe. David wasn't sure what to do, unwilling for the moment to attempt to find who he was, or leave and inquire the Princess whether or not the Captain of the Guard was a loud snorer. It was during this *briefest of pauses*, as my brother later described it, when I'd hastily stormed in and toppled my cautious brother onto our sleeping host—who was *not* in the storeroom as a prisoner, but instead, as a lazy guard who'd stolen away for a nap.

The troll guard woke as unpleasantly as one might expect, and tried immediately to dispatch with our heads. Screaming unintelligibly, we found ourselves scrambling for the hole in the ice from which we'd come. We were neither fortunate nor silent enough to make it down the hole without our assailant taking notice. If it wasn't for a badly maintained rope ladder, our day would've ended much differently. As our fortune played out, the third rung from the top was the first rung the troll stepped onto, and it was weak. The rung snapped, sending him down the hole quite a bit faster than he planned, and bringing his chin in contact with the edge of the hole with considerable speed and force. We spent no time deciding whether he was dead, or merely unconscious. Thankfully, I risked a quick jab to relieve him of a dagger at his belt, as David recovered a sword skittering away from him, as he slid to a stop on the ice, a motionless heap.

The Princess led us away from the troll, through hidden doorways in the ice once again, until I suspected we were back-tracking toward her cell. She insisted there was only one other place the Captain of the Royal Guard could be kept. I couldn't bring myself to say what I feared most. From my brother's worried expression, I guessed he'd come to the same conclusion: her Royal Guard may have already been killed by the trolls. Whether they'd been saving the Princess for a ransom or for a meal, the chances of our survival didn't seem hopeful.

We made our way silently through the icy tunnels, me holding the dagger and fish tooth, and David holding his newfound sword. It was a hopeful stance—one we wouldn't have held long if we'd met up with a more-conscious adversary.

Soon, Princess Schelli was convinced we were beneath the room holding at least one of the Royal Guard.

"There aren't many rooms they could use as holding cells," she defended herself wearily. More desperation had grown in her voice. Perhaps she feared just as we did.

With little hope left, we began to chip away at the ice, David with his sword, and me with the dagger. I worried we'd be overheard chipping through the ice, and there would be a crowd of trolls standing ready when we broke through. Fortunately, the Princess's second guess was correct. The ice finally broke and a large piece fell to the ground, larger than we'd intended.

I stood on David's shoulders to reach the hole. Once my elbows were through, he shoved at my feet to help me up into the room. Inside, it was dark and foul. One corner was stained, and the adjacent corner held a low wooden table with a human tied onto it. He was lying on his back, and stretched to his full length with ropes tied to his hands and feet. At first, I thought he was dead.

I approached the man cautiously, making as little noise as I could. He drew quick, shallow breaths.

"Release me or kill me," he whispered, his eyes remaining closed. I reached for the rope tied to his left arm first, and used the dagger to saw through it. His free hand grasped my wrist with surprising speed, and clamped down on it like a vice. I dropped the blade onto the table and jumped back, holding my breath. He grabbed the blade and cut himself loose, then dropped it and dove for the hole in the floor. He slid through head first. His hands grasped for the opposite edge as he passed through the hole.

I snatched up the blade and reached the opening in time to see him right himself in his decent, then land, sliding on the ice. He was back on his feet in an instant. Before anyone spoke, he grabbed the sword from David's hands, and pushed him hard, sending him sprawling down the tunnel, sliding on a thousand shards of ice. When he saw the Princess, he let out a tiny gasp and placed himself between us, sword raised and ready to strike. The Princess shrieked, and told him we were friends. He looked at us skeptically, keeping his sword still raised, but not quite so high. His eyes regarded us for an uneasy second before he turned his back on us, as if he'd decided we could pose him no threat. As I dropped clumsily through the hole, I saw him kneel before the Princess and whisper something to her. She nodded quickly.

He spun around and held out his hand to me.

"*Knife*," was all he said. I handed the dagger to him, and he was off at a sprint, out of sight before anyone else could muster a word.

"*He* is the *Captain of the Guard*", the Princess said with a proud smile.

Within minutes, he returned with three more members of the Royal Guard, all of them wielding swords or staffs. The Captain wore a red welt on his forehead, trickling blood. The sword he held had streaks on it, as though it had been too hastily wiped clean. He left two guards with us and disappeared once more down the tunnel. Within moments, he'd freed the remaining soldiers and guards—fourteen of them in all.

No sooner than they had assembled, they were on their way to the Courtroom of the Winter Palace, where a self-proclaimed *troll prince* sat and ruled. They met only a few trolls along the way, who by then were nearly running scared. They locked them in the very rooms where they'd been held, save for the three rooms with holes in their floors.

When they found the troll prince, he had left the Courtroom in an attempt to flee. They bound him in a wooden cage on top of an oxcart meant for moving goats, under guard, in a stone and wooden stable outside the ice palace. David and I eventually followed some of the Royal Guard to the stable, and I heard the imprisoned troll shrieking nearby; it was an awful sound. While David and I waited there, trying to stay out of the way, I heard one of the Princess's attendants talking to one of the guards.

"I'd hate to be the one who snuck in to set us free, if the ice troll ever catches him."

By the end of the day, the last troll had been captured. The royal attendants had all been set free, and were restoring the Princess's chambers to something like normal. This was a lot of work; since the trolls had taken the Winter Palace, they'd nearly let it fall into ruin. David and I met the Princess's guardian, whom the Princess called *Sally*.

Lady Sally, as the others called her, looked us over before showing us where we'd later sleep, in a room nearby the Princess's suite. She explained we would share the room with her and several guards.

She was a silver-haired woman who held the look of deep wisdom in her eyes. She walked slowly and gracefully, almost as if she were gliding over the floor. Other attendants—and even some of the Guard—tipped their heads to her in respect.

At first entering our room, I didn't recognize the strange squared, curtained piles as *beds*. They were designed to keep a body warm in a palace made entirely of ice. Each bed consisted of a low block of ice topped with tightly packed snow, then straw. On top of the straw, a soft mattress was laid, and on it were many thick blankets. The curtains surrounding each bed were thick and heavy.

That night, Lady Sally told us a little of their captors, and how they'd fallen captive. She began by praising our brave actions and scolding us for taking such risks—though I noted she offered no alternatives. She explained the troll's leader had gathered many conspirators, and taken the Winter Palace while there were only a few caretakers there. The trolls had hidden themselves and waited for weeks until the Princess and her party arrived. With larger numbers, they captured the Princess, most of her guards, and all her attendants.

"The Captain and his men fought bravely," she told us. "If the scoundrel hadn't captured the Princess and held her at knifepoint, the Royal Guard would never have been taken captive." There were only two outcomes, I realized, the Royal Guard were willing to accept rather than surrender.

After we'd rescued the Princess—it sounded strange to hear what we'd done called a *rescue*—the troll prince soon learned she was missing, from the guard posted at her door. He flew into a rage, and sent nearly all his guards to search the palace. Many guards entered the tunnels from the Princess's cell, only to waste their time on a path filled with loops and dead-ends. Schelli had turned the revolving door panels more considerately than I could have guessed. Even the trolls guarding the Captain were pulled from their posts to join the search for the Princess.

When the Captain and the first men he'd freed began to fight and capture the trolls, their leader heard nothing from them, and became even more enraged. More and more trolls were sent, including the ones who guarded the cells holding the remaining soldiers of the Royal Guard. If the troll prince had only taken time to think, he might have sent a large group of guards together, and the Captain and his men could have been recaptured or killed. He wasted his superior numbers, even neglecting in his fury to send for his troops of green trolls, assigned to patrol the grounds. The foolish leader's soldiers were defeated alone or in pairs.

When Lady Sally's tale was over, a soldier led us to a room with wooden floors, where we were allowed to take warm baths in glass tubs while an attendant washed our clothes. We were told to keep from dripping the warm water onto the floor as much as we could. We were given long underclothes, thin and smooth like silk. After we put our cleaned clothes over them, we were the warmest we'd been since reaching the Winter Palace.

To be certain, it had been a long and traumatic day. However, we were spending the night in safety, suddenly guests of an entire palace full of grateful and capable hosts. In our beds, with a bulky guard standing at the entrance to the room, I had the most restful sleep since we'd arrived.

Part II

2.0 The Long Trail Down

We were awakened by one of the guards in our room. He explained to us the Captain of the Guard had decided we'd begin our march down the mountain trail in a few hours. It was a long, gentle slope all the way to the desert, where we meant to follow a trade road to a nearby duke's outpost, instead of continuing to Thraen Kholl, their capitol. We wouldn't soon reach the duke, however, for reasons dire to my own health.

I was glad when the guard told us he would take us to the Captain for questions. As we followed the guard, I was nearly frantic at the prospect of finding our way home. We'd already seen adventure several times in the days since we'd arrived, and I only wanted answers to the many urgent questions building in my head.

I should have known from the start it was the *Captain* who had questions *for us*. How could he not? No one knew who we were, where we'd come from, or how and why we'd arrived at the Winter Palace. By some stroke of ignorance, I entirely missed his point, and didn't even think it odd when he asked my brother to wait outside the room while he spoke with me.

I entered the room and closed the door behind me, as the Captain took a seat behind a large wooden desk, and motioned to a chair across from him. I sat and immediately began asking him every question I could conceive. Of the many questions I had for the Captain, he had patience enough for half.

First, I asked why we didn't go directly to their king's palace at Thraen Kholl, to return the Princess to her worried father. The Captain explained the King expected his daughter was well taken care of and enjoying her retreat at their winter vacation home. Normally the entire Royal Family would have arrived much earlier, but for the troll-merchant disputes. Before I could interrupt to ask about the disputes, he went on to explain they needed to first warn the *Duke of Enthicia* of the trolls who had taken the Winter Palace. He needed to be ready in case the trolls should attack his outpost at the far end of the desert. Eventually the King would send more soldiers to guard the Winter Palace.

I asked if this man was related to the mute duke we'd already met. The Captain was surprised we'd met him, and asked if he was well. It seemed the Captain was some sort of fan or follower of this duke—he'd studied letters the duke had written long ago.

The Captain explained this duke we'd met was a cousin of the King, and *the duke in the desert*—for Enthicia is a desert—was a distant cousin to them both. The *silent duke* was further down the line of ascension than the King's children, but not as far as the *desert duke*.

Finally I asked the Captain if he had ever heard of my hometown, or the nearby larger cities I could name. He hadn't; in fact he hadn't even heard of the United States. When I asked him if he'd heard of Earth, he seemed insulted.

"*Of course*. But you must know," he said as his eyes narrowed ever-so-slightly, "*Earth* is a very old name. We use the word *Terra*."

"Well then," I continued, sensing his impatience growing, "what part of the *Terra* do you come from?"

"The North Forest."

"Oh—in what country is the North Forest?"

"It's in Terrance County," he replied.

"No," I repeated slowly, "not what *county;* what *country* do you come from?"

"I'm not sure what you mean," the Captain replied in a low voice.

"Well, what do you call all your counties put together?"

"Why, Terreldor, *of course*. It's all the King rules, and all there is."

"But what's beyond your *kingdom*—on all sides?" I asked.

"Only the lonely ocean." He paused, then looked at me with compassion, and in his eyes I saw a sudden realization, as if he had decided I was mentally slow. He began to talk more slowly. "I've never sailed far from the coast, but those who have, never found other lands. I don't know why this is important to you *now*," he added, his impatience showing once again.

"How big is the kingdom?" The Captain paused at this question, looking at first perplexed, then skeptical. Finally, he heaved his shoulders in a shrug and answered me.

"From east to west, you can sail along the southern coast in about a week in favorable weather. To sail the eastern coast from north to south would take six days, and ten days from south to north. The western coast would take six days to sail from north to south, and seven or eight from south to north." His reply sounded as if he were reciting an answer from a geography textbook.

"And the northern coast?" I asked him. "How long to sail along the whole thing?" He eyed me with suspicion once again, perhaps realizing I was not dull after all.

"No one has tried to sail the whole north coast in many years. It's dangerous, filled with shallow, rocky shores, and bad winds. I have no idea how long it might take, supposing it's even possible."

I tried to guess how big the island was. I didn't know how far a ship could sail in a day, or even what kind of ships they had.

"How long to ride horses from the east coast to the west?"

The Captain gave me a strange look. As far as he knew, no one had attempted to travel from east coast to west—or west to east—in a single journey. While the coasts were well mapped, it seemed there were inland areas too dangerous or difficult to travel, and no one had ever mapped them completely.

"Do you really believe water surrounds the entire world?" I asked, foolishly hoping he'd change his mind.

"Well, not literally. The kingdom is surrounded by water, but Terra itself holds land and water together as a globe...not floating...but not falling either. Look, I know you're curious, but I really can't educate you on these matters right now. And it's obvious you cannot answer the questions *I* have for *you*..."

I hadn't heard the Captain sound so irritated yet, so I held my tongue. He patted me on the shoulder brusquely, asked me to send my brother to see him, and finally told me to see if I could help Lady Sally in any way. For all my questions, I hadn't received a single helpful answer.

Outside the room, I told David the Captain was ready to see him. Instead of letting me pass by, David surprised me by grasping me tightly by the arm.

"What did he ask you?" he whispered nervously.

"What? Nothing. I asked *him* questions. Why?"

"Are you *crazy?*" David asked, his eyes wide. "What's *wrong* with you?"

"What are you talking about?" I responded, still confused.

"We're here to answer *his* questions, *you toe-head*. Don't you think he's curious about who we are, why we came upon the Winter Palace, or who sent us?"

"No one *sent* us. What's wrong with *you?*"

David threw his hands in the air and shook his head as he walked past me. Looking back, I can only guess the Captain found me too oblivious to be a threat, and decided to get more useful answers from David. Perhaps he decided to defer any judgment on us until we reached the King.

Not long after our questioning, we started our journey down the long slope from the mountaintop to the desert. It was late morning when we began. They had only three carts whereas nearly a dozen had ridden up the same trail when they'd arrived. The remaining carts had nothing to pull them; the trolls had eaten all but six of the oxen after taking the Winter Palace.

One cart led our group, holding the Princess and her guardian. The other two carts were farther back, one carrying the firewood we would need until we reached a more temperate altitude, and the other holding the imprisoned ice troll. The rest of the caravan—maybe thirty-five of us in all—walked.

Before long, David and I found ourselves near the end of the line. I decided to venture near the ice troll and finally get a glimpse of him. I knew he was surrounded by heavy guard in the middle of our party, and so I struggled to reach his cart. When I finally saw the fallen troll leader, I fell back and squawked out a little *yipe*. The troll must've heard this, and turned toward me. His eyes grew wide, his nostrils flared, and he let out a terrible shriek—first unintelligibly, then in slow, even speech.

"I see *you who undid me*. I'll get you—I'll choke the life from you, and freeze your veins," he hissed.

I fell back yet again, and slipped on the icy trail. As long as the troll saw me, he snarled and shrieked. He said awful things, and when he could no longer see me, he asked many times for the boys *who dared to undo him*. I swallowed hard. Stumbling back toward my brother, I paused to ask one of the guards what was wrong with him. The guard only laughed.

"Haven't seen him yet, eh? He's not like the greens or browns, he's a Lyssiltik—you know, an *ice troll*. They live only on tops of the coldest mountains."

It seemed fearfully unlikely to me this strange world should have three species of monsters, and have such simple names for them. It would be far from that mountaintop palace, and months later before I would learn the complex relationship and history of the Chrutghanies, Luskidians, and Lyssiltiks. It was enough at the time to discover the antelope prince had meant the ice troll was a different kind of troll altogether.

He was a Lyssiltik, covered with the thick white fur of a polar bear. His face had about as much hair as a man who didn't shave. His skin, where it showed on his face and palms, was a dull blue-gray. He had long, sharp fingernails almost resembling claws. His blue-within-blue eyes burned bright with hatred for me. From then on, I worked diligently to stay out of his sight.

Eventually David caught up to me, and I was happy to put some distance between the troll and myself.

We talked about how frightened we'd been before we set loose the Captain, and how nicely the Princess had treated us after her friends had been freed. It didn't feel like we were walking slower than the others, but soon we found ourselves once more at the end of the caravan. As the last guard in line passed us, he paused to warn us, "You'd better pick up your pace boys, or you'll fall behind and freeze."

We walked faster and kept up for a while, but the group was moving too fast for us to match their pace all day. We'd walked too many miles in the past few days, and our feet and ankles ached.

When it became obvious we couldn't keep up, the rearmost guard shouted forward to another guard in the caravan. We could hear the next guard shout even farther up the line. Before long, I noticed everyone ahead was walking around something in the trail. Soon we saw it was the firewood cart, which had completely stopped in the middle of the path. The rear guard told us to climb aboard and rest.

"You've earned it," he said with a wink and a warm smile.

Sitting on a pile of firewood certainly isn't comfortable, but it felt so good to rest, it took some time before we realized it. Our rest came with a cost; the bitter cold began to seep through our clothes once we stopped walking. We sat on the logs and kindling, shivering and wishing we were home.

Not long afterward, two guards fell back and asked us to follow them as fast as we could. Curious, we went with them past the troll's cart, all the way to the front of the caravan.

The Princess's cart wasn't the fancy coach in which she normally rode. It had been an open oxcart, recently fitted with benches for seats and a hastily-built frame around it. Lush carpets were stretched across the newly added framework, for shelter from the cold. As the guards we followed reached the makeshift coach, they chatted quickly with the guards posted behind it. I wished they would hurry, as I'd grown breathless from hiking at double speed. One guard pulled back a curtained flap in the cart's woolen covering, and told us to hurry inside the ramshackle coach. It was dark but warm, and we heard the Princess talking to someone. I realized we'd hardly seen her since we'd left the secret tunnel. I very nearly didn't recognize her, inside the cart—even with a small lantern lit. As my eyes adjusted, I saw she'd been talking to her guardian, Lady Sally, sitting beside her.

"...for some warm food, too. Oh *there* you are! I'm so sorry you two were left out in the cold. I *just* heard, and ordered you to be brought in here where it's warm." She hardly stopped talking while we sat in the only free space, on the shoddily upholstered wooden bench across from Lady Sally and the Princess, nearly hidden by piles of blankets. "Our cart isn't much, but I'm grateful for it. They had so little time to put this together, and it won't be for long..."

The Princess thanked us again for saving her, and setting free the Captain. She began to tell us how sad she felt for the trolls. I assumed I'd misheard her, but didn't interrupt. She told us how beautiful the Winter Palace had been before they took it over.

Princess Schelli wore heavy furs, and even her hair was covered in a fur hood. A long ringlet of dark hair dangled across her face before she tucked it back under her hood. Her eyes were dark brown, nearly black-around-black in the dim light of the coach. She explained how her family spent Christmas in the Winter Palace every year, but this year the King was too busy with some troll-merchant disputes.

This was the second time I heard of these disputes, and I still had no idea what they were. The Princess offered little more information, other than they had prevented the King from leaving home for long. She'd begged the King to let her visit the Winter Palace for a while in the early spring instead, and he agreed. It was high above the summer frost line, so it hardly mattered to the Princess what season it was.

Apparently, the trolls who guarded the Princess liked to talk. She knew intimate details of many things the ice troll had done, beginning long before she was captured, and lasting nearly until the day she was freed. The trolls had imprisoned the few year-round caretakers of the Winter Palace, and set a trap hoping to catch the entire Royal Family, presumably to kill them all. When no one came for Christmas, the troll prince waited. When only the Princess arrived, he hoped to use her as bait, or ransom to find some leverage on the King. In the time since, he'd lost some of the trolls following him, and sent others to gather more troops, leaving him with few guards to keep their prisoners.

Soon after taking up residence, the ice troll ordered salt by the cartload, and barrels of saltwater from allies in Enthicia, and begun creating the saltwater moat. Tons of salt, and many barrels of saltwater were enough to create a slurry, which in turn dissolved enough snow and ice to create a shallow moat. Just months before, it had been called *the Ice Garden,* and had been filled with ice sculptures, skating rinks, elaborate snow slides, and even small hills for sledding. The wooden door we'd discovered beneath the drawbridge was a maintenance entry for the palace's security tunnels. The Princess had used the tunnels and the old door to sneak out and wander the Ice Garden on moonlit nights, during her more pleasant stays there. The damage to the Winter Palace, Schelli worried out loud, would not soon be undone.

As she talked, I looked around the cart. Its rough wooden frame was less obvious from the inside. It might have been made in haste, but the materials used were obviously from the royal chambers of the great ice castle. Fine furs, rich blankets, and silk rugs covered every inch of the interior. Under the many thick blankets we'd found on the bench, I was finally warm, and soon became sleepy.

Making myself as comfortable as possible, I removed my heavy coat and wrapped my arms around myself. My mind wandered, and I found myself fingering a tear in my shirtsleeve. Until that moment, I'd been unable to remember how my shirt was torn. Unexpectedly, a flood of memories returned to me. They fit so well in my mind, I felt immediately they must be true, but at the same time they were so implausible, I wished I could call them only a dream.

2.1 Memories from Day One

This new set of memories—nearly an entire day had been lost to me—came to me with unexpected context. I knew immediately these events had occurred before we met the silent duke, on our first day in Terreldor.

My first memory was thick with fearful overtones. David and I were panicked, running through a most unusual forest. The trees were arranged in colonies: massive banyan *villages*. Flying buttresses of wood grew a hundred feet or more from central trunks, each tree an ancient canopy. They were thin enough to run through with room to spare in most places, but their boundaries, where one colony ended and the next began, were chaotic tangles of aerial roots and young trunks. I feared they were homes to untold numbers of spiders and snakes. We struggled through boundary after boundary, at times finding ourselves lodged in these strange walls.

We came across one of these tree-walls thicker than the rest, where the small gaps between roots and trunks were filled with wiry vines, covered in long thorns. I couldn't remember what drove us to do so, but we struggled recklessly—and *painfully*—through it. There was no surprise my shirt had been torn, rather it was no small wonder our clothes weren't ripped to shreds. The stiff thorns left us with painful scratches, for which I could still find evidence on my forearms.

Emerging through this all-but impenetrable wall, we saw it formed a protective ring around a strange village of tiny people. They were impossibly small—no larger than my thumb. Time passed with a corresponding empty page in my memory, as may be expected in dreams. In my next recollection, my brother and I sat beside each other, before two rows of tiny men and women, arranged in a half-circle around us. Most of them looked old to me, but their ages were difficult to tell.

The *head councilman*, as they called him, spoke of a banquet they'd prepared in our honor, we were soon to enjoy. But first, he promised to explain where we were, and how we'd arrived there. He claimed some of them remembered seeing us, or, depending on perspective, would meet us one day in the future. He went on, acknowledging what he said was difficult to believe, which I considered an impressive understatement. He gave a detailed explanation of a Path between our two worlds. He paused, and I leaned closer, straining to hear him.

His next words are burnt clearly into my memory, though they meant nothing to me as he first spoke them. Certain I'd misunderstood, I repeated them over in my mind several times as the head councilman waited patiently. Though they sound like nonsense, I'll produce these words of his exactly as I remember them.

"You traveled to our world through *the Path*. Our worlds exist in different dimensions, or at least very far apart in space—we cannot know for sure. The Path is a link between them, and it is *unstable*. The last time we know the link to our world was open, it was about a century ago from *our* perspective, and, judging by your appearances, won't open on *your* end for another five or ten years in *your future*."

David was just as convinced he'd misunderstood him, and eventually we both told them so. Again, the tiny man explained his strange theories to us, several times, even giving complex examples. He made it abundantly clear they believed two things neither I nor my brother could accept. Firstly, many of them were older than a century, some by several decades. Secondly, my brother and I had come to their world by some mysterious path, which existed in a complex relationship of *divergent timelines*.

Finally, the village's miniature leader returned to his seat, and the different members of their council took turns addressing us. They read from an old book one of their people had written long ago, listing many things our older selves had done—or would someday do. The book's author was said to be one hundred and forty years old. I wasn't listening particularly carefully, but thought instead on the quickest way to politely leave them.

Their story began at a time when their race lived alongside full-sized humans, as they had done for many years before the narrative began. It described the day-to-day particulars of a tiny man called Linker.

Linker and his entire people were slaves. He and his immediate family made braided gold jewelry for a wealthy merchant; he specialized in forging miniscule gold links. Their family heard of two strange brothers, who'd learned of his people and wanted to help them. Hope rose and fell for Linker's family as their weary days passed, and they gathered scraps of rumors and tales of what the brothers did in their attempts to help Linker's race. The brothers petitioned the King to outlaw the slavery of the tiny people. This king seemed to be influenced more by rich merchant's guilds, than for any sense of fairness to Linker's people. Eventually he decided to appease the few influential subjects who cared for their plight. He believed if he freed them, they wouldn't be able to survive on their own, and would soon go back to work for the same merchants who had enslaved them. The brothers heard of his plan, and conspired to lead the tiny people completely outside the kingdom, to live in peace outside the king's rule.

The story told at great length the details of their journey: how they travelled, how the brothers helped them plant the thorns in the boundary wall of their great banyan tree, and eventually taught them how to make a life for themselves, isolated from all others as they chose to be. The longest part of the story dealt with some problem at the start of their village, some rift I didn't understand. It seemed the tiny people held so much hatred for the humans who'd oppressed them, it somehow caused them hate each other. The two brothers helped them in some compromise or negotiation, thus—according to their story—saving them twice. It made little sense to me. The book seemed to be more about a lesson in hatred than the tiny people or their old lives.

Their lengthy story went on, again describing the two brothers. It seems they'd appeared in Terreldor just as we had, confused at first, but gradually regaining their senses. After all their time helping the tiny people, they simply disappeared into the jungle, never to be seen again. They went on to tell us more about the link between our worlds, and how the brothers pointed out the nature of the *Path*, and had remembered visiting their village when they were younger. I was fidgeting by the end of their story, wishing it over.

I found I couldn't remember the banquet they promised, or exactly how long we stayed with them. Sometime the same day, they pointed us toward the thinnest point in their thorn-wall, and we scraped our way slowly and painfully through it. As we started, they apologized for the new cuts and scrapes we would get on our way.

When I tried to push further back in my memory, I hit a foggy wall of amnesia. Our hazy first hours in Terreldor were lost to me—perhaps, I thought, for good. My mind focused instead on the strange explanation the tiny villagers had given us. It seemed like nonsense, both their existence *and* their theories, though I later became convinced our experiences with them were real. Our day with the tiny villagers alone—of all my improbable memories—had offered an explanation of where we were, and how we'd gotten there. I felt betrayed in that the explanation was too fantastical to take seriously.

As my mind adjusted to our surroundings, again I wanted very badly to compare my memories with my brother.

"Hey," I said, jabbing him with my elbow, "do you remember the tiny villagers?" David only grumbled an incoherent reply, so I jabbed him again.

"I said, *leave me alone*," he mumbled, slightly louder than before. The Princess and Lady Sally were both sleeping.

"C'mon, this is *important*." We both knew he didn't hesitate for lack of sleep. It can be very distressing to recall an impossible memory; it seems to indict your sanity just to *think* it. After the briefest pause, I added, "Do you remember the same things I do?" David raised his head, with guarded hope in his eye. He felt it too—the chance to have his disturbing memories confirmed by another.

"Well, what parts are you unsure about?" Perhaps he didn't want to be the first to recite our memories.

"What happened after the long story they read to us?"

"You mean the banquet? I remember you went hungry, rather than eat what they cooked for us."

Mice. The image of a dozen roasted mice, individually skewered over impossibly small fires, flashed through my head.

"No," I objected, "*before* that. Something between the story and the banquet—I can't remember what it was."

"The medals? They gave us each a tiny medal, if that's what you're thinking about." David spoke in noncommittal tones, but I knew he felt every bit as uncomfortable as I did.

"Medals?" I asked. No sooner had I spoken the word, than I flopped over to reach into the pocket I'd been laying on. I turned it inside out, and just as I'd hoped, there were two metal disks, clinking together at the end of a loose thread. They were very flat, and seemed thin enough to cut me, if I were to press them hard. The head councilman had presented us with two miniature medals, as a token of gratitude for saving their people.

"You tried to refuse, right? Because…" David wanted me to finish his sentence, still testing his memories against mine.

"…we *didn't* save them." I still felt somewhat guilty, accepting a reward for something we'd obviously never done. I'd tied them to a loose thread hanging from the seam in my pocket, to be certain I wouldn't lose them.

"Anything else I might've felt guilty about?" I asked. It was my turn to have my memory confirmed. David smiled.

"They advised we head to *the King's side of the kingdom*, if we wanted to find our way home. We didn't plan to take *any* advice from them, but you thanked them on our way out." David rubbed his forehead, where he'd received a particularly nasty scratch from their thorn barrier. Inwardly, I sighed. "It didn't matter much, did it? We found our way to the King's *daughter* soon enough."

"What happened before? What happened before we found…the little village?"

"The *Village Peaceful*," David reminded me. The name was familiar to me. He paused before continuing in a more subdued voice, "It's as far back as I can go." He sounded afraid, or perhaps defeated. "All I remember from the day before the village is cloudy. I remember feeling confused and afraid, but nothing else." He added with a scoff, "I'll remember soon enough. Yesterday, I couldn't even remember the village."

Though we'd spend hours trying, we would never remember how we found ourselves in the banyan forest. At the time, I felt comforted, knowing my brother was going through the same doubts and discoveries. And why shouldn't I be comforted? Whatever was happening to us, we were safe, warm, and fed, but most importantly, we were in the company of normal-sized humans, who for the moment, did nothing *impossible*, and seemed willing to help us.

Lady Sally and the Princess woke before long. The Princess took a long drink of water before she began to speak again. If I had to guess, I'd say she'd been talking nonstop before we were brought to her cart. She spoke of *so many* things. She appeared younger than David and I by a few years, but I couldn't be certain; despite her knack for talking, she acted much older than she looked.

One thing she talked about took me entirely by surprise. It was just after she was interrupted by the snarling squeals of the ice troll, bound in his cart somewhere behind us. After all he'd done to her, she told us she felt *sorry* for him.

I'd seen how frightened she'd been by the way she spoke of the time she'd been imprisoned. She even knew he wanted to kill her and her parents, and yet she spoke as if she'd already forgiven him. When I asked her about this, I could only meet her response with shock.

"Yes, I *have* forgiven him," she told me decidedly.

"How can you *say* that? You know he wants you and your family *dead*."

"That poor troll is a hate-monster." she replied. "Even though we know very little of him or his people, I'm convinced his life has been full of hatred—giving *and* receiving it. He's consumed with hate in the same way we should all be consumed with love. I believe he's never felt love, and was never given the opportunity to *show* love." Her eyes welled up with tears. "I hope one day he gets to feel love from someone," she went on, "maybe from me."

"How could you love that thing?" David objected. "He's *pure evil*."

"*He isn't*," she insisted, with unexpected ferocity in her voice. "He still has the ability to make choices. He's never even *seen* the choice to love—this is the only thing wrong with him."

We gave her pat responses, unwilling to excite her any more. I turned away and pretended to fall asleep. It made me angry to hear her say such things. It reminded me of the silent duke and the hill troll. What would become of him? Would his kindness be the end of him?

My mind wandered back to the Princess and the ice troll, though I didn't want to think any more on them. The ice troll was a monster who wanted to kill us. I hoped he would be put in a cell forever, or killed.

Soon after it grew dark, the cart stopped and the Captain opened the curtain and asked me and my brother to follow him. He told us our party needed to make camp for the night, and invited us to sleep in his tent; we quickly agreed. I was certain he was an important man to their king, by the way the other guards treated him, and by his responsibilities. I thought his tent would be like a cloth house, with sleeping bags and a stove—but it wasn't even a real tent. It was just a bunch of cloths or blankets set around a wooden frame, open on one side and facing a small fire. The Royal Guard, I later learned, had found most of their equipment when they searched the Winter Palace, but their tents were all missing. The Captain let us sleep in the front of his *tent*, closest to the fire.

The roof of the tent was higher in the front than the back, so it didn't fill with smoke. Even so, I wouldn't call the air trapped inside *fresh*. When the front of me grew hot from the fire, my backside froze, and I rolled over. Back and forth, I rolled, all night long. I was still tired, but very glad when a guard woke us and asked us to follow him back to the Princess's cart. We were about to continue our descent. I looked back, but the Captain wasn't anywhere to be seen. I realized he'd probably been up for hours, getting everyone ready. *Perhaps*, I thought with a smile, *he chose to be away when we woke so he wouldn't have to answer another set of my questions.*

As we walked to the Princess's cart, the guard told us a group of the blue-gray ice trolls had attacked our Caravan during the night. It was the most ice trolls any human had seen in one place. He told us they hadn't fought very hard, and no one had been badly injured in our defense. He didn't mention if any of the trolls had been harmed, and neither of us asked. He delivered us to Lady Sally, who we found leaning against the cart. She wished us well, and told us there was food for us inside. We nearly tripped over each other on our way in. I was embarrassed to be greeted in the dark interior by the Princess's giggles.

"Oh—good morning, Princess," I offered awkwardly, trying to focus on her in the poor lighting. I also glanced quickly around in search of the breakfast we'd been promised.

"No one who's rescued me is permitted to call me *Princess*," she said with a smile. "Call me Schelli." She passed a small basket with a misshapen loaf of bread, and sharp cheese. "I'm afraid this is all we have for breakfast," she offered, and as an afterthought, added, "only for a few more days, though."

By the time Lady Sally joined us, the cart began to move. I was just finishing my bread when I noticed a strange odor in the cart, something like smoke and mud. Embarrassed, I thought David or I must have walked through a campfire on the way to the Princess's cart. If Schelli or Lady Sally noticed it, they were polite enough not to say so.

We talked about many things, but weren't able to learn any more about the island than I had talking to the Captain. David asked why we couldn't sleep in the cart with her and Lady Sally. At first she seemed startled, but after a quick glance at both of us, she relaxed and gave a warm smile in reply.

"Well, that's the Captain for you; he has so many silly rules. He says a princess has to be protected from her enemies, *and* her friends, and even from *herself*. Can you imagine that?"

She began to tell us stories of all the silly things the Captain had done under the guise of protecting her. She made us laugh. I was sure some of the things she told us were meant as jokes. In one story, the Captain wouldn't let her eat any cake for a month, because he claimed it might be poisoned. She found out much later he'd simply believed it was unhealthy to eat cake more than twice a year.

The weather began to warm as we rolled downhill. The snow we rode over began to crunch under the wheels of the cart, and then became silent as the cart slipped sideways a little now and then. I made a habit of peeking out a small flap of carpet left unattached as a window—so much so, it irritated my brother. By the late afternoon it was cooler again, but there was very little snow. We came upon a rise just before the trail grew somewhat steeper. The rise was topped with a snow drift, the last deep bit of snow before the trail gave way to dirt and mud.

The Captain called for the entire party to halt, then called for his Elite Guard: a small group of his most trusted men. Then he had us regroup, and divided his best men between the Princess's cart and the ice troll's cart. He re-arranged the caravan, putting the troll's cart ahead, and the Princess's cart toward the middle of our party. David and I had to walk behind the cart, and guards were given our seats across from Lady Sally and Schelli. I hoped we wouldn't be hiking for long.

As we started moving down the trail again, I wondered why the Captain rearranged everything. Several times I thought I saw something move in the corner of my eye before I spotted one clearly. I'd snatched glances of the white fur of several ice trolls, hiding all around us in the snow drifts. They looked taller and thinner than the troll prince, but unmistakably the same type of creature. Only after I caught a glimpse of a blue-gray hand or face, did I make out their white outline against the snow.

As we approached the last snow drift across the trail, guards ran up to the oxen of both carts. They slapped their backs hard and tugged at their yokes. When the first cart's wheels hit the peak of the snowdrift, they began to sink. There was mud under the snow, and the prisoner's cart lurched to a halt. More guards ran to help, pushing the cart from behind. The cart eased slowly through the messy snow, and onto firmer ground. Then the guards rushed to the Princess's cart and did the same. Even the guards sitting around the Princess jumped out and helped push, leaving their weapons in the mud.

I glanced around at the high drifts to the side of the trail and saw the ice trolls walking back and forth, talking to each other. They were no longer trying to hide. They moved as if confused or distraught, but none of them came toward us. As we rolled downhill and away from the last bits of snow, they turned and stood silently watching us. An eerie shiver rolled over me, as they disappeared behind the last snowy rise, immobile and unspeaking.

2.2 Near Miss

When the sun rose enough to warm us, the ice and snow seemed a distant memory. I caught a glimpse of the ice troll, bound in his caged cart, and he seemed sad—almost less dangerous. In the warming surroundings I thought he even looked smaller. His hair seemed thinner, and his demeanor was subdued. I wondered what the King would do to him. After so recently wishing him dead, I found I nearly felt sorry for him—though not quite.

I was tired from walking and decided to climb back in the Princess's cart. When I told David, he decided to race me there. We were far behind both the troll's and Princess's carts, and we were out of breath when we reached them.

I stepped in a small puddle of foul-smelling mud on my way forward and soaked my left boot. The guard outside the Princess's cart insisted I remove the soiled boot before I entered. He tucked it under the heavy cloth of the cart's covering, then held me in the air as he inspected my other foot, and most of my clothing as well. By the time he finally caught up and hoisted me into the cart, David was already inside and asking the Princess more about Terreldor.

"Did you find out anything new?" I asked, hoping for an explanation without timelines or magical interplanetary trips.

"Not really," he replied. "I learned a little about the island we're on, and how it's made of counties—and a few dangerous places no one visits. But I still can't find out where this island *is*." The Princess looked irritated.

"Why do you keep asking where the kingdom is? Do you think someone *misplaced it*?"

"Sorry, Schelli," I answered her. "We're just very lost right now. We come from very far away, and have been wandering—often with no memories—for at least a week now." The Princess only frowned.

"Well, if my father's scouts can't find your home," she said with a shrug, "then it can't be found."

David asked about the strange stand-off with the ice trolls, and the Princess told us all she knew of it.

The Captain had already suspected the ice trolls would attack again. He saw the low snowdrift as their last chance before we crossed the snowline. He took every precaution, and it paid off. No one was hurt, and the ice troll was still on his way to stand trial before the King.

That night we camped just as we had the previous night. Fortunately, it was less windy and the cold didn't seem nearly as severe. The Captain and a dozen guards sat around a campfire just as I supposed they'd done the night before, talking and even singing a little. While my brother was tired enough to go straight to sleep, I left the Captain's tent and walked near their campfire to listen from a distance. I overheard stories about the way they lived, battles their fathers fought, and the like. The Captain saw me and smiled, but didn't invite me to join their circle. Other than the Princess, David and I were the only ones in the caravan who looked younger than thirty. I realized a band of traveling soldiers wouldn't seek out the only nearby teenager to join their party.

The next day we started later, and I had a chance to sleep in a little. Well past the danger of ice trolls, the Princess's cart returned to its place near the front of the line. Whenever I found myself falling to the end of our caravan, I hurried to the front to ride with the Princess.

The caravan seemed to be moving more slowly on our third day down the mountain—or maybe I was better rested and walking faster. I was able to keep ahead of the wood cart for long periods without getting tired. It seemed every time I found myself out of breath, I made the mistake of stepping in another puddle, and my boots were growing messy. It was never much mud, but the worn trail was hard-packed earth on both sides.

As we traveled, the trail began to resemble a dirt road. On a whim, I walked ahead of the entire party to get a better view downhill. A stone's throw from our party, I stepped in the middle of the trail and looked as far down the path as I could. I remembered the mud, and looked down at my feet. Oddly, there were no mud patches in the trail ahead of us, as far as I could see.

I thought David and the Princess were missing a fantastic view, so I waited at the trailside until the Princess's cart rolled past me. I'd guessed Sally wouldn't let her outside the cart as long as it was muddy, and I wanted to let her know the trail was clear, but when I saw David was walking with the soldiers at the end of the line, I decided to wait to talk to him first. I can't even remember what I wanted to tell him, though this tiny decision would cost me great pain.

I noticed someone had covered the troll's cage in blankets as it rolled toward me—perhaps so he couldn't see out. At its nearest, I could hear the ice troll breathing. He sounded sick, or at least out of breath. As his cart passed me, it veered close to the edge of the trail, and I was too distracted by his labored breathing to step back.

In an instant, I was snatched off the ground by a beam hanging from the cart—or so I thought. It was a wiry arm, thrust from the cart. It plucked me from the ground and held me dangling, gasping for air. Flailing wildly, I tried to scream, but couldn't. The furious glare of the ice troll flew through my mind, but the arm holding me seemed far too small to be his. It was a pale blue-gray and had only sparse patches of fur. The arm was thin as a child's, but its claws pinched the skin around my neck, pulling me tight against the wooden bars of the makeshift cage. I kicked and tore at the arm to get free. A guard was yelling and furiously poking the wooden end of his spear through the cage. I imagined a smaller, hairless troll was in the cage with the troll prince. *He'll never find it in time*, I thought of the guard with the spear.

As I began to lose consciousness, an eerie calmness fell over me, and the troll spit strange words at me through clenched teeth.

Thilstatt monunorsett hrinnic destalgh. Lymgkha tsinhrol.

They were the first words I'd heard in Tlaltsihk, the mother tongue of the Lyssiltiks, or ice trolls. He spoke them in a strange cadence, and while I knew nothing of their meaning, I was sure they were a curse. Finally the arm released me and I fell to the dust of the trail. The guard scooped me up before I was crushed by the cart's rear wheel. I was weak and dizzy. Two guards rushed me to the Princess's cart and roughly slid me on the bench across from Schelli and Sally. My neck was very warm, I thought from finally being released from the troll's tight grasp. But it was wet, and when I turned my head, it hurt badly. I touched my neck—though Sally tried to stop me—and saw my hand was covered in blood. I remember thinking about the poor little troll. *Why did the guard stab it?* This was my last thought before I lost consciousness.

The troll had done more harm than I could have known—more than anyone could have guessed at the time. I had a deep gash in my neck, and it thrummed painfully with each heartbeat. I'd lost a lot of blood. I woke up with a bandage wrapped thickly around my neck. My brother was the first person I saw when I woke. The look on his face frightened me more than the pain from my wound.

The Princess looked just as worried. Sally was busy pushing a canteen into my mouth. She calmly told me everything was *just fine*— though she didn't sound very convincing. She too looked scared, though she hid it better. Sally told me I would have to ride in the cart for a few days and drink as much water as I could. I asked about the smaller troll, but she shushed me and told me not to worry about trolls. David tried to give me an awkward hug, but the bulky bandage around my neck got in the way. So he squeezed my shoulder and told me we'd find a way home soon. Schelli's eyes were red and swollen, as if she'd been crying. I didn't ask why.

I slept the rest of the day. I was woken by the noise of the soldiers setting up camp for the night. I felt much better, and so I asked Sally if I could walk to the Captain's campfire. She looked like she might say no, but for the fire's warmth. She sent me with a strict warning not to wander, and to yell for help if I felt dizzy.

I stepped out of the cart and began to walk up the trail. The Princess's cart was kept in the rear of the caravan at night, but the fire wasn't far. My head throbbed as I jostled to the ground and began my way. I hoped the pain would fade when the initial head rush from standing wore off, but it only grew worse. Distracted, I stepped into a large patch of mud. I scolded myself again for forgetting to look for mud patches, though it was dark. I was careful enough to step completely off the trail and walk far around the ice troll's cart. When I stepped back into the trail, I kept a careful eye out for any puddles, but found none.

Something seemed very wrong. I found dry ground in front of the cart, mud under and behind—my mind strained for an explanation. The jumble of thoughts sifted and fit themselves together, and the wild revelation they left me, almost made me cry out. I told myself it was impossible. I told myself to walk and not run. I heeded none of my wiser thoughts, and instead fainted on my way to tell the Captain the ice troll was melting.

2.3 Of Dreams and Visions

When I woke, I was lying next to the Captain, close to the fire. I heard him talking while another soldier tried to get me to drink.

"I would have killed him where he stood," he said, "but only the King can pass judgment on him. We *must* bring him to Engdynlor *alive*."

I opened my eyes and sat up. I noticed with detached curiosity, I was covered by many thick blankets. I turned and whispered to the Captain.

"The ice troll is melting, isn't he?" He *wasn't*, but it would be months before I would learn this.

The Captain gave me a shocked look, then glanced away and sighed.

"It would seem he's very ill—he may even die. We're deciding what we will do. This isn't your worry; you need to rest. Lie down and see if you can drink some more water."

I followed his advice and wondered where my brother was. I guessed he was sleeping in the Captain's tent again. Since I took up half of Schelli's cart, he would probably walk all day or ride on the wood cart. We were far enough from the snowline, there was plenty of wood near the trail, and the wood cart was being used to carry the older royal attendants.

I began to feel comfortably warm—even too warm, and I inched back from the fire. I heard the men talking in turns, each saying in their own words how the ice troll deserved to die. I must have fallen asleep again. The Captain woke me when he raised his voice.

"*Enough*. Whatever we do, I will not willingly cause the troll to die. It is our duty to deliver him to the King."

The Captain and his men talked further about what they might do. They spoke of sending a group of men back up the mountain to guard the ice troll where it was cold, while a fast runner went to get instructions from the king. They also considered setting it free, close to where the snow still lay in drifts.

I fell asleep again and dreamt several guards had climbed back up the mountain with the troll, as the soldiers had mentioned. In my dream, the other ice trolls easily overpowered the guards. Some of the guards were killed, while the others were captured and died later, bound and lying in the snow. I woke up shivering, and rolled closer to the fire.

Again I fell asleep, and had another dream. This time the soldiers let the ice troll go free into the snow. I dreamt he ate fistfuls of snow until he grew bigger and stronger. He grew twice as large as when I'd first seen him. He took control of the ice castle again, and subdued the brown and green trolls into his service. He sent green trolls after us, and a great army of them caught us in the desert. They left us to die, bound face up, lying in the scorching sun. I woke sweating, and squirmed farther from the fire. I sat up confused, still half asleep. I couldn't shake the feeling of these dreams. They felt real, like fresh memories.

I tugged on the Captain's arm until he turned toward me, wearing a look of tested patience. Suddenly, all the other men became quiet, and I was embarrassed. I am sure they were not accustomed to having a child speak during their meetings. I whispered quietly to him.

"If you let him go, he will grow again, and send green trolls to kill us all. We will die tied up, trapped in the sun."

Even as I said it, I felt foolish. Then the memory of the first dream distracted me. It too felt real. Against my better judgment, I burst out, even louder than before.

"But if you leave men behind to guard the troll, *they will all die.* They will freeze to death, tied up and in agony."

All the men murmured. The Captain's look changed from impatience to frustration, glancing here and there among his men. His expression calmed as he turned back to me and spoke with a curious voice.

"Why would you say that? Were you listening to us?" I told him of the two dreams I had.

Others in the group started to talk. I heard someone say, "…only a *child,*" and another "…visions—*he knows,*" and yet another hoarsely whispered, "…in the *Prophecy?*" I began to worry what they thought of my dreams.

Still half-convinced I should remain silent, I told them, "*Never mind.* These were only foolish dreams—I'm sorry I interrupted. I was far from the fire and felt cold. Then I was too close to the fire and felt hot. That's all they mean."

They didn't seem to hear me. They kept talking about the dreams and what else they might do. The Captain quieted everyone and told me to go back to sleep. He called for a guard to bring him something, and put yet another thick blanket over me.

"Don't worry about your dreams tonight," he told me. "Now you will be warm enough, and far enough from the fire."

I remember smiling and thinking, *Does he really think I will sleep after all this? I'll be awake all night, and hear everything they plan.* And yet I soon knew I couldn't keep from falling asleep, no matter how badly I wanted to hear the soldiers.

When I fell asleep, I had one last dream. I saw the Captain's Council talking on and on about the ice troll. I dreamt I fell asleep and had *another* dream. I soon realized I was dreaming and woke. I told the Council what to do, and they all nodded thoughtfully, as if I had given them some wise judgment. In this dream of mine, the soldiers sat behind a half-wall, like a jury at a trial. They wore white robes and long white beards, and went on nodding and commenting on the wisdom of my words. When I *actually* woke up, for a moment I had the sadly familiar feeling I *might* be dreaming, but couldn't be certain. I opened an eye for a second and caught a glance of the Captain beside me. He was not dressed in white, only his same worn clothes he'd worn since I'd first seen him. I relaxed a little—I was truly awake. I smelled the smoke of the fire, and heard its familiar cracks and pops. My face was warm, but my foot was cold where I'd pushed it out from under the heavy blankets. I could also hear…whispering. It was the guards. They were talking about *me*. I heard only bits and pieces, all crammed together as they spoke over each other.

"Did he fall asleep yet?" "Could it really work?" "Will he dream again?" "Shhh, he's *waking*." "Did he really sleep?" "I saw his eyes twitching—that means he slept, doesn't it?" I rolled over onto my back and looked up at them. My mind was still slow from sleep, and I thought they already knew what my third dream was.

"But I *still* don't know what I *told* you," I said hoarsely.

Some cheered or laughed, while another moaned, "This is a *waste of time*."

"What did you dream, young man?" asked the Captain.

I sat up and shook my head—*ouch*. Did they really want to hear my dream? Could they possibly think it would tell them what to do?

"You're wrong," I whispered to the Captain, thinking I knew his thoughts, "It doesn't mean anything."

"And yet, I want you to tell me." A stern look in his eye hurried my reply.

"I dreamed I fell asleep, and had *another* dream. I dreamed I woke up, but I was really still dreaming. I told you what to do and you listened. But it doesn't mean anything—*I don't remember what I said.*"

The Captain was patient. "Think carefully. Do you remember anything from your dream-within-a-dream?"

"I remember it was about the troll, but that's all." I felt horribly worn. The members of the Captain's Council began to murmur, then argue. The Captain stared into the fire as if his mind was busy. The other guards became louder and louder, but the Captain said nothing. I was almost asleep, but couldn't take my eyes off the Captain, looking so intently into the flame. All the sounds blurred together, and it seemed almost quiet. A log shifted heavily in the fire and a shower of sparks erupted silently and swirled slowly—*too* slowly, into the air. Everything seemed to move impossibly slow, and all I could think was, *What is the Captain planning?*

Finally the Captain stood and spread his arms for the men to be quiet. "I've heard enough. This Council is over. We will continue moving down the mountain in the morning." At that, he turned and walked slowly away. Two soldiers lifted me, though I tried to object. They carried me after the Captain, but soon left the road and took me to the Captain's tent. They laid me next to David, already sleeping. It seemed the Captain was headed somewhere else. David rolled over and whispered to me.

"I thought you'd never get here. Sally said you went to the *Captain's Council*. Why couldn't I come?"

"I don't know. I fell asleep anyway. I slept and dreamt most of the time I was there.

"*Sleeping and dreaming,*" he scoffed. "Couldn't you stay awake? The Princess said the Captain would only call for a council if a very important decision has to be made."

I didn't reply, though David badgered me with more questions. The next morning, I had no memory of them. Just before I fell asleep, I yawned and said to my brother, "I almost forgot…the ice troll is *melting.*"

2.4 For the Greed of Gold

I woke the next morning to the cropped view of my brother staring at me. I sputtered in his face.

"What's the matter?" he asked quickly.

"You're close enough to bite my nose, for one. Are you trying to look up it, or eat it?"

"*Neither*," he replied angrily, and backed away, though not by much. "I wanted to wake you, but Sally said I had to let you sleep. Now, what did you mean about the ice troll melting? Were you dreaming when you said it?"

I told him all about the puddles of water dripping from the troll's cart and how he'd shrunk. He sat speechless, either in awe, or disbelief. I told him of my dreams and how the Council was trying to use them to decide what to do.

"Are you serious?" cried David. "They think *you're* going to know what to do? They should've asked *me*, I'm the older brother."

"Only by a year."

"Two," he insisted. He always called it *two years*, and I always called it one. In truth, we were exactly eighteen months apart.

"Anyway," I replied, "I don't think age had anything to do with it. Maybe everyone here thinks dreams are really important. Maybe when the troll scratched me, they thought it gave me some kind of mysterious knowledge about ice trolls," I guessed wildly. Even as I said it, it seemed unlikely.

"I can't believe they *listened* to you. You should tell them to throw the dumb troll *into a pit*. Yeah, go to the Captain now, and tell him you just remembered the dream. Tell them to dig a pit and throw him in, before you have a dream we all *jump off a cliff*."

I chuckled. I *could* have a dream about jumping off a cliff. Suddenly it didn't seem so funny. What if I *did* dream of doing something crazy? How could I let them do whatever I dreamed? And yet, I didn't want to lie to the Captain.

"I can't *lie* to him."

"What's worse?" David asked, "Lying, or telling him of some crazy dream, and getting us all killed?"

I thought about it for a long time. To my surprise, found I *couldn't* lie to him. We stood to walk to the cart, but I found I was too dizzy to walk.

"Wait," David said, "I forgot—you're not supposed to walk. *Wait right here.*"

He ran off. I tried to follow, but felt even dizzier, and my stomach objected. I sat down impatiently. Soon two soldiers brought a makeshift stretcher, and I reluctantly climbed onto it. They carried me to the temporary royal coach, and I carefully entered.

Princess Schelli was not there. Lady Sally gave me water and bread, and told me to drink as much as I could hold. She removed the bandages from my neck, and I felt the last wrap peel painfully from my wound. She dressed my neck in fresh bandages, and asked if they were too tight. I shook my head and realized, not for the first time, turning my head was very painful.

"Good *morning.*" I turned—again, painfully—to see the Princess enter the cart under the door flap. "Have any good *dreams* last night?" she asked with a smile. I felt a warm rush in my face as I blushed.

"How did you know?" I asked. She only smiled. "It's not my fault," I offered defensively, "I didn't tell the Captain to do as I dreamed." The Princess was too calm about it, as if it were a joke.

"You don't have to worry about the Captain doing as you say," she finally replied. "He's so stubborn, sometimes I don't think he even listens to the King."

"But last night, they listened so..." I trailed off, not knowing what else to say. Did I misunderstand? Were they only playing with me? Just minutes ago, I felt certain they were ready to do whatever I told them. When the Princess saw the look on my face, she laughed.

"Oh, they were listening to you, all right—but the Captain makes his own decisions. Sure, he might hold councils and listen to dreams, and talk to a lot of people, but he decides against what he hears as often as not. Just like my father, he says it's important to have all the information before making a decision."

"Well," I asked impatiently, "what did he decide?"

"He decided to decide *later*," she giggled. "He said he still needs more information."

It worried me to hear her say this. I was almost ready to take David's plan and deceive the Captain, but still, I knew I couldn't lie to the Captain.

After eating all the food Sally gave me, and emptying half the canteen, I felt very tired. When I lay down, the cart began to roll. It rocked back and forth as the cart was pulled over the trail.

After a fashion, the rocking grew worse. The cart was jumping wildly, bouncing high into the air and crashing back down on the trail with a deafening noise. When I sat up, everything had turned quiet, and I was frightened to discover I was alone in the cart. My stomach turned as I felt the unmistakable sensation of falling—then tumbling. I looked out from the door flap, but saw only sky. The cart tumbled and I saw I was falling into a deep pit. The bottom was dark and somehow I knew it was *cold*. The cart crashed into the pit's floor, landing in a deep pool of water. I swam furiously to a rock jutting out from the surface. I shook violently and felt feverous. I saw something high above me tumbling, falling down into the water with a great splash. I looked closely and saw in horror—it was the ice troll. He swam toward me, all the while eying me with a ghoulish scowl. I looked for a place to hide, but there was none.

I woke up. I lay still, savoring the grateful feeling of realizing *it was only a dream*. I felt cold, and realized the cart had stopped moving. The flap of carpet was open, and through it, a guard was conversing with Lady Sally. When he left, Lady Sally turned to me, and asked me to sit up and drink. When I finished, she told me the Captain was coming to talk with me.

When he arrived, I was happy to tell him about my dream. I knew it was probably only a result from David's suggestion, but it was better than nothing.

"Thank you," the Captain replied somberly. "That's all I needed to know." Without another word, he left. Lady Sally stared at me with wide eyes, while the Princess wore a sorrowful expression. Neither of them spoke, and an awkward silence hung over us.

I lay back down, exhausted. It wasn't long before David opened the flap and poked his head in.

"Are you feeling any better?" he asked.

I wished I could tell him I was, but I only shook my head in response. *Ouch.*

"Did you *really* dream that," he asked, "or did you dream we all jumped into the ocean, and were too afraid to tell him?" Apparently, he'd been listening from outside the cart.

"Well, I kind of dreamed *both*. I dreamt the cart was falling down a big hole filled with water, but I don't think it really matters. Then I saw the troll fall after me, down into the same pit."

"Schelli said you were moaning and making noises in your sleep. Are you sure you're all right?" David was uncharacteristically concerned.

"My neck and head hurt, but that's all. I feel dizzy a lot, and my stomach doesn't feel so good…"

David climbed in and sat on the floor between the two makeshift benches, crowding Sally's feet.

"Can I ride in here with him?" David looked at Sally.

"I suppose you should," she replied with a cautious smile, "I think it may do him some good."

The cart began moving again, and I wished for a soft mattress under me. David pulled back the door flap behind him to take in the view. I caught a glimpse of a long arc in the trail ahead of us.

"Hey," I strained to yell, "Keep it open."

Impossibly, I thought I recognized the road ahead of us. Deja vu always sent shivers down my spine, and this was no exception. *Where have I seen this before?*

Just beyond the edge of the road was a cliff—a long drop-off, not far from the wheels of our cart. The worn trail led us along its curved edge, and I looked out from it. I couldn't see the bottom, but far past the cliff, I saw another rising from the mist. I followed it until I realized the edges of the two cliffs curved to meet at both ends. I labored to sit up and stick my head through the flap, again painfully turning my neck. The cliff was the rim of a giant crater, colossal in every dimension. I thought back to my dream. *If I dreamt of a pit because David mentioned it*, I thought, *what made David think of a pit, only hours before we reached one?*

"Did you know we were going to pass a big crater like this?" I asked him, looking to Princess Schelli and her steward for confirmation.

Lady Sally explained, "The Princess and I have passed it many times, but I don't think your brother knew of it."

David shook his head, and Lady Sally continued.

"This place has a long and horrible history." She paused, as if to see if she held my interest. "Centuries ago, there was a great mine in place of this pit. The miners followed gold so deep under the mountain, it became hard to breathe. They found a way to recycle their air, but hit an underground aquifer. They re-routed an underground stream, and ran into yet more problems."

"*Really?*" David remarked, "It must've been some gold mine."

"Yes," Sally replied. "It was indeed. What I've described so far took place over a century. Eventually, it became too dangerous, and the King declared the mine closed. A few decades later, a group of rich trolls asked for the King's permission to work in the mine, and trade with him for the gold they found. They claimed trolls don't need quite as much air as humans, and it would be safe for them. Trolls dealt with humans more often back then, you see, when the Princess's great-great-great uncle was king."

Lady Sally smiled at me and patted me on the head. David's eyes were fixed on her intently.

"The trolls found great amounts of gold deep under the mountain, and for many years it was prosperous for much of the kingdom. Farms sprouted up in the nearby area to sell food to the many trolls working here. Blacksmiths paid high wages to crowds of apprentices, struggling to meet the tooling needs of the mine. The King, and eventually his heir, saw their treasury grow large with the gold the trolls mined, and the trolls were growing rich too. Their leaders called themselves lords, though they held no such titles from the King.

"No human knew how many trolls were deep within the mine; no humans were allowed to enter. Eventually, the surrounding areas were crowded with farms, and they sent all their food down into the mines. It is said there was a steady line of trolls and mules with food and supplies leading down into the mines, and a steady line of mules loaded with gold and rock and dirt coming out.

"After many years, the new King became worried. No one knew how deep the mine was, or how wide it had grown underground. The rich troll lords claimed all was fine, and kept telling the King how much gold was *just a little deeper.*"

"Were they right?" asked David.

"It seems they were," Sally answered. "The rate at which they pulled gold from the mine seemed to always increase. It was rumored at the end, they were limited only by the amount of food available to the mine site. If they had redirected food from farms of Terrezia Plain, they would have affected food prices across the entire kingdom, and brought more notice to their growing numbers."

Sally paused to take a drink. She reminded me to do the same, advising once more, I should drink as much as I could hold.

"Where was I now?" she asked. "Oh yes. The mine lords claimed everything was fine, but the King was wise, and didn't believe them. He suspected things were anything but safe in those deep channels under the mountain—both for the trolls who worked in them, and for his human subjects who lived and worked nearby.

"He knew the trolls had grown in number. Eventually, he called for his advisors to estimate their number. Their results were shocking— far larger than the troll population *throughout the kingdom* was previously believed to be. The King knew closing the mine would cause a revolt, so he began to gather a great army to enforce its closure without forewarning the troll lords. While he was gathering men from across the kingdom, something terrible happened. It caused a dreadful noise; some say the King heard it all the way from Engdynlor, still a few days' travel from here."

"What was it?" David interrupted.

"Why, the mine of course. It collapsed."

"*What?*" I asked, somewhat shocked. I should have guessed where the story was leading.

"Yes," Lady Sally replied. "The entire mine, and many of the farms in the surrounding area; they *all* collapsed. They dug so deep, so vast were their tunnels, the entire area became unstable. Some say," she added with a mischievous twinkle in her eye, "the roots of Golden Mountain were shaken, and this is why it's now shorter than its neighbors." David eyes grew wide, and he leaned closer, drawn in by her tale. She lost her smile, and her expression grew sorrowful.

"All but a few of the trolls died, some of those who guided the mules in and out of the mine. Many farmers died too. The great pit you see now is all we have to remind us of their folly. This pit, the Spill Hills, and a tiny slice of the Spill Plain."

"*That's awful,*" I blurted out. "They all just *died? None* came out?"

"There was nothing left to come out *from,*" she said. "The entire area sunk as far down as you can see the pit is deep. Their greed for gold killed them all."

We were all silent for a moment. My mind turned to a strange word she'd used.

"Where did the King hear the noise from—some place a few days from here?"

"Eh?" Lady Sally responded in surprise. "Oh—from *his palace*; it's called *Engdynlor*. It's in the center of Thraen Kholl, our capitol." It seemed odd to me they would have a special name for a building, even if it was a palace. I was about to make sure I'd heard her correctly, but David spoke first.

"What are the *spill things* you mentioned—hills and plains?"

"They are two of the three massive changes the troll miners brought to this mountain range. All the dirt and rock they pulled from the ground had to go somewhere, so they formed the Spill Plain and the Spill Hills. We'll see the last of the Spill Plain farther down the mountain today. It was a small plain built downhill of the mine, for farming. They created level ground where before, there was only sloping mountainside.

"The Spill Hills are older, created before the Spill Plain. In fact, the Spill Plain is built upon a number of these hills. The hills were built before the mine's growth was limited by available food. They're a result of carrying the excess dirt and rock only as far as necessary. If you imagine how much work it is to move enough rock to build a hill, you will understand why they carried it as short a distance as possible. The trolls simply carried their loads as far as they needed to, and dumped them to spill down the far side of the growing hills. Over generations, they created an artificial set of foot hills, built on the gentle slope of this mountain.

"The Spill Hills surround the mine on three sides—every direction but uphill. The Spill Plain—what's left of it—surrounds the mine on the same three sides, closer to the mine.

"What happened after it collapsed?" David asked. He'd hardly taken his eyes from Sally since she'd begun her story.

"The King declared the entire area abandoned, and illegal to enter. Soldiers were posted around the perimeter for many years to keep people out. They arrested men for trying to enter the pit in search of gold. Those who snuck past the soldiers never returned from the shifting ground down there; some say it is still sinking today. The sides of the cliffs are too steep to climb up or down without long ropes. *This* is why I reacted to your dream as I did, Mark. You dreamed of throwing the troll into this pit, it seems—without hearing of it first."

"Will he melt down there? Or die of thirst?"

"Oh, I don't think he'll melt," she chuckled. *Doesn't she know?* I wondered.

"It's very cold," she went on, "And there are plenty of cold streams, fed by snowmelt. I imagine he'll find a colder climate down there than any place but the top of the mountain. It's shifting ground, and could give out under his feet if he doesn't stay at the perimeter of the pit, near the cliff."

"Where do the streams go?" I asked.

"See for yourself. They disappear into the rocky ground of the pit floor. What half-filled tunnels lie beneath, no one knows."

"Yeah, half-filled with *gold*," David chimed. "Didn't the King *ever* let people go back down to look?" he asked, obviously disappointed.

"No. And neither did he let his soldiers go down into the pit to rescue the dying trespassers. Many greedy men died of minor injuries, simply because they could no longer climb back up the cliff. They snuck past the guards to find gold in spite of the King's law, only to sink into a pile of rocks. The King declared he wouldn't allow more to die in trying to rescue the dead. *No one* came out, young man," she told David in a scolding tone, "*not one.*"

I was surprised to hear her speak such brutal words toward the trespassers. I shivered to think of those who died trapped in the pit looking for gold, and of the soldiers who wanted to help them. It must have been a horrible way to die, and also a horrible way to live—to hear them screaming and yet be forbidden to help. *Well*, I thought, *at least now I know why it's called* Golden Mountain. Another thought occurred to me. *Why do the antelopes of the plain believe the surrounding mountains once glowed?*

Soon, my thoughts returned to the mine. I thought of my dream, and what the Captain said when I described it to him. *That's all I needed to know.*

"Do you think the Captain threw the ice troll down there?" I asked.

"The Captain did what he decided was best," replied Schelli, who had been silent for some time. "It's his responsibility to decide. He's a wise man, Mark."

I didn't feel much better, though I knew in my mind she was right. I lay down again and tried to rest. After a long while, the cart seemed to be rolling a little uphill. When the road became steeper, I decided to look outside. There were scrub pines not far from the cart. Ahead of us, the gravelly road climbed up a long, wide hill. Sally saw I'd noticed.

"Can you feel the difference?" she asked. "We're no longer riding on level ground. We've passed the Spill Plain and we're climbing the first of the remaining Spill Hills. Long ago, travelers rode downhill where we are now riding uphill. See if you can find the stream running down this hill, over the last remnants of plain and into the pit."

I searched for it, but I didn't find it. We saw so many massive hills around us, I found it difficult to believe they were all built by hand.

"Wow," David remarked, "Everything in all these hills came out of the mine?"

"All this, and more," teased Sally. "Remember the *gold*—they certainly didn't leave any in these hills. Don't forget; some of these hills have worn back into the pit over the past centuries. This is why the downhill side of the mine pit isn't quite so deep. When we begin to roll down the last Spill Hill, you'll be able to see where some of the spill dirt has eroded *away* from the mine, too. The last spill hill has the longest downhill slope.

"See if you can find an apple or cherry tree; there once were many of them here. The Spill Plain grew crops, and some of the Spill Hills were long ago covered with orchards. Without the extra sunlight, this mountain is no longer hospitable to fruit trees, I'm afraid. It's simply too cold most of the year to support them."

"Extra sunlight?" I asked, "What do you mean?"

"Just what I said. This mountain received brighter sunlight, and received it *longer* than the rest of the kingdom. But," she added with a smile, "I'm sure you've heard more than you care to hear of Golden Mountain's history."

I began to doubt I could put any faith in what the Princess's steward said. Surely it was legend, or superstition. *One mountain can't get more or brighter sunlight than the rest*, I thought. And yet, she spoke with the authority of someone wise and inquisitive enough to discern fables from history.

"How do you know so much of the mines?" I asked.

Lady Sally smiled. "Did you think the King would appoint a fool to instruct his daughter?" I hadn't realized she was also Schelli's teacher. *We might learn more from her than anyone else*, I thought. I turned a little to face her.

"Do you know of any places *outside* the kingdom?"

"The stars and the sun—and the moon, and the distance between. *Some* say the kingdom includes those too—but if you include only where people are ruled by the King; this is all the land west of the Daggora Mountains."

I decided to ask another way. "If you could sail far away from land, is there other land you might see, not connected to this land?" I hoped she might have learned more geography than the Captain.

"There are a few small piles of rock, and the tiny islands of the Broken Coast. Most are too small for even a house to be built upon, but a half-dozen or so could fit a house and a farm, should someone desire badly enough to live there. As far as I know, no one ever has.

"Whether there is land farther out to sea, no one in the kingdom knows. As far as ships have sailed and still returned, they never saw any. Scientific expeditions have measured the depth of the oceans, and they seem to grow deeper the farther out they sail, with no sign of shallowing." I guessed this could be true of a large island in the middle of the ocean.

"What about the extra sunlight?" I asked. "I'm not bored—I really want to know."

Lady Sally looked at the Princess and flashed a friendly grin. I would later learn the doomed mine era was Lady Sally's favorite, of all their kingdom's long history.

"Princess, it seems you've picked some rather studious friends," Sally joked. "If only you were as eager to learn our history as they are." The Princess stuck her tongue out, then smiled to cover it up. I was glad for Lady Sally's stories. She'd said very little before the Captain had spoken with her, almost nothing before I began asking her questions. *It's not so unusual*, I supposed, *for a teacher*. Sally shifted in her seat and began lecturing once again.

"Then I suppose I must begin with another people. I must first tell you of the Korvotians."

"The who?" I asked excitedly. "Are they from a different kingdom?"

"*Of course not*," replied the Princess, visibly irritated. "They were a different *people* in *our* kingdom."

David wrinkled his brow and asked, "If everyone belongs to the same kingdom, aren't you all the same *people*?" Sally looked surprised.

"Oh, our King is wiser than *that*," she replied. "He values each people for their uniqueness; their customs and cultures are each their own. This is part of the greatness of our kingdom—our peoples are different, but choose to be ruled by one wise King." Her face turned a shade less serious and she added, "If you are done interrupting me, I will continue…"

I hadn't even realized we'd distracted her from her lecture.

"The Korvotians were a people who worked with metal, or rather building complex structures with metal. They were contracted by the trolls when the mine began its second expansion: when they saw they would one day be limited by the amount of food they could redirect to the mine site. It was an unimaginable goal, one of the largest single accomplishments in our history. It serves as a reminder of the many ways greed can motivate. After all, if we aren't motivated *by love*, it is often *greed* who is our master. For all their foolishness, the mine lords had the wisdom to plan well ahead, and the *desire* and *discipline* to achieve the impossible."

David and I looked at each other, and I held back a smile. To Lady Sally and the Princess, I supposed I seemed as eager as David.

"The trolls believed there was a near-infinite supply of gold under this mountain; in fact, they claimed the root of the mountain was made of pure gold. As I've said, they were wise enough to see how large their operation would grow. Some say they believed they would eventually have the entire kingdom growing food for their miners. It is said they would have eventually conquered the kingdom through expansion."

"What do you mean?" David interrupted.

I glared at him as if to say, *another interruption?* Sally glared at him too, but answered nonetheless.

"Can't you see? If the entire kingdom committed all their resources to bringing food to the trolls, it wouldn't matter if they *really* ruled or not. In practice, we would all be working for the trolls. The mining lords would control the resources of the kingdom, and with an uncountable army underground, it wouldn't have been long before they ruled from the throne as well."

Her eyes gleamed with excitement. She paused to regain her composure—or perhaps for dramatic effect.

"Now, where was I? Oh yes, the farmland. They knew they would need farmland nearby, when the mines had grown steadily for another century or so. The climate was too cold for productive farming most of the year, so they hired the Korvotians to build the Great Mirrors. We should be able to see some of their remnants now."

I looked out the door flap, but when I realized I didn't know what to look for, I lay back down. Before she went on, Sally looked at me knowingly and smiled.

"This mountain is part of a long range. The nearest mountains on both sides were of great interest to the mining lords. The mountain they called Westward lit up with sunlight a little earlier each dawn, and the mountain called Eastward stayed lit with sunlight a little later. They contracted the Korvotians to erect gilded mirrors to cover the closer sides of both mountains. They would reflect sunlight from those mountains down onto the long, gentle slope of Golden Mountain all day long, including the extra time in the morning and evening. So Golden Mountain received the sunlight of three mountains, stealing it from Eastward and Westward." *Stealing sunlight* sounded dramatic to me, but I said nothing. David wasn't so patient.

"How could they?" he interrupted once again. "How can you build a mirror big enough to cover a *mountain?*"

"They didn't", answered Lady Sally with a smile. "They covered both mountaintops with many, *many* mirrors. So many, when they were finished, no sunlight touched the ground of the other mountain faces. Let's look out and see if we can see Eastward and Westward yet." She looked out first, then let each of us follow her example.

"Look carefully and see the tiny steps carved in some places. Look for roads built in the rockier parts. The Korvotians built all the mirrors the same size. Each one was made of the same parts. Only one in one thousand were made to be adjusted. After they set each of the adjustable mirrors and fixed them to strike in the correct place, the gaps between them were filled with mirrors set in their positions permanently. Watch and once in a great while you may see a flash of light where a mirror is still erected. Of course, most have been torn down for their *precious gold.* Perhaps one in a hundred thousand remain." As she said this, she turned quickly to watch David with a playful grin.

"*Really?*" he asked, hopefully.

"Forget it, David," said the Princess. "People have spent *months* looking for just one mirror. What you can see clear as the sun from here gets lost in all the rubble, so far away."

Sally smiled and continued. "For half a hundred years they worked on those mirrors. How it must have gleamed, though—can you imagine? Both mountains lit up like the sun all day, every day…" she trailed off, apparently lost in thought.

"Look there," said David, "I can see a little gleam *right now*." I turned my head quickly to try to see out the flap he held open. I tried to shriek and suck in my breath at once. Sally scolded David and told me to lie down. Gently, she removed my bandage and looked closely at my throat. David's head poked up from behind her, trying to see. I saw his eyes grow wide while he let out a tiny gasp. His fearful reaction made me shudder.

"Why does it look like *that*? Why is it blue and...*shriveled*?" David whispered.

Sally *Tisk-Tisk*'ed him away, saying, "Oh, never mind about that—it's only some bruising. You'd also be black and blue, if I squeezed you long enough." Despite her reassurance, her voice had grown more concerned.

"Why don't you let Mark rest," Sally continued, "and go see if you can find the Captain. I wonder if he knows all about the Great Mirrors." David looked a little doubtful, but soon said he would go. I imagined he was excited about seeing the Captain without me. He jumped from the cart and ran off to find him.

"You need to get some sleep, my dear boy. But drink some more water first, and eat this." Sally handed me a canteen and some more bread. I was beginning to worry my injury would only grow worse.

I tried to sleep, but my mind was too full of thoughts. I looked over at the Princess and saw she was sleeping. I turned to ask Sally another question.

"What were you before the King appointed you to care for the Princess?" She looked at me with a sharp eye.

"In a word: *lost*. Before I found myself in the King's service, I didn't know who I was."

"Really?" I asked, then added, "I hope you don't mind me asking such personal questions."

"Not at all. How else would I share what lessons I've learned?" She added with a wink, "I may not look it, but I haven't been a teenager for a long, long time."

"Then may I ask; how can you find who you are by serving someone else? Wouldn't you find out who the King is, more than yourself?"

"Exactly," she said. She wore a smile far too wide to match her words.

"I don't understand."

"I've known people who spent their entire lives trying to *find themselves*. And do you know what? They never do. Finding yourself isn't about focusing your life upon yourself. That's infinite introspection—you *lose* yourself within yourself. It limits your horizons, relationships, and success. It destroys your capacity for change, and in the ultimate poetic injustice, your happiness as well. No, it's not a healthy path for anyone…" She looked lost for just a moment, as if recalling an unpleasant memory.

"When you dedicate your life to a *cause*—and not just any cause mind you—*then* you will find yourself. I was no one before I served the King and his family. My service is my life—and it is a joyous one."

"Lady Sally," I replied, "I envy that in you."

"Why do you say that? Of what are you envious?" I was surprised by her confronting manner. I had only meant to compliment her.

"Why, your ability to dedicate yourself to a cause so trustingly, I suppose."

"I believe we all have that ability. In fact, I believe it's what makes us *alive*."

Though her words made no sense to me, they irritated me. I smiled weakly in her direction, then rolled over and finally fell asleep. I was still sleeping when David and the Captain returned. Later, David told me Lady Sally spoke quietly with the Captain for a long time. She got angry at one point, and told him something he clearly didn't want to hear. David seemed to think it had to do with me sleeping in the cart while I rode with them.

2.5 Race for Engdynlor

When I woke, it was dark outside, but we were still moving. I asked Lady Sally why we were traveling in the dark.

She replied, "The Princess is becoming very homesick. She misses her father very much."

If the Princess was homesick, I hadn't seen any sign of it. I gave more thought to my throbbing head. I felt too hot or too cold no matter what I did. I fell asleep once more, and woke when our cart came to a stop. I heard guards talking outside. David sat on the cart's floor in front of me. He looked very excited.

"I'm going to spend the night in the Captain's tent while you stay here. He's going to tell me about all the famous battles fought near here."

I suspected Sally had asked the Captain to let me sleep in the cart. This made me worry all the more for my health. I took another sip of water and fell into a deep sleep. Sometime during the night I know I woke, hot and drenched. I had strange dreams about trying to sleep with no relief. When I woke in the morning I was shaking with cold.

Though I remember little of this night, I remember learning how the soldiers kept the small cart warm for Lady Sally and the Princess. They dropped large rocks into their campfires when they first lit them, then used large sticks and boards to roll them out and lift them into the cart, onto a bed of mud and wet leaves or grass. In this way, when I woke, the cart was much warmer than the cold air, which blew in whenever the flap was raised. I remember waking to the smell of dirt and old leaves.

It seemed to me we started earlier in the morning than we had on the previous days. Just after a pair of soldiers scraped the leaves and mud away, David climbed into the cart and sat on a bed of fresh leaves they'd brought.

"Do you feel any better?" my brother asked me.

"I think I have a fever."

Sally looked at the two of us, then met eyes with the Princess. Schelli's eyes were red and looked as if she'd been crying.

"Boys," Sally said quietly, "There's something I need to tell you."

She looked directly at me. Her eyes were kind, but fretful.

"The injury the ice troll gave you is infected. It's the reason you have a fever. We're still three days away from Engdynlor, but we can make it in two if we ride farther each day. When we get there, I know you'll be fine." She paused and patted my head. David's gaze never left her.

"As soon as we arrive," she continued, "the King will set you straight. For now, it's important you drink as much water as you can."

"What about the duke of the desert?" David asked.

"Duke *Ward*, of *Enthicia*," Lady Sally corrected. "Runners will be sent to carry our news to him. We must cross the desert instead. Enthicia is narrow, so crossing it to reach Engdynlor is much shorter than traveling along it to TerkEtmek." Sally sounded very serious, as if she spoke of life and death.

"Terk-*what?*" David asked, scrunching his nose.

"Terk*Etmek*," she explained slowly. "It's the desert trade city where the duke lives." David seemed about to ask her another question when I interrupted, frustrated with his distraction.

"Is the King a *doctor?*" I asked,

Sally gave me a funny look, as if I'd changed the subject.

"He often makes the sick well, if that's what you're asking." She spoke so resolutely, I guessed this response was all I would get from her. David and I spoke for a little while, but I had to fight to stay awake. Finally, I lay down and went to sleep. It felt good to sleep; it was my only respite from the pounding headache and burning pain in my throat.

While I slept, I dreamt I was lying on soft grass beside a tropical pool. Tall trees towered over me, and shorter trees and palms surrounded me on three sides. Taller trees filtered the sunlight to soft tones. The water sparkled deep blue. I dreamt David and Princess Schelli were splashing in the pool and laughing. David swam near a small waterfall feeding the pool. He swam toward it as fast as he could, then let its current push him away.

The contrast from the dream to my next waking was terrible. Weak sunlight shone in my eyes. I was very cold, and shook uncontrollably. I wondered if I was trapped in a nightmare, and tried to make groggy sense of my surroundings. I was no longer in the cart—people were carrying me. David ran beside me and tried to hold my hand, but fell short. My head was throbbing and bouncing, and my whole body felt frozen—except for my neck. My neck burned as hot as fire.

This memory is still fresh in my mind after all these years. I had no sense of time—how long they carried me or even how long I was awake. I have no recollection of being set down, only of being carried. When I woke, I was in a warm bed with white sheets and heavy blankets. I felt much better, and for a while I thought I was completely healed—until I turned my head.

Ouch! Suddenly, the wound on my neck hurt as badly as ever. If I kept my head straight and moved slowly, I felt close to normal—or at least a very tired version of normal. My fever was gone, my head didn't hurt, and I was *hungry*. For the first time in days I was *very* hungry. There was a glass and pitcher of water beside my bed. I emptied them both. There was a bathroom built right off the room, and I used it. Standing and walking, I realized my throbbing headache wasn't far away. I was dizzy, and not a good kind of dizzy, either. I felt sick to my stomach and for a moment I lost my appetite.

As I stepped out of the bathroom, I saw a very large man sitting in the chair beside my bed. The Captain stood behind him. *They weren't there before, were they?* I couldn't say why, but he looked *important*. The man smiled and seemed to look sad, both at once.

"Are you the one responsible for saving my daughter's life?" he rumbled. His voice was peaceful, even gracious, but low, as if it might shake the floor.

"Yes, Sire," the Captain answered for me when it became apparent I would not—or *could* not—answer for myself. "A brave boy indeed." He too, wore a smile while he spoke.

"Come now, lay down; you're not better *yet*," the stranger said. "It was a nasty strike the enemy made when you stood too near to his cart."

"Yes sir," I sheepishly replied. *Is the ice troll his enemy?* I wondered.

The Captain leaned toward me and added, "That's *yes, Sire.* This is our *King.*"

"Enough of that for now, Andrew," the King replied, and his voice caught with a low chuckle. "The boy can't be expected to follow court etiquette in his sick bed." Again, I had to wonder if the floor had moved a little, or if I was only dizzy. I had to ask myself whether or not I was dreaming.

"No, son, you are not," said the King with a smile. I was embarrassed—I must have unwittingly whispered my thoughts, as I've often been told I do. The King looked at me and winked. "Your friends will visit you soon. Rest and heal, and be careful not to tell others of your encounter with the ice troll." Before I could respond, he rose and left. The Captain followed behind him.

As I lay there wondering what had just happened, David burst into the room. He squeezed me in an embrace as I sat up, carefully avoiding the bandages on my neck. Sally followed. She stood just inside the door, and nodded to someone behind her. Finally, the Princess joined them. Schelli sat on the chair while Sally stood and David leaned on the side of my bed. David and Schelli raced each other to instruct me on all I'd missed while I phased in and out of consciousness.

As they reported, the Captain had been afraid I would die before we reached Thraen Kholl. He decided he and a portion of the guards would travel nonstop with the Princess's cart. We stopped only once to water the oxen, at a place called the Green Oasis, or Tume Belor, as Lady Sally called it. They described it exactly as I'd dreamt, somewhere in the middle of the narrow desert we'd crossed.

When the Captain had told Sally it would take at least an hour to water the oxen, she'd had me carried to the poolside, and let the Princess and David play in the water. My heart swelled to know such a place truly existed.

"How sad you didn't really get to see it…only through a half-dream," Schelli said.

"I wish I could go back and see it again," I replied.

"And you shall," boomed a low and familiar voice from the doorway. It was the Captain. All eyes were on him as he entered the room. "I will take you to the Duke of Enthicia, by way of Tume Belor. The King sends us."

The Captain stood beside Sally, and tried to calm us as we assailed him with questions.

"One at a time—*slow down*. First, there are some things you need to know about the ice troll. It's as you've probably heard, we let him down into the mine-pit of Golden Mountain. He'll remain there until the King's fast messengers reach him. In fact, they've most likely reached him by now. The mark he gave you," he said, motioning toward my wound, "is a vicious one." My hand floated to touch my neck…it still burned, and *itched*.

"You're much better now," said the Captain, "but you are not healed. If left untreated, the infection could return, and even kill you."

David's eyes grew wide, and the Princess let out a quiet gasp. My face turned hot, and for the briefest of moments, I felt as if I'd lost my breath. The Captain continued.

"According to the King, the only way you can be fully healed is to make a trip through the desert. I shall accompany you, all the way to the Valley of Abandon."

"Is it near the Green Oasis? What did you call it—*Tume Belor*?" I asked. The name *Valley of Abandon* would seem less intimidating if it were near the oasis the Princess had just described.

"It is *not*," the Captain answered grimly. "We turn to the desert path at the Green Oasis—Tume Belor is its ancient name. We follow the trail to the duke's mansion at TerkEtmek, then turn east to find the Valley of Abandon. It is a long journey."

Schelli seemed angry, and Sally, troubled, but neither spoke. David gave no hesitation.

"How can he go on a long journey if he's sick? Won't it make him worse?"

"He will continue to get better over the next weeks. He will be strong enough to ride a horse, and to fight, if need be."

"Fight?" I asked quietly, "Who would I *fight*?"

"We'll be crossing dangerous land. It would be wise to be able to fight before traveling there."

"Are you *crazy*?" David burst out, "My brother's on his *deathbed*, and you want to take him into some dangerous land where he has to fight for his *life*? If he gets better in the next few weeks, he'll keep getting better until he's *back to normal*."

I shuddered violently to hear those last three words. Suddenly there were too many memories resurrected in my mind, and too many parallels between the present and another recovery I'd made in the past year, after an accident I'd tried hard to forget. Deja vu had never been less welcome.

I shook off my paramnesia, but not before it was noticed. My demeanor had changed so abruptly, everyone in the room but the Captain had fixed their gaze on me. Lady Sally seemed worried, and turned as if to say something reassuring. I don't know if she looked less certain of what needed to be said, or who needed to hear it. The Captain broke the silence, speaking to David instead of me.

"Be cautious what you say, young man. This is what the King has said; I will not try to prove it to you. You see, to *me* there's no proof more valid than *the King has said it*. Mark will have his choice in this. Only the sick can choose to be made well, and only Mark can choose to take this journey. If he does not, he must take his chances with the future his wounds will bring him." Then the Captain turned to me and his face softened a bit—though not by much.

"Let me warn you, the longer you hold onto a wound—*any wound*—the deeper it becomes." He paused just long enough for David to reply, though the Captain interrupted him abruptly. "And David, what if *back to normal* isn't a place your brother wants to go? Can you choose for him?"

When he turned back to me, I was sure his eyes held the answers to all the questions I'd been consumed with so long—the questions weighing on my mind since the accident back home. For just a moment, I was certain the Captain could see right into my mind.

Unwanted memories I'd fought back for months rushed over me: a horrible car wreck on the way to my first pro ball game. My best friend had chosen me as his guest, a birthday present from his parents. The irony of their gift hadn't been wasted on me; so much pain and suffering had come from a *gift*. It left me in the hospital for months, and trapped in bed at home even longer—and yet my friend and his parents had fared much worse. It took a long while before I'd felt whole again. The feeling was recent enough, I'd just begun to feel guilty for it. Soon afterward, my sense of normalcy and my hopes to return to a peaceful life were interrupted by the mind-retching trip across worlds—our arrival in Terreldor.

What if I didn't want life to go back to normal? I didn't want a blindly-led life, lacking substance and meaning. I wanted my friends' life—cut off so unfairly—to mean something. Then suddenly, as unexpected as it was surprising, I felt determined *my life* would mean something—*I would make sure of it.*

These errant thoughts flew through my mind in a few short seconds. I looked quickly around—had anyone noticed? They were talking about the journey across the desert, only I hadn't been paying attention. David seemed calmer. I knew he was no longer worried about the journey, because he believed I would never embark on it. As soon as the Captain said I'd have a choice, my brother had the answer he wanted. He believed he could convince me not to go, and normally I would have expected he could. *Just maybe* I was so desperate, he'd have no ability to sway me.

Too many ideas sapped at my strength. They whirled about my head until I was dizzy and tired, but most of all, frustrated. I was sick of missing things, only to be told of them later. I wanted to be part of what was going on, and yet I found I was falling asleep again. Sally saw my tired eyes and hushed the others.

"My dears, nothing needs to be decided today. Mark is tired and he needs his rest. Let's let him sleep, shall we?"

She gently ushered the others out of the room. The Captain followed them, but turned back, leaving his head poking through the doorway.

"Not to worry young man; you *will* feel better. And when you do, you'll never worry about feeling left-out again."

I sat up to ask what he meant, but he was already gone. Could he read my face so easily? It was unnerving to have my thoughts so exposed. I told myself I was tired and I must've misunderstood him, but I only half-believed it. Aggravated and spent, I fell into a restless sleep.

Part III

3.0 Recovery

In the weeks to come I *did* feel stronger—and eventually busier as well. In a few days I was moved from the lonely sickroom inside Engdynlor, and joined David in a small unused barrack, still within the palace wall. I was just as eager to find a way home, but I soon decided being a guest of the King in the center of Thraen Kholl was as good a way as any to bide our time.

While I wasn't well enough to travel, I hoped to learn as much as possible of the layout of the kingdom from whatever maps I could lay my hands on. At the very least, we had plenty to eat, and we were safe. Knowing there were real-life monsters lurking around this new world—some of them bent on murdering me—occupied a sizable portion of my mind at night. Having a place to sleep inside tall, well-guarded stone walls was a welcome thought most nights.

The first night after I was moved, we ate dinner with the Princess. During the meal, David asked if we could talk to her father about finding a way home. As she awkwardly began to answer, Sally interrupted.

"I know you aren't accustomed to our practices, but asking the Princess to petition her father on your behalf is…well, it isn't allowed. The King wouldn't tolerate someone using his daughter to bypass proper protocol." Princess Schelli looked regretful, but held her tongue.

"There are proper channels you must follow," Sally continued. "I will ask a page from the court to take your petition for an audience. But remember, the King is caught in very delicate interests right now. It's likely he couldn't see you right away, even if he longed to with all his heart." She surely saw the doubt in my eyes. It seemed unlikely to me the King couldn't do as he pleased. She added, "His responsibilities to his kingdom come first. If this weren't so, our dear Schelli would be taking her meal with her parents tonight."

Sally's words evoked another regretful reaction from Schelli. We resolved to patiently wait, but would eventually learn the *proper channels* took weeks and months rather than hours or days. For the rest of the evening, our conversation was light. Mostly, Schelli kept us busy with questions of our home. I enjoyed our time with her, but it was stained by the unspoken questions I wanted her to carry to her father.

In the following days, we began to wonder what was expected of us while we were guests in the palace grounds. While we hardly expected to be entertained, it seemed odd nothing was asked of us at all. We spent our time exploring the grounds and meeting the interesting people who lived and worked within the palace walls.

The palace itself—called Engdynlor by all—was the largest structure in the *palace grounds*—the official term for everything within the palace wall. The other buildings in the grounds circled Engdynlor. They were used for anything as lowly as the Royal Guard's stables, or as stately as the Grand Banquet Hall, the building used for coronations and other lofty events. The palace grounds were surrounded by the rest of the city, which was encircled by a second wall, both taller and thicker than the wall around Engdynlor.

There were several parks in the palace grounds, and even more in the surrounding city, filled with ornately trained shrubs and finely carved statues. In all the grounds, there was hardly an intersection without a garden, accompanied by a bench or decorative fountain. One day we would learn of a private garden, an open courtyard hidden within the palace itself. Even among those who lived and worked in the palace grounds, few had seen it.

I knew the grounds would hardly represent what we might find in the rest of the kingdom, and I badly wished to see outside the palace walls again. By the end of my second day in the barrack, we had a fair idea of the layout of the complex, but nothing else to show for our time. We began to feel a severe lack of occupation. Everyone around us was so *busy*, I felt like a loafer among them. On this same day, David brought up the subject.

"How long can we be expected to...do nothing?" I asked him, while we walked to our barrack.

"Why do you think the whole kingdom is arranged around us?" he replied, sarcastically. "Everything going on around us has nothing to do with us. Haven't you heard about the trade problems the King's busy with?" He could hardly know more than I did about the trade problems, which was close to nothing.

"Well," I countered, "What have you heard of them?" He glared at me.

"Oh, you know," he went on, "they've been keeping the King busy all the time. He probably forgot all about us. If he had time to think of us, don't you think we'd get our audience with him?"

"I think we ought to do *something*," I protested.

"You're walking around pretty well, right?" I nodded. I didn't tell him how badly my neck ached and burned, even from doing so little as turning my head. "Well, let's ask someone in the other barracks if there's anything we can do to help. Maybe we'll see the Captain there."

I also hoped we would find him—but as far as I could tell, if the King was busy with something, it was likely the Captain was busier.

We walked to the barrack beside ours early the next morning. When we knocked at the barrack door, it was answered promptly by a soldier not much older than the two of us.

"Yes?" he asked.

"Is there anyone…uh…*in charge* in there?" David asked, nodding past the soldier, farther inside the building.

"Yes, wait right here," he replied with a smile, and shut the door.

A moment later, the door opened again, and we were ushered in. I nearly tripped as we walked past a row of cots, unadjusted as my eyes were to the dim lighting. We were led to a desk in the back with a lantern chandelier hanging overhead. There were cobwebs between the oil lamps, and I couldn't shake the feeling they were swaying a little. The man at the desk spoke to us first.

"I am Lieutenant Underhill, the day-lieutenant. What do you need?" His brazen question did nothing to calm my nerves, but his manner was warmer than his words.

"Nothing," I answered him. "I mean—we don't *need* anything. We just want to help." How could I have spoken so clumsily? David, probably hoping to do better, jumped in.

"Is there something we can be doing, while we wait for an audience with the King?"

"Ah," replied the lieutenant. "Had enough sight-seeing?" The young soldier beside him chuckled.

"Yes," I replied, hopeful to show them I could actually speak. "That is—uh, *I guess so.*" Though I couldn't be sure, I suspected we'd been insulted. The Lieutenant seemed friendly, but the way the other soldier laughed made me wonder. Looking back at the incident years later, it was obvious they'd assigned someone to watch us. Two teenaged boys showing up with no history, just after a conspiracy to kidnap the Princess, would be highly suspicious. The safety of the Royal Family belonged to the Royal Guard, along with the security of the palace grounds; it was their *job* to suspect us.

"Well," Lt. Underhill went on, "I'm sure we can find something to keep you busy."

Each day afterward, we spent time doing chores around the complex. We were assigned to any tasks not requiring training or direct access to Engdynlor. We cleaned the stables, swept streets and floors, hauled garbage, and scrubbed pots and pans in the Guard's mess hall. David worked harder than I did, and I took frequent breaks during any task involving head-turning. After a week of drudgery, we found ourselves again at Lt. Underhill's desk, at his request.

"Well done, boys," he started. I winced. Were we only boys in his eyes? Though my pride was hurt, I tried to keep my face from showing it. "Thank you for your help. You've worked hard over the past week, more than paying for your food and lodging. I know your plans aren't settled yet, but anywhere you might go, it's likely to be on the back of a horse. Do either of you know how to ride?"

We both shook our heads. The lieutenant's eyes squinted with suspicion. He smiled as if he'd just confirmed a doubtful rumor.

"We'll start there. Tomorrow, I'll have a page bring you to a sergeant in the Calvary, and we'll see how much you can learn."

And so our days were spent outside the palace grounds, with the Calvary. The Calvary's stable was within the walls of Thraen Kholl, not far outside the palace wall. Cavalrymen of low rank trained us, while giving us a large enough share of drudgery for the time to pass quickly.

We met a different trainer each day. When I asked about this, I was surprised to learn in all the Calvary, there were very few men who were paid for their service. Most of them volunteered their time one or two days a week, and held jobs or owned businesses in and around Thraen Kholl.

On most nights we ate as guests of the Princess, along with Lady Sally, in Schelli's private quarters. Normally the Royal Family would eat together, but the King grew even busier with the trade disputes. With David learning to ride and working beside me, we were hardly apart. I was well enough to do nearly as much work as my brother.

After we'd been learning to ride for a few weeks, the Captain brought us to the Guard's mess hall, and seated us at a table along with Lt. Underhill. When the Captain asked if I was ready to begin some light battle training, David gave me such a stern look, I nearly refused. Lt. Underhill interrupted David's glare.

"The training is offered to *both* of you, actually." While he spoke to the two of us, he was facing David. My brother couldn't resist, and was suddenly too excited to dissuade me from joining.

We learned basic self-defense, or something the sergeant assigned to us called *battle survival skills*. This basically translates to: *how to keep your head on your shoulders in a battle*. We practiced with clubs, though the sergeant told us the basic skills we learned wouldn't change much for any weapon we might hold.

When another sergeant offered to take David to a more advanced sword fighting course, he jumped at the chance.

"Sorry," David told me, "you're not well enough yet—it's *too strenuous*."

I had to admit he was partially right. I could walk and even run a little, but my throat still burned in pain when I moved my neck or stretched my throat. Days when I tried to ignore this were followed by painful nights with little sleep. I learned to keep my head cast downward and my eyes upward. It earned strange expressions from most strangers I passed. It was awkward, but I managed at most tasks. If only my wound had improved in its appearance, I would have been content to heal slowly. The area around my long scar was still blue, as if I were bruised. It had been too long for it to be a bruise, and the dark-hued patch of skin didn't seem to be shrinking. I tried not to think of it, but it began to worry me as time wore on.

After my first morning of sitting alone in the barracks, I decided to go for a walk. I wandered around the palace grounds with no particular goal in mind. Eventually, I met a man walking in the same direction, and I followed him as we talked. When we parted ways, I found myself in an empty courtyard with a stone statue of an armored soldier at its center. At the feet of the soldier was a stone plaque engraved with the single word: *glory*.

The stone soldier had a helmet in his left hand, down at his side. His right arm was raised high, pointing his sword to the sky. His head was tossed back a little as if he were laughing. His right foot stood on his apparent enemy, lying on the ground. I stepped back and looked at it from different angles. Something didn't seem right about it. His stance and expression seemed a little forced, as if he'd worked up too much pride. I wondered why the title on the plaque wasn't capitalized.

A young girl about the age of the Princess—perhaps a little older— entered the courtyard and must have noticed me standing there. She walked so quietly, she startled me when she spoke.

"An impressive statue, isn't it?"

"I suppose," I replied, noncommittally.

"Oh, don't you think so? It was hewn to honor a great warrior, don't you think?"

"I'm not sure. If so, maybe the sculptor carved it wrong. Doesn't he look...I don't know...*braggish*?" I strained to see the statue's face better. At that point she noticed my scar.

"Hey, you're the one who rescued the Princess all by yourself," she exclaimed. "Yes," she went on excitedly, "you saved the Princess and the entire Royal Guard, when they were imprisoned in the Winter Palace."

"No, not quite," I replied. "I had help from my brother in setting the Princess free—we couldn't have done it without each other. Then we both had help from the Princess in setting the Captain of the Guard free. Without her knowledge of the Winter Palace, we'd have been caught for sure. Then the Captain was free, and he did everything else." I paused for a moment, my eyes drawn back to the statue, "...it wasn't all that...*glorious*." I smiled back at the statue. I was reasonably sure I finally understood it.

"Oh." She looked disappointed. "Well, I bet they couldn't have done it without you," she said politely.

"I'd like to think so." I returned her kind words with a smile. "But really, I think anyone with their wits about them could have done the same." She looked almost embarrassed for a moment, then suddenly looked back at my throat excitedly.

"I heard you were attacked by an ice troll...is it true? Was it the troll prince who gave you such a vicious wound?" My ears perked up and I got ready to launch into the story.

"It was *horrible*. You should have seen it..." I stopped mid-sentence. Something had caught at the back of my mind. Before I was able to continue, I remembered the King's words. *Be careful not to tell others of your encounter with the ice troll.*

Would it really matter, I wondered silently, *if I tell this young girl, inside the palace grounds? Surely she's trusted, if she's allowed through the palace wall.*

"Yes, yes? Go on, *tell me*," she insisted, eyes bright and smiling. My heart sunk as I realized I couldn't.

"I'm sorry, but I need to be somewhere…right away." I left her quickly, and didn't look back. As I walked away, I reminded myself I had no idea why the King had told me to remain silent, and therefore I couldn't guess what harm it might cause. The King had put us up in his barracks, and it was his soldiers who trained us. I found I couldn't betray his trust. I marched back to the barracks, all the way thinking through the story the way I wished I could have told it.

3.1 Of Piteous Circumstances

By the second day of David's new swordplay, I was in a foul mood. I moped around the vacant barrack, wishing I could go with him. As I sat on the edge of my cot, I thought of the ice troll and my wound. Why did he have to grab *me*? Why did I walk so close? Why didn't the guards near the cart stop me? It was their fault—*they* should have my wound. My throat burned worse than it had for days. Just then, I heard the familiar voice of the Captain.

"Our troubles are still our own, when we blame them on others."

I turned, and at first I was glad to see him, but when his words sank in, I felt embarrassed. I must have been mumbling again, loud enough to be overheard.

"*Oh*—I didn't mean it; I was only thinking out loud. My throat is hurting much worse this morning..." The Captain wore a sad smile when he replied.

"Was it hurting so badly when you woke? Or did it feel worse when you sat down to think about it?"

A flash of anger welled up in me. Who was he to judge me? But he hadn't judged me, had he? I looked carefully at the Captain's face—he held no contempt. His manner was one of someone who'd come to visit a friend.

"Maybe you're right," I said, standing. "I haven't seen the Princess for a few days. Is all well with her family?"

It was a common greeting I'd learned, to ask of a mutual friend's family, though it felt odd asking about the Royal Family. I knew the Captain was charged with their safety, but I had only seen the King once, and had never even met the Queen. The surprised look on the Captain's face showed he thought it odd also.

"They are well." His expression changed, and his voice shifted. "Do you know what an honor it is for you to eat with the Princess? Or even to live in these barracks, within the palace grounds?" I nodded.

"I didn't think it had anything to do with *me*. I thought we ate with the Princess…well, because she *wanted* us to. I thought we were allowed to stay here as the King's guests until I healed—or until we get our audience."

"How *humble* of you," laughed the Captain. "Did you forget you rescued her, and myself as well?"

Actually, I nearly had. It was easy to feel humble around the Captain. But other than the girl I met at the statue *glory*, I hadn't given it a thought since we left Golden Mountain. But I couldn't say so; it sounded far too unlikely.

"I thought the King felt sorry for me, I guess." The Captain's face turned grim.

"It's time *you* stopped feeling sorry for yourself. You can't fully want to be healed while you hold self-pity. As long as you do, you're asking others to pity you as well. And why should they pity you if you're fully healed?"

I turned my head from him. It hurt to hear such words; I wasn't yet ready to consider whether they might be true. So I did my best to ignore his comment *and* my embarrassment. I turned back to him, still red-faced, and changed the subject.

"What brings you here? Can I do something for you?"

"Maybe you can," he replied. "Since your brother began learning swordplay, I thought you might also."

"I'm not well enough. Otherwise I would have gone with him. As it is, I can hardly lift my head."

I stretched to lift my chin high, as if he could feel the pain it caused me. Then I hung my head even lower than the pain gave me cause to.

"So you mope all day, looking at the floor? You're right about training with David and his new teacher—you're not well enough by a long ways. But I'm waiting for a new assignment from the King, and have some time on my hands. Would you like me to give you some training? There is plenty you can learn without hurting yourself." I looked up at him.

"*I surely would*," I answered, excitedly. "But why would you waste your time teaching *me*?"

"I wouldn't," replied the Captain. Then, to answer my confused look, he added, "If you don't give it your best, and make the most of it, I *won't* train you."

"Oh. I didn't mean..." His literal response shocked me, not for the last time. "I only meant...you're an important man in the kingdom. Surely you have more important things to do."

"We are all important in the King's service, my young friend. As for your *skills* being worth my time...*you may surprise yourself yet.*"

His words puzzled me. I thought about it as he led the way to the palace. *I might surprise myself? What does he think I'll do?* I hoped he didn't expect some heroic feat from me. Even as I thought this, I realized the pain in my throat was nearly gone. I wondered if the Captain was right. Perhaps my thoughts played a greater role in my recovery than I could have imagined.

3.2 New Training

I didn't realize the Captain was taking me to his private quarters until we arrived. No sooner had we entered his quarters, than he excused himself, asking me to be patient while he attended to a critical task. While he was gone I glanced around at my surroundings. I was surprised to see how humble they were.

There were a few hangings on the walls, and the floor held even fewer pieces of furniture. He had a simple bed, not much different from the cots in the barracks. The room wasn't bare, but no one could call it messy. One item cried out among the few things in the large room. I saw it the moment we entered, even before the Captain left. Something shiny lay under his desk, brightly reflecting the sunlight falling through the window. I bent and picked it up. It was a magnificent jewel, set in a gold decorative frame. It wasn't jewelry to be worn, but looked instead like an award. The entire piece fit easily within my palm. I fingered the inset jewel, then set it on the Captain's desk and continued to study the sparse furnishings around me.

When the Captain returned, he seemed happy to get started. There wasn't much room for sword fighting, but when he moved a few items to the walls and rolled up a carpet, there it was plenty of room to draw swords and move around.

"First you'll learn to fight hand-to-hand. Let me see the battle stance you learned. Good. Now it's a little different when using a sword..."

The Captain began to teach me the fundamentals of swordplay. He was patient with me, except when my wound slowed me down. After a while, this seemed quite inconsistent to me. *If he knows how badly my wound hurts*, I thought, *can't he show a little more compassion?* I understood this better in time. At the end of the day, my legs and arms hurt worse than my throat.

That night I didn't tell David of my time spent with the Captain, and he didn't ask. He clearly felt guilty for enjoying his own training, assuming I had only chores to keep me busy. The following morning and the next, I waited until David left before I headed to the Captain's quarters for training. He didn't have all day to train me, and I was able to reach the barracks before David returned. When my training ran later than normal, I made sure to do some of the cleaning chores we were assigned before heading back to the barracks.

After a few weeks of training, the Captain led me to the stables and started teaching me how to use a sword and lance while riding a horse. We used a small parade field outside the palace grounds, not far from the gate.

"This is the preferred way to enter battle," he told me.

He went on to show me his most basic rules for riding against an armed enemy. After a few short hours I was spent. When it was clear we were done for the day, he turned his horse around and spoke.

"On a *journey*," he paused to look directly at me, "one would hope to fight only from this position, if at all."

The rest of my training with the Captain involved horses. I learned how to quickly mount and dismount in battle, and how to control the horse in situations where it may want to flee or dodge.

At this point, my training became considerably more difficult. He began to setup battle simulations on the field. He would ride through stacks of wooden crates or hay bales, striking at one with his sword, driving his lance into another, and avoiding still others with poles jutting out from them. I can remember growing angry on days when he pushed me to try difficult moves I wasn't ready to learn. On these days he was quietest. On the last of them I became so angry, I jumped off my mount and swung my sword wildly into one of the bales of hay topped with a helmet.

"*Congratulations*," he said disapprovingly, "You managed to give up a superior position in battle."

I swung around and yelled at him, "*It's a stupid exercise.* I'll never come across a situation like this in battle...*it's too ordered.* How long did it take you to arrange this puzzle of enemies?" My voice sounded strange. It was raspy, almost foreign to my ears. I wondered if the wound over my throat could affect the inside of my voice box.

"Oh, is it your turn to teach me what battles are like? I'm *surprised indeed* at your performance today."

He sounded angry, but his face was gloomy. When we were finished, he told me there were some duties he needed to attend to the next day. He asked me to come early the next morning, so he could check on my technique, and leave me to practice until I left for my cleaning chores.

I felt horribly guilty. Perhaps he wanted to spend less time with me because I'd acted so badly. Either way I knew I'd hidden my training from my brother long enough. I *had* to tell David, or I'd be living a lie—something I was unwilling to do. On my way out, I looked at the bale of hay I'd sliced into when I lost my temper. I'd cut clean through the helmet, the bale, and stole a hefty chip from the cobblestone beneath. I hefted the practice sword, then looked along its edge. It was *bent*. Could *I* have bent it? I was growing stronger, downcast head or not.

After washing, David and I ate with Sally and Schelli in her private quarters. I remembered the Captain's humble furnishings, and noted how unlike them the Princess's were. Sally was always there when we visited, and several attendants as well. I still hadn't brought up my training with the Captain when David began telling us of his training. Schelli sounded impressed with his progress, and asked how my own training was going.

"Oh, Mark doesn't come, he's still too weak," David replied for me. Sally glanced toward me, and seemed to watch my reaction with interest.

"Actually," I said hesitantly, "the Captain's been showing me some sword fighting moves while David's at his training." My words answered the Princess, though I faced my brother.

"*What?* Why? Are you planning on battling someone?" He was angry, just as I knew he would be.

"Are *you?*" I retorted.

"Well, no," he said quietly, then redoubled his frustration. "*But I'm well enough to train.*"

"And so am I. It's a little slower, but I'm learning to use a sword *because I like it*. What else do I have to do?"

"You're planning on going to the desert with the Captain, aren't you?" he asked, accusingly.

Here we go, I thought. As I prepared to argue why *I might* go, I realized I'd known I *would* go all along. David questioning my ability only strengthened the resolve of my response.

"Yes, I *am* going. I'm strong enough to ride and to *fight,* just like the Captain said I'd be."

"Then you don't have to go," David half-shouted, pleadingly. "If you're all better, why put yourself in danger?" I was shocked to hear deep concern in his voice.

"But I'm *not* all better, am I?" I lifted my chin toward the ceiling to show my scar. I'd cast my head down so regularly, I hadn't realized none of them had taken a close look at my wound for the past few weeks. It *hurt* when I looked up, no less this time than any other. As I did, I heard a gasp. I looked down to see Sally glaring at the Princess, her hand cupped over her mouth. David's face had grown pale.

"What's wrong?" I asked them all, *"What is it?"*

David tried to re-assure me. "It's nothing. We just didn't..." His voice trailed off uncertainly.

"Where's a mirror?" I asked, equal parts fearful and angry. I jumped to my feet and ran to a mirror on the far wall, again lifting my head high. *Ouch.* What little of my throat I saw, made me stumble back in shock.

"How long has it looked like this?" The three of them approached slowly. David answered first.

"We didn't want you to worry. You were moving around so well, and you were feeling so much better, I just—"

"How long?" I insisted.

"It's been growing slowly ever since the troll attacked you." Sally stated calmly. "We all wanted to believe it would go away, or perhaps it was only some internal bruising. It doesn't appear to be bruising any longer."

My entire throat had become a dark shade of blue—nearly black. The raised skin of my long scar was a pale blue-gray—the same blue-gray of the ice troll's skin. I tried to recall how long it had been since I'd seen a mirror.

"Did you see the color here, in the middle?" I whispered, still glancing in the mirror and straining to keep my chin high.

"No, not until just now," said Lady Sally. Suddenly, her expression turned resolute, and she reached for my hand. "We will go and ask if the King will see you. He may be able to help."

I felt horrified, but also somehow betrayed. I'd been feeling so much better, I had no way of expecting I might be getting worse.

The exercise from my training had done me well. As long as I didn't lift my head much, I felt fine, and in some ways I felt stronger than ever. Earlier, when I heaved my sword through the bale of hay and bent it, I felt *powerful*. I had no way of suspecting some infection, or perhaps blood poisoning, had been creeping across my throat.

Lady Sally led me straight to the King's Council chamber. *If it's this easy*, I wondered, distractedly, *why have we been waiting so long?* Even so, I suspected Sally would invoke some protocol reserved for emergencies to ask for an audience. I realized it might not be certain the King would see us, even so.

At the door to the King's chamber, an armed soldier asked our business. His eyes darted back and forth between Sally and my neck. I was sure he could see some of my wound even while my head drooped toward the floor.

"We need to speak to the King urgently. Tell him it's about *the troll injury*."

When the soldier went through the door, another came out to take his place, and barred the door. Before long, the door opened, and the two soldiers switched places again. One of them told us we would go in soon. While we waited, I began to wish for a chair. Finally, the Captain opened the door from within.

"Come in Mark, Lady Sally."

The Captain sounded very proper. I'd later learn to call this demeanor his *King-mode*—an extra reverence he showed around the King.

The King sat behind a large table, covered with maps and long lists. I suspected others had emptied out of the room from another door while we waited.

"Are you feeling...at all ill?" The King asked cautiously.

"Not really, Sire," I replied. It was only the second time I'd seen him, and I'd already forgotten how imposing he could seem. Sally kneeled beside him and spoke softly.

"My lord, his scar has grown, and...appears very troubling. I thought you would want to see him right away."

"Come near, son," said the King.

I nervously approached, and lifted my head to show him my throat and neck. With his thumb and forefinger, he lifted my chin higher. I winced from the pain, but kept silent.

"Hmmm. What do you say, Captain? Is he ready to travel? Has he grown...*stronger?*"

"Yes, Sire, he's taken to his training well—*and* shown new strength."

If I was doing well at my training, the Captain had never told me so. I felt a little better to hear a rare compliment from the Captain, especially spoken to the King. Something in his voice sounded almost like pride—though I may have imagined it. The way he said *stronger*, troubled me; this part didn't sound like a compliment.

The King released my chin, and I let out a sigh as I lowered my head. The King noticed.

"This scar has dropped your sights some, I see. Have you made your decision about the journey I requested you take?"

Requested? The Captain hadn't called it a *request*. If I had any doubts left, they vanished. I felt nervous and was afraid my tongue would mangle my words.

"I will go," was all I trusted myself to say.

"Then Captain, you are released to make ready for your journey. Leave when you see fit." Then he laid his hand on my shoulder and lowered his voice.

"This is a time of maturing and growth for you; don't fear it. Your decisions on this journey will alter the path of your life. You just may return to us a different person." His words shocked me. Before I could make sense of them, he added in a muted tone, "Make me proud, son."

I think my mouth may have actually dropped open. The Captain placed his hand on my back and led me dumbfounded, out of the room. Lady Sally followed. When we reached the Princess's quarters, Schelli and my brother were somber. David looked toward the Captain doubtfully, then turned resolutely to me.

"I'm going with you," he said, his very tone daring me to challenge him.

"Sorry, David," the Captain replied, "the King says this journey is for your brother alone. I am going only to protect him, and to lead him when he needs it." David's face turned gravely solemn. "I did say I would *protect him*," the Captain added with a smile.

David looked distractedly to the Captain and smiled weakly. The Captain told me what I'd need to pack. It didn't sound like much.

"Don't worry," he said, reading my thoughts from my expression once again. "My list is somewhat longer. Come by my quarters tomorrow, and together we'll begin preparing."

The Captain soon left, and the rest of our evening was tainted by worry. I remembered fretting about telling David of my sword training, though suddenly, it seemed trivial. We tried to play a tile game, a favorite of Schelli's, though none of us were interested in it. Finally I stood and broke the uncomfortable silence we'd fallen into.

"Well, I'd better get to sleep. I think tomorrow might be a long day."

David walked beside me on the dimly lit road back to the barracks. Without warning, he blurted out at me in an accusing tone.

"Has the King or the Captain even mentioned what spectacular thing on this trip will heal you?" I was taken back a moment. Seeing the King had distracted me, and for the first time I realized I'd never given it a single thought.

"You know, they never did. I don't know *what* they have planned. I'm sure there's a special doctor in the desert."

"I hope he's close."

Then I stopped, frozen in place on the dark road to the barracks. David turned back to see what was wrong. "What is it?"

"I just realized—*I had an audience with the King.* I could've asked him about the way home, and it didn't even cross my mind."

"I can see why," he responded. "I mean, you had a lot on your mind." David paused a moment. When I didn't reply, he spoke again. "Hey, I didn't think of it either. It's been a busy night, for both of us."

We walked a little farther in silence. I continued to wonder how I could have let our return home slip my mind. Being in the King's presence was difficult to describe.

"What am I going to do while you're gone?" David finally asked. "I'll just worry about you."

"I'm sure the Captain or the King has something in mind."

"I still don't want you to go—but I don't want you to get worse either. Be careful...and stay safe. I really wish I could go with you."

I wished he could too—or at least part of me did. He was my older brother and would always look out for me. I wondered if I might learn something important without him beside me. The possibility of something important happening without him, somehow made me miss him already.

3.3 Into Enthicia

The next morning we started our preparations at the armory, where a smithy measured me for mail and armor. Then the Captain took me to the palace stables and told the stable master he would need a smaller warhorse—one I could ride—in a day or two. Once we'd begun preparing, I actually forgot to ask him what on our trip would heal my wound. Mostly, I didn't want to think of it, and was content to assume it was a faraway doctor. It was far better I didn't ask; if I had, I would have never started the journey.

For the rest of the day, the Captain drilled me on the small parade field outside the palace grounds. I practiced all the lessons he'd taught me, while I wore ill-fitting armor and a helmet. I fell asleep easily that night. The following day, the Captain brought me to the armory and had me try on a chain mail shirt, a helmet, and a breastplate of armor. The smithy handed me a bright sword—much newer than the one I'd used in practice. He also had an axe and lance for me. I desperately hoped I wouldn't need to use any of them, despite my training. We left the smithy with instructions to change the breastplate and mail shirt somewhat for a better fit.

After a short practice, the Captain told me to be ready to leave in the morning. David and I ate dinner with the Princess again, another somber meal. Everyone seemed either sorry or worried to see me go, and yet hopeful I would soon be better. It astonished me no one asked what *exactly* would heal me in the desert. Perhaps they already knew and said nothing.

That night sleep didn't come easily. When I finally fell asleep, I woke only a few hours later, and lay restlessly in bed. My head was full of thoughts on all the things I'd seen in this strange land. Once again, I questioned the ones I didn't understand, but no answers came to me.

David rolled over, and his snoring grew louder. Finally, listening to his sniffs and snorts, I found sleep again. I dreamed we were home and I was lying in bed. The door to my room was open, and I could hear David's snoring down the hall, in his own bedroom. All felt right again; all was back to normal.

No sooner did I think this in my dream, than a question rang aloud from no direction, or perhaps from all directions at once. "What's so great about getting *back to normal?*" The last three words rung over and over in my mind, until finally I woke.

It wasn't yet dawn. When I was certain I wouldn't be able to fall asleep again, I picked up my practice sword and walked outside the barracks. There was an open area nearby, well lit by oil lamps placed around its perimeter. I took advantage of the light and space to practice. By sunrise I felt tired enough to sleep and headed back to the barracks. The Captain was there, waiting for me.

"Meet me at the stables when you've said goodbye to your brother. We'll begin our journey as soon as you're ready."

I nodded. David was snoring peacefully and I didn't want to wake him. Instead, I wrote him a short letter, and hoped it would bring him some peace when he read it.

When I reached the stables, the Captain was checking over the packs on two donkeys, and our horses. Both our horses were fitted with armor, saddles and saddlebags. The saddles had various sheaths or scabbards to hold our weapons. When I approached, the Captain turned toward me as if he knew exactly when I would arrive.

"Are you ready?" he asked.

His tone seemed to imply a meaning much deeper than *are you ready to leave.* Unsure, I nodded and went to hoist myself onto the smaller horse. As I did, I saw chain mail lain across the saddle—obviously for me to wear. After a short struggle, I made my way through the neck and arm holes. I took the lap armor meant to protect my thighs, and put it on as well. I left the shield and helmet strapped to the saddle, but accepted my new sword as the Captain held it out for me. I sheathed it in its scabbard where I could easily reach it while riding.

"Your horse's name is Yashel," said the Captain. "She is a good horse."

I was tired and had nothing to say, so I only nodded. The Captain nodded back, walked to his large horse, and swung up easily onto his saddle.

I strained to look up at the Captain, and felt searing heat on my throat and neck.

"Do you think we'll meet trouble on the road to Tume Belor? I thought the road was busy—and *safe*".

"Did you think your training was over just because we're going on a journey?" The Captain paused long enough to give me a suspicious smile. *"This is where it truly begins."*

I was sure I didn't like his response. I tried to follow his example in mounting my horse, but with the extra weight of the armor I wore, it took more strength than I could have guessed. My first try left me short, and I fell onto the cobblestones. My natural tendency was to lift my head up as I swung, but that wouldn't do—*maybe on the return trip* I thought with a wry smile. My second attempt nearly sent me sailing over the top of my horse.

I thought the Captain was being kind in overlooking my sloppy mount, just as he looked back and teased, "I can see your training should have included more instruction on mounting your horse."

Soon we were riding through the large gate in the palace wall, and down the streets of Thraen Kholl. We passed through a second wall—the wall running around the entire city—before we followed the Desert Road east, down into the countryside. The road was empty, as early as it was. I followed the Captain closely, and our two donkeys trailed faithfully behind us. When we'd first started, the Captain called out a loud *Jack!* and *Jenny!* to them, but seemed to pay them no mind ever since.

On the road down from Thraen Kholl, I couldn't any longer ignore the burning question in my mind, but felt foolish for not asking earlier. When the narrow street widened, I rode beside the Captain and asked him *other* questions.

"How long is the ride to the oasis?"

"Much shorter than when you rode it last. We have no marching soldiers or oxcarts," the Captain replied.

"What time do you think we'll get there?"

"We'll be there by late afternoon. By then its cool waters will be a welcome sight indeed."

"Why's that?" I asked. I felt like he was baiting me.

"It's no longer spring. We'll be riding under the hot desert sun by noon."

"Oh." I shifted restlessly in my saddle. "What will we do when we get there?"

"Drink."

"And then...?"

"Ride."

"We'll ride until..." he wasn't offering information, it seemed. "Until what?"

"Until we make camp and sleep."

Finally I could hold back no longer.

"Captain, *what's supposed to heal me on this trip?*" Again he smiled.

"Oh, you don't know...?"

"No, I don't know," I replied in anger. "Who would've told me?" I realized I was yelling as I would at my brother, not as I should address the Captain of the Royal Guard.

"I mean...no, sir." He paused just long enough to worry me.

"Beyond TerkEtmek, at the far end of Enthicia, the ground is rocky and unstable. The melted rock from deep underground is closer to the surface and sometimes escapes..." He paused.

"Yes?"

"There are geysers there, and sometimes even small eruptions or spills of lava."

"Is there a special doctor there?" I asked, hopefully.

"*What?* No, no one lives there. There are pools there, heated by the earth...mineral pools."

"*Mineral pools?*"

"Yes. They are thick with minerals from deep underground. It's not quite water...though they're not sandy. They're more like..." he trailed off.

"Mud?" I asked, sarcastically.

"Yes, I suppose they *are* like mud." The Captain had turned away from me, but his voice told me he was smiling.

"And...?"

"And what?"

"What about the mud pools?" I asked.

"You are to bathe in one particular pool. Then you will be healed."

"I'm supposed to *sit* in *mud?*" I asked, "*That's* what this whole trip is about, the reason I'm risking my life?"

I turned and looked back the way we had come. *I know the way...* But the Captain was already speaking again.

"These pools are considered rejuvenating by the desert traders. Some consider them magical. The minerals in the pools are said to come from deep within Terra. It's something you've never experienced…"

"Is it worth risking my life over?" I yelled back. I was losing my temper, worse than before. Even as I ranted, I knew I should keep silent. "This is the worst idea I ever heard of."

The Captain stopped in his tracks. My horse kept walking, until I noticed and pulled back on the reins. The Captain spoke in an even, hushed tone.

"It was the King's idea to send you on this journey, to save your life. I will give you *the benefit* of doubting you remembered this. I won't tolerate insubordination toward the King."

I turned back toward him, ready to argue, but stopped as soon as I saw his glassy stare and the heavy look on his face. For a split second I thought he might draw his sword.

"I wasn't thinking," I said apologetically. "I know the King sent us…*and* I agreed to go."

My face flushed hot with shame, and I turned away. The Captain's horse started walking again, and I slowed to fall farther behind him.

We rode in silence the rest of the morning and early afternoon. I was hungry, but didn't want to break the silence. The landscape was changing as we rode mostly downhill. The trees thinned and the grass in the fields became dry. Eventually the grasses broke way to open sand, and I knew we weren't far from the refreshing waters of Tume Belor.

I began to notice things I'd missed when we'd crossed Enthicia on our way to Engdynlor from the mountains. The Desert Road—or *Desert Trail* as it was often called—wasn't really a road *or* a trail. It was only a collection of stone posts set into the sand to mark the shortest path across the desert, by way of Tume Belor. We didn't pass many of them before I could see the oasis ahead of us, a tiny dot on the sandy horizon with a backdrop of the distant Golden Mountain and her sisters. We rode over low dunes, barely perceptible while on top of each, but visible when seen from a distance, gazing over many of them at once.

3.4 Tume Belor

As the oasis grew on the horizon and became clearer, I wondered when the Captain would speak again. I wished I knew how to break the uncomfortable silence. I couldn't apologize to the Captain; he was angry for what I said against *the King*, not against him. We rode the remainder of the way in silence.

I remembered seeing Tume Belor for the first time. I wasn't fully awake, and I'd assumed I couldn't trust those hazy memories. Seeing it again, I realized it was far more beautiful than I had remembered.

There was a large outcropping of smooth rock on the south side of the oasis, two or three stories high. Its north side was covered with green plants and mosses. Outside this rocky spire, the entire oasis was encircled with lush palms and taller trees, many of which seemed to belong in a forest rather than a desert. I couldn't see any water; the wall of flourishing greenery blocked it completely from view. My mouth felt full of sand and I waited impatiently to drink from the clear pool ahead.

When we finally reached the oasis, neither of us had spoken. I wondered what was wrong with me, why I had acted so rudely. The Captain turned to the right and spoke quietly. I had to strain to hear him.

"Go ahead and cool off in the water. I'm going to climb the rock and have a look around."

He clicked at the donkeys and they seemed to read his mind. They remained with me, and he rode toward the tall rock. He didn't sound angry anymore, but I still felt uneasy.

I led Yashel and the donkeys over the green grass and mosses of the oasis. I brushed against palms both high and low and every other type of plant I could have guessed to find there. I heard a faint chirping from somewhere, but couldn't quite find the birds making the distant sounds. I aimed for the end of the pool nearest the rock outcropping.

Even before I approached the pool, I heard something I'd thought I'd only dreamt was there: a tall and gurgling waterfall. I hurried through the greenery to see it, and found myself at the pool's edge, staring in awe. *How is this possible?*

At the water's edge, I hurried to remove Yashel's bridle, and let her drink. I led the donkeys to the water beside Yashel, then carefully removed my chain mail and lap armor, and laid them across my saddle, causing Yashel's back to quiver.

The pool was larger than I expected. As tired as I was, it would have taken the rest of my energy to swim across it. I wished I could jump in. What would the Captain think of me then? When we were last there, David and the Princess swam in the oasis, but I knew no one else had. Was it considered childish? I removed my boots and socks, then rolled up my pantlegs. I looked around for the Captain, but found him nowhere in sight.

The pool was deep near the rock formation. At the other end, there was a shallow shore like a beach, but I could see a steep drop-off in the water beyond the large rock on which I stood. The water was a deep blue everywhere but the shallow end. I sat on the stone ledge, dangling my legs in the water. Surely the Captain wouldn't think it childish to cool my legs. Just then I heard the Captain shout from the top of the giant rock. He was so high, and the low palms so dense, I could hardly make him out. My neck stabbed with pain as I searched for him.

"*Armed enemies approaching!* Catapults launching—first volley coming…*now.*"

This is it, I thought, *the ice troll has finally caught up with me.* Then I saw the Captain falling past me as if in slow motion, knocked from the top of the rock and yelling the whole way down. He splashed as he landed in the water, and an unshakable fear assured me he was dead. *Wait a minute,* I thought, *is he…laughing?*

Drenched, I found the Captain treading water, apparently in only his underclothes. He wore a big grin on his face, and slapped the surface with his arms, sending peels of water after me. I laughed, then joined him. I didn't bother taking off my shirt; it was already soaked. I jumped into the pool as close to him as I could, knees tucked up under me and yelling *catapult away* as I splashed him back.

We swam and splashed until I was too tired to tread water. Standing on the bank, I wrung out my shirt and pants while the

Captain walked around to get his horse. When he returned, he pulled some bread and fresh cooked meat from one of the donkeys' packs, and set it on a cloth he'd placed on a large boulder near the water.

"Last fresh food until we reach the duke's," he said.

I ate more than I expected to. While we washed, he told me a little of the simple environment surrounding the oasis.

There were small fish in the pool, and a few species of small birds in the trees. There were tiny black crickets and also a few small rodents; other than these, no animal life could be found. Once again the Captain's broad knowledge amazed me. Was he a scientist or a soldier? When I asked how the water got to the top of the rock outcropping, he explained the oasis was fed by a spring under pressure. Part of the water feeding the pool leaked up through the sand, and the rest of it was squeezed up through the giant rock and found its way out near the top.

I asked him where so much water could come from, out in the middle of the desert. He explained we weren't truly in the middle of a desert, but near the edge.

"If you climb the rock, you can look past the oasis. Looking back the way we came, you'll see Thraen Kholl, and in the opposite direction you'll see Golden Mountain. The rock tower feeding the oasis is actually connected to the mountains by a layer of underground rock. Long ago, there was lush vegetation all around here—the last green forest before the desert. Enthicia encroached over the forest, reaching close to Golden Mountain. This oasis remained as an island of life, fed by the spring in this tall rock."

"How does the water get from there to here?" I asked, "How can the rock carry the water like a pipe?"

"The roots of the mountain carry it here. There's a layer of rock running from under the mountain to here, deep under the sand. Water can't flow up through it until it reaches here, where it finds a hole in the rock it can sneak through. The weight of the water higher up, trapped under rock, pushes it up through a hole in the stone, and through a few places on the pool's bottom."

"So if everything you described hadn't happened perfectly, this oasis wouldn't exist?"

"It isn't as impossible as it sounds. If the water found its way out of the rock in a different place, the oasis would be there instead. If the desert hadn't encroached into an ancient forest, we would be resting near an ordinary spring and pool in the forest, instead of this oasis. The unlikeliest part is a spring occurring in this tall outcrop of rock."

Learning more of the strange oasis, Tume Belor seemed evermore magical to me. *Too bad I can't be healed by bathing in this pool*, I thought as we got ready to ride. Wisely, I kept my thoughts to myself.

Leaving the oasis behind, I wondered how the rulers and scientists of Terreldor could understand some things very well, and others not at all. *They certainly seem intelligent*, I pondered, *but they hold onto old superstitions*. I hoped none of them proved dangerous to me. It was worrisome they could believe a mineral-mud bath would heal the scar and infection in my neck.

Well, I thought in anger, *they can send me to their stupid mud-bath; I'll even sit in it for them—then they'll see how wrong they were*. My plan didn't bring me any comfort. In the end, I'd still be sick.

I looked back, taking one last look at the oasis receding behind us. It was the most beautiful place I'd ever seen. A dry wind blew over me, pulling my thoughts back to the present. I cleared my throat and called to the Captain.

"What will be the most dangerous part of our journey?"

"Tomorrow we'll come across a region called the Great Dunes. This region has three dangers, the first of which is the terrain. There is one safe path through the deep valleys between the dunes. It is the *only* known way around the many pools of quicksand. Most of the springs feeding the quicksand pools are not sweet, like the waters of Tume Belor, but bitter—and poisonous. As for animal life in the Great Dunes, there are deadly scorpions, poisonous tarantulas, and sand-colored vipers. We won't spend the night there, and we'll dismount as few times as possible." The Captain paused, perhaps to see if I had any questions.

"And what is the third danger?"

"There are rumors among some of the merchant families of marauding trolls. Other traders claim no knowledge of them."

"Why hasn't the King sent people to investigate this?" I asked.

"What do you think we're doing tomorrow?" he replied with a smile. "The King has far too many errands for me to perform them one at a time."

"Really?" I felt a little hurt. I guessed I wasn't as important as I thought.

"Don't look so sad, my young friend. The King wouldn't have sent *anyone* to take you; he wanted me specifically, to protect and train you.

As you know, I'm the head of the Royal Guard, and I've had to find others to tend to the many duties I normally perform so I could bring you. As you may *not* know, the Royal Guard is a peacetime order. In times of war, I command all the King's armies. So it's not a hasty decision when the King sends me away from Engdynlor."

A sense of self-importance swelled within me, and the Captain noticed.

"Don't be too prideful," he said, though in a kind voice. "You should know you're highly valued by the King, but being prideful about it won't help you in the end." Uncomfortable, I tried to change the subject.

"Are there any other missions from the King you'll be working on, while we're out in the desert?" I asked this as a joke, but his voice was serious in his reply.

"Nothing we can discuss now." At the time I thought he was only teasing me.

3.5 The Great Dunes

We rode mostly in silence for the rest of the afternoon. It was hot and dry, tempting me to stop and get more water from the sacks the donkeys carried. Before long, I could see the ground swell in front of us before it disappeared into sky: the first of the Great Dunes. The stone markers for the Desert Road had been evenly spaced on our way to Tume Belor. Ahead of us, however, there were no markers in sight.

We stopped to make camp near the foot of the first dune. The sun was low in the sky. Again, the Captain scouted the area—a task much easier in a near-featureless desert—while I shimmied out of my armor. While he removed his own, he told me there was a hidden well nearby, and he suggested I try to find it. I tried to imagine what a hidden well might look like as I scanned the area. If there was a very low well, or if it were buried just a bit, how could travelers be sure a sandstorm wouldn't bury it forever? I didn't see anything resembling a well, or much of anything at all in our immediate surroundings. I looked back the way we'd come, and focused on a nearby stump. It was horribly out of place, with nothing like it in view. It had just come into view when the Captain first mentioned we'd be stopping soon. I turned back to the Captain, but he only smiled.

As I approached the stump, I noticed there was some dry grass around it in the sand. It was the only vegetation in sight. I thumped the side of the stump with my boot…it felt more like stone than wood. I looked at the top of the stump carefully. The top *was* made of wood: a wooden plug fit into the top of a stump made of stone. The plug looked weathered, stained gray with age. Though it looked rotten, it was very hard. I reached down into a hole near the center of the plug, where it appeared some wood had rotted away. My finger found a large metal ring fixed into the bottom of the rot-hole. I pulled hard, and the entire wooden plug slipped up a little. The Captain walked over with a coil of rope in his hand and slapped me on the back.

"*Congratulations*—quite a disguise, eh?" He helped me lift the wooden plug from the stump and set it in the sand. The underside looked smooth and glossy, like it had been coated with something.

"But how?" I asked, bewildered.

"It wasn't by accident. This well was dug by hand and lined with stone. The top half is a petrified log, brought in from another part of the kingdom. Most of the log is underground—a *long way* underground. This way it looks like an out-of-place stump instead of a well."

As he spoke, he tied one end of the rope around the stump, and dropped the other end down the hole. The end of the rope had a ball of cloth attached to it.

"Why hide it?"

"Most travelers need to bring many extra pack animals with them to haul water. They must haul water for their animals too, unless they plan on eating them on the way." I thought of eating a donkey, and looked over at Jenny. She brayed contemptuously—not my idea of a meal. "The King's servants," he went on, "must cross Enthicia quickly from time to time. This convenience allows us to do so easily. If the King's enemies knew of it, they might foul the well. And so, it was built in secret."

When he'd retrieved the rope from the well, I saw it had a light fabric sack attached at its end. After it had been down the well, it filled with water. At the top of the cloth sack was a metal loop holding it open. A small rock dangled from its bottom, dripping water slowly onto the dry sand at our feet. He took a small sip and relished its taste.

"Here," he said, "have a drink."

As I drank, he walked back to Jack and unloaded a large wooden bowl from his pack. He filled the bowl and set it before his horse.

"There, Rider, drink deep," he said, stroking its mane.

"Captain?" I asked hesitantly, "Your horse is named...*Rider*?"

"It's a long story." His smile told me I would not yet hear it.

I fetched my canteen from my saddlebag. When I got back, the end of the rope was back in the well. I hauled it up and filled my canteen, and the Captain did likewise.

"Drink as much as you like now, it's the last water we'll see until we reach TerkEtmek."

When I'd had my fill, I led the horses and donkeys to the stump, and pulled the packs off the donkeys. The leather-cased water skins in their packs were still full, so I left them alone. I unloaded Yashel and asked the Captain if he'd like me to unload Rider. He nodded. By then he was filling the watering bowl for Yashel. We rested, leaning against our packs and talking as we took turns watering the donkeys and then the horses again. We ate dried meat and bread from the donkeys' packs, drank more water, and refilled our canteens. When the animals would drink no more, I fit their grain bags over their mouths. The Captain lifted the wooden plug and returned it to its place in the petrified stump, sealing the well from the sun. I felt almost proud to be treated as an adult by the Captain, taking turns with the night's chores before we bedded down in the sand, each under a thick stack of blankets.

I woke just as the sun began to rise over the horizon. It was *cold*. I'd heard deserts had cold nights, but never really imagined it possible until then. I got up and checked the animals, wearing two blankets around me as I went. I started to load the donkeys, first Jenny, then Jack. I was nearly done loading Yashel before I realized the exertion of packing had warmed me.

The Captain woke and checked the donkeys, giving me a quick nod. He looked like he was still asleep.

"Did you sleep well?" I asked. He only nodded and attempted a quick half-smile. I decided to give him some time before attempting conversation again. We ate more bread in silence, and drained a little from our canteens. After the Captain loaded his horse, we put on our armor and rode uphill, still climbing the first of the Great Dunes.

I soon realized the Captain had understated the Great Dunes in his description. I'd thought the dunes were more pronounced, or maybe twice as large as the ones we'd ridden over the previous day, but they were not. They were great mountains of sand; each would have been a wonder in its own right.

Over the Great Dunes, the stone markers were limited to the peaks of the dunes we needed to cross. They were offset from the exact peak of each dune, guiding us to the valley on the right or left. The Captain led our small party toward the marker near the first dune's peak, then veered to the right, choosing the valley between the dune and its rising neighbor on the same side. I could see the next dunes were larger still. It was slow going, and I rocked back and forth as Yashel climbed. The donkeys huffed and snorted, but were otherwise silent. Before we crossed the first ridge, the Captain let out a great yawn.

"*Well.* Good morning, my young friend. How did *you* sleep?" He spoke as if not a moment had passed since he first woke.

"Pretty well." I smiled. I'd discovered another curious bit of the Captain's private life; he was *not* a morning person.

When we crested the ridge of the first large dune, we were able to see down into a real valley. It was quite a sight. Looking behind me, it appeared as if the valley in front of us was lower than the desert plain behind us, and I wondered if it were possible. The dune ahead of us was taller still. I felt like we were on a ship at the peak of a giant sea swell, about to dive down into the trough between colossal waves made of sand. It made me dizzy. I shivered as we rode down the back of the first great dune. We'd had the sun to our backs on the way up, but the ride down brought a chill back to me. When the sun was overhead later in the day, I wished for such a shadow.

We rode slower as Jack and Jenny stepped more cautiously downhill. My gaze was fixed on the sunlit peak ahead of us, jealous for its warmth. When I told the Captain I saw *something* moving in the corner of my eye, he seemed to snap from his thoughts.

"What do you think it was?"

"I don't know. If tumbleweeds grow here, I might have seen one rolling by."

"Be cautious, it might have been a sand-colored snake. They are hard to see, even up close."

My mind suddenly fixed on danger, I asked him, "We've been in armor since we left, with our swords at hand. Do you think we'll meet any threats?"

"Today it's more likely than any other. As I've said, we'll be in the Great Dunes all day, and this is where the troll sightings are rumored. If there is trouble to meet us, I'd wager it would be today."

We rode on down the long slope of the dune in silence. I tried to imagine what would happen if we saw trolls. Would they attack us? Would they threaten us, or try to negotiate first?

"Do you get used to it?" I asked. "The waiting, I mean."

"If we meet danger, remember your training. Don't try to figure everything out; your training will take care of most of your thinking."

I tried to remember all the sword and riding techniques I'd practiced. Sometime after, while we were riding up yet another dune, I found myself still wondering if I'd seen a snake. I was distracted when the Captain shouted to me in a firm, clear voice.

"Turn around *now* and ride up the last dune, as fast as you can. *Go!*"

He smacked the flank of my horse with the flat of his sword. I headed quickly back downhill, wondering if it was a test of some sort. Soon, I knew it was not. I heard a chilling shriek from behind me, then the Captain's quiet *cluck* at the donkeys as he slapped their rumps to set them trotting. They brayed and snorted as they scattered.

Everything happened in slow motion. My body was sluggish, and I worried I wouldn't be able to fight. I lurched forward as Yashel hit the bottom of the dune valley, then started climbing fast, up the last dune we'd ridden down. The Captain passed me on the way up and turned, facing me and the shrieking trolls I was riding away from. I remember thinking, *his horse must be far faster than mine.*

When I reached the Captain, he was silent. Surely he expected me to turn around and fight…or did he? For a quick second I thought of continuing past the top of the dune, and riding away from the trolls as fast as I could. It lasted only a second. It was as if the thought didn't fit in my mind well enough, and so it was rejected. To this day, I wonder if I was foolish, or merely *young*. When I turned around, I saw a half-dozen trolls, snarling and shrieking as they charged up the hill after us. Each of them waved a sword or an axe. I stopped and turned to face them, alongside the Captain. I imagined I saw the trace of a smile in his face as I turned.

The Captain spoke calmly. "Now we have the higher ground. Be glad they are not on horses." He paused just a moment before he cleared his throat, and said a little louder, "On my call, we ride down upon them. Hold your sword *tight*." As I sat there on my horse, I felt like I was in a dream. I looked at my hand…*I hadn't even drawn my sword.* I yanked it from its scabbard. As soon as I held it ready, the Captain yelled, *"We ride!"* and we thundered down the long dune toward them.

The Captain was right about my training in one way; I didn't question myself or wonder what to do. It didn't prepare me, however, for what I *felt*. My heart was like a ship lost in a storm during the three or four times we rode past them, dodging their weapons and striking at them with our own. I didn't know whether to feel afraid or excited, disgusted or proud, as we killed them all, and so I felt a little of each, bobbing back and forth between emotions.

When it was over, the Captain slid off his horse and went to check each troll. He tore a shirt from one, and used it to wipe his sword. He tossed it to me and I caught it by the bloody patch. I jerked a little, but didn't drop it. I wiped my sword too, then dropped the cloth to the sand. The shirt had a strong, foul smell. The blood was warm, and while I should have expected this, it surprised me.

I half slid, half jumped down from Yashel and fell to my hands and knees, retching. I emptied my stomach, and let out a stifled sob. *What will the Captain think of me now?* I wondered. Just then, I felt his hand on my shoulder.

"You did well, Mark. You did well."

I felt a surge of pride at his approval, but it was washed away by a tide of disgust. *You feel pride at this?* My mind demanded of me. I retched again, leaning over my breakfast as it sunk into the sand.

The Captain turned and dropped heavily to the sand, sitting while he waited for me to finish. When I turned and sat up, he spoke in a hushed tone.

"I need to find the donkeys. Why don't you get back on your horse and head up the dune to see if you can spot them?"

I did as he said, but the Captain found both before I reached the top. They had followed the lowest path possible, at a right angle to our own. Perhaps he wanted me in a safer position than sitting in the sand, while he looked for the donkeys. Perhaps he just wanted to give me something to do.

Death. I had killed someone...*two* someones. They weren't human, but they were *people*. *How could I have done this?* I wondered if I would feel shame and disgust for the rest of my life.

The Captain signaled me to ride down to him, and we continued on our way up the same dune we'd scaled, seemingly a lifetime ago. I steered far clear of the trolls' bodies, and found myself extremely attentive as we approached the next ridge.

After a moment of silence I asked, "When we rode far enough from the trolls, why couldn't we have run away and left them alone?"

"There are two reasons," he replied in a resolute voice. "Firstly, they were on foot, so their caravan is not far. They would've reported us to others who would have chased us, maybe too many for us to escape. But more importantly, their intent was to murder us. They would have done the same to the next humans traveling across the dunes. As Captain of the King's guard, I cannot allow this. You must realize, it would have been impossible for us to take any of them prisoner and still make it out of the desert alive."

He looked thoughtful for a moment before he spoke again. When he did, he wore a painful expression.

"You can't know what to do with the feelings you have right now. We *had to* do what we did, but it doesn't make it *easy*. It's hard to kill for a reason. Remind yourself, it's *supposed* to be hard to kill; we weren't built for it. You're *meant* to go through pain after killing an enemy. If there's an honest way out, we should take it. I'm glad you asked why we didn't do just that—it shows you have a strong desire *not to kill*, which belongs in all of us."

The Captain paused to let his words settle into my mind. I still felt repulsion in my gut, but I felt better to know it was normal and right for me to feel it.

"It was fortunate they were all on foot. If one had been on a horse, it would've been much easier to slip away and report us to the rest of their caravan. I meant to talk about this before we met any trolls, but I didn't expect to see any this close to the desert plain. If we are attacked again, and some of them are mounted, we may need to split up. If we stop them, their caravan may assume they met with some other danger in the dunes, such as snakes or scorpions. At the least they'll have a harder time tracking us, if their sentries don't live to warn them immediately."

We rode in silence while I wondered if I would stop shaking soon. Before I did, the Captain spoke again.

"Do you know why we turned, and rode back up the dune when the trolls attacked?"

"It was like you said," I replied, "so we would have the higher ground." The Captain nodded.

"Do you know why they attacked when they did?"

I thought about it for a bit.

"They attacked just as we were approaching the top of the dune. This gave *them* the high ground, and left us furthest from getting back to high ground ourselves."

"Right you are. The last time we rode against them, when there were only two left standing, *that* time we rode uphill. How was it harder?"

"It was much more dangerous, I think. It felt...well, it felt *scarier*."

"Right. Do you know why we rode uphill against them the last time?"

I wondered, *was it because they were fewer and wounded, so it wasn't as dangerous?* No; it might be part of the answer, but there was something else. We could have rode around them in a wide circle uphill, just as we'd done before. My mind found an answer, but I didn't like it.

"Was it...was it *to train me?*"

"Yes." He let his answer soak in before he continued, and for a moment, I thought I might be sick again.

"I didn't know this skirmish was going to take place," The Captain explained, "but I knew it was likely we'd see one before we passed the Great Dunes. I had to see how you would react. You fought bravely, Mark."

I felt ashamed. He didn't know how scared I was. If he knew how clumsy I felt and how I almost forgot my sword, he wouldn't have said these things. I rode in guilty silence for a while, then burst out in frustration.

"But I *was* afraid—I wasn't brave at all!"

The Captain clicked his tongue, as if correcting me.

"*Of course* you were. If you weren't afraid, how could you have shown bravery? Bravery isn't needed where there isn't fear; then only duty remains."

"But I was so clumsy...*I didn't even remember to draw my sword.*"

"I know," he said with a smile. "Why do you think I told you to hold your sword *tightly*? What did you think I was waiting for, before I called us to ride?"

A chuckle fell from of my mouth. He'd known all along.

"Nonetheless, by then you'd already passed the biggest test," said the Captain.

"I did? What was it?"

"You turned around to fight. I never told you to. You could have kept riding away; you even would have been somewhat justified. You knew I'm an experienced soldier, and more equipped to battle the trolls. When you turned to fight alongside me, you told me volumes about your character."

"No I didn't," I objected in a shameful tone. "I *thought of* riding right on past the next dune, and the next." I stared at my saddle, not wanting to meet his gaze.

"I *know this*," he responded to my astonishment. "But you didn't think of it for long. The *choice you made*, along with the pain I saw in you afterward, these are the important lessons. It's not about the fear you felt, or what you were tempted to do. Your *actions* are what speak the loudest."

We rode on, over the next dune and the next. It was a long time before the Captain spoke again.

"Yesterday you asked if there were other missions on this journey you should know about," he started. "There *is* another mission I couldn't discuss with you then. There is a possible conspiracy I'll be investigating on our trip."

"*Really?* What is it?" I asked, excited to hear of it.

"As you may know, there have been bitter disputes between the Trade Merchants and the gypsy troll caravans. These same disputes kept the Royal Family from going to the Winter Palace this past Christmas."

"Who are the Trade Merchants and the gypsy trolls?" I interrupted.

"The troll caravans are the only trolls who do business with humans, and they deal only with the Trade Merchants. They are nomads who travel the length of the desert, and the near side of the Vuori Mountains.

"The Trade Merchants were once a powerful group. They've been known to control weaker kings in our long history. Our King treats them fairly, if not so in their own eyes. The merchant families own vast tracks of land and trade what they yield from them. Recently, the Hapsteads and Neerfals have been trading lumber back and forth, and I find this suspicious."

"Why? What's odd about trading lumber?" I asked.

"Lumber is one of the costliest items to move, and the Hapsteads and Neerfals are on opposite ends of Enthicia. Moving logs or lumber across the desert is very difficult. Obviously, the two families would normally keep their own lumber and trade it with those closer to their forests. It may be a simple evasion of trade taxes, or something more sinister. Of course, it could be as the families claim and they prefer each other's lumber for specific uses: oak for furniture and pine for building. I need to be certain. The duke may know something of it too."

"What are the disputes about?" I prompted.

"Anything you can imagine. I can't remember the trolls and merchants ever bickering so much. There have been anonymous raids on both sides, and we fear a long feud between the two groups may begin."

"Why couldn't you tell me before?" I asked.

"I wasn't at liberty to share it. The King wanted no one else to know what we suspected."

"Then why did you tell me about it now?" I asked, surprised.

"The King permitted me to share this mission with those I truly trust."

I beamed at hearing this. *"Really?"*

"You've responded well to your training, Mark. I've pushed you to your limits."

"I haven't learned my sword skills *that* well." I said, blushing.

"I know."

I twisted my head around so fast, my neck burned with pain.

"What? Then why..." The Captain cut me off.

"Mark, I haven't only been training you for battle. I've also been testing your abilities in patience, boldness, submission, honesty, loyalty, humility, and compassion. These, and others you will learn, are far more important than skill with the sword. Swords may help win a battle, but they're not what we need in building a kingdom."

I thought immediately of the jewel I found lying on the floor, when I was alone in the Captain's quarters. Was it a test? I remembered when the Captain asked if I'd like to train with a sword while my neck hurt so badly. I thought of the girl who wanted me to tell the story of the ice troll, when she tried to give me more credit than I was due. Were they also tests? When the Captain pushed me to anger, when he tested my patience and told me things I didn't want to hear—when I chose to go on the journey against my brother's warning, when I'd yelled at him the previous day—was the Captain testing me during all these times?

I asked him outright. He smiled wide and said to me, *"Those and more.* I had to be sure you could be trusted with the secret of the Honor Knights".

"The honor nights? What are they—and *when* are they?" I asked.

"Not *when,* but *who.* We are a group of men bound in loyal service to the King. Our order has existed for centuries, with no one but our own membership aware. It is a *secret* service."

"Then why are you breaking tradition to tell *me* about them?"

"I'm not," smiled the Captain, "I'm keeping with the Knight's Code in telling you."

"How? You said only the knights themselves are aware of the...*order?*"

"Yes, only the knights, and whenever they are chosen, *apprentice* knights." He turned to me and lowered his voice. "I am inviting you to join our order."

Part IV

4.0 Apprenticeship

I swallowed hard. *Did I hear him right?*

"How?" I asked doubtfully. "I don't even belong here. Someday David and I will find our way home...won't we?"

"I've talked to the King about this, several times. I'm sorry to say so, but I feel that you may never find your home. For your sake, I hope you do. But for the kingdom's sake...well, I think you would make a fine apprentice, and one day, a fine knight. I think you could be a great help to our kingdom. Even so, the King is convinced you *will* return to your home."

He saw my expression and knew the question I was about to ask.

"No, I'm afraid I can't explain why he thinks you'll return. You'll have to be content he has good reason to suspect you will. The King also believes the things you will learn as an apprentice will be a gift from our land to your own. This is the first time an apprentice has been chosen when we know you may not stay in our order for life. It's caused a lot of...discussions among the other knights."

"Who are the other knights?" I asked.

"You can only know this if you are accepted as a full knight one day. This rule protects our order from annihilation. Only full knights know who the others are. This also protects our apprentices. If an enemy wants to kidnap an apprentice, they can only discover the name of his mentor. If they know who the apprentice is, it would already be obvious to them who his mentor is. If you accept the apprenticeship, you will be known as my armor bearer."

"I didn't even know your kingdom *had* knights. I knew you had sergeants, colonels, lieutenants and captains, but I never heard anyone talk of knights."

"Our order is secret. Our knightly duties are in addition to whatever else we do. Because we serve in secret, no one can be drawn to our order for glory. The *glory test* was one of the first I sent you. Do you remember the girl in the courtyard?"

"The girl who asked me about the ice troll?" I asked.

"She was sent to test whether you would obey the King. You didn't even remember her trying to give credit to *you alone* for the Winter Palace rescue, did you?" asked the Captain.

"Yeah, I guess she did. She didn't know how small a part I really played."

"Your part was *not* small. But it's important you didn't seek personal glory by taking credit for the actions of your brother, the Princess, and my soldiers. The glory test is very important. If someone desired to become a knight for their own glory, they might one day be vulnerable to bribery or even treason."

"*Aha,*" I cried. "I *thought* I understood the statue, but wasn't sure. It wasn't commending anyone; it was making a point about seeking glory."

"The statue in the courtyard? Yes, you're right. Those who want such a statue erected in their image do not make it far in the King's service."

It was a lot of information, and for a moment, I felt overwhelmed. We rode in silence, as if the Captain knew these ideas would take a while to sink in. I was proud the Captain trusted me enough to share these things with me. Eventually, more questions gathered in my mind.

"Why did you say my sword skills aren't important?"

"I didn't—they may determine whether you live or die in battle. Even so, there are more important skills for you to learn. These will determine what you may do with your life *after* you survive a battle. Of the many things you must learn to become a knight, most of them don't involve weapons at all."

That was unexpected. "Well, how did your mentor find you?" I asked. Joking, I suggested, "I'll bet he didn't find you chipping through the floor in an ice castle."

At this, the Captain dropped his eyes to the path, and a great heaviness seemed to come over him. *I shouldn't have brought up his being rescued by boys*, I thought. When he spoke, I saw this wasn't his concern at all.

"My father was a soldier. He died in battle when I was a young boy. I bounced from job to job in Thraen Kholl until I was taken in by a blacksmith. After working for him almost a year, I learned he was a knight when he invited me to be his apprentice."

"I'm sorry." I wished I had something more to say.

"I was too young to mourn him then. My biggest regret is for the lessons he never got to teach me. You see, after I became a knight, I learned my father had also been a knight. Even a knight's family doesn't know of our order."

We rode up another long dune and down the other side without talking. The sun was directly over us, and it bathed us in dry heat. I didn't want to take off my armor, remembering the trolls. I rubbed my side where one of the trolls' swords struck me and pressed the chain mail hard into my ribs. I was sure I'd have a large bruise by nightfall. I wondered sarcastically if the Captain's magical mineral pool could heal bruises too. I no longer wondered if this trip would be a waste of time—the Captain's invitation was more justification than I needed.

Just over the top of another dune, we stopped to pull food from our packs and break for water. From that point, we were most likely to see approaching trolls or other attackers. We refilled our canteens from the water sacks on the donkeys and watered the animals with the wooden bowl, this time only one bowlful each. I had to dig a bowl-shaped depression in the sand before each animal so it wouldn't spill. Between watering them, we sat on blankets we spread on the hot sand, being ever cautious of snakes and scorpions. I turned to the Captain with another question.

"What type of things does an apprentice knight learn?" The Captain cleared his throat before he spoke.

"These are the first things you'll learn as an apprentice: Boldness, Humility, Submission, Leadership, Compassion, Strength, Conviction, Forgiveness, Loyalty, Patience, Wisdom, and Honesty."

"Some of those sound like opposites." Each topic sounded important, but I wondered how long he could talk about them. Perhaps he'd give me a quiz to see if I understood each one. Either way, they didn't sound very *knightly* to me.

"That's only because you don't understand them well enough. We grow up learning to use these words as society misunderstands or abuses them. I can assure you, none of them are opposites."

"Somehow I thought there would be a lot of sword training involved." I must have sounded disappointed.

"And there will be. I will also teach you in the areas of government and politics, commerce and trade, negotiating, and even psychology."

"*All* those?" I blurted in surprise.

"Just maybe," replied the Captain with a smile, "you have a lot to learn. It looks like someone's done drinking," he said, nodding toward Jenny, who stood over the empty bowl. "We'd better get going. We need to clear the last of the Great Dunes by nightfall."

While I packed the bowl, the Captain secured the water sacks. We rode on, and I began to relax. By early afternoon I felt confident we wouldn't see another attack. When we reached what seemed to be the highest dune—an entire *mountain* of sand—I could see we were over halfway to the desert plain beyond the Great Dunes. In the distance, I could see the small city of TerkEtmek.

It sat at the far edge of the desert, encroached by rocky terrain leading to mountains to the east and south, and a road leading to a more welcome region to the southwest.

The only sound to be heard was the *ssshh—ssshh—ssshh* of the animals' hooves shuffling over warm sand. Suddenly, the near silence was interrupted by a terrible bellowing. I carelessly spun my head in the cry's general direction—*ouch*—beyond the dune to our left. The Captain clucked his tongue and the donkeys stood still. He motioned for me to be silent as we reined our horses to a stop. I reached for my sword, but the Captain motioned me away from it. We heard the noise again. It was a horrible noise, and I imagined a large animal being brutally slaughtered. The Captain motioned me to follow, and we rode most of the way up the dune lying between us and the cries. By the time we stopped, the sound had ended.

We turned our horses facing downhill. The Captain opened his pack and removed three items, handing two of them to me. The first was a glass bottle of thick liquid, and the other, a strapped roll of thick, hard leather. The item he held turned out to be two thin sheets of pale cloth, rolled together. He unrolled them and cut two holes in the center of one. Then he *wore* the sheet over his head, like a ghost costume, and peered through the eyeholes. I looked nervously around. *What is he up to?* He spread his sheet on the sand again, and cut two holes in the second sheet as well. Nervous as I was, I bit my tongue to keep from laughing. Did he want us to dress as ghosts?

Next, he took the bottle of liquid from me and poured it carefully over both sheets. I had to stand on their ends to hold them in place as he used the bottle to smear the syrupy liquid evenly over their surfaces. Then he flipped the sheets over, so the sticky sides were in the sand.

Finally, I understood. We rolled over the sheets and turned them back over. The Captain had made sand-colored sheets for us, to camouflage us against the dunes. I wondered what the last item was, even as he unfurled it.

The thick leather roll held two glass lenses. I watched as he rolled the leather around both lenses and used the leather straps to tie it tightly together—a portable telescope.

We wore the sandy sheets over our heads, and padded clumsily the rest of the way to the crest of the dune. We knelt at its peak, just high enough to see down the other side. I clenched my teeth together, willing myself to remain quiet. The next valley was filled with dozens of green trolls, arranged in a caravan of carts.

I soon saw what had made the noise. An animal carcass was being butchered, and near it, a long line of trolls waited for fresh meat. I saw no fire. Maybe they used the sun, or maybe they would eat it raw. The Captain was busy scanning the group with the telescope. A moment later, he handed it to me, and I looked through it as well.

I searched to find how many horses there were: not nearly as many horses as trolls. I tried to count how many of them were armed; most of them were. There were many mules and donkeys tied to carts. Some carts were smaller, with clay pitchers dangling from ropes—for water, I guessed. Suddenly, one troll attacked another. They fought violently until the largest, best-armored of the trolls struck them both with a heavy club. One troll fell, face down in the sand, and the other stood to face the one who struck him. The larger troll dropped his club and unsheathed his sword, and the smaller troll turned and walked away. Finally, the larger troll walked to a horse and rested his club in a holster on its saddle. His horse was huge, much bigger than the Captain's. I noticed a large, jagged scar covering most of the horse's rump. I wondered how the horse lived through such an injury.

The Captain tapped my shoulder, and receded from the trolls' line of sight. I crawled backwards after him, not wanting to take my eyes off the caravan. When we reached our horses, he stowed the sand-sheets, wrapping them around the sticky bottle, and collapsed the leather-tube telescope. Walking quietly, we led our horses back to the donkeys, and continued in the way we'd been traveling.

We made as little sound as possible over the next several dunes. Finally, the Captain asked me what I thought of the troll group.

"Well," I started thoughtfully, "they must be one of the caravans who trade with humans, and carry goods across the desert. It looked like they were just about to eat a donkey. Most of them were armed, and they had carts of water. I think I saw the leader break up a fight. Did you see his horse? What could have scarred it like that?"

"A *mule*," he corrected. "But yes, they were about to eat it. They are too heavily armed to be a simple trade caravan. It *was* their leader you saw, and his horse was probably scarred from battle—specifically, while *running* from a battle. It must have been slashed while its rider was running away. I've never seen such a large scar on a healthy horse. I know this, though; a troll would never ride a horse if it proved he ran from battle. It must be the horse of someone he's killed." The Captain seemed annoyed by something, where I expected only fear.

"I don't know why they're armed so heavily," he continued, "but I'm sure it's not for peaceful trading. Their carts were mostly filled with water, and it's certainly not for trade on the either side of Enthicia. They must plan to spend some time in the desert. I hope the duke can shed some light on this. Either way, we'll be out of the dunes soon, and relatively safe."

The sun was getting low, and I kept repeating to myself, *only a few more dunes to go*. We were at the bottom of a valley between dunes when a group of trolls appeared over the dune in front of us. Before we saw each other, the Captain drew his sword and rode in front of me, grabbing Yashel's reins from my hands and turning me around. As we passed the donkeys, he slapped their backsides with the flat of his sword once again. We rode halfway up the dune we'd just come down, and turned around. They'd spotted us and were riding hard toward us. There were four of them on horses, and three or four on foot. One of the mounted trolls split off from the group and veered left, toward the troll caravan.

"*Here*," the Captain yelled, grabbing the lance hanging from my saddle. "Go after the fleeing troll. *He must not reach the caravan.*" He held the lance out for me to grab, and I knew what I must do.

The battle was as gruesome as before. The only thing keeping me from freezing in fear, was the thought of the entire caravan surrounding us, ready to kill us. My horse was faster by far than the horse I chased. I caught the mounted troll at full speed, and stopped it with a hefty thrust of the lance. When I was sure he would not get up, I retrieved my lance and raced back to the Captain, who by my count was facing six or seven trolls by himself. When I nearly reached him, he was facing only two mounted trolls, and two more on foot. When they saw me, they turned their backs on the Captain and raced for me, swords and axes raised. I felt my heart catch in my throat.

The Captain immediately jumped off his horse and slapped its backside, and it trotted away from him. Then he yelled loud enough to get the trolls' attention, and stood holding his sword and lance high in the air. The two trolls on horses saw an easy opportunity and wheeled around to ride down on the Captain, though they had nearly reached me, and I was by far the easier target. The Captain began waving toward himself, and I realized his plan. He wasn't waving to the *trolls*, he was waving to *me*. I jabbed my heels into Yashel's belly. Steering clear of the trolls on foot, I rode fast after the two mounted trolls. I left my lance in one and struck the other with my sword. By the time they reached the Captain, neither was in shape to do him harm. The Captain was still waving me on, so I rode up to him. He jumped onto Yashel, behind me, and we both rode her the short distance to his horse. The Captain and I rode down on the remaining trolls, and left them dead on the desert floor.

We found the donkeys a short way off, and rode on our way in silence. We were driving the donkeys to go faster now, doing our best to get clear of the dunes in decent light. I was surprised to find I felt much less disturbed after the second battle, though in truth, I was not at all equipped to judge such things yet. I wondered if I was still shocked from the experience of the first encounter, or if I had gotten used to death a little more. Or, seeing the caravan of trolls, perhaps I was too scared to worry about anything but *living*. Either way, I was tired and wanted to sleep somewhere safe.

I was relieved when we rode down the last of the Great Dunes. We stopped a good distance past it, and I watered the animals, while the Captain remained on his horse. I filled our empty canteens, we drained them, and I filled them again. When I thought we were going to unload the blankets and sleep, the Captain told me to load the empty water bags and bowl back onto Jenny and Jack. *Surely we can't ride all night*, I thought, but this was exactly what the Captain had planned. I was angry again, but also a little scared. What would happen when we reached the mud baths and nothing happened? Would they blame me?

By the time it was too dark to see the ground in front of us, there was a tiny glowing light on the horizon for us to follow. The Captain insisted we must reach TerkEtmek before we stopped. As the minutes passed, the lights of the small city grew. I must have fallen asleep a dozen times, though I never fell from my horse. I dreamt I was on the back of a giant antelope again, hanging on for dear life. I dreamt I felt its bony spine press into my backside, and woke with a start. My backside hurt, and I realized I was sitting on my lap armor. I pulled it around over my thighs and tried to get comfortable again.

Finally, we approached the gates of TerkEtmek. The Captain yelled ahead to the guards on the wall.

"A messenger from the King comes to see the duke. *Open the gates.*"

Lanterns were lowered on ropes, partway down from the top of the wall. Next, great doors in the gate opened, just as we approached them. A large number of armed guards on horses encircled us. They escorted us through the main road of the small city to the duke's mansion.

Even with the excitement of being led by guards through a new and wondrous city, I was falling in and out of sleep. Each time I woke, I felt scorching hot or freezing cold. Whenever I reached my hand up to my throat, my wound felt more sensitive than before—and very warm. I shook and sweated, sick with fever.

The last thing I saw was the duke's mansion. I thought it looked just like the palace, only smaller, and I wondered why it wasn't called a palace. I have a dream-like memory of the Captain demanding the duke be woken, and see us immediately. He said he had an injury for the duke to see. I also remember dreaming the King and all his relatives were magical healers. I dreamt the Captain was injured, but he hid it from me. I dreamt the duke was an ice troll, and tried to turn me blue.

For the second time since arriving in Terreldor, I woke in a bed I'd never seen before, made up with white sheets and blankets. The blankets were rough wool, and I was hot. It was dark, but there was a candle burning nearby. There was a woman there trying to calm me, though I couldn't understand why. Some kid was screaming at the top of his lungs. *If he would only stop*, I thought, *maybe I could get back to sleep.* I struggled against the woman, who began to hold me down. When I opened my mouth to protest, only screams came out. I realized it was *me* who had been screaming all along. I closed my mouth and soon fell back asleep, confused and afraid.

Sometime later I heard voices and felt light on my eyes. It seemed to shine through my eyelids, and my head pulsed with pain. I heard low voices.

"He screamed like a child last night, don't you think?"

"Sire, you should have seen him yesterday. He fought harder than some soldiers I've served with. He's not thirsty for blood, either. He took his first battle as hard as should be expected."

"Yes. Well, you place more importance in this than I. A little bloodlust in soldiers wins battles. I think you'd better bring him to the pools as soon as he can ride; there's nothing else I can do for him. Now as for you, I think your shoulder will be back to normal any day now."

"Yes sire, it feels fine."

"Captain Williams, when it comes to your own injuries, I'd trust a troll's word over your own."

My throat was dry. I coughed and choked, and my eyelids seemed glued shut. A third person, someone on the other side of my bed, helped me sit up and put a glass to my lips. Her delicate hands told me it was a woman helping me. Eyes still closed, I emptied the entire glass without stopping for breath. She put another into my hands and I drained it also, then rubbed the sleep stuff from my eyes and finally opened them. I was out of breath from gulping down the water, and had to yawn. My mouth opened wide, locking my ears shut, so I had no idea how loudly I yawned. By the time I finished and looked around, I could tell by the look on the faces staring at me it was a loud yawn indeed.

"*By fire,*" said the man, in a low voice, now wearing a lopsided grin. "Does this boy do *anything* halfway? I should hope he doesn't want to eat, or we may be gobbled up alive."

The man was sitting in an ornate chair, and the Captain stood behind him. I knew immediately he must be the duke. The Captain sounded stern, but tried to hide a proud smile on his face.

"Mark, this is Duke Cornelius Ward the third, a relative of the King. He is royalty, and we call him s*ire.*" It seemed so much like a morning not long ago, when I woke in front of the King. This time I resolved to do things right. Though I was dizzy, I stumbled to my feet and saluted him as I'd seen soldiers in the King's palace do.

"*Sire,* I am Mark, armor bearer for Captain Williams—at your service." My eyes popped open a little in surprise, as did the Captain's. My throat felt different, and my voice, rough. It hurt to talk.

The duke stood up at once and cried, "By the skies, you do go all the way, don't you? I will call you By Halves while you're in my house, for everything you do *by double.*"

The Captain's smile grew. The duke turned to leave and we both bowed.

"I leave you to make your plans. Captain, send word to me if you need my help."

When the duke left the room, the Captain slapped me on the shoulder and tousled my hair. It was the warmest gesture I'd seen from him yet.

I was too dizzy to stand, and I half-fell, half-sat on the edge of my bed. The Captain saw me stumble, then told me I'd need to rest more.

"What happened last night?" I asked him.

He smiled. "Nothing. You slept all night long."

"Really? I hardly remember arriving here. How did I get changed, and cleaned, and into this bed?"

"That was the night *before* last. You've been sleeping for two nights and a day. As I'm sure you recall, I intended for us to camp just outside the Great Dunes, but I had a small injury from the second troop of trolls we met. I didn't want to risk another battle until we both felt better. I should have known such a long ride would be too hard on you. You had to be carried into the mansion. Why, when we got inside the gate, you nearly fell off your horse. The duke's nurse, the lady who was just here, changed and bathed you."

He saw my expression and added, "Don't worry, you're not the first male she's treated."

"I just feel tired, that's all," I said, though my face flushed red.

"Tired and *embarrassed*. But we made this trip for a reason, remember? You're not as well as when we left Engdynlor. Your injury is ready to be healed."

I felt a pang of guilt. What would happen when their silly mud bath didn't heal me? I felt angry at the same time, but tried not to let it show. The Captain spoke on.

"We'll ride to the Valley of Abandon tomorrow, where the mineral pools are. It's not a hard ride, and I don't want it to delay any longer. For the rest of today, you'd better try to sleep."

I sighed. He must have known I would be bored alone in the room. Just then he took a satchel from his shoulder and opened it. He removed a large roll of something resembling brown paper. It felt smooth like cloth, but tougher. It was oiled, and looked like I might see light through it if it weren't so thick. I realized it was some type of leather. He unrolled it before me.

"This is a map of the south end of Enthicia. When you are bored and can't sleep, you can study this map. In fact, here…" He pulled a smaller piece of the same papery leather from his satchel. "You can make a copy of the areas with the mineral pools if you feel strong enough to sit at the desk."

He nodded toward a small desk at one end of the room, I'd somehow overlooked until then.

"Just be careful not to spill ink on the original," he added. "It's from the duke's private library."

I thanked him, grateful for some task to stave off boredom.

"Rest well," he added on his way out of the room. "I'll come back tomorrow, late in the morning, to wake you."

I immediately began poring over the map. The leather was smooth, and very thick. I studied the edges to see how thick it was. It looked like two thin pieces of leather glued together, frayed in places. I laid it out in front of me, wondering what the symbols meant as I searched for a key.

Though I had planned to stay up studying and copying the map all day, I soon gave in to sleep. I had strange dreams I cannot remember. They were bits and pieces jumbled together, none of which lasted more than a few seconds. When I woke again, it was night. My body was still tired, but my mind was wide awake. I found a candle on the nightstand beside me, but nothing to light it. I wandered in the darkness across the room to search the desk. I nearly knocked over an inkwell before I found a tin of oversized matches. I lit the candle and fetched the map from the bed stand.

Looking at the map again, I felt a rush of excitement and I knew I wouldn't soon fall back asleep. I had to hold the map up to the candle to see anything at all. After I thought I understood the markings, I tried to trace a portion of the map, but soon found it was impossible. Even if I held the candle very close, I couldn't see through the blank page to the original. I decided instead to draw a miniature version of the entire map on the smaller piece of leather. My eyes became strained. The candle wasn't bright enough to see all the details in the map. For fear of dropping wax on it, I held the map upright. I found if I allowed my eyes to adjust to a dark corner of the room, I could hold the map in *front* of the candle, and see more of the map at once. I copied the content of the original onto the smaller leather by moving the candle so close to the smaller sheet, I dripped quite a bit of wax onto it. The work was slow; I wasn't quite familiar with using a quill pen.

When I was finished, I quickly looked at the two maps side-by-side. It seemed there were more details than I remembered from when I first saw the original, but I was finished, and I was happy to see I'd drawn the proportions fairly accurately. The faintest of the symbols weren't listed in the map's legend, but had their own strange captions. They were underscored by odd symbols reminding me of Japanese characters. By then, the first dim glow before dawn was falling through the single window in the room. I felt tired again, so I left the map on the desk. Once the ink was dry, I rolled up the smaller map and stuffed it into a pocket of my pants, and laid them over the chair beside my bed. I fell asleep when I laid my head on my pillow, and had no dreams the rest of the night.

4.1 Coals in the Valley of Abandon

When I next woke, the sun was shining brightly through the window. I turned to find the noise I assumed had wakened me. It was the door, creaking loudly as the Captain walked through it.

"Are you ready to ride?" he asked.

"Absolutely. I feel like I've been sleeping for a year."

Something seemed different about the Captain; he was much more energetic than I expected, so early in the morning. I felt like it would be a good day. And why shouldn't it be? I had my strength back, and since my fever had broken, I felt nearly as well as I had before the incident with the ice troll. As long as I didn't drown in the mud bath, I knew I'd be fine.

The Captain stood, waiting for me in the doorway. I got ready to leave, and turned to follow him out of the room.

Don't forget the map," the Captain said, pointing behind me. "Bring it, and we'll return it to the duke's library after we eat."

"Don't we need it?" I asked, walking over to it.

"No. I know the path well enough."

As I rolled up the duke's map, it looked much simpler than I remembered. *Why'd it take me so long to copy?*

"I must've been sleepier than I thought," I said, mostly to myself.

"Eh?" mumbled the Captain, his mind obviously on breakfast.

"It seemed so complex last night, with so many symbols on it...but it looks almost plain today."

"Is it safe to assume you stayed up late copying it?"

I nodded. If he thought my memory was faulty from staying up so late, he was probably right. I followed the Captain to the service kitchen. Workers were busy preparing lunch for the duke's table.

There was enough food for a small army, and each plate was impressive. The Captain caught the look in my eye and smiled.

"The duke sets a fancy table for his guests, eh? Too bad we'll be on our way to the Valley of Abandon when this is served."

The head chef let us eat anything we wanted, and asked if there were other things he could prepare for us. I asked for some eggs and fried ham, and ate them with biscuits from the table—they tasted like cornbread, only much sweeter. The Captain asked for a steak and washed it down with every kind of fruit juice they could squeeze for him.

"It's not every day you get a breakfast like this," he said with a wink.

With a full belly, I followed the Captain to the duke's library. We left the original map with a page at the door, and headed for the stables. The duke's mansion and the surrounding grounds amazed me. Even the stables were made of stone and painted white. The Captain noticed my fascination.

"Impressed?"

"It looks very…clean. And expensive, too."

"Only near the mansion," he replied. "The duke allocates his funds…*differently* than our King." His tone told me his statement would stand alone; I would get no more from him on the subject.

We finally reached our horses and found our armor hanging near them. We donned our armor, then dressed our horses in theirs as well, but left the donkeys in the stables. We left by another gate, across the city from the way we'd entered, called the *needle's eye*. Not far from the mansion I lost all hope of direction in a tangle of narrow, twisting paths I would hardly call streets. Everything I saw was in poor repair, and generally dirty. The people we passed looked unhappy, even hungry.

"Is the rest of the city like this?" I asked.

"All but the duke's mansion," the Captain replied. Again, his words held an air of disapproval. We rode on, and left our thoughts unsaid. We needed to dismount and lead our horses by their bridles when we reached the smaller gate. I saw at once how it got its name; it was hardly more than a hole in the city wall. The guards there hardly acknowledged us as we passed.

Outside the narrow alleys and three story buildings, I could see enough sky to know our direction.

"We turn east-by-southeast around the wall of the city, is that right?" I asked.

"Very good. I can see you stayed up late studying the map," the Captain replied.

We rode along the city wall a while before the trail led to the open desert. The sand was littered with rough stones, which gradually gave way to boulders. As we rode, the large rocks became increasingly dense. Soon we followed an obvious trail winding though boulders as large as small huts. I drank often from my canteen and thought of my throat. *As long as I drink a lot, it doesn't hurt,* I thought, *I can live with that.*

The sun was high above us, well past noon, when we heard something ahead of us on the trail. The Captain motioned for me to dismount. We led Yashel and Rider off the trail a ways, winding past rocks and boulders. We tied their reins to a tall, jagged rock and walked cautiously in the direction of the noise.

It was a large group of trolls, meandering though the rocks and boulders at a right angle to the path. They crossed the path from left to right—they were headed away from TerkEtmek. My miniature map showed what I thought were the ruins of an old city in the direction they were headed. There were at least thirty trolls, perhaps many more. We watched quietly as they passed into the rocks again on the other side of the trail. When the steady stream of trolls had ended, several stayed behind. They tied their horses and sat on low rocks as if they planned to remain there all day. The Captain motioned me back to the horses.

When we reached them, he spoke in whispers, telling me we would need to lead our horses far from the trail, to avoid being seen or heard by the trolls. I sat on my horse at the Captain's insistence, while he walked ahead, leading both horses northward. When we were far from the trail, I felt safe enough to talk to the Captain.

"Why is this place called the Valley of Abandon?" I asked. "It doesn't look like a valley."

"It's actually the beginning to the desert valley we've been in for days. This place looks particularly abandoned though, doesn't it? Even so, it's not named for the people who abandoned it, but for the things *others* have abandoned here."

"*What* things?" I wondered aloud.

"This is something you need to discover for yourself. You will learn it later today, or I fear you never will."

His words were nonsense to me, though I knew the Captain well enough not to ask him more on the subject. *Maybe he plans to show me later*, I thought hopefully.

A short while later we heard more noises ahead of us. We repeated the process of tying the horses and creeping toward the noise, peeking between rocks as we went. This noise was nothing like the last—no horse or donkey hooves striking stone or grumbling trolls. It was a gurgling sound, almost like water boiling. It seemed to grow fainter as we followed it, and I wondered if we'd accidentally passed it. We were both shocked by a great bellow rising up from the earth ahead of us. It was immediately followed by a tall spout of water rising into the sky, over the large rocks in front of us. After walking around a few more boulders, we found a pool of water covering the geyser spout. We touched the pool—it was very hot—and tasted it—it was bitter—and finally spit it out. The Captain seemed excited.

"I think we've discovered something new. This geyser wasn't on the map."

"Then shouldn't we add it?" I asked. "I mean, add it to my copy?"

I pulled the rolled leather out of my pocket and held it out for the Captain to see. The Captain looked surprised when he saw my map was a full copy, instead of a full-sized replica of only a small portion, as he'd suggested.

"Ah, so you made good use of the blank page I left." I smiled, proud of my work. "Well," he went on, "we'll tell the duke about it. He'll send cartographers to find exactly where on the map it belongs. I'm sure they'll want to test the water, though I don't think it's good for drinking."

Instead of taking the map from my hands, he handed me a short lead rod I'd seen him use as a pencil; he wanted me to guess where we were on the map. I saw a strange symbol just north of the trail, near where I thought we stood. It looked almost like a geyser. I handed the map to the Captain.

"It looks like they already added it. I guess we didn't discover it after all."

The Captain eyed my map suspiciously.

"This isn't a copy of the map I brought you. This symbol wasn't on the original...nor was this, nor...*this*—what *is* this?" He pointed to the symbol I thought looked like ruins; something like a broken fortress.

"I don't know. It wasn't listed in the key; I checked. I think these markings were in the lighter ink. Maybe you didn't see them." I wondered if the Captain's eyesight was growing worse with age, and he hadn't discovered it yet. My grandfather once told me his eyesight got worse *overnight*, sometime after he turned forty.

"Before we left, I borrowed the map from the duke's library specifically to see if there had been any recent additions or warnings. I studied the original map sitting at a desk in full sunlight." He paused to glance back to the map, and furrowed his brow. "Did you use a magnifier? Maybe you saw only scratches or stains, and imagined the rest."

"No, *I'm sure of it*. These were fainter than the other symbols, and a little…blurred."

He squinted to read further detail from the map, though he held it at arm's length. "Is this…did you write something *below* these symbols? Did you label them with abbreviations?"

He pointed to the same symbols, his fingernail each time underscoring them, pointing out a smaller figure, or pair of figures accompanying each of them.

"*No*. They looked like boxes, or little doodles below the blurry symbols. I thought they might be a code. What *are* they?"

"Draw some of them for me, here in the dirt," he said, handing me his dagger. I drew several of the simplest shapes, the ones I could best make out the night before. The Captain's face grew ashen, and he kicked at the dirt, destroying my drawings.

"What did you mean, they were *blurred?*" he asked.

"It was like they were rubbed out, or out of focus. I did this at night, in front of the candle." The Captain paused at hearing these words.

"'*In front of the candle*'?" he repeated cautiously. "In front of *what* candle?"

"Well—I was afraid to drip wax on the original, so I held the map upright, in front of the candle on the desk."

"Then you saw this when the map was lit from *behind?*"

"I guess so. What's the difference?" I asked, confused.

"Don't you see? Did you notice how thick the map was?" he asked, poring excitedly over my copy. I nodded slowly, trying to remember. "When an old and valuable map begins to crack or tear, it is often bonded to a new piece of leather, one already trained to roll in the same way as the old. The duke's map was very thick, though neither side appeared stressed. I wondered why it had already been bonded."

His eyes lost focus as his gaze drifted to the sky. *What is he thinking?* I wondered in vain.

"You said these details," he started, pointing back to my map, "were drawn in a fainter ink…and they were *blurry*. *And* you saw them when the map was lit from *behind*. What does this tell you?"

My mind wasn't putting the pieces together. Then all at once, the idea snapped into place. I felt like I'd just invented electricity.

"They're *secret* symbols, hidden between the two pieces of leather—*which is why they're not in the map's legend*. But what are they…and what are the symbols below them?"

"These are *logograms*—picture words, and they belong to a forgotten language. It is called Lusidek, though few recognize its characters. It was once spoken by the brown trolls, back when they were still separated from the greens." He spoke distractedly, then his voice dropped an octave, and he caught my gaze in his own. "You must speak of this to no one. I need to think on this." He paused in deep concentration before adding, "I need to learn what these newly mapped locations have in common." He rolled up the map and slid it into his pocket. "You don't mind me borrowing this for a while, do you?" It wasn't really a question, though I shook my head anyway.

When we reached our horses, I climbed back onto Yashel and tried to rest. It was a slow, bumpy ride back to the path. It felt like we'd passed the trolls by miles in our off-trail wandering.

The rest of the ride was uneventful. I had a lot of time to think. *Why am I so resistant to the possibility the mineral pool might help me?* Whenever I thought this, my mind seemed to rebel. Even then, I knew it wasn't like me to throw away an idea so easily. *Then why am I doing it?* I asked myself repeatedly.

Something the Captain had said provided a welcome distraction to my thoughts.

"What did you mean, *when the browns were still separated from the greens?*" The Captain turned back to me and smiled.

"Still so interested in our history?" I nodded, trying to appear studious. "Over a millennium ago, the brown and green trolls were separate nations, Chrutghan and Luskidia."

"The *who* and the *what?*" I interrupted.

"Not the *who*," The Captain corrected. "The brown trolls, or Chrutghanies, made up the nation of Chrutghan, and the green trolls, or Luskidians, made up the nation of Luskidia. You didn't think they were always called green and browns, did you?" The Captain scoffed. I only shrugged in response. "Anyway, he went on, "the two nations didn't interact, short of territorial wars. They both grew to roughly the same height, though they were separate races."

"Aren't they still?" I asked.

"No. Though the brown trolls are now shorter than the greens, today they belong to a common race." It didn't make sense to me, and I told him so. "After a terrible war, both nations entered into a peace treaty, and the king of each nation took a daughter from the other, to marry one of his sons. It was a political arrangement, though it broke a strong taboo from both peoples. The green troll prince fell in love with his new wife, and to the surprise of both nations, she bore him a son: a green troll. He grew quickly, and it soon became obvious he would be larger than any troll then alive."

"Really?" I asked, dubious such a thing were possible.

"Yes," he insisted. "Soon after, the brown troll prince decided he should treat his own marriage as more than a political concession, and his wife soon bore *him* a son. Their child was brown, and he was healthy and strong, though no taller or shorter than was expected of any other troll family. As the legend goes, the green prince was rewarded for accepting his wife from his father's enemy, while the brown troll prince was destined to remain jealous as punishment for *his* intentions. This is, of course, ridiculous, but it's what the legend claims."

"So why are some still brown, and some still green?" I asked, pointing him back to my question.

"Many a green troll desired a brown troll for his wife," he replied, drawing out his words slowly, "to bring him large children. Huge dowries were paid to the fathers of all the brown troll girls. So many of the green troll men married brown trolls, the male brown trolls who were poor either took green wives, or went unwed. Within a few generations, nearly all trolls had both nations in his ancestry."

So what? I thought, still waiting for my answer.

"Today," he continued, "every brown and green troll now carries the genes of both species. It isn't uncommon for two green parents to have a brown troll born to them, or for two brown trolls to have a green child. This has made all the difference in their history ever since."

"How so?" I asked.

"Any troll who desired to associate only with others of the same color, must deny some of his own family—be them cousins, or nieces, or uncles."

"And any brown troll father," I went on, seeing further implications, "who keeps his daughter from marrying a green troll, turns down a dowry—is that right?" The Captain nodded his confirmation.

"Despite some problems the dowries caused, the browns and greens have treated each other as equals ever since. Then, when one king died with no heir, his subjects agreed to be joined into the other's kingdom. Soon after, they came to speak the same language, and the language of the brown trolls—Lusidek—was abandoned. Finally, they were no longer two nations, *or* two species.

"Eventually the names Luskidians and Chrutghanies fell out of use, as troll families called their children greens or browns, I suppose just as we call our children blondes or redheads. For a while, their combined nation was called Chruskolia, and their new, combined race was called Cha'roles. As time wore on, their nation fell, and Cha'roles became shortened into *trolls*."

What an odd history, I thought to myself. Something seemed missing, and it took me a moment to discover it. "Which king lived?" I finally asked.

"Neither," he replied in a mocking tone. It took me a moment, but I guessed his meaning soon enough.

"You know what I *mean*," I complained. He smiled again, and laughed.

"We'll never know. There are two versions recorded, and as many experts are convinced one version is true as the other. Since Chrutghy—the language of the green trolls—survived, many assume it was the brown troll king who died with no heir. But *look*—now we've arrived."

I looked up, surprised. We'd finally arrived at a pool of steaming mud. It was mid-afternoon. The Captain dismounted and pointed it out, though there was little need. He seemed suddenly bored, as if he were distracted. My nose wrinkled when the wind carried the pool's odor my way. My mood soured immediately.

The pool was small, and near to the trail. It didn't look noteworthy. The Captain explained I was to wade in up to my chest, and then carefully submerge myself, all the way into the mud. It bubbled as he spoke, and the wind shifted again. The odor grew stronger. It smelled like rich soil at best, with a generous helping of sulfur.

"Won't I sink, like in quicksand?" I asked, clearly not wanting to touch it. The Captain climbed back on his horse and turned as if to go.

"It's mostly water," he replied in a monotone. "It won't be difficult for you to wade into it." As he spoke, he turned Rider back the way we'd come.

"Where are you going?"

"A little way back on the trail, to wait for you. You don't need me here for this." He disappeared behind the rocks. I was almost certain I wasn't meant to wade into the smelly muck with my clothes on. I was glad for the privacy, even if it left me feeling unprotected.

I laid my armor on Yashel's back, remembering to tie her reins to something; I found a nearby boulder, almost pillar-like. I took off my shirt and pants and walked toward the mud. Its unpleasant odor grew tenfold. When I reached the pool's edge, I set my boots on a half-sunken boulder and piled my remaining clothes on top of them. I felt ridiculous. My feet sunk in the mud and my toes made a sucking noise with each step. *This is going to be very messy*, I thought. Then I stopped. I felt a deep, inexplicable resolve not to go any farther. *The Captain isn't jumping in this stinking mud-hole*, I thought. *He isn't even here to watch. I know it won't help, so why should I throw myself into this smelly mess?*

I thought of only smearing the mud in my hair and face. If the mud had such wonderful healing properties, I'd even smear it over my scar.

Again, my thoughts surprised me. The Captain had taken so much time and effort to bring me there, why was I unwilling to do this one, simple thing? *Because it's stupid*, my mind rebelled against the idea once again. I felt the words ring in my heart, and I knew I believed them. *Why am I acting like this?* It was as if my head and heart were settling an argument, only it wasn't an argument—it felt more like a war going on inside me.

I'm going in…No, I'm not; it's foolishness…I'm going in right now…I could drown, there might be dangerous animals in the mud. This last thought seemed so desperate, so grasping, I couldn't believe I'd thought it. I wanted to rid myself of the inner conflict forever.

If I go against this desire to stay out, it will be gone. My mind went back to a time when I was a young child. David and I had found a rope swing hanging far over the lake near our house. The bank was steep, so the swing would launch the rider far out into the lake. I hated being afraid of swinging on it, and I eventually forced myself to do it. After a few tries, my fear went away.

I stepped farther into the mud, and my leg muscles twitched. *Why do I feel so weak? It's only dirt and water.* It was hot, but not painfully so. *I'll drown*, I thought in panic, but I knew the fear was unreasonable. When

I stepped again, it was over my waist and I gasped—hotter still. I made it in up to my chest and waited. I tried to gather my strength, but there was none. I felt like the mud had stolen it from me. I took a big breath and dunked my head under. Just as I did, fear washed over me. With my eyes tightly shut to keep out the mud, I could see the ice troll in my mind, large and intimidating—and screaming at me.

I popped my head out of the murk, gasping and clawing at my eyes to wipe the mud away. The fear was overwhelming. With my eyes finally clear, I looked around. Of course, I was still alone. *Foolishness,* I chastised myself. I filled my lungs and dunked in again. I felt the fear wash over me again, this time not as strong. I popped my head out of the muddy water and willed myself not to open my eyes. I took another breath and dunked in one last time, deeper than before. When I surfaced, the fear was gone and I looked up at the sky. I realized the sludge hadn't clung to my eyes as I'd expected it to. I gazed up at the sun. It seemed somehow brighter than it had been only a moment ago. I watched it spin tight circles over my head and realized I was *spinning*—spinning and laughing. I felt tired, but not as weak as I'd felt on the way into the pool. I heard a snapping noise, and I began to turn, following it. Again, then again I heard the sharp noise, and realized someone was clapping.

The Captain had returned and stood barefoot at the edge of the pool. He walked right in beside me and held out his hand. I thought he was going to grasp my hand and use it to pull me out of the mud, but instead he shook it heartily. I felt a lump in his palm, and at first I thought he was trying to hand me something. When he released my grip I saw a white bandage wrapped around his palm. He wore a smile so wide it seemed to run clear around his head.

"I knew you would, Mark. I *knew* you would do it."

He turned, stepped out of the foul mud, then walked to his horse and opened a saddlebag.

Dazed and confused, I stumbled out of the pool and toward my clothes. The Captain returned with two towels and an extra canteen. He handed me the first towel, and I used it to scrape away as much mud as I could. Then he handed me the canteen and the second towel. I rinsed, dried, and got dressed. Suddenly, I realized my throat didn't hurt, no matter how I moved. I stretched my neck as far up as it would bend, and felt no pain at all. I felt the scar. There was a small bump of hard skin, but no pain, even if I pressed hard. I couldn't wait to find a mirror. I knew the large patch of gray and blue skin would be gone.

I put on my armor and got back on my horse. We rode at a faster pace along the trail, still in silence.

"Well," I called to the Captain ahead of me, "I guess it was some very special mud after all." He only turned his head halfway toward me to respond.

"Oh, I think you know better than *that*."

"I didn't mean it's *magical*," I quickly replied, "I understand how minerals can—"

"Heal severe wounds in a matter of seconds?" He interrupted, his words steeped in sarcasm. He was right; it didn't make any sense.

"Then how *did* the mud heal me, if it wasn't by some special mineral?"

"It had nothing to do with the mud," he answered quietly, almost too quietly to be heard.

"What do you *mean*?"

The Captain slowed to a stop and sighed before he turned around to face me.

"Your *own actions* healed you. Think carefully about this: have you been acting differently at times since the ice troll wounded you? Anything new?"

I knew what he suggested was right. Hot flashes of anger, moments of unusual thoughts, suspecting I knew much better than the Captain or the King—these were things I couldn't explain. And the almost-unconquerable desire not to go into the pool—the urge I'd just overcome—*what did it all mean?* I had an idea, but my mind all but refused to consider it. Feeling another strange aversion, so soon after overcoming the last, troubled me, and I told this to the Captain.

"It's hard for me to say it, but you're exactly right—I *have* been acting...*different*."

"Is it still so hard to say?" asked the Captain.

I tried it again. "I'm not usually so angry or likely to shout at someone." I paused to weigh my feelings before answering his question. "No, it wasn't as hard the second time. Why wasn't it?"

"This is an important lesson. The more you admit you're wrong, the easier it is. The easier it is, the more you'll do it. The more you do it, the more you'll learn to know what's *right*...and the more you'll *be* right. More importantly, this stands true for *many* bad habits we pick up. The prideful habit of not admitting you're wrong, a tendency to act selfishly or brashly, a habit of avoiding work we know we should do…all of these bad habits lessen once we confront them and purposely fight against them."

What he said made sense to me; it was logical. But it *felt* almost magical—as if my mind understood but my heart didn't.

"But why?"

"It's the very action of going against the natural tendency you're trying to break. If it's a cycle you've gotten used to, you need to *purposely* break the cycle before you can overcome it. Sometimes this comes with great difficulty. But the next time you feel the same tendency, it won't be so hard to overcome, and the next time will be easier still. Eventually, you make a habit of the opposite action, a *good* habit. I've seen this pattern many times in my life, in conquering *many* old patterns. I'm sure I'll discover many more before I die, poor habits I haven't yet discovered—even patterns I've deceived myself into believing are harmless."

I realized I'd been lying to myself in a way, trying not to think about the new behaviors I'd taken on since my injury.

Many questions crowded into my head, too many to think at once. Instead of asking the questions I really wanted to ask, I blurted out another.

"Why is your hand bandaged?" Then before I could even pause for an answer, I asked another question. "And what does the ice troll have to do with the mud?"

The Captain smiled and continued slowly down the trail.

"All right, from the beginning. How well do you remember being attacked by the ice troll?" he asked.

"What do you mean? I remember him holding me."

"Really think about it for a moment. How long did he hold you? You said he scratched your neck, but you didn't realize it until you felt your throat and saw your own blood—am I right?"

"Yes…but I was struggling. I can't remember exactly how long. I *was* in a bit of danger, you know." He ignored my wry comment.

"When you discovered how badly you were bleeding, you were surprised. Does that mean whatever he did to you, didn't hurt enough to expect such a large gash?"

"That's right; I was afraid. I guess I went into shock for a minute."

"I think you're probably right. But this could mean you might not remember exactly what happened to you."

"What do you mean? I remember he *hurt* me—and mumbled strange words at me. What does it matter?"

"Did he?" the Captain asked, surprised. What did he say?" I recited the word as best I could remember them. "It sounds like Tlaltsihk. This is the language spoken by the ice trolls."

"They have their own language too?" I asked.

"Yes. It's nothing like our language; neither is it similar to Chrutghy. The ice troll who bit you must've spoken all three."

"Oh, because he commanded brown and green trolls?"

"Yes. We know very little of the ice trolls. What we *do* know is little more than rumor." After seeing my frustration, the Captain began his explanation again.

In the King's library, he explained, there were sketchy reports of people who had been attacked by ice trolls. The survivors claimed the trolls can poison their victims by *biting* them. Based on these reports, and what he'd observed, he theorized after the troll grasped me, he'd infected me with a poison, and this caused a growing wound. It festered under the skin of my neck, but its effects didn't end there. If the Captain was right, the ice troll had poisoned me with *rebellion*. To this day, I don't know exactly what this means, or how it's possible, but I was at the time convinced. From the moment he bit me onward, my health grew worse and my attitude began to change. These were the changes I found so difficult to admit I'd had, only moments ago. I called to mind a few of the times when I'd flashed out in anger: in my training, in the barracks with David, even during the trip across the desert. Worse yet, I'd shown a general inability to acknowledge someone might be right when I disagreed with them.

Soon after I'd reached Thraen Kholl, most of my outward symptoms were healed—but inside there was no change. So the Captain said as little as possible about my condition, knowing I wasn't yet able to hear the truth. And how could I have? He knew my infections couldn't be healed until I had dealt with the seeds of rebellion the ice troll had planted in me. This could only be done once I was ready to deal with those poisonous seeds.

The strangest part, the thing I was amazed to ponder was this: the very thing I was healed by, was my recognizing the need *to be* healed. When I chose to submit to the King's plan of going into the mineral pool, the very act *undid* the rebellion—it cancelled it out. This is the only way rebellion can be destroyed, he explained, to go against the grain of the rebellious desire, to kill the desire through refusal to give in to it. The King believed I would need to accomplish a significant act. The trip to the Valley of Abandon was the traditional demonstration of submitting to the King's service, though I had no idea at the time. It was an extreme version of the tradition, strong enough to undo the troll's poison. I was shocked to realize I wasn't the first person who'd been sent to the mineral pools—and worse yet—everyone I knew back at the palace understood exactly what the trip meant.

This was the Captain's riddle, the lesson he'd said I would learn then or would never learn: the Valley of Abandon was a place where people abandoned unwanted things—seemingly *needful* things. I'd abandoned *rebellion* there. Who knows what things have been left there, by generations before and after my visit?

I'll never know how a poison or infection can change one's attitude or character. Did the troll use a drug that affected my mind? Was his saliva poisonous? Did he hold on to me longer than I remembered, and hypnotize me? I never regained any memory of being bitten, only of being held.

The Captain kept silent for a long while, letting me mull these things over. Just as I thought I grasped an understanding of it all, doubt crept in, and settled on the ill-fitting bits and pieces I couldn't explain. I called ahead to the Captain.

"But rebellion isn't *always* bad, is it?" The Captain slowed until our horses were nearly side-by-side on the narrow trail.

"When do you think it can be helpful?" he asked, cautiously. I thought of several examples.

"When I stood up to the hill troll at the silent duke's house…or when oppressed people stand up to an evil government—aren't those good? How about standing up to my brother, when he said I shouldn't go on this trip?"

"Ah, I see; this is a problem of semantics. Those things are not rebellious in the way *some* use the word. Different peoples often have different uses for a word. The important thing is the *concept* I used the word *rebellion* to describe—this concept is always harmful. Others may use the term more liberally, but I use it to describe a collection of actions of one common motivation: standing against what is *right*, to replace it with what you *prefer* or *desire*. The actions you described are more fitting of the word *boldness*. Boldness is standing up to what is *wrong* to declare or uphold what is *right*. Boldness requires strength, much more so than does rebellion, which is more likely to use *anger* or *force* than true strength." I thought about this for a while, and it seemed to fit what I knew to be right.

"So did my wound also make me a little bolder?" I asked.

"No. The ice troll was bent on evil. You never would have seen him acting boldly. You've been growing bolder because you've been growing more mature. You're growing into the shoes of a wise and upright man. Your actions today demonstrate this."

My face burned red to hear him say these things. The Captain was looking only at the trail ahead of us.

He continued, "Rebellion is a *false reflection* of boldness, just as *anger* is of *strength*. They aren't opposites; one is a dim imitation of the other. When we get back to Engdynlor, I'll show you other characteristics on the Table of False Reflections, and the other Tables...if you accept our offer for apprenticeship." If my face was red before, it turned doubly so.

"What do you mean?" I quickly responded. "*Of course* I accept. I thought...I thought you already knew."

The Captain turned to me and smiled. "You never actually said so. I thought it was good you were taking time to consider it; it showed you weren't making a hasty decision. Then I began to worry you might never decide."

"When were you going to say something?" I asked, afraid we might have gone on misunderstanding each other forever.

"Just a few seconds back," he replied.

Of course, I thought, *he brought it up, didn't he?* The Captain cleared his throat and spoke, his voice a little lower.

"There is an oath you must swear, and an accompanying ritual to perform. I'll show you tonight, after we reach TerkEtmek."

I wondered what the oath and ritual were...the Captain sounded grim when he mentioned them. I wondered about the Table of False Reflections he'd mentioned. It sounded almost *magical*—or at least somewhat mysterious.

"What else is written on the Table of False Reflections?"

I wondered what it looked like; was it carved out of precious stone? Was it perhaps solid gold? Maybe it was kept in a secret room of the palace, hidden from all but the secret order of Honor Knights.

The Captain answered, "The *characteristics* on the table are no secret. Most of them I've already mentioned to you: Honesty, Loyalty, Leadership, Boldness, Strength, Wisdom, Patience, Freedom, Conviction, Forgiveness, Submission, Humility, Love, and Compassion."

I took them more seriously after the Captain explained they were characteristics I would be expected to show.

"What do they have in common? Some of them don't even sound related."

With a knowing look on his face, the Captain turned to me once again. "These characteristics are the steps to maturity, and also the steps to becoming a good leader."

"Really? I mean...I didn't expect *love* or *submission*, or even *forgiveness* to be on the list."

"*This is why we keep a list,*" he said with a smile. "Imagine this: how could a knight serve a kingdom or a king he didn't love? And how could a knight take orders from the King if he didn't submit? A knight who doesn't walk in forgiveness will always show a bias against some, and favor for others. This would eventually make him unable to properly serve *or* rule."

"I wouldn't have guessed it...though it makes sense," I replied. "But which do the knights do? Do they serve, or rule over people?"

"Why, *both*," he exclaimed. "How could you effectively lead without serving? And how could you rightly judge and rule over a people you didn't also love and serve?"

"Well, if I'm going to be your apprentice, you'll be leading me a lot. But *you'll never serve me*," I said, astonished he could suggest such a thing.

The Captain smiled even wider. "Oh, no? Then who walked to find a trail through the rocks earlier today, while you rode on your horse? Who carried you into Engdynlor when you were unconscious? Who carried you into the duke's mansion when you were yet *again* unconscious? And who stayed beside your bed watching you slowly recover? Serving someone doesn't mean doing whatever he wants."

He turned and saw how uncomfortable I was at hearing these things.

"I don't tell you this to embarrass you; and I don't serve you out of obligation. As my apprentice, I hope you won't serve *me* out of obligation either."

I was quiet for a time. I finally found it in me to reply in a subdued voice.

"I just didn't realize..." I trailed off, uncertain of what to say. "Thank you for doing all those things," I said eventually, "Thank you very much." My face flushed crimson—I could feel my pulse coursing through my temples.

"Don't worry," he said, "in a few weeks all this will seem normal to you, as if things should *always* be like this—because in truth, *they should.*"

Not long after our conversation, we dismounted and led our horses off the trail, to the north side. We were getting close to where we'd seen the trolls guarding the trail. I hadn't realized it was such a long walk, earlier that morning when I'd ridden Yashel over the same course. We walked in silence. For some reason, it was important to me to *walk* instead of riding Yashel while the Captain led. I felt strong enough to do it, and the Captain didn't object.

When we finally returned to the trail I was glad to ride again. Walking even in the light armor we wore wasn't comfortable for any distance. Again I rode close to the Captain's horse so I could hear him. He noticed how close I rode and turned to face me.

"What did you mean about the things on the list being 'steps to maturity'?" I asked him.

"I meant they are the characteristics by which a man's maturity can be measured. Of course, *humility* would prevent us from trying to measure another's maturity to compare with our own, but maturity must be measured in those the King considers for the positions of leaders, rulers, or judges. We knights use them as a way to make sure we continue to mature, and to teach our apprentices to follow in our steps."

"Do all knights have apprentices?"

"Yes. It is a very important step to teach these things to another."

"How many apprentices have you taught?"

"I will answer this tonight, during your Oath Ceremony."

The Captain seemed unwilling to answer any more questions about the apprenticeship, and so I didn't ask any more. I thought of the characteristics he talked about and I wondered what they might mean to the Captain.

"What is the opposite of compassion?" I asked.

"Indifference. The worst thing a ruler can feel for his people is indifference."

"Is compassion like love?"

"The two are similar. You can't have compassion without love, but compassion can be defined many ways. For our purposes, we measure it as showing mercy, or being willing to sacrifice to give others the chance to choose to do right."

"*Like the silent duke,*" I said absentmindedly.

"Did he demonstrate compassion for you?"

"There was a troll who stole from him. He lived inside the walls of the duke's manor. He said he couldn't refuse the troll a chance to choose to do right, even if the troll hurt him. In fact, it's why he was banished to the other side of the kingdom, because he allowed people to swindle him. Then, when we left, he gave us supplies even though we were strangers to him. I couldn't understand why he would act this way."

"He sounds like a very compassionate man," said the Captain. "I wish I'd met him—I suspect I could have learned far more from him than his letters." After a short while he added, "*And* I hope his actions make more sense to you as we spend time together."

Talking about the silent duke, I was reminded of the others we'd met on the far side of the island.

"We also met a village of tiny people who were very big on forgiveness. They told us a long story about hatred. They said hatred for their enemies had somehow caused them to hate *each other* as well. It nearly destroyed their village, they told us, but I'm sure I must have misunderstood."

The Captain gave me a strange look, as if I'd surprised him by speaking of something he expected I couldn't have known. But he went on, perhaps sounding a little doubtful.

"Yes, unforgiveness is an act of irony. After someone causes us pain, it's foolish to multiply it by holding it close. Even a fool knows better than to swallow poison to kill his enemy—and yet, this is what unforgiveness is. I certainly believe it could destroy a community."

"What do you mean? Who would hold onto *pain?* And who swallows poison to hurt *others?*"

He paused for a moment, as if reaching for another way to explain it.

"When someone hurts you badly, it's like dropping a hot coal in your hand. It makes sense to drop the coal, to let it go immediately. But we often close our fist around it instead; we hold onto it. By holding onto the pain, we multiply it many times. If we drop it quickly, there is little damage, and it will soon heal. *Unforgiveness* keeps the pain alive and allows it to grow, *and* to cause lasting damage.

My mind brought back other strange memories.

"We met a herd of giant antelopes on Otlak Plain. Their prince was so obsessed with honor and loyalty, I thought he might be crazy. Now I wonder…"

"Loyalty can be misused if you are loyal to the wrong cause," offered the Captain.

Looking back on these experiences, I was excited to understand a few of them. My mind was hungry for more. Could the Captain be wise enough to explain all of them? I thought of Sally and how she explained her service to the King. When she first shared it with me, I found her story unimaginable. I told the Captain this, and he nodded knowingly.

"Think on these things, Mark. It's an important point in our maturity when we can see positive examples in the lives of others. Our natural tendency is to dismiss maturity we see in others, out of pride or jealousy. It's so much easier to call their actions unreasonable, unnecessary, or even wrong. You're learning to see the good qualities you lack in others. This is actually a *skill*. Without it, we quickly reach a limit in our maturity. It is part of the difference between having the heart of a trusted son and the heart of an orphan."

By the time we talked through these concepts, we were clear of the craggy rocks, and once again riding side by side over the sand. I could see TerkEtmek's high walls in the distance, and my mind's eye turned to follow it. I preferred to let my mind become busy with our return, rather than with memories I wasn't yet ready to recall. The Captain seemed so wise to me just then, so ready with an answer to any question I had for him. Even so, I would discover I had many questions left I wasn't ready to have answered.

I turned my thoughts to the strange tales of the ice trolls.

"What else is known about the ice trolls? How are they different from the brown and greens?"

"The brown and greens claim they and the ice trolls are *incompatible*." I asked what this meant, and he launched into his story-telling voice. I was content to listen as we rode.

The ice trolls, he explained, had intermarried with browns and greens as soon as intermarriage was no longer taboo. The blue-gray trolls who married either browns or greens were also able to have children. Some were covered in the white fur of the ice trolls, and some were smooth-skinned, resembling their brown or green ancestors. One thing, however, was common to all their children: they were never able to reproduce, no matter *who* they married. Once this was known, these two *incompatible* races were no longer willing to intermarry, and in so doing, condemn their children to never have children of their own. The ice trolls remained in their icy mountaintops, living as isolationists. Not until the plot at the Winter

Palace, were they ever known to interact with the other trolls, through all the centuries since then.

When his story was over, I felt almost chilly, though the desert was anything but cool. While we rode over hot sand, we ate bread baked that morning in the duke's kitchen, though it didn't taste fresh. I found I didn't miss the feast the duke was sharing with his friends. I wouldn't have traded that day in the desert for all the fine food in the world.

4.2 Scars and Blood

When we unloaded our horses in the duke's stables, it was early evening.

"I know you feel fine, but I need a rest," said the Captain. "Why don't you go back to your room and relax while I take a nap? When it's dark, we'll walk out into the desert, and I'll tell you of the oath I mentioned."

Excited, I quickly agreed. When I got back to my room, I was sure I wouldn't be able to sleep. After I'd washed and lay down on the soft bed, however, this notion changed. I had a strange dream of fire and blood. It wasn't a scary dream, but I didn't enjoy it either. It was so unclear, I dismissed it from my mind.

Dream or no dream, I woke feeling very much refreshed. I found a clean set of light clothes in my room, and put them on. I remembered a mirror in one of the drawers of the desk, from the previous night when I searched for a match to light the candle. I went back to the desk and found it. It was fancier than I'd remembered, with a heavy silver handle ornately decorated. I paused before looking at my neck and throat. With a sudden resolve, I lifted my chin and angled the mirror so I could see. There was a dark line of red scar across my throat, with a bump of scar tissue. It itched when I ran my fingernail over it. Other than the scar, there was nothing left: no bruising, no tenderness, and no pain, no matter how far I stretched my neck in any direction.

Setting the mirror down, I decided to look for the Captain. I walked out to an open courtyard in the middle of the mansion, wondering where he might be. I didn't know my way around, but I could see there were others there, eating and talking. The Captain had told me the duke entertained a lot of guests, mostly members of the rich merchant families. He had sons who were apprenticing with the wealthiest merchant families to learn a trade before taking places in government. Enthicia was becoming a crossroads of trade, and its scant cities were growing quickly.

I sat in a wicker chair and studied the people in the courtyard. I was happy to be out under the sky in the cool of the night. Servants came and lit many covered candles around the courtyard. The guests wore fancy clothes, light and thin as the borrowed clothes I wore. They talked and laughed incessantly. I heard someone approaching from behind.

"*By Halves, the armor bearer*," the duke roared. "Would you like to join the party?" I stood and saluted him.

"No, sire. I was looking for the Captain. I'm supposed to meet with him."

"It's a cause for celebration, your recovery," the duke went on. "Why don't you join us and tell your story to my guests? I'm sure they would like to hear it."

I was tempted, but something held me back. My mind raced to find a polite way out of the party.

"Sire, I know the Captain would be honored to have you invite his armor bearer to your party, but until he hears of it, he would consider me as disregarding my duties. I'll go find him now, so he will know."

The duke's eyes narrowed for an instant, and I thought I saw anger hiding in them. A broad smile grew on his lips, and he laughed generously.

"You are loyal to your Captain; this is a good sign. I'm sure you'll prove as loyal to the Royal Family in your service. Go, find your Captain and do as he likes. You'd better check the barracks and stables though; I'm sure you won't find him lounging with my guests."

I thanked him and left. I wasn't sure if he was insinuating something with his last remark, and made a note to ask the Captain about it.

I found him in the barracks, a short walk from the duke's mansion. He'd just woken and was getting dressed in clean clothes on loan from the duke. He still wore the dirty cloth wrapped around his right hand. Most unusual, I thought, was something more subtle.

"You look so strange without your uniform," I said in realization.

"I *feel* strange without it. It's been a long time since I wore such fine-spun linen. If the duke expects to see me at his parties, he'll be disappointed."

"I saw the duke while I was looking for you. He wanted me to tell a story about my recovery to some of his guests."

The Captain looked up with a start. When I didn't go on immediately he prompted me, "*And you said...?*"

"I wasn't sure *what* to say. It seemed like a strange request. I told him you expected to meet with me, and I would go to find you first."

"Good job," the Captain said as he slapped my shoulder. "I don't trust all the duke's guests, especially some of the trading families he deals with. If they make it through the dunes so frequently, it may be they've made agreements with the trolls, whom we now know are unusually armed, out in the desert." Then he added, almost as an afterthought, "Why do you think his request was strange?"

"I felt like there was no room to do what was right. I couldn't disobey the duke, but I felt wrong about telling the whole story to all those people."

"Let me say this about you: you have a wise conscience. I know very well what you mean about too little room to do what's right. You'll surely remember this experience when you take your politics course. How did he leave it?"

"The duke? He dropped the matter, but said I wouldn't likely find you at one of his parties..."

The Captain's right hand had been patting at his waist involuntarily as we talked. He seemed ready to leave, but hesitated, and finally lifted his sword and belt from his bedpost where he'd hung it.

"We're not going far in the desert tonight, so we don't need our armor. But for me, leaving my sword behind feels like I'm wearing nothing at all." He unbuckled his heavy belt—unusual for the light clothes he wore—and added his sheathed sword to it.

On our way from the barracks, he noticed me turning toward the stables.

"We won't need the horses tonight—just a short walk outside the walls."

We used another small gate when we left the city. It was even smaller than the door we'd walked our horses through that morning. It didn't look like a horse could fit through it. It was dark, but we had a full moon to light our way.

The Captain was in a talkative mood, so I decided to ask him a question long on my mind.

"Captain, will you tell me how your horse got its name?" He smiled immediately.

"Oh, I don't know…it's a tale few have heard," he teased. I did my best to feign patience. "…I suppose an *apprentice of mine* can hear it.

"Some years ago I was leading a troop providing protection to a merchant caravan under contract to the King. Actually, my job was more *babysitting* than protecting. We didn't yet know if the caravan could be trusted to stay out of the cargo.

"I became friends with the caravan's cook, who was also in charge of caring for the horses and donkeys. One night, he brought a nice cut of meat to my tent when it was time for dinner. He told me it came with a request he hoped I would be willing to grant him. At first I was offended he might try to bribe me, but I soon saw it was an honest enough gesture."

I saw something in the darkness ahead of us and became distracted by it. The moon gave enough light to notice it, but not enough to distinguish what it was. For all I knew, it might have been a man or a rock—or a band of bloodthirsty thieves. My eyes darted back and forth between the object and the Captain, though it was too dark to make out his expression. Apparently it hadn't bothered him, and he went on.

"The cook told me one of his mares was pregnant. This much I already knew. More accurately, his news was the mare was *no longer* pregnant, and we now had a foal in our caravan. He thought the mare would survive the trip if we went a little slower the next day, and stopped later, to make up the lost time. This part of his request I could not grant him. The schedule a caravan keeps cannot be changed for any small reason. At the time, I couldn't be sure he wasn't trying to influence our schedule to coincide with a band of thieves, or some other plan to harm us. So I made a concession for him. I told him I would allow the meal wagon to leave early with an escort of one of my men, and travel later than normal so he could travel with the mare."

I nearly tripped on something jutting out of the sand—a piece of wood, I thought. The shape in the dark was directly in front of us; I assumed it was what we were headed for. The shape resolved into a tight group of *several shapes* as we drew nearer.

"His next request was for the foal. The day-old horse simply couldn't make the journey. It had bent its leg during birth, and would not be a strong walker for some time, if ever. Not able to walk well enough to survive our trip, she could only survive by riding in one of the wagons. Now, he knew how precious the cargo space was on the trip, and he was not allowed to enter the cargo carts. But with his meal wagon loaded as full as it was, the foal could only fit on one of the cargo wagons. The cook made a gift of her to the King, and said he would hate to see the young horse die because her mother delivered her a few weeks early. If I would only lift her into a cargo cart each morning, and take her out each night for the next few days, the King's stables would have another foal, which might grow up to be a strong and healthy horse." The Captain added, "He didn't mention I would also need to clean the back of the cargo cart each night, as I was the only one with legal access to the cart."

Finally, we were close enough to see the shapes ahead of us were trees. As I listened to the Captain's tale, I wondered idly if there was a spring nearby to bring them water.

"I agreed to take the foal in my care, and I eventually became good friends with the growing filly after the trip was over. She grew to be a strong horse, and when she was ready to be ridden, I asked the King's stable master to have her assigned as my own horse. He knew of our history together and was happy to agree."

The story was an interesting one, but I still didn't make the connection to her name. The Captain let the riddle hang long enough to know I hadn't guessed the answer.

"And that is the story of the first horse to travel across the desert as a *rider*, instead of being ridden."

I laughed; mostly at myself for missing the connection. I wondered how many years ago it could have been.

By then we'd reached the small cluster of trees, a tiny island of life surrounded by dead sand. The Captain asked me to gather the dead branches and twigs from around the trees. I found several long dead stems of oversized palm leaves, but only a few of the half-dozen trees were hardwoods. He pulled the largest dead branch from one of the gnarled hardwoods and broke it over his knee, then slammed the two halves against the ground until he had a half-dozen pieces.

To my surprise, he pulled a very small knife from a concealed compartment in the back of his large belt buckle. He used it to whittle a few of the dead sticks I'd gathered until he had a pile of wood shavings under the dry branches and twigs. Then he pulled several clumsy-looking matches from his pocket, and lit the shavings. Before long we had a small fire to warm ourselves in the cool desert night. Not long after I learned the Captain's purpose for the fire had nothing to do with warmth.

"Now we're in the open desert," the Captain began, "where we know no one can listen in. There is a secret oath you must swear to accept your apprenticeship. Listen carefully, because the results of your decision will be life-long. I'll answer any questions you have at the end."

He paused long enough for me to nod before lowering his voice an octave, and launching into his soliloquy.

"To accept your apprenticeship with the Honor Knights, you must swear lifelong loyalty to the King, his family, the knights, and his kingdom. You must swear to keep our order secret, including its existence and our membership. You must swear to keep all secrets and private knowledge you will learn as part of your duties. You must swear to serve as an Honor Knight in addition to your public duties, and to do so without compensation. You must swear an oath of obedience to the King first, then to myself as your mentor, and finally to other ranking members of our order. You must serve in conformity to the Characteristics of Maturity as I've begun to explain them to you, and will continue to teach you in the ways thereof."

He kept his hands busy as he spoke. First he unraveled the cloth from his right hand and wound it around the metal handle of his small knife. Then he used the knife to stoke the fire and to pull some coals and ash from it. He laid the knife in the coals for a while, and finally laid it in the ash pile as he finished speaking. After a short pause he asked, "Do you have any questions?"

"Yes," I answered, a little nervously. I cleared my throat. "What happens if I'm not accepted as a knight?"

"You will still be bound by your oaths. It has happened before, when an apprentice was not accepted as a knight, but still served the King loyally for life. It is not merely an honest and good man the knights look for in a fellow member. There is no shame in becoming an apprentice and not an Honor Knight. If there is any strong resentment left afterward, a former apprentice may be ordered to relocate to another city. Any order but those which are urgent, can be appealed, in a private review with the King. He is a fair man."

"What if I find a way home? Will I be ordered to stay?"

"I've spoken to the King about this. As long as you are not in the middle of an urgent assignment, you will be given permission to return to your home land on the condition you will someday mentor another in our teachings."

"Can't I tell anyone I'm an apprentice, or maybe someday a knight?"

"Never. Not your brother David, not the Princess, and not her guardian Lady Sally. While you're an apprentice, you can only discuss the existence of the order or your apprenticeship with me and the King. Even then, you can only do so if you are certain you are not overheard."

"You mentioned you would answer another question when it was time for me to take the oaths—"

"Yes, the number of apprentices I've taught. The number of Honor Knights is constant; we don't need more than we have. It is the intention for each knight to select one apprentice, and for each apprentice to be accepted as a full knight, and in turn have his own apprentice when the time comes. Once in a while the chain is broken, and an elder knight will take on a second apprentice. This is not common. You are my first and probably only apprentice." Hearing this silenced me for a while. "Do you have any more questions?" asked the Captain.

I thought a while before shaking my head.

"Then are you willing to take these oaths?"

I nodded as solemnly as I could. I'd never seen the Captain so somber—he seemed almost mournful.

"I will lead you through each oath."

Then he picked up the small knife and held its blade in his closed right hand so the cloth-wrapped handle hung below his fist.

"When you complete your oaths, you will take this knife from me, signifying my blade, in service to the King, will pass to you, just as my teachings will." I opened my mouth to ask a question, but he cut me off. "The time for questions is now passed. You may ask any further questions when the ceremony is complete."

He led me through each of the same oaths he'd explained, his fist held out curiously before me. Time seemed to slow to a crawl as I watched the Captain's glowing face flicker in the fire's warm glow. When I swore the last oath, I reached up to take the knife from him, but he held onto it. I opened my mouth to object, but his eyes sparkled and he shook his head. *No questions* his eyes seemed to say. I pulled the knife handle down a little ways, confused. My arm froze when I saw blood trickle from the bottom of his fist. I could only stare at him, my eyes pleading for an explanation—but none was granted. I received only a slow, deliberate nod in response.

I couldn't do it. My hand dropped from the knife handle, but he took my hand with his left and placed it back on the knife handle. I winced and imagined the pain I was causing him. Rather than stare at his hand I locked my gaze on his face. He showed no hint of discomfort. *Is it a trick?* I wondered hopefully as I slowly pulled the knife from his closed fist. When at last I held the knife and his fist was empty, he spoke.

"I will protect you though it will harm me, and you will bind my wound."

That's a strange thing to say, I thought. But when he opened his hand I saw a thin line cut across his palm and fingers, partially covered by a small pool of blood. Shocked, I unraveled the cloth from the knife handle and wrapped it around his hand. There was ash in the cloth though, and I knew it would sting.

The Captain tied off the bandage and stood. I stood too, unsure of what to do. He shook my hand and slapped me heartily on the back. He called me his armor bearer, and apprentice, and son. When I told him I was sorry for cutting him, he told me the ritual was complete.

"Why did I have to hurt you?" I asked, with a hint of frustration in my voice.

"Will you ever hurt me again? Will you ever betray me?"

"*Never.*"

"The ritual added resolve to your answer. You will never try to hurt me, and you know I'm willing to be your mentor, even if it brings me harm. Don't you see? This is the same lesson your friend the silent duke taught you, the lesson of *compassion.* Not only have you heard the words of this lesson, but now you've felt them in your heart."

"Does your hand hurt much? The cloth is too dirty for a bandage, isn't it?"

"This is why I added the ash. I'll have a scar across my palm and fingers when the cut heals. Other knights in the order will know I've chosen my one apprentice, whether you become a knight or not."

"Didn't you say knights sometimes have another apprentice, if their first apprentice isn't chosen?"

"No. Only if a knight's *first* apprentice is chosen, may he ever receive a second scar, on his left palm. The Knight whose first apprentice is rejected will never have another."

"Scars and blood! Who thought of this ritual?" I asked, upset, if not angry.

"It's been used for centuries. Not only knights use it, or our scars would reveal our entire elder membership. Some others use it for marriage, some for a business partnership or an important contract. Some artisans use a similar ritual for their own apprenticeships."

The Captain kicked sand over the fire and choked it out.

"Be careful with your new knife, please. I took it from my mentor many years ago in the same way you took it from me. When you get back to your room, look in your belt's clasp and you will find a place to keep it. One day you can pass it on to an apprentice of your own, and before then it may come in handy once or twice."

We walked back in silence while my mind raced with thoughts of the long day. I knew I would fall asleep a different person than I'd been when I'd woken that morning, only hours earlier. As I marveled at all I'd seen that day, I had no reason to suspect it was far from being over—and no way to guess by morning, the entire kingdom would be thrown headlong into turmoil.

4.3 The Duke's Secret

When we returned to the mansion, I realized I was not yet tired. I had expected to fall asleep right away, but as the Captain walked me to my room, I knew I was too excited to sleep.

"I think I'll take a walk before I turn in," I said. His eyes flashed a knowing look.

"…mind too busy to sleep?" he suggested. I nodded, embarrassed he could read me so easily. "Stay close to the mansion," he added, "there are corners in this city you don't want to find after dark."

I promised I would, and he left me to explore. There were probably a lot of things I could have seen, but there was one place I wanted to go more than any other: the stables where Yashel was kept.

I expected to find the stables dark as late as it was, but I found them well lit by lanterns. I approached slowly, not wanting to wake all the horses and cause a commotion. I walked into the short stall where Yashel was kept, and I brushed her like I'd seen workers at the stables do in the palace grounds. She seemed to like it.

A few minutes later I realized I wasn't alone. I heard loud voices, too loud for me to have missed before. Others had entered the stables.

They were laughing and teasing each other. One of them made a joke about the Captain's horse, then said something about claiming her in the morning. My ears perked up. They spoke as if the Captain was dead. Could it be another Captain they talked about? I could tell by their voices, they were approaching Rider's stall, near the larger horses.

I crept to the back of Yashel's stall, and crouched low behind her. I stroked her back and kept my hand on her leg so she would know where I was and wouldn't get so scared as to kick me. As I crept, I heard the men continue.

"What makes you think *you'll* get his horse? I'll bet the duke has other plans for her."

"Nah, the duke doesn't want her. She's a nag and everyone knows it. Too old, just like the Captain."

I heard Rider let out a whinny, and I hoped the speaker hadn't struck her. I heard a third voice try to quiet the first two.

"*Shhh*—what if the Captain hears you?"

"*Forget it.* He'll be dead the next time we see him. As long as Nigel hasn't fallen asleep, he'll take care of the Captain. The old prude went to the barracks early after riding out in the desert all day—who knows *where*. We know it wasn't where he *said* he was going, or the trail guards would've seen him."

The trail guards? My mind raced to guess what they were talking about. *Who is Nigel, an assassin?* I had to warn the Captain, fast. Hopefully, this Nigel went to the barracks while we were out in the desert. How was I going to leave without the men seeing or hearing me? The outside walls of the stables were stone; there was no way to break out. I would have to take my chances waiting them out. Just then Rider whinnied again.

"All right, morons, you've had your fun poking at the old nag. Now report on the horses and we'll head back to the tavern."

I breathed a sigh of relief. When I could no longer hear them, I got up and pulled my armor and sword belt from the pegs in Yashel's stable where I'd hung them, and put them on clumsily. Looking down at my hand, I saw I still held the tiny knife I'd taken from the Captain. How had I brushed Yashel down? I looked at the clasp on my belt, and sure enough, there was a groove in the back I saw would hold the knife perfectly. I slid it into the groove and noticed a tiny piece of wire to hold it in place. I saddled Yashel and put on her armor as quietly as I could, calming her as I did. I changed my mind and removed my sword and belt, and slung them over my saddle, in case I had to run or move quietly.

I waited another minute, hoping the men were far enough from the stables to miss me. I led Yashel out from her stall and opened the door to Rider's stall. I almost forgot to load the Captain's armor onto Rider, after fitting her with her armor.

I led both horses out of the stable, in case the Captain would want to leave the city. Knowing the men who wanted him dead had access to the stable, I thought it best not to return there. I was just about to leave when I saw a larger stall with several horses in it. Something in the stall was tragically out of place...I felt for a moment like separate worlds were crashing together. I walked back, chastising myself for wasting time until I saw clearly what seemed so strange to me: the scar. It was the horse I'd seen in the Great Dunes, in the troll caravan.

The scar was too large and jagged to be a coincidence. My first thought was the horse had been captured; perhaps the caravan met the duke's men in battle. I assumed the men I'd overheard were working with a group of traitors among the duke's soldiers. I should have thought more carefully about what I'd overheard. I left in a hurry.

The barracks were near the stables. As I approached, I saw two soldiers posted at the door. I left the horses out of sight and tied their reins to each other, then nervously walked up to the soldiers.

"Who's there?" the first soldier insisted.

"I'm an armor bearer, bringing a message to a soldier in these barracks." I told them. While it was the truth, I wasn't volunteering anything about the Captain until I was sure they weren't part of some plot against him.

"Come back tomorrow," demanded the second soldier. "These barracks are closed."

I turned to walk away, disappointed I didn't learn anything from the soldiers. Before I got far, one of them called after me.

"Wait. Have you seen the Captain, or the duke's guest who came with him?"

"No," I lied, without giving it a second thought. I told myself it was necessary, the Captain would say I was in some kind of war condition, and not breaking my oath of honesty. The truth is, I would have lied either way. I wasn't going to betray the Captain to those men, or let them capture me for further questioning.

While my mind raced with panic, I walked back to the horses. *Where'd the Captain go?* I wondered. *He might have gone to check on me, in the guest quarters.* I wondered if it would have been better if I'd stayed in the barracks with the Captain, but I hardly had time for self-doubt. I needed to get to my guest room in the mansion.

I led Yashel and Rider on foot, holding both their reins. I didn't go into the main entrance of the mansion, but instead headed for the kitchen, which was on the backside of the mansion. I planned to go in the same way we'd left that morning, through the kitchen's servant entrance. Upon reaching it, I tied the horses outside and went in.

As soon as I entered, I began questioning my actions. If I'd taken the time to think it through, I could've saved myself some frustration, but I wasn't yet ready to accept the magnitude of the problem facing us, so I questioned myself irrationally.

Maybe my imagination had gotten the better of me. Was there a simpler explanation of the things I'd heard? Maybe the men were drunk, and only wanted to tease the Captain's horse. Maybe another soldier noticed the Captain was missing from the barracks, and reported it to the duke. And maybe the duke sent someone to search my room too, and found it empty. He *could* have posted soldiers to the barracks, I reasoned, so he could find out sooner if we were safe. Or maybe there was an assassination plot against the Captain *and* the duke. I made a hasty decision; since I had sworn to protect the King's family, I must warn the duke there might be a plot against him.

I walked into the courtyard where I'd seen the duke earlier, hoping to find him. If he wasn't there, I would have to ask whoever I could find where the duke's private quarters were. I didn't want to tell anyone else what I'd heard before talking directly to the duke or the Captain.

The courtyard was in the center of the mansion, but open to the sky. It was square, and had entrances from the mansion on all four sides. By chance, when I walked into the courtyard, it was from an entrance not lit by lanterns. I assumed the party was over, as there was only one area still well-lit. I could see people in the candlelight, but I couldn't yet hear them over the bubbling fountain in the courtyard's center. I was nervous about disturbing whoever was still in the courtyard, obviously in the middle of a conversation.

As I drew nearer, I could see the man in the center tilt back his head and laugh; it was the duke. I nearly ran up to him and blurted out everything I'd seen and suspected. But again, I doubted my suspicions, and thought I would probably make a fool of myself if I acted so rashly. My approach was somber rather than rushed.

I walked slowly and quietly so as not to disturb the duke until I heard a lull in their conversation when I could politely interrupt. I wouldn't say I crept, but I was definitely trying not to gain their attention until I knew exactly what to say. While I was listening for the group to pause, another soldier entered the courtyard, from the entrance the duke was facing. Something he said had angered the duke, though I didn't hear a word of it. What was said next sent chills down my back.

"Sire, they will return…and when they do, we'll take care of it. Nothing is undone yet. My soldiers found the Captain's horse is still in the stables, and the other horses are all accounted for. They cannot cross the desert *on foot.*"

"And what of the other horses? Those of our special guests staying *outside* the city tonight?" the duke snapped. He spoke in guarded tones, but sounded ruthless nonetheless. All trace of humor had left his voice.

Then I saw clearly: *could the trolls be his guests? Their patrol attacked us just before we left the Great Dunes.*

"Yes, Sire. All of them are accounted for. I assure you, the Captain and his guest won't make it through the night alive." There was little room for doubt before he spoke, but these last words jolted me. I tried to pay attention, but found it difficult. Meanwhile, the duke responded in a voice so filled with hatred, it shook me a second time. He threatened the soldier's life and seemed to blame the Captain for stranding him in the desert, calling him some name I wasn't familiar with. He brought to mind an image of a venomous snake.

I backed away slowly, heading for the fountain. I held my breath until I crept around it, and let its gurgling swallow the sound of my breathing. I tried to convince myself they hadn't seen me. How could they not have? There were several soldiers facing the duke, and therefore facing me. Maybe I was in the shadow the duke's body cast. As soon as I left the courtyard, I sprinted through the halls of the duke's mansion.

I fell back to my original plan: to find my room and see if the Captain had gone there to check on me. I realized I might attract attention running through the dark halls, so I slowed to a swift walk. As I turned the last corner into the hall leading to my room, someone fell from the ceiling, landing behind me. I saw an arm with a knife reach out in front of me. Then, before I could scream, another hand covered my mouth.

I remember my thoughts, blurred together in no more than a few seconds' time. *I'll never get to say goodbye to David. I hope he finds his way home,* and, *what will he tell mom and dad?*

I expected the arm with the knife to strike me, but instead, it disappeared, back from where it had come, and I heard a whisper in my ear.

"It's your Captain. Don't make a noise."

And then I was released. As I spun around, the Captain whispered, "What's wrong with you? You didn't even *struggle.*" Could he really be *angry* with me?

I whispered back, "They're trying to kill us! *We have to leave.*" The Captain was tense behind his smile as he whispered his reply.

"Well, I didn't stop by to see if you wanted a *snack.*" And then, more grimly he hissed, "Let's go, *in silence.*"

"Wait," I whispered back, "Our horses—I tied them at the kitchen entrance."

He nodded and led the way through the mansion, sword in one hand and dagger in the other. We left through the kitchen and rode through the city undetected. The Captain expected a fight at the needle's eye, but no one questioned us as we led our horses by hand, out through the small hole in the city wall. Only once we were out of the city and on the trail to the mud pools, did the Captain let me speak. I began to tell him what I'd heard.

"They're trying to kill us—*and the duke knows.*" His head whipped around at that.

"How do you know this?"

"When I couldn't find you in the barracks, I went to the courtyard to tell the duke. I snuck up on him and some soldiers while they were talking. I didn't really mean to *sneak*—"

"What did you *hear?*" he interrupted.

"Oh—the soldier promised the duke we wouldn't live through the night. The duke said his life depended on it."

"You *heard* the duke say that? Could you be mistaken?"

"No," I replied testily. I remembered who I was speaking to. "I mean, I heard him clearly; I'm not mistaken."

"What else did he say?"

I tried to remember exactly the words he used. "He called you a name, and said you stole something from him, or left him stranded in the desert." The Captain looked thoughtful.

"If he thought I stole from him, he would need to try me in court—not send an assassin after me in my sleep. I must go and talk to him, to see if this is something we can straighten out."

"Back to the mansion?" I asked, shocked. We'd been lucky to get through the needle's eye so easily, and I had no desire to go back through it.

"Not for you. You need to wait someplace safe. Do you think you can find the geyser we saw earlier today?"

I nodded.

"Wait for me there. Ride slowly, and listen for sounds ahead and behind you on the trail—and be glad it's a full moon."

"What about you?"

"Like I said, I must talk with the duke."

The Captain had already stopped and dismounted. I wondered what he was doing. It seemed as if he were half-undressing before me. I realized he was removing anything capable of making noise. His armor and his horse's armor came off first, then many items I never guessed he kept on his person, from more pockets than any set of clothes had rights to have. In the end, he kept only trousers and boots, a long undershirt of sorts, and a long dagger. His horse wore only a saddle blanket, and a long coil of rope. All the rest of the items were loaded onto Yashel; she was quite loaded down.

The Captain mounted Rider and turned to leave. He paused long enough to turn back to me, with a great sense of urgency.

"I will sneak into the city and find the duke in his mansion. This will take some time. If Rider is discovered where I tie her outside the city, it could take me most of tomorrow to return. Try to get some sleep once you reach the geyser. I'm sorry I can't take you there, but this must be done right away. Will you be all right?" I nodded unconvincingly. "I'll see you as soon as I can. If I'm longer than a day...try to head to the cities past the desert. Your map is among my things," he said, waving toward Yashel's burden. "There's little hope in crossing the desert without donkeys to carry your water. *You* might last long enough, but your horse would never make it, and she can't carry all the water you'd both need."

"*The donkeys*," I lamented. "I didn't even think—"

"You thought of plenty. I needed to get you safely out of the city first. Just make sure you *stay* safe." He turned to leave.

"*Captain*," I called. He turned back impatiently. "When you get back will you tell me how you clung to the ceiling so long? You know, outside my room in the mansion?" He smiled back.

"Just a bit of rope and a lucky hole in the beam above me." Then he was off, riding fast toward the city.

4.4 Long, Lonely Night

I rode in silence, straining to hear any noise around me. There seemed to be a hundred tiny sounds, none of which were loud enough to be a horse or donkey walking through the sand. When I reached the trail through the rocks, I kept thinking the troll guards were just ahead of me, but I was never as far along the trail as I thought. I got tired of dismounting and looking ahead of me, wondering if I were nearly upon the trail guards. So I rode on, with my lance in one hand and my sword on my belt, ready to draw.

I'd taken Yashel's armor off, and tried to arrange her double load so it made the least amount of noise. This left my hands full, but at least they were filled with weapons, as I used the lance's strap and my scabbard to secure the Captain's gear. I didn't know what would happen if I ran across a troop of trolls. *Perhaps my extra gear will act as a shield for me—or better yet, maybe they'll laugh themselves to death at the sight of me.*

Finally, I recognized an oddly-shaped rock up ahead, and knew I was at the place we'd left the trail much earlier in the day. I dismounted and crept onward to make sure. It was farther than I remembered. I saw trolls sleeping on the trail, ahead of me. Still on foot, I led Yashel off the left side of the trail, looking for the way to the geyser.

Walking in the dark was much more frightening than riding, I found. I moved so slowly in the dark, it seemed I heard every insect in all Enthicia. And to me, each one sounded like a troll rousing from its slumber. A few times I paused, paralyzed with fear. It couldn't have been more than a few hours, but to me it seemed to take days. Panic wrung me dry of all other feeling, long before daylight. When I found the geyser, the sky ahead of me showed a dim arc where the sun would rise. I arrived hollow and numb. It had been the longest day and night in my life.

It was cold, of course. After I found a spot nestled in the rocks on the far side of the geyser, I put both Yashel's and my own armor back on, just in case we were roused by charging trolls. In the pale early dawn, it seemed as likely a scenario as any. I leaned against a rock with my sword at my side, and finally slept.

When I woke, my legs and shoulders ached, and I was *hot*. I looked up and the sun was well overhead. *How could I have slept so long?* Only then did I notice the rhythm of hooves striking sand and clicking over rocks. What direction was it coming from? It sounded like far too many hooves to be one rider. I jumped up and climbed onto Yashel, remembering the Captain's words from my training, "...one would hope to fight only from this position, if at all."

I grabbed both my spear and sword, and hoped Yashel would know where to charge when I yelled. I prepared for the worst as I heard the animals getting closer. Finally, I saw motion between two rocks.

It wasn't half a dozen riders...it was merely a dozen *hooves*: the Captain on Rider, and our two donkeys following.

"Are you all right?" I yelled, jumping off Yashel.

"Aside from being tired enough for three men, yes." He still wore a smile, but looked as weary as I'd ever seen him.

"What happened?"

"Many things, Mark, many things. We're in far worse danger than I thought."

"Well, I guess things didn't go well with the duke, or you wouldn't have brought the donkeys. How'd you get them?"

"One thing at a time," he replied. "Let me talk uninterrupted for a minute."

He paused, as if to collect his thoughts, or perhaps to decide where he would begin. By the length of his hesitation, I guessed he would be talking far longer than a minute. To be sure, I was getting better at faking patience.

"Grave events are taking place," he began at last. "We cannot return to the duke's mansion or any desert settlement. We must reach Engdynlor as soon as possible. There are difficult decisions I need to make. Wait—there's one thing I must know *now*. Is there anything else you heard the duke say, or the people he was talking to?" The Captain dismounted and unloaded the large wooden bowl from Jack.

"I don't think so," I said—too soon, judging from the Captain's expression.

"Take a moment and think. First recall what you *do* remember, then see if anything else comes to you." I took off my armor and sat on a low rock.

"First, I remember a soldier talking to the duke—in the courtyard. He said not to worry, our horses weren't missing, and we couldn't cross the desert. Then the duke asked if any of their *guests'* horses were missing. He called them *guests who were staying outside the city*—the trolls. I saw the horse with the jagged scar in the stables."

"Go on," he urged, speaking over his shoulder.

He filled the wooden bowl halfway from one of the water sacks on Jenny's back, and let Jack drink. I knew he was interested in what I said, but also in a great hurry.

"The soldier answered, 'none of the horses are gone.' He promised the duke we would be dead by morning. The duke told him his life depended on it. Then he called you a name...*serper*, I think. He said if we made it back to Engdynlor, his plans would be ruined."

I tried hard to remember the exact words he's used. "No, wait, that doesn't make sense... He said if *the serper* found out his plans, everything would be ruined. But if he was going to kill us, it wouldn't matter if you found out first. Let me think a second."

The Captain waited patiently. Next it was Jenny's turn to drink—again, he gave the donkey only half a bowl.

"He didn't call *you* a serper. He said if *you serper* finds out, all his plans would be ruined. The duke vowed to punish him for casting him into the desert."

The Captain's face looked as if he'd received grave news. In a way, he just had. I remained ignorant, but dissatisfied with how I recalled the duke's words.

"...'If you serper finds out, all my plans will be ruined.' Was he calling the soldier a serper? What *is* a serper?"

The Captain interrupted me, his tone low and hollow.

"The word is *usurper*, Mark. It means someone who steals the throne, who forces his way into being king without the right."

He turned away long enough to give Rider her turn at the half-filled wooden bowl. His tone rose a notch when he continued.

"Commit these words from the duke to memory. You heard him right, and you will need to testify before the King."

I played the words over in my head until I was sure I had them memorized. At least the sentences made sense, if I didn't know who he was talking about.

"But who is the usurper? Who stole the King's throne?"

"Before our King ruled, there was an older king. He had a…well, a *different* way of ruling. *And* he had no children."

"Oh, like the silent duke told me. I wasn't going to mention this, but I don't think he liked the old king."

"Yes. And when he died, his nephew didn't qualify for the throne, so it was legally passed to the other Royal House, and our current King was crowned. The nephew who *wasn't* crowned king is the *duke of Enthicia*," he said, spitting the words out in distaste. "We now know he wants the throne; worse yet, he believes he *deserves* it."

The history lesson was an unexpected view into the kingdom's past. I wished the Captain would skip the details and get to his point.

"His mother tried to skirt our ancient law and install him as king. She tried to gather an army to take the throne by force. When she failed, our King sent her away to the desert, which at the time, was not on any trade route.

"By the time the duke had grown, his mother had built a small trade city around her lavish mansion, on a route she worked hard to create. When his mother died, the King named her son a duke, and gave him authority to rule Enthicia in the name of the King. He was to protect and improve the trade route and monitor the activities of the troll and merchant caravans."

By then, Rider and Yashel had drunk their water, and the Captain began to pack his things onto Rider. I swallowed my questions, telling myself I'd find their answers sooner if I didn't interrupt.

"So *it would appear,* the duke means not only to kill you and me, but also the King and his family. The duke's mother hated not only the King and his family, but all his loyal subjects. I'd hoped the duke hadn't inherited the same hatred from her. Out of this hatred and unforgiveness, the duke planned the attack on the Winter Palace. He was behind the ice troll, and provided him with the knowledge and help needed to take it over."

I realized my mouth was open.

"How did you find all this out? And how did you get Jack and Jenny?"

The Captain turned to our canteens. Tilting his head back, he emptied his own, then refilled it from one of the water sacks Jenny carried.

"Is your canteen empty?" he asked.

I nodded and tossed it to him. He refilled it and stowed it in my saddlebag. By then I was convinced he was determined to trickle his story out as slowly as possible. While I waited for him to answer, he took the empty water sack from Jenny, and I helped him fill it in the hot pool. It wasn't easy, and we got a lot of mud mixed in with the water.

"Will we have to drink this?" I asked.

"I hope not. We'll ration what safe water we have, but if it isn't enough, we'll have to chance *this* water. Now where was I?"

"How did you figure out the duke's plans?"

The words leapt from my mouth in hopes it might speed his reply. It didn't.

"Oh yes, I'll get to that. But first, we need to get going. We need to make our way through the eastern edge of the desert, to the Great Dunes, as soon as we can."

I swallowed my impatience as we turned our back on the geyser and made our way north, leading our horses by the bridles through the rocky divide between Enthicia and the Daggora Mountains.

4.5 Nemesis in Abaddon

We walked through the sea of boulders for a half-hour before the Captain was willing to answer my question. There was no way for us to walk side-by-side through the twisted landscape, and we knew there were trolls guarding the trail not far behind us. Even though I saw the wisdom in his choice, I didn't like waiting.

"All right," he finally started, "here's the short version. I went to the stables first, to get the donkeys. I left them tied near the gate I would later use to leave the city."

"Wait," I interrupted, "how did you get *back into* the city?"

"I climbed the wall. There are a few places where it's possible."

"What about Rider?"

"I left her outside the wall. Did you think I might have *carried her over?*" His tone reminded me how unwelcome my interruptions were. It returned to normal as he continued. "I made my way to the mansion's roof and found the duke's private quarters. I climbed down my rope and entered his window."

"*Really?* What about his wife? Did you have to bind and gag her?"

I'd already resolved not to interrupt the Captain again, but I couldn't picture him climbing into the duke's bedroom and taking his wife hostage. The Captain answered in frustration.

"He's a widower," he glowered over his shoulder. "Now then, I entered his window without waking him, and walked to the door before approaching his bed."

"Captain…" I said, hopefully.

He sighed heavily. When he paused to drink from his canteen, he grimaced and didn't continue immediately. I took it as permission to speak.

"It's too hard for me to hear half the story," I pleaded.

"We have a long ride ahead of us. You can question me for details the entire ride if you like; just keep quiet until I finish." It certainly wasn't what he intended, but I took advantage of his pause and asked another question.

"Why did you enter from the side of his bed near the door?"

"Last question," he said sternly. "I wanted him to think I silenced the guard posted outside the door instead of arriving through the window." He paused, as if confirming I would not interrupt again. "He was fearful at first, but grew cocky when he realized I wouldn't harm him. He's still a member of a Royal House, and I am bound to protect him.

"I questioned him about the assassin in the barracks, pretending to know more than I did. When he feigned ignorance, I made as if to leave through the door. As I'd hoped, he was ready to tell me the truth to keep me there with him. No doubt he believed I killed his guard, and he expected reinforcements would arrive soon. He was willing to tell me his entire plan, in hopes to stall long enough to capture me. To his surprise, I leapt out the window as soon as I'd heard what I needed."

He looked at me expecting another interruption, but I remained silent. In my mind, I counted the questions I would ask the moment he finished.

"I went back and found the donkeys, and made it through the needle's eye just before dawn. I rode to meet you at the geyser, as quickly as the donkeys would allow." I waited for more, but it seemed he was finished.

"Are you done?" I asked, immediately realizing how brash my question sounded. He turned back and smiled at me.

"Ask away."

"Didn't the duke see you climb up the rope, and send soldiers after you?"

"Doubtless he *would have*, but he didn't see me climb the rope. I hoped to give him some cause for confusion."

"How? I mean, why didn't he see you?"

"I was *fast*. I tied large knots in the rope to make it easier to climb. I made it to the roof and pulled the rope after me before he even parted the drapes."

I wondered if I would have thought so far ahead. "All right…then how did you get out of the city with the donkeys?"

"I tied the donkey's reins together, and held them in one hand. Then, dragging them as fast as I could, I fought my way past two guards posted at the needle's eye, and ran out of the city."

"How'd you do that? Did you kill them?"

"No. The guards posted to the gate hardly resisted. They fled the city rather than face the duke after letting me through—little good it will do them without water or horses."

The Captain paused to take a drink from his canteen, then spit. He grimaced as he continued in response to my question.

"If either of the guards had sounded an alarm instead of running, the duke's soldiers could have easily caught me. Even so, if the donkeys had resisted any more while I dragged them through the gate, I wouldn't have made it."

Suddenly, I realized how thirsty I was. The dry desert air stabbed at my throat. Reaching back to Yashel, I found my canteen. I realized the donkeys hadn't had water in their sacks when I left them in the stables.

"How did you manage to fill the donkeys' water sacks?" I asked. I knew the well we used the previous morning was in a common area, well-lit and probably too risky to use.

The Captain looked over his shoulder and saw me lifting the canteen to my lips.

"I'll tell you in a minute," he replied through a wry smile.

I was very thirsty. I took a long swallow from the canteen, then another, and another. When I finally tipped the canteen nearly upside down, I received a nasty surprise. The water had bits of dirt or hay in it, and I realized it *tasted* like hay. I spit out the last mouthful, gagging.

"*The water's bad.* Did you fill my canteen with the geyser water?"

"No, I used the same water in my own," he replied in an even tone.

"What's wrong with it?"

"I filled the empty water sacks in the duke's stables." It took a minute to realize his implication.

"You mean you used the *horses' water?* You filled the sacks from the *trough?*"

"If it's good enough for the horses…" He trailed off, smiling. I held my tongue while my mind flooded with things I would have *liked* to say, but wouldn't have been especially helpful.

"What if we get sick?" I finally asked.

"Then our horses and donkeys will be sick, too—which would be far worse for us in the long run. I don't like it either, but look on the bright side...we won't have any trouble rationing our water. With a little luck, we won't have to try the geyser water at all."

This set my mood for the rest of the morning. The next time I took a drink, we'd emerged from the rocks enough to ride again. By then we were far off the Desert Road from TerkEtmek to the dunes, and under the hot mid-day sun.

I was so thirsty I hardly minded the foul water. Grateful for what water we had and forgetting my sour mood, I began to pelt the Captain with more questions.

"Was there anything else to the duke's plan? Did you figure out anything else?"

"What," he smiled, "planning to kill the Royal Family isn't enough?" I didn't respond. "Unfortunately," he continued in a grave voice, "there *is* more to his plan. Like I said before, the duke certainly believes the King stole the throne from him, regardless of the well-known succession laws. He has an agreement with most of the trolls in the kingdom to help him seize the throne. In exchange, he'll give them the homes and businesses now belonging to loyal citizens.

"He clearly hates the King's loyal citizens as much as his mother did. He wants to turn us into slaves for the trolls. The human soldiers who fight with him are promised positions in the palace. Some have been promised slaves with the right to sell them or their labor. The merchant families siding with the duke are promised trade monopolies. One merchant family expects to re-open Abaddon using slave labor— with no regard for their lives, I'm sure. The kingdom the duke would create is a dark one indeed." The Captain shuddered visibly. As much as he was telling me, he left me with more questions than I could keep track of. More than anything else, I was afraid the duke might succeed in all his plans.

"Does he stand any chance of winning?" I asked, worry plain in my voice.

"It's hard to say without knowing how many families will side with him—and how many trolls there are. He could have a real army by now."

"*Really?*"

"The duke gave the trolls weapons and trained them in fighting. In fact, it was the duke who approached the *ice troll,* and plotted the Winter Palace takeover. He was the one who gave the ice troll the false title of *prince.* The duke swore he would make him a prince after he secured the crown."

"How big could the duke's army be?" I asked.

"I don't know. I *do* know he has several troll captains out in the desert, training their own platoons. They're building barracks and gathering an army in the Great Dunes."

Then the Captain slapped the side of his head and moaned, "Of course—*the timber trade*. The Hapsteads aren't trading timber with the Neerfals. They're both selling their lumber to the duke, who's using it to build barracks in the Great Dunes. This is bad news; they're both powerful families, now enemies of the King."

"What about the trolls we saw in the desert?" I asked. "Were they part of the troll army?"

The Captain nodded. "A scouting troop, most likely. The duke seemed very confident of the size of the troll army." The Captain turned toward me and added, "And yes, it *was* the leader's scarred horse you saw in the stables."

It seemed impossible for the duke to be involved in such treachery with no one the wiser. I said nothing, sensing it wasn't my place to judge such things. My mind turned to what the King might do to counter the duke's attack.

"So we're riding straight for the palace to warn the King, then?" I asked.

"Not yet," said the Captain. "This is what I'd *planned*, but unfortunately there is little we can say without more proof."

"We both heard the duke admit to *attempted murder*. What other proof do we need?"

"We could warn the King of a dangerous army of trolls in the desert, but the King will not hear an accusation against a member of the Royal Family without three witnesses—it's an ancient law. When we *do* return, I'll most likely be arrested on sight—"

"*What?*" I blurted, "Why?"

"The duke knows we may spoil his plans, so he'll try to kill us. If he can't, he'll try to discredit us. He could have already dispatched fast riders for Engdynlor, with false charges against us. The King may not believe them, but he'd have to investigate the claims. You must realize, when you told me what you overheard the duke saying, it changed everything."

"But how?" I asked, "We're still only *two* witnesses. Can we kidnap a soldier?"

"I would have, if I thought we could bring him across the desert alive. None of his soldiers would come willingly, knowing the King could sentence them to death for treason. It's too long a trek to survive tied up, lying across a horse. And we would need another donkey loaded with water sacks for the soldier and his horse. However, there is one more witness not far from our route—one we could easily bind and take with us over a much shorter distance."

"*Who?*" I asked.

"I hate to reunite the two of you...but I have no choice," the Captain replied with a pained look on his face.

"You mean...the *ice troll?*" My face grew warm and my neck tingled. My ears seemed to close up and my head felt foggy. I didn't want to see that hideous beast as long as I lived.

"I'm afraid so. We know where he is; we left him no chance of escape. By now he's probably light and weak enough to be tied to the back of one of the donkeys. More importantly, we don't have to cross the long Desert Trail with him. We only need to take him from Abaddon to Engdynlor."

It was the second time he'd used the word. "*Abaddon?*" I asked, not quite sure what I'd heard him say.

"It's the old name for the mine pit, where we left the ice troll. I don't know where the name came from, unless it merely means *abandoned*. Centuries ago it was declared abandoned by royal edict..." The Captain went on, but I wasn't listening. My mind focused on my memory of the troll, screeching in pure hatred for me.

"Mark," the Captain finally interrupted my thoughts, speaking slowly in a resolute tone. "You must face this. You know it's irrational; when a fear is more than a healthy respect for danger, we call it a *phobia*."

I looked up at him with doubt, and yet not without hope.

"The troll is weak and sickly now," he went on. "You're trained in battle, and you'll be wearing armor the entire time you're near him. He poses little threat to you."

I said nothing. Inside I felt hollow. We rode in silence for some time, until the Captain chose once again to wake me from my daze.

"You can do this. We *have* to."

"I know...I just don't *want* to." He sighed and let me return to my contemplations.

While the route we'd taken through the rocks was more difficult and therefore slower, it was also a more direct path from the geyser to the Great Dunes. When we reached the first of the grand mountains of sand, we rode around its east side. We went off-route to flank the

Great Dunes, traveling over the dunes closest to the Daggora Mountains. To ride completely around the east side of the dunes, would've meant leading our horses by hand through another maze of boulders. Not only would it be slow, it would also risk one of the animals breaking a leg on the uneven and sometimes jagged footing.

We took extra time to dismount and crawl near the top of each dune we were forced to transverse. We used the sand sheets again, just as when we'd spied on the troll caravan. Several times we veered to the right or left to avoid being seen by trolls. After we learned about the growing troll army in the desert, there was no point in engaging them if it could be avoided. We knew the desert was unsafe to cross, but moreover, the kingdom might soon be at war. Nothing we did on our trek could make the dunes safe for those loyal to the King.

Since they might conceal quicksand, we needed to avoid the valleys between dunes, and any steep area likely to give way and send us sliding *into* a valley. In this way we were able to avoid the deadly quicksand springs. Once, a sand-colored scorpion tried to sting me as we crawled to peer over the top of a dune, but it only got its tail caught on the sandy sheet I wore. I brushed it off with the back of my hand and squashed it with the pommel of my sword.

We saw the *troll city* being built in the Great Dunes. Once we saw it, we knew exactly where we were. My copy of the duke's map had a box drawn among the eastern dunes, in the same place we suspected we were, when we found the growing barracks.

We'd been skirting a long valley when we heard banging sounds over the dune to our left. Investigating the noise, we found the missing lumber, just as the Captain had guessed: being slowly transformed into a growing cluster of barracks. There were trolls, human merchants, and even a few of the duke's soldiers in the valley, all working on the construction of the slipshod buildings. There was a shifting pool of quicksand in the center of the valley, with a large ditch shaped like a V, probably to scavenge water. We quietly backed down the dune and gave the whole camp a wide berth.

Our trip was slowed by our repeated checks at the top of each dune. It was very late by the time we rode down the last dune, and we weren't anywhere near the hidden stump-well. We drank our fill of the dirty water in the donkeys' water sacks, then gave the rest to the animals. The water sack from the geyser was still untouched. We would be thirsty the next day when we reached Tume Belor, but as long as we weren't delayed, we wouldn't need to risk the bitter water of the geyser's pool. The Captain tried not to let on, but he didn't seem to think it would be a healthy choice for us.

When we finally saw the oasis on the horizon late the next morning, the horses picked up the pace. They seemed to recognize the speck of green on the horizon, and we let the donkeys trail farther behind as the horses hastened. Before long we could make out the individual trees and palms, and then finally, we were among them.

We led the animals straight to the pool, but the horses wouldn't drink. Something didn't smell right. The Captain lifted some water to his mouth and smelled it, then tasted it, and immediately spit it out.

"*Fouled*," he cried, and looked carefully around. He wore a look of disgust on his face.

"Stay here while I check the top of the rock," he said, moving with a sense of urgency. The animals busied themselves with the grass of the oasis, their first meal they'd had all day.

When he got to the top of the small waterfall, I could tell from the way he moved—something wasn't right. I walked around to the desert side of the rock to better see him. He threw three large wooden barrels down from the top of the rock, and they burst onto the desert floor. To me, they smelled like gasoline.

While I waited for him to climb down, I returned to the pool and its lush banks. With a little searching I found four more barrels lying around. The once pure water had been changed from delicious refreshment to poison. When the Captain came down from the rocks he spit out the word *turpentine*.

"*What?*"

"They fouled the water with turpentine. Three barrels were each half full, and dribbling into a tiny pool the spring feeds, on top of the rock. We could wait all day and there still might be enough up there to poison us."

"Then do we go back to the hidden well, under the stump at the first Great Dune?"

"If we found it was fouled too, we could die before we found clean water—even if we find the geyser water is safe."

"Then do we head for the Palace?" I asked, worry creeping into my voice.

"If we did, the animals might not make it to another water source. Also, we'd lose valuable time in getting our third witness to the King. There's one more chance for us to find pure water here."

I followed him as he headed to the rocky spire, where it spilled its water into the pool. It came down in a great sheet and churned the water of the pool where it entered. The Captain closed his eyes and stepped directly into the waterfall. I knew there was rock behind it; I'd swum up to the waterfall when we were last there. Apparently there was a hole in the rock just a few feet over the pool's edge. I closed my eyes and followed him through the water…and tripped right onto the Captain. I should have guessed there couldn't be a giant cavern on the other side of the waterfall; the rock formation had a very small base. When I stood up and stepped out of the Captain's way, I could see the *cave* was no bigger than a closet. He was fiddling with something close to the ground. I jumped back out of the waterfall and slipped, sending myself right into the pool.

When I climbed out, my eyes stung and my mouth tasted bitter. Worse, I had no water left in my canteen to rinse my mouth. I tried to spit the taste out, but my mouth was dry. I decided to see if I could dribble a few drops from the water sacks we'd emptied the previous day, so I walked around the rock to find the donkeys.

They were still eating, milling around a broken turpentine barrel near the side of the pool. Jenny sniffed at a broken barrel now and then as if the turpentine in it might suddenly turn to water.

"Jenny—*get away from that.*"

The sacks were empty. Bored and looking for a distraction from my thirst, I wandered around to the desert side of the stone obelisk. As I bent over to inspect a broken barrel the Captain had thrown down, I heard gurgling behind me. I turned around to see a tiny jet of water pouring from the rock and spilling onto the sand.

I rushed over to it, wondering if I'd witnessed some kind of miracle. I smelled it, and it seemed fine. I rinsed with it until my mouth tasted better. By then the Captain had stepped through the waterfall once again, and found his way to where I stood.

"It isn't spoiled, is it?" he asked with a worried look on his face.

"I don't think so. I fell in the pool and got water in my mouth, so I can't taste very well."

The Captain knelt and tried the water. "It's fine," he said, smiling back at me.

He let me drink my fill as he unpacked the wooden bowl and water sacks from Jack and Jenny, who were still eating grass around the other side of the rock. Then he drank, with the wooden bowl in the sand beneath him. I brought Rider around and let her drink several bowls of the pure water. We took turns bringing the animals back and forth so one could drink as the others ate. Between trips, the Captain explained the new spring.

"I already told you it was unlikely a pressurized spring would find its way to the surface at the top of this rock outcropping. I *didn't* tell you this was by design. In the hollowed-out space we just stepped into, behind the waterfall, is a hidden access point to the sealed pipes carrying the water to the top of the outcropping. In this tiny room, there is also a valve—I just opened it—which lets some of the water pass through a bored hole, out the back of this rock." He patted the stone above the spout of water. We'd just filled Jack's water sacks, and I turned to the Captain to ask a question.

"Should I go get Jenny now?"

"Sure. I'll bet she's thirsty enough to run, if she knew we had fresh water."

I pulled Jack with me, leading him back to the grass by the pool where the other animals were feeding. I returned with Jenny and led her to the wooden bowl to drink.

"There you go, Jenny," I told her, "drink up, girl."

The Captain wore a curious smile as he asked me, "When exactly did you decide to name her?"

"What? *I* didn't name her; you told me their names before we left the palace."

"I did? I don't think they even *had* names. What did you think I called them?"

"Why, Jack and Jenny," I said. "Just when you told me Yashel's name." The Captain laughed out loud.

"You're part right. I did call them Jack and Jenny, but those aren't their names...at least they weren't *yet*."

"What do you mean? If you called them Jack and Jenny, weren't those their names?"

"A male donkey is called a jack. A *jenny* is a *female*."

"Well," I scoffed, "I guess I named them after all." While filling Jenny's water sacks, my mind turned back to the oasis. The mystery surrounding its water fascinated me. Somehow Tume Belor seemed more ancient, even more wondrous, after I heard its secrets.

"Why is the valve secret?" I asked the Captain.

"Every water source around the desert is important to the King. To prevent them from being fouled in time of war, they are kept secret.

We used the hidden stump-well on the way to the Great Dunes—what, five days ago?"

"Why didn't the duke know the secret?" I asked.

"Remember, he was raised by his mother, an enemy of the King. My guess is our previous king didn't trust her. I was more worried another servant of the King—a traitor who chose to side with the duke—might have damaged the valve."

"Anyone specific?"

The Captain wore a pained look. I waited for a response, but it soon became plain I would get none. I changed the subject.

"Are there secret pipes under the desert sand, all the way from the mountain to here?"

"Honestly, I don't know. Whether the spring was under pressure and its water once rose from the sand near here, or if miles of pipe had to be laid to carry the water here, maybe the King knows—I do not."

He paused to load the last sack onto Jenny. It was the sack we filled at the geyser, and he'd rinsed it clean before filling it.

"With the sacks full," he started, "it's time we moved on to Abaddon, to find our cold little friend."

I shuddered as I tied the last of the donkeys' packs. The Captain went back through the waterfall and closed the valve once again, and the tiny spout trickled to a stop. We led the animals together and turned eastward along the Desert Trail, toward Golden Mountain.

We rode side by side, and the Captain explained more of the virtues I would learn in my knight's training. I began to see I wouldn't learn these lessons in a classroom. He asked if I thought I understood the concepts he'd explained so far, and I responded with a nod. As I did, I wondered what role the knights played in the kingdom. If they had jobs everyone knew of, what did their roles as knights mean?

"Are all the Honor Knights in the military?" I asked.

"You might be surprised to find what other jobs are held by some of us. If we were all in the Army or Navy, many of our assignments would look like unwarranted military interference."

"What other jobs do knights have?"

"You can't know who any other knights are unless you are accepted into the order, Mark. I'm afraid I can't narrow the list for you."

"Oh, I didn't mean to—I was just curious. What types of things do knights do...you know, as *knights*?"

"Well, there are some duties all knights have. There are many things we do simply because the King needs them done by someone he trusts.

The purpose of the Honor Knights goes far beyond that. It plays into the theory of government the King's family has held for centuries. You need to learn more of the two Royal Families to fully understand."

I settled into my saddle for the long ride ahead of us. He paused thoughtfully before he explained the differences in the two families.

The King and silent duke are both from the royal line of Harringtons, while the Duke of Enthicia belongs to the line of Wards. Though they rarely inter-married, they are distant relations.

When there are no sons or daughters of a king in the Harrington family, a cousin or uncle or aunt can inherit the throne. But if a king from the Ward family dies with no children of age, the crown falls back to the Harrington family. In this way, the crown will always return to the Harrington family eventually. The Ward family was first named because they do just that—they *ward* over the kingdom while there is no king to rule from the Harrington line.

The theory of government held for so long in the Harrington family has a very different goal for the kingdom than what most of the Ward kings believed, and was central to the schooling of every Harrington child. The knights call it the New Rule. The goal of the New Rule is to prepare the kingdom for self-rule. When the entire kingdom voluntarily submits to the King's rule, and there are no wars or rebellions, the new government will be introduced. First, the Honor Knights will be installed as judges to interpret disputes and passed laws. Meanwhile, the people elect representatives to perform the administrations of government. Eventually, the knights are replaced by judges elected by all the people.

"As Honor Knights," the Captain concluded, "we will have the privilege of implementing the age of self-rule, of peace and prosperity."

"Why can't you do this now?" I asked. His theories seemed unrealistic to me.

"Well, our theory of government implies any people who cannot submit to a benevolent king, cannot successfully rule over themselves."

I wondered if such a simple view of government could be accurate. *What about my own country?* I wondered. It seemed unimaginable a King with absolute authority could peacefully rule over a modern nation, but the Captain had begun talking again, and I was missing what he said. I remembered my plans to interrupt him less.

"...so this system couldn't work if the kingdom were split into separate self-governing kingdoms. The New Rule theory holds war would be too likely, and such wars would be much worse than we know of today." At hearing this, I lost all resolve to keep silent.

"How can you say that? Do you really believe two separate governments can't live at peace with each other?"

"It has been tried many times in our history. The longest any two separate governments lived at peace with each other is only a few centuries. More often than not, it's even shorter." I couldn't grasp his perspective.

"Do you count it as a *failure*," I asked, "when two governments keep peace for *hundreds of years*? Why isn't it a great success? Think of all the suffering prevented, spread across hundreds of years of peace."

"Actually, our history shows the opposite is more likely; the longer the peace lasts under such governments, the worse the destruction and suffering are, when they eventually fall."

The Captain could tell I disagreed, though I knew I could not change his mind. He shook his head regretfully before he went on.

"This is why the duke's plans are so harmful. He means to split the kingdom in two: a kingdom of Trolls and one of Humans. There could be no lasting peace between them."

"But isn't the island split in two now?" I asked.

The Captain sighed. "In some ways, yes. The King would like to see the trolls living alongside humans—*partners* who treat each other as equals. But the King can only lead where his people will follow."

"So if we win this battle or war the duke is trying to bring, won't the King rule over the trolls?"

"I haven't asked him that yet." Before he went on, he paused enough for me to realize I was asking him hypothetical questions he couldn't definitively answer. When he spoke again, he sounded thoughtful. "I imagine the King would exercise some amount of *defense* from the trolls to protect the kingdom. Otherwise, he must allow them to act as separately as they desire, or they will never submit to his rule voluntarily. The King will stop their attempt to make war, and punish the guilty as necessary to protect the kingdom, but he will not rule over them as a conquered people. The King must have suspected the *possibility* of the duke trying to take over, but his nature is to give him the chance to do what is right, just as you explained his distant cousin, the silent duke, would do."

I remained in quiet thought for a while. It certainly would be exciting, to be a knight who ushers in a new form of government—in effect, to change the world. The *Benevolent King* theory seemed strange to me, as did their distaste for multiple governments. I imagined the goal he spoke of was likely to be far away, as badly as the trolls and humans were getting along.

"What do the knights do before then, before the new government comes?"

"Well, we all hope to be in the generation of knights who bring in the New Rule. Until then, we have a common task: to prepare the people of the kingdom for the New Rule. A people who submit out of weakness or fear, will never form a lasting government. The values I'm teaching you need to belong to the majority of the people in the kingdom. Then the elected can rule from a position of mature responsibility, instead of greed or power-lust. Only when the people pass their values on to their children, can the kingdom become stable and peaceful. Even if I never participate in the New Rule, I can help bring it to pass by teaching these values to others, enriching their lives in the meanwhile, and fostering peace—the environment in which the New Rule must grow. So you see, learning these values is more than an exercise for you, it's training on how to be a knight, *and* how to help bring in the New Rule."

I was no expert in government. Still, I was doubtful so many people would choose to give up their positions and authority, as the Captain expected of the knights. It would be some time before I could put my doubts into coherent form.

4.6 Up the Mountain Slope

We rode in silence as the afternoon wore on. I tried to enjoy the landscape, but there wasn't much to appreciate. All differentiation in the terrain lay far behind us or far ahead of us. Eventually, the Captain noticed my boredom and added an afterthought to my lesson in the New Rule.

"The truths we hold as knights, we give away. The knights who get to usher in the New Rule will give away their authority, just as the King will. This is what we believe *authority* to ultimately mean: to train up and to give away. The duke, he has different ideas about authority—or the abuse of authority, I should say. He wants to rule the kingdom by force. He's eager to murder those who oppose him."

I thought about the two dukes: the silent duke and the duke in the desert. Two men could hardly be less alike. As we rode toward Golden Mountain I also remembered our trip down the same trail we'd taken, not so long ago. I wondered how much farther it was to the mine pit. The Captain had led us in a nonstop ride from the pit to the palace before, to save my life. Sally had said it was two long days of riding to the palace, while we were a half-day past the mines. Already the sun was getting low and I could see grass tufts growing here and there…we were coming to the end of the desert, and the end of the day's ride.

"Will we stop to sleep soon?" I asked, breaking the silence.

"Yes, we have no choice. The animals need it more than we do. We'll ride until dusk, and then stop to let the animals bed down. We'll light no fire, and start at dawn. We should make Abaddon by late morning."

I knew the Captain wanted to get the ice troll to Engdynlor as soon as possible, but I wondered what price he was willing to pay. If he thought the animals could survive it, would he have us ride nonstop? Hearing him talk of knights and government had distracted me for a while, but soon I could think only of the ice troll. I knew he was weakened. I knew I could easily strike him down; so why was I afraid? I wasn't looking forward to sleeping in the open with no fire. I wished my brother was with me.

By dusk we were well on our way up the gentle slope of the mountain's skirt. The terrain had become rocky with large boulders here and there, but also held an occasional tree or bush. When it was time to stop, we rode far off the trail, winding around bushes and tall boulders. The Captain selected a spot where the horses wouldn't be seen, should someone pass on the trail. We quickly unloaded the donkeys' packs, and I watered the animals while the Captain laid out our blankets. The Captain handed me a long piece of salted dry meat for dinner, and a flat, stale piece of bread.

"Not much to eat tonight, I'm afraid," he said.

While Jack and Jenny drank their bowls of water, I lay back against our packs and watched the sun's last rays disappear from Eastward's peaks. By the time the animals were watered, I could hardly see. I took the bowl from the horses, not bothering to pack it, and climbed into my stack of blankets, wearing everything but my armor. It wasn't very cold yet, and just a little windy, but I preferred being too hot during the night than too cold.

To my surprise, I was so tired I had no problems falling asleep, though my worries continued to plague me. I dreamt I was stranded in the snow of Golden Mountain, freezing. I was surrounded by howling ice trolls, towering above me, all of them trying to bite me. I kept trying to go back to sleep—I had some notion I was dreaming—but the trolls wouldn't give me any peace. It felt like it went on forever. Finally I woke to hear a distant howling. Without opening my eyes, I thought, *it's only the wind. It's too far from the pit to hear him. Go back to sleep.*

A few moments later, I became convinced the night held no more sleep for me. Resolved to wait out the rest of the night in fear, I opened my eyes to see a welcome but dim blue band over the mountain; it was morning. I listened carefully and found I'd been right; it had been only the wind I'd heard. The sound came and went with the gusts I felt blowing over me.

I stood and rubbed my legs to warm myself. I even hopped up and down for a while. I threw a blanket over my shoulders and began to pack while the Captain slept. I remembered how slowly he woke. *At least there's something I can do faster than him*, I thought.

When I bent to pick up the wooden bowl, I drew back my hand quickly, even before I fully understood why. There was a large sand-colored scorpion in the broad bowl. I picked up a small boulder to drop on it, but thought better of it, cautious of breaking the bowl. I went instead to where Yashel lay, to fetch my sword. When I drew it, I heard a great whirl of motion behind me, and turned to see the Captain facing me, dagger drawn and eyes darting back and forth. *Wow*, I thought, *he can move faster in his sleep than I can move awake.*

"A scorpion in the bowl—I didn't want to squash it." It couldn't have made much sense, but it was all my mouth could manage at the moment.

He put his dagger away. "Did it sting you?"

"No. It just crawled in and got trapped."

I walked over to the bowl and skewered it with the tip of my sword.

"See?" I asked, turning back to the Captain—but he was already lying under his blankets and once again asleep. I flung it far from our camp. I was more careful the rest of the morning.

I gave the animals each a bowl of water. The Captain could tell me later if he wanted them to have more. By the time I packed my things, the Captain was rolling his own blankets and adding them to Jack's load. We were set to go, and I realized I was finally warm from the effort of packing. I told the Captain the animals each had a bowl of water, and he nodded as he mounted Rider. We left without another word.

I watched the great Westward Mountain as we rode. Its peak was ringed in sunlight. I saw several sparks of light on the peak to our left—the few golden mirrors left on Westward's east face. I wished I could have one as a souvenir. I loved the history of the mountains, tragic as it was.

Before long, the Captain finally spoke. First he yawned, then he coughed heartily.

"I had a dream early this morning," he started. I waited. He paused a bit longer and then continued, "...of a silly young man, trying to scare me to death in my sleep." He turned to me wearing a broad smile.

"Oh, really?" I replied. "In *my* dream there was a mean old knight *pretending* to sleep, trying to scare *me* to death."

He laughed heartily. I'd almost forgotten about my actual dream.

"I really *did* dream though. There were giant ice trolls, tormenting me all night in the snow, howling and biting me."

"It's easy to tell what your mind was on as you fell asleep," he said, then added in a comforting tone, "However, you know we're not going as far as the snowline. We'll see only one ice troll in our journey."

We rode on, talking about the ice troll and Winter Palace. The Duke of Enthicia had promised to send soldiers to take back the Winter Palace and hold it against further attack. By then, of course, we knew this was a lie. We guessed at what false charges against us the duke might have sent to the King. The duke knew he was not completely trusted by the King, so we had some hope he might not have sent any message at all. If the duke took the wisest route, he would probably send assassins to search us out, but send no one to Engdynlor.

When the Spill Hills were in view, we passed a stream not far from the road. We watered the animals and rested for a short while. The terrain had already begun to change drastically from the desert floor, with full-sized trees all around us. My thoughts wandered until I remembered the impression the Captain had made on me when we'd first met. Though I felt like it had been *many* months, I realized it was closer to three, since our trip down Golden Mountain.

"Why were you so interested in my dreams after I was bitten by the ice troll?" I asked.

The Captain took a long breath and sighed. "Some legends claim a young man's dream can hold true wisdom. I don't have much use for legends, but fresh perspectives weren't abundant at the time. Just like now, a difficult time can mean your oaths and obligations make your choices *for* you. There may be little room for error. Unlike today—when what we must do is clear—I hadn't yet found an acceptable path of action.

"Dreams put concepts together in such strange ways, sometimes they can stumble upon ideas we might not otherwise see. To be honest, your dreams didn't help much. I'd all but decided to leave the troll at Abaddon, but was hoping for another solution. I thought it unlikely you could have dreamt of the pit, having never heard of it before." Then, smiling, he added, "Perhaps the legends are right."

"I worried I was responsible for everything you did—I should have known better."

"You didn't know anything about me then," the Captain responded, suddenly in a much lighter mood.

We mounted our horses again and returned to the uphill road. We rode in silence for a while, left to our own thoughts. Before long we were climbing the first of the Spill Hills, and I pondered at how even their uphill sides were. It seemed like a giant staircase. I knew the collapsed mine pit was not far.

"How will we find him?" I asked the Captain. He gave no pause to wonder about whom I was asking.

"We will lower ourselves by rope down into the pit. We must be careful to stay near the edges to avoid further collapsing of the pit's floor. Breaking a leg down there could mean death. I've been thinking of a way to hide the rope at the top of the pit so no one could pull it up and leave us stranded."

"And what if the troll finds the end of the rope while we're down there? Couldn't he climb up and take the rope with him?"

"Not likely. I don't think he could survive the long trek to the snowline, and I suspect he knows it. I think we'll find him asleep near an ice-cold stream near the pit's walls."

I tried to think of a solution to both problems, just in case. "It's too bad we can't take the rope down there *with* us, and somehow throw one end back up out of the pit."

"It's too far, even if we had a grappling hook. If we had a bow and grappling arrow, it might work."

"Could we make one? I mean, make a bow to fire the tip of a lance?"

"It's worth some thought," he replied, though from his expression I suspected he was humoring me. I welcomed the distraction. "It would be a crude bow, with rope for a bowstring. I don't think it could fire a lance head far enough. Why don't you keep your eyes open for a straight sapling, almost as thick as your wrist? We'll be at the pit soon."

The Spill Hills had many pine trees on them, but I found none small enough to cut and bend into a bow. Hill after hill, I saw no sapling the right size. Finally, we reached the pit, and the Captain led us from the road, following the rim of the chasm northward.

We came across a place where our descent would be nearly vertical. There we found a large groove in the side of the cliff wall, wide enough for two men to lie in side-by-side.

"Look," said the Captain, "I think this was a ventilation shaft to the mines." It made sense to me—along its way down the cliff face, the groove was eroded in places, but remained more or less visible on its way down to the pit floor. We'd found our hiding place for our rope. It would be nearly impossible to see from any angle, other than the very spot where we stood. I stared down the channel all the way to the bottom of the pit, and took a step backward.

We led the animals into the trees and tied them in the grassiest area we could find. They hadn't eaten regularly since we fled the duke, and they were surely hungry. While they ate, the Captain unbuckled Rider's bridle and detached some metal rings from it. He tied the leather straps of her reins in knots where the metal rings had been.

We ate some dry bread and drank from our canteens. After a short rest, we pulled both ropes from our packs and put on our chain mail. We left, taking only our swords and canteens—and of course the rope. We found the groove again and secured the longest rope tightly to a large boulder, making sure to avoid any sharp edges on the stone. Just before he tied the rope to the boulder, the Captain slid the rope through the metal bridle rings, though I couldn't yet guess why. Then he tied a stick to the other end of the rope and threw it. It fell short of the pit's bottom. He pulled it back up and added half the smaller rope to its end and made sure the knot fit through the metal rings. He tossed the lengthened rope down the groove again; it hit bottom with some length to spare.

The Captain used part of the remaining rope to tie a safety line around my waist and to the main rope, in two loose loops, a hand's breadth apart. If I slipped and fell, the safety line would catch on the rope and bind it so I wouldn't slide very far. I might get a good burn from the rope around my waist, but I wouldn't fall farther down to find a worse injury. He had me practice unbinding the rope from the safety line. When he was sure I could do it, he showed me how to use one of the metal rings from the bridle to rappel down the cliff. I had the ring attached to my sword's belt, and the rope went through the metal ring. If I wrapped the rope off around my back, the rope couldn't slide through the ring, and I would stop. It seemed easy. The groove from the old ventilation shaft wasn't straight down, just very steep. The Captain asked if I thought I could do it safely, and I nodded.

"Well then, do you want to go down first or second?" he asked.

"You mean, do I want to slide down ahead of you?"

"Not exactly; we have to go down one at a time. Otherwise the person on the bottom would pull the rope too tight to rappel."

The thought of me waiting up at the top didn't seem very attractive, but I liked it better than waiting alone at the bottom of the pit. I asked to go second. He checked my safety line and belt, then used the same technique he'd explained, to rappel down the cliff. He seemed to descend very slowly, and I soon became bored. I looked across the enormous crater, and wondered in amazement what the area of the pit's floor might be. We hoped to skirt the mere edge of it, and with any luck, only a small fraction of its circumference. I pondered what direction we would first take. I followed a tall thin waterfall trickling down the cliff, nearer to the trail. *Maybe the ice troll is there*, I thought. I saw a flicker of motion farther out from the edge, but couldn't find what caused it. I wondered if rocks were still caving in after so many years. When I finally looked back down the rope, I saw the Captain had reached the bottom, and was waving an arm at me. *How long has he been waiting?* Embarrassed, I started down the rope, rappelling slowly just as he'd explained.

Halfway down, I realized it was much harder work than I'd expected. I wished I could stop for a drink. I was weighed down by my sword and chain mail, and both made it difficult to maneuver. Parts of the large groove in the rock were smooth, and others jagged. I stepped down carefully, and found it went faster with one leg pointed straight below me, and the other bent high so my foot was close to my waist. In this way, I could feel for the rock below me as I backed down, and keep from banging against the rock in front of me. Soon I met the knot where the shorter rope was tied to the longer one, and knew it wasn't much farther. It was then, just as I let the knot pass tight through the metal ring, I slipped.

The groove was smooth and nearly vertical immediately below me, and I got the rope wrapped around my back far too late. The safety line caught tight and pulled its loop around my waist, up *hard*, toward my chest. My weight was hanging by the safety line, and the rope loop was pulling tight, constricting my chest painfully. I closed my eyes and tried to breathe slowly and force myself to think. I tried to gain footing beneath me, but there was none. I pushed out from the wall with one leg bent in front of me, and was able to lean back some. The farther I leaned back, the closer the loop in my safety line slid down toward my waist. It scraped painfully as I worked the loop back down.

Finally, when I was standing straight out from the rock, I could reach the safety line where it bunched the main rope tight. I loosened it as quickly as I could, but nearly slipped again when I realized, too late, I wasn't holding the main line behind me. I went much slower the rest of the way down; it was nearly a straight drop. I didn't know I had reached the bottom until the Captain reached up and slapped my back, startling me.

On the ground, I breathed a sigh of relief. The Captain cut off the excess rope, and tied it to his belt in a loop. Then he elected to hide the bottom end of the main rope, just in case the ice troll saw us descend and came by looking for it. I stood on his shoulders, leaning against the wall, and stuffed the small bundle of the rope's end into a crack in the cliff face. I jumped down from the Captain's shoulders and asked where we would start to look.

"There's a stream over this way," he said, pointing back toward the mountain trail. "We'll see if we can find any signs of our *friend* there."

The stream didn't seem far, but the ground was an uneven jumble of rocks and boulders. It was more like climbing than walking. My sword hung from my belt and got in the way. It kept my left hand busy tilting the sword's hilt downward, to keep the scabbard's tip from clanging on every rock I passed. There were places where soil had filled in between the rocks making for easier walking, but they were few.

We kept close together and whispered back and forth.

"There are some things I should tell you about the ice troll before we hope to find him. Do you remember why we left him here?"

"He would have died if we took him across the desert, and we couldn't let him go back up the mountain." I wasn't sure if he was trying to hold my interest, or quiz me.

"Well, he *might* have died; we don't know for sure. There wasn't as strong a reason to risk his life then. Anyway, we didn't plan to leave him here forever."

"That's right," I remembered. "You said it was temporary until the King could decide what would happen to him. What did he decide?"

"The King sent messengers to talk to the troll. They described a place near the stream ahead of us where they found him."

"What did they do to him?"

I knew they hadn't killed him or set him free, or we wouldn't be looking for him in the mine pit.

"They made the troll an offer. If he would go to Engdynlor to learn from the King, and swear allegiance to him, the King would let him return to his mountain home, and would help him establish a trade route over the mountains where none exists today."

"What kind of punishment is *that*?" I blurted, a little too loudly. The Captain sent me a concerned look, and I didn't need to guess at his meaning.

"Perhaps the King wanted to give the ice troll a chance to do what's right." I remembered recent conversations with the Captain, and felt a little ashamed. "The King has made every effort to make peace with the green and brown trolls with little results thus far. This is the first contact with the ice trolls in a very long time. The King wants to begin a peaceful relationship with them, if such an endeavor is possible."

"And he refused the offer?" I guessed.

"He did. He wouldn't trust the King after imprisoning his daughter—*and* clearly planning to murder him and his family. He chose to stay in the pit and live in despair. Before they left him, the messengers warned the troll what the King would do if he escaped." Then the Captain turned to me; his expression turned solemn. "What are the important things to remember as we talk to the ice troll?" I thought for a moment. I didn't think very much of the ice troll, or his ability to tell the truth.

"He already planned to murder the King's family, and refused his second chance to follow the King—which says a lot about him." The Captain looked grim.

"Yes, those are important points. They are the troll's history with the King and they show he isn't trustworthy. It's also important to remember he once led a large number of trolls, and if he *did* choose to be loyal to the King, he might bring peace between humans and trolls. This is important to the kingdom, and even more important to the kingdom to come."

"I didn't think of this at all, even though you just talked about it." I muttered, half to myself.

"Perhaps you hold unforgiveness toward him. The Princess forgave him, and I could argue she has the most reason to hate him." I wasn't excited about being compared to the Princess—especially not on the topic of forgiveness.

"If the King forgives him," I asked, "how can he protect his family from what he might do in the future?"

"Forgiving the ice troll doesn't mean he won't be punished, no more than it means he'll be trusted. The King is still responsible for his family and his kingdom. When the King forgave him, he opened his heart to the possibility the troll might choose to change. In some cases, when the King must pass a sentence, his forgiveness may not change his actions at all—only his attitude toward the guilty. I have seen the King deeply moved and saddened when a death sentence is carried out for a murderer. He still wants to see the person change, and he is burdened by knowing it's too late.

"It's much more than this though; forgiveness frees *you*. Remember what I said about unforgiveness on the way back from the Valley of Abandon? Unforgiveness is like a hot coal in your hand. A wise man would drop it immediately, and let it fall to the ground. Only a fool would wrap his hand around a live coal and hold onto it. The harder you hold onto the pain, the more it hurts you. Even worse, unforgiveness won't cool down like a coal from the fire; it gets hotter the longer you hold onto it. Its effects spread to other areas of your life. The village you told me of before…I can believe it was in danger of being destroyed by unforgiveness. I have seen firsthand the pain it can cause."

"How?" I asked, "I mean, what have you seen?"

The Captain looked around and stopped. He lowered his whisper even further.

"It's not a short tale. But if you're ready to hear it now, I will tell it. It will take some time to reach the stream, and you'll have to stay close to hear me. Are you sure you wouldn't rather hear it another time?"

I thought a moment. I assumed he wouldn't tell me during our ride to the palace if the troll was with us. Who knew what would happen when we reached Engdynlor? It might be a very long time before I heard his story.

"I can hear you—I mean, if you want to tell it now." He started moving again, whispering in my direction.

"This is the tale of my first *LifeGrowth*," he said as he turned to catch my curious expression. "I'll come back to that word later." The Captain seemed to relax somewhat, as he launched into his story.

4.7 LifeGrowth

The Captain was young when his father died—something he explained more easily than I would have expected. The phrase he used to tell me how old he was struck me as odd: *at an age when a boy chooses to leave his childhood, or remain a child for life.* He'd come to blame the army for his father's death, and even the King, for sending him into battle. He nursed his anger until it turned to hatred. The young Captain held onto it tightly, and like a coal, it burned its way deep. Fortunately, he never reached the end of the road he'd started. A smithy hired him as an assistant, but not because he was a hard worker or a worthy employee. On the contrary, the teenaged Captain-to-be had changed jobs frequently since he first began to work to support his mother. Mostly, he was fired for not taking instructions reliably—something I found unimaginable for him. He worked shamefully for the smithy, and fought his instruction at every turn. Still, the tradesman didn't fire the Captain, for he'd hired him out of *obligation*. He'd known the Captain's father, and had served with him in battle.

In time, the smithy began to see something in the Captain no one else had. He saw promise where others saw a waste of time, a rebellious child. He chose to give the Captain compassion and mercy, where others had merely doled out justice.

Working for the smithy was not easy—not by any means. He worked the Captain hard, and several times the young Captain meant to quit. Each time the smithy talked him out of it, and gave him another chance to prove himself. Once he gained his trust and loyalty, he showed the young Captain how harmful his hate and unforgiveness was. By then, he'd redirected his feelings toward the trolls who killed his father, though it was hardly less harmful.

Fortunately, the feelings he held for the trolls were nothing compared to the duke's or the ice troll's hatred. While the Captain had a short time to learn to hate them, the duke's mother taught her son to hate from birth. The ice troll would have had generations of trolls to thank for teaching him to hate humans. The trolls were poisoned by hate every time a human showed he thought himself better than a troll. Trolls are capable of good, the Captain insisted, though they have so much hatred to overcome, most humans can never see it. He ended his story by tying the ice troll's hatred to his own.

"If I can understand a fraction of his hatred," he went on, "I can guess at his plan, and it isn't to help the duke take over as King. Far more likely, the duke doesn't know his co-conspirator's true intentions. I believe he plans for the trolls to take the kingdom for themselves, and set the trolls over *all* humans, as slave drivers. Knowing hate as well as he does, the duke should be able to see this. He hates the King, his family, and all his loyal citizens with a blind fury. Still, he can't see the logical implication; the trolls he recruited hate humans even more. He trusts the trolls to help him take over the kingdom, but when he empowers them for war, he has no idea what he's unleashing."

"You aren't painting a very hopeful picture for the ice troll," I interrupted. "You make it sound impossible for him to change."

"When hate runs this deep, it isn't easy to be freed from it, though I *have* seen it happen. When it *does* happen, it isn't by any great feat of the person holding onto the hate. He is set free by the compassion *others* show him. Hatred this deep takes a long time to undo."

He gave me a lot to think about. I thought of the King forgiving the ice troll after he imprisoned his daughter and tried to murder his family. I remembered the Princess forgiving him also.

"I still can't see how they could forgive him after all he did to harm them—especially knowing he would do them *more* harm if he could."

"I can't explain it to you, Mark. It's something you have to see for yourself."

He was right, and I couldn't see it yet, though I wanted to. I wanted to understand such a transformative forgiveness. I didn't want to have the feelings I had whenever I thought of the ice troll. I walked on in silence, thinking intently on these things.

When we finally reached the stream, we walked along it as far as we dared, away from the place where it ran down the cliff into the pit. The banks on both sides of the stream were mostly soil, and some small bushes grew there. We found a small cave-like hole under large boulders where the stream had left gravel and soil to make a level floor. It was large enough to get out of the rain, and was littered with tiny scraps. The Captain quietly drew his dagger and stooped down to inspect them. The litter on the floor was made of small bones from mice or rats, picked clean and white. The Captain said it was exactly as the messengers described: beside the closest stream to the trail, sheltered from the rain, and with signs something had been capturing and eating small animals there. The ice troll was not in sight.

The Captain had a plan for capturing him. If the troll saw us, he might be frightened into running away from the pit walls and into the dangerous rubble. The Captain, much heavier than the troll, wouldn't be able to follow. So we laid in wait for him. The Captain crouched in the back of the troll's scant shelter with his dagger drawn. He had me hide between two rocks where I could see the troll if he approached from nearly any direction. He told me to get comfortable, and prepare to wait a long while in silence. I was to give him a warning if the troll approached, by clicking two hand-sized rocks together, a sound not too uncommon in the pit.

I lay down so only one eye could see between two large rocks, and propped my head up. I had a lot of time to think while lying there. Soon, I needed to concentrate on staying awake. Then I felt hungry, which helped keep me awake, but wasn't any more enjoyable.

When the ice troll finally showed himself, I nearly missed it. My eyes blurred with fear as he appeared from behind a boulder. *He's grown.* I thought for a quick second he was back to his full size, but I relaxed when I saw it wasn't so. He was horribly thin, and seemed much shorter than when I first saw him as we left the Winter Palace. His hair had all but fallen out, leaving only white patches here and there. He seemed nearly doubled over as he slid over the rocks, dragging a stiff leg in an almost snake-like manner. His ribs jutted out from his chest as if he were starved.

I finally remembered to signal the Captain and fumbled to find the two rocks I'd laid aside for this purpose. When I clicked them together, the ice troll went rigid. He looked around, sniffing the air before slouching even lower and continuing toward his hole. I saw the Captain ready himself and I hoped he would catch the troll easily. The ice troll looked sickly and frail. He was so puny, I wondered what had happened to him. The leg he favored seemed shorter than the other— it hadn't been so before, as far as I could recall. The way he winced as he walked made it clear he was in pain. Even his wheezing cough was still with him. The Captain hardly needed my warning he was coming.

As the ice troll picked his way through the rocks, I wondered about his size. Had he really grown? I didn't get a very good look at him after he shrank in the wagon. Was it possible he hadn't gotten shorter, only thinner? By then the troll had almost reached the Captain, and I turned my attention to them both.

Several dead mice hung from his hand, swinging by their tales; he'd been hunting. *He must be fairly fast to catch mice without a trap*, I thought. Just then I saw a flurry of motion as the Captain jumped out of the hole and grabbed the troll by the neck with both hands. The troll shrieked and spit, and screamed strange words. He writhed desperately, clawing uselessly at the Captain's mail. Soon the Captain had the troll's hands behind his back, and bound him. He tied his feet together as well, and drew them behind him, near to his hands. He leaned the troll's contorted body against a large boulder. The Captain collected the dead mice and piled them on the bank beside the troll. I walked down to the Captain as he addressed the troll.

"You may remember me; I am the Captain of the Royal Guard, whom you imprisoned in the Winter Palace. This is Mark, whom you bit and poisoned. He helped me recapture the Winter Palace from your troop. He is well now, which is more than can be said of you."

"*Ciphthghor, Ciphthghor ut nestthver,*" we wailed, then looked straight into the Captain's eyes and seethed, "Death…*death and pain.*" My heart pounded while I hoped the troll didn't notice.

"Is that what you think is in store for you?" asked the Captain, starting back at him just as fiercely. Then he drew his sword and laid it against the troll's chest. "No more Tlaltsihk from you—*guard your lips.*"

As I got closer, the troll tried to kick at me, but instead only tipped onto his belly. He was thin as a skeleton, and so pale I could see through his skin to his veins in places. He writhed on the ground, trying to roll off his belly. He was so grotesque, I felt pity for him. I walked behind him, grabbed his bound hands and leaned him against the boulder. He tried to scratch me with his sharp, claw-like nails. I remember thinking his body seemed light as an empty shell. His hands were cold to the touch. He stopped struggling, lowered his head, and wailed.

The Captain laid his sword on the troll again, this time, against his neck. "We need you to be quiet. Do you understand?"

The troll looked up at us with swollen eyes and said, "Kill me now then. Don't make me wait."

"We're not here to kill you," answered the Captain. "We know of your plans with the Duke of Enthicia. We know he was behind the plot at the Winter Palace, and his plans to become King."

The troll's eyes grew large with horror.

"More than this," the Captain pressed, "I know what roles you have in mind for trolls and humans after you depose of our king, in spite of the duke's ignorance."

The troll let out a gasp, then tried immediately to hide it. *So the Captain had guessed right,* my mind raced. He caught the look in my eyes as I glanced at the Captain, and he knew he'd given us more information than he'd meant to. He let out a quiet moan and the sound of it chilled me.

"Why do you wait? Kill me and be done with it."

"As I said, we're not here to kill you. I have some important questions for you. But first I want to know—what happened to you? You were thin and sickly when we let you down into this pit, but since then you've gotten worse. Why didn't you take the King's offer his messengers brought you?"

"It's *your* fault," spat the troll. "You pulled me from the cool of the mountain. I choke every day trying to swallow enough of this *water*," he said with disgust, glaring at the stream, "to stay alive in this heat. I need to take water so often, I can't even leave this stream. But *you knew* this would happen. I vomited constantly while I was tied in your cart. My bowels haven't stopped since we left the snow." I thought of the muddy patches on the trail I'd stepped in so long ago and felt sick. When I made the connection, I blurted out before I thought any better of it.

"So you *weren't* melting," I exclaimed. I felt foolish I'd misunderstood for so long.

"*Melting?* Of course I wasn't, you little fool! Did you think I'm made of ice? You should have died when I infected you, *idiot*." He snarled, glaring at me. The Captain turned and slapped the troll with the back of his hand.

"This is a servant of the King. You will treat him with respect, troll."

He grumbled a reply under his breath, but said nothing else. His words were filled with violent hatred, but his body was frail and dying. He seemed *sad* to me. Suddenly, I saw him through different eyes. It was a shift in my perspective, and it made all the difference in the world. He was a hurt little being who was to be pitied, not hated or feared. I imagined I could see all the pain thrust upon him as a child, all the hate nurtured in him by his injured parents and relatives, misshapen in spirit, if not in physical form. I imagined the agony he surely felt—and I wished him free of it. It was as if a veil had been pulled back, and I saw the troll for the first time without the foggy lens of my own perspective.

Is this how the King sees him? I wondered. I imagined it was. I found I could no longer hate him after seeing him in such light; he had no hope of a meaningful life, and he knew it. Any ill will I had for him dissolved as I watched him writhe. To my great surprise, I nearly felt ready to forgive him. It made no sense after what he'd just said, but nonetheless I looked back at him and spoke.

"I forgive you."

It was a ludicrous thing to say just then, like talking of drought during a catastrophic flood. As I spoke, I reached to feel the knot of scar tissue on my throat. My fingers tingled as they searched for it in vain. I rubbed my entire neck and couldn't find the scar I'd felt only earlier that day.

The Captain looked at me and smiled warmly, as if to say, *finally you understand.* The troll spit at me and hissed.

"Is that why you refused the King's offer?" I asked, "Were you too sick?"

"I don't believe a word you say—I know you'll kill me before sunset. You might as well know—*see if it brings you any peace.* I refused his offer because I believed I could escape. But thanks to *you two,* I broke my leg trying to climb out of this forsaken hole, the very next day. Then I knew I'd spend my dying days in this pit—*may it be on your heads.*"

"You have only your own choices to thank for your situation," the Captain replied. "The King was lenient in his offer to you. After you planned to kill the Royal Family, you *deserved* death. The King truly wants to make peace with your people. I can't speak for the King on this, but I think his previous offer may still stand, if you cooperate and swear your loyalty to him. You have little other choice, I may remind you. If you come with us, you might stay in the ice room under the castle. It is a stone room, and would be under constant guard, but I think it's your only chance at feeling cold again." The look on the troll's face changed quickly.

"Fine then—*I swear my loyalty to your king.* Will you untie me now?"

"I'm afraid not. We can't allow your escape. You cannot go back to your home until you've proved your loyalty and trustworthiness. You must come to Engdynlor."

"I might survive the journey, but what life would it mean for me? Locked in a dark room underground? Let me stay here in this pit; I want to die here."

"You've given me what I need to know," the Captain replied coolly. "You might survive the journey. You will stand witness before the King. We will bring you, bound, to Engdynlor. This will be your first step in learning allegiance: agreeing to come with us."

"I'll die on the way for certain," hissed the troll.

"I don't think you will." The Captain spoke with finality; he was decided. His face turned apathetic as he decided to explain. "We have two donkeys loaded with water sacks, and you will ride bound to one of them. You'll have all the water you can drink, and we'll travel in darkness. If we start at dusk, we should make Engdynlor by dawn."

The troll looked as if he might explode with fury, but instead clenched his teeth and remained silent. Finally he spoke in a low tone, spitting his words at us.

"Be careful how you tie me. I'm half dead already—and I'm *sure* you wouldn't mind finishing the job." The Captain ignored him.

"You'll understand if we treat you as a prisoner on the trip. After all, we have no proof of your allegiance *yet.* You'll be bound when we bring you up the cliff wall. I can wrap you in my mail to protect your skin, but I cannot untie you before we reach Thraen Kholl."

The Captain untied the troll's feet, but used the rope to bind his arms behind him, by first tying the rope around his waist. Then he tied a slipknot around his neck, leaving extra rope at both ends, so either end could draw the knot around his throat. With each of us holding the rope ends taut, he couldn't lunge at either of us. I led the way, and we carefully brought the troll over the rocky terrain, back to where we'd hidden the rope.

Once we reached the cliff, we retrieved the end of the rope from where we'd hidden it in the cliff wall. The troll eyed the rope cautiously. The Captain took the last of the remaining rope to make two double-loop devices with a complex-looking set of knots. Each one was wound around the main rope we were about to scale. With the troll bound beside us, he showed me how they worked. He stuck a foot into each of the long loops he'd tied onto the main line. The tops of the loops were in his hands as he stood in them, just off the ground.

Quite easily, he used the long loops to climb a few feet up the main line. While he rested his weight on one foot, he raised the other foot and loop with his opposite hand. Then he raised the other foot while standing on the first. After a few short steps he slipped his feet out and jumped down.

"You see? These loops hang on these knots. We use the *ascenders* so we can use our legs to climb, rather than our arms. I'll go up first, then pull the troll up. Afterward, I'll throw the rope and ascenders down to you, and you can make the climb yourself."

I nodded in acknowledgment and the Captain turned to the troll.

"I need to know you are healthy enough for what we need to do. How well can you breathe through your nose?"

"Well enough. What does it matter if—"

In one quick motion, the Captain stuffed a balled up rag into the troll's mouth. The rag ball had a short piece of rope tied to each side. The Captain tied these together behind the troll's head, securing the rag in the troll's mouth.

"We can't have you screaming aloud once you're halfway up the cliff, can we?" smiled the Captain.

Finally, he tied the end of the main line around the troll's hands and arms a few times, and once more around his chest. Then he removed the rope tied around his neck and used it to tie his chain mail to the troll's back. The troll could move his legs and feet well enough, but it was plain he'd be mostly dragged up the cliff. If he slid over onto his belly, he could probably use his legs to right himself. I realized the rope around his hands would be the only thing keeping him from falling down the cliff, and by the way the troll eyed it, he knew it too. He would make no attempt to claw through it during his ascent.

When all this was ready, the Captain set to climbing the rope up the cliff. I sat and watched, my attention divided between the Captain and the troll. I was glad the troll was gagged; I didn't want to hear what he might have to say with the Captain gone.

Soon after the Captain disappeared over the top of the cliff, the troll began to lift off the ground. He used his legs to kick downward and speed his ascent. It seemed he didn't want to dangle at the end of a rope any longer than he must.

After the troll disappeared over the top of the cliff, I stood back, expecting the rope to come tumbling down. I put on my chain mail and sword, wondering if they would get in my way much. Just before the Captain threw the rope, I changed my mind and took them off. Eventually I tied both of them to the end of the rope. When I put the safety line around me, I slipped my feet into the ascender ropes and began to climb.

I made quick progress for the first quarter of the climb, then stopped for a little rest. I reached the knot joining the two ropes I was ascending, and began to panic. I soon realized, while the Captain might have forgotten the ascenders couldn't get past the knot, he'd remembered to send some help my way, down the rope. I saw a tangle of rope dangling just a few feet above the large knot; the Captain had fashioned a second set of ascenders. I was more than glad for them, having no idea how to tie a prussic knot myself. Shaking, I carefully stepped out of the old ascenders, and into the new pair above them.

The second quarter of the climb took me longer, and my legs began to burn. By the time I was three fourths of the way to the top, I was using my arms to help pull my legs up for each step. My legs felt like they were made of clay. I could feel my feet, but from the tops of my thighs to my ankles, I felt only burning. *How did he make the climb so fast?*

As I got to the top, the Captain leaned over and grabbed my outstretched hand. I was grateful for the help, and let him half-drag me over the edge. I collapsed to the ground, my legs shaking.

"Where are your sword and mail?" the Captain asked with a concerned look.

"At the end of the rope," I gasped. "Did you think I could climb all this way with those *too?*" The Captain laughed.

"Then I'm glad you thought of it. You were taking so long, I was afraid I'd have to pull you up like the troll."

The troll sat behind the Captain, bound hand and foot, but without the rag in his mouth. He didn't seem happy to see I'd made the climb safely.

We led him by rope, from the front and back as we had before, until we found the horses. The Captain transferred some of the water sacks to Jenny to offset the troll's weight. The troll rode nearly on Jack's neck. The Captain tied another rope under Jack's belly, to hold the troll's feet tight against Jack's sides. The troll's hands were still tied behind his back, so he had to lean on Jack's neck.

"Time for a little trim, troll," said the Captain. "Those long nails of yours might scratch something along the way."

The troll let out an angry hiss—some curse in his own tongue, perhaps. The Captain turned his back to the troll while he pulled a small knife from his belt clasp, like the one I'd taken from him. He made quick work of trimming the long, thick, nails on the troll's hands. Finally, he picked up a rock and used it to smooth them down to round nubs, nearly even with his fingertips. Finally, he untied the troll's hands and retied them in a different fashion.

His right arm was tied around Jack's neck, to the far side of Jack's load. His left arm was tied only to a canteen. He could use his left arm to drink, but if he didn't wrap it back around Jack's neck soon, he would lose his balance, slide down Jack's front, and risk being trampled.

"Drink as much as you need," the Captain told the troll, "but no more. We'll be riding all night."

While the Captain tied the troll, I pulled the rope up and claimed my sword and mail. I stowed them both and filled my canteen. When I mounted Yashel, the Captain pulled a half-empty water sack from Jack's pack and laid it on the front of his saddle. He mounted Rider and we were off. It was just turning dusk as we left.

"Troll, do you have a name you'd like to be called?" asked the Captain.

"I do, but you can't say it."

"Try us," I said.

"Ssphotchhh," hissed the troll.

The Captain smirked, "I think you're right, troll. How about Sphotch...or Spoch? Close enough?"

"Call me what you will," he snorted.

"Sphotch it is then. Now then, *Sphotch*, remember you're learning to be loyal to the King. Your cooperation will be needed in the weeks to come." Another labored sigh escaped the troll. The Captain went on, unstilted. "I know what you've seen of humans hasn't left you with a good impression of our species, but I think this will change if you get to spend any time with our King. Still, after your crimes, you must realize you'll need to work hard to earn any trust."

The Captain looked around, surveying the area. "When your canteen is empty," he added with just a little menace in his voice, "let me know *quietly*, and I'll refill it *as we ride*." Then the Captain turned to me, and his voice returned to normal. "We'll stop at the stream ahead and fill all the water sacks the donkeys can carry."

We rode as fast as Jack would allow. We reached the stream past the Spill Hills before it was too dark to fill the sacks. Many times along the way, Sphotch grumbled and the Captain took a water sack from his saddle to dribble it into the canteen in Sphotch's hand. The troll hacked and choked whenever he drank, and I wondered if he was trying to alert some unseen enemy.

Several times we stopped to unload another water sack from one of the donkeys. By the time we reached Tume Belor, over half the sacks were empty, and the troll was asleep. We rode on without stopping to water the animals. After passing the oasis, I rode closer to the Captain.

"Do you think we can trust him at all?" I asked.

"I'm certain we can't. He'll lie whenever he thinks it might serve his interests. I expect he hoped to escape with a donkey and water, his only sure way back to the snowline. This is why I told him in the pit he would be tied to one of the donkeys carrying water. I gave him incentive to come."

"Isn't it risky to tease him with escape?"

"Yes. It's also why I took so many precautions. And don't be fooled by his raspy snoring. He's probably listening to us now—*isn't that right Sphotch?* He doesn't yet understand forgiveness. He has no forgiveness for himself, so how could he receive forgiveness from someone he's wronged so badly? He can't imagine why we don't kill him. Honestly, I don't know the King *won't* sentence him to death. I suspect Sphotch will get leniency from the King, and if he proves loyal someday, even a chance for freedom. Remember to guard your words, Mark, so you don't let out any secrets."

I kept quiet after that. I thought how hard it would be to edit my thoughts each time I spoke with my brother or the Princess. My mind turned back to our trek. We were fortunate to be traveling over desert. With only the stars and moon to light our way, rough terrain could have cost our animals a split hoof or broken leg.

I was just starting to fall asleep when the Captain slowed to a stop and clicked his tongue. Jenny and Jack stopped, as well as Yashel. The Captain turned his ear to the Desert Trail and sniffed the still air.

"Follow me off the trail for a while, but ride behind Sphotch—and *watch him.*" He clicked at the donkeys again. "If he begins to make any noise, use your sword to threaten him. He must not make any loud noises."

What does he expect me to do, I thought, *stab him?* I hoped Sphotch was truly sleeping, and would stay asleep the rest of the trip.

We rode off the trail at a right angle for a long while, then slowly rounded back in the direction we'd been traveling. A half-hour or so afterward, we turned back and found the stone markers of the trail again. The Captain stopped and pulled out his telescope. He looked back at the portion of the trail we'd skipped. He didn't say a word as we continued on our way to the palace. By the time the sky began to grow a light arc over the mountains behind us, we were riding uphill, passing grassy fields and an occasional tree. Before the sun fully appeared over the horizon, we could see Thraen Kholl.

When I asked why we rode off the trail in the darkest hour of the night, the Captain surprised me.

"I thought I heard something. I know for certain I smelled something—a troll, and I was upwind of Sphotch. I saw what looked like two green trolls and their horses, when I looked back on the trail afterward. If Sphotch wasn't asleep, he picked the perfect time to remain quiet. We would have had little chance of outrunning them, and I might have needed to kill our new friend here, rather than let him be captured."

His casual tone surprised me. I realized again I no longer wished him dead. I still hoped the King would punish him, but I didn't want him to die, not on our ride back to Thraen Kholl, nor at the palace. The Captain interrupted my thoughts.

"Mark, when we enter the city, I don't know what will happen. Just remember to be truthful, and don't betray any of the things I told you were secret unless the King or I are present and allow it. If the duke sent messages ahead of us, I may be arrested when we enter the gates. It will be temporary though, as the King will make a thorough investigation."

"Do you really think you'll be arrested?"

"Only if the duke sent messengers. And if he did, you're most likely implicated by the same lies. The troll will certainly be jailed either way. We'll cause quite a commotion, riding into the city with an ice troll. Be brave, and trust the King to make sure it all works out in the end."

When we finally reached the city's gate, the Captain beat the great wooden doors with the pommel of his sword. Guards looked down from the wall and whispered excitedly. The doors were opened only wide enough for one horse, and we rode in single file. I was the last to pass through, and stopped short as soon as I entered. The doors were closed behind me, and I heard the *clang* of iron as they were bolted shut. A half-ring of soldiers faced us, each shouldering a crossbow and ready to fire. I swallowed hard as the troll woke and started to howl.

Part V

5.0 The Trial

The Captain held his hand up and spoke loudly, "We are three witnesses with an urgent message for the King. Please send a runner to His Majesty."

"Yes sir," replied one of the guards, though he didn't move. "Now please separate yourselves from the troll."

The Captain dismounted and clicked his tongue to Rider. The Captain's horse followed me as I rode through the semicircle of crossbowmen. I sighed with relief. They were aiming only at the troll. Why hadn't the Captain come out of the ring? I dismounted and tried to get back to the Captain, but was stopped immediately by a soldier.

"*What are you trying to do?*" he asked accusingly.

I had no answer for him, since the Captain could clearly take care of the troll himself. I retreated, and climbed onto Yashel's back for a better view.

"I'm going to remove the troll from his donkey, and bind him for safe transport," the Captain said aloud. I heard him continue more quietly, "Troll, don't make any sudden movements, and I promise you'll live to be questioned by the King. Beyond this, your destiny is out of my hands, just as I've explained to you."

When the Captain brought him down from the donkey's back, he was nearly limp. The Captain bound him the same way as when we'd led him before, and handed one of the rope ends to a surprised solder.

"Lead us to a cell under the castle with no windows," he commanded. "This prisoner is frail and will need a cool place, if he is to live."

They made their way into Engdynlor on foot. I tried to follow, but was shoved aside by a crossbowman. I decided to take the animals to the stables and figure out what I should do next. The Captain had warned me we might be separated, but nothing he'd said prepared me for the commotion our entrance caused.

I told the stable master the horses and donkeys had been through a hard ride, and needed food and water. He shook his head in disapproval when he saw them.

"Did you try to ride them to death? Where's the Captain?"

"He has urgent business with the King," I said, and left it at that. I was too exhausted to be polite. The stable master raised an eyebrow, but said nothing else.

After the stables, I went straight to the barracks to find David. His barrack was completely empty. With nothing else to do, I decided to bathe and change. I badly wanted to see David, but I realized it was for the better I hadn't found him. I didn't know exactly what I needed to keep secret.

Certainly I couldn't mention the Honor Knights, but what about the duke? If the King wouldn't hear accusations against him without three witnesses, it was surely forbidden to accuse him in private as well. What about the troll? His involvement might be a state secret. David would want to know why we brought him. He'd have countless questions I couldn't answer. It would be painful to hold back so much; I was never good at keeping secrets from him.

By the time I'd washed and returned to my bed, there was a messenger waiting for me.

"The Captain sends for you. You must come at once."

"I'm ready," I responded quickly. "Lead the way."

The messenger turned and *ran*. I lost my breath keeping up with him. Once in the palace, I was led to the same room where I'd last seen the King, before our journey. There were half a dozen armed soldiers at the door. They lined up along both sides of the door, while the messenger remained with them.

When I walked into the room, my eyes were ill-adjusted to its dim lighting. The Captain called to me and told me to sit beside him. He sat in the middle of a short row of chairs with the troll at his side, tied to his own chair, his canteen still in hand. The troll writhed in his ropes as I sat at the other side of the Captain, furthest from the troll.

Then I saw the King. He was sitting on an ornately carved chair with a high back. There was an older man standing behind him, dressed in shiny armor, though to me it seemed only decorative. The cloth of his pants looked frail but expensive, perhaps silk or velvet. The old man spoke in a grave voice.

"These proceedings have now begun. I will swear in each of you in a moment. The three of you are about to bring accusation against a member of the Royal Family of Wards. This is not a trivial action on your parts. If your testimonies are judged false, you may receive death as the penalty. You may only speak of events you have witnessed firsthand. You may not offer interpretations or assumptions. Do you understand these laws as I've explained them?"

The Captain answered boldly, "Yes sir, I do."

I answered likewise, though my worries of the death penalty were surely apparent in my voice. When Sphotch did not answer, the Captain spoke up.

"Sir, the Lyssiltik, named Sphotch, is a reluctant witness, and I request he be so treated."

"Conceded. Be reminded, his testimony may be deemed invalid due to his criminal history," the older man added. The Captain nodded but remained silent. The man in armor continued. "Now then, have any of you let your accusation be known to another?"

The Captain spoke first again.

"I have discussed my accusation with my armor bearer, only after hearing his testimony of treasonous words spoken by the duke. I have not discussed it with anyone else."

I added, "I told the Captain what I heard the duke say, and I told him the duke's guards were after us. I didn't talk to anyone else about it."

The Captain added, "I can vouch for the troll thus far: I placed him in the pit Abaddon after we captured him at the Winter Palace. Since I pulled him from the pit yesterday, he has been in my presence and has spoken to no one but my armor bearer and me. We sought him at the pit as a third witness."

There was a pause as the man who stood spoke quietly with the King. He turned back to us and spoke aloud.

"Normally, you would be questioned separately. Since you have admitted to speaking to your armor bearer about your accusation, you may be questioned together. Since the troll—*Sphotch*—is a reluctant witness, you may be present while he is questioned, but he will not hear either of your testimonies. Let me remind you Captain, this does not look well for your case so far. Your actions fit many of the characteristics of *conspiracy*."

I had no idea there would be so many rules to follow. I chewed my lip nervously. The Captain sounded so deliberate in everything he said, it scared me. It sounded as if the man questioning us already doubted us. I hoped the King would be thorough, and find we were telling the truth.

"Your armor bearer will be questioned first," continued the older man. "Before this," he said, turning to me, "please state your name, each of you."

"I am Andrew Williams, Captain of the Royal Guard."

"I am Mark Adams, armor bearer to the Captain of the Royal Guard."

"Ssphotchhh...*Prince* of the trolls," hissed the ice troll, and took a drink from his canteen. His hateful manner nearly made me flinch.

The King shifted in his seat, and spoke in rumbling tones, "Thank you, Nathan. Please have the troll removed." The older man bowed to the King and left the room for a moment. Two guards came and carried the troll, still bound in his chair, out of the room. Nathan, the older man, sat at a miniature desk behind the King, and began to write on large sheets of paper.

"Now Mark, tell me what you heard, and when and where you heard it," said the King.

"The duke was talking to his soldiers in his courtyard...four nights ago, after my trip to the mineral pools. A soldier told him—"

"Did he know you were there?" interrupted the King.

"No, Sire. It was dark and I was waiting to politely interrupt their conversation. I approached from the dark end of the courtyard. I wasn't *trying* to eavesdrop..." I paused to remember exactly what I'd heard. I was glad the Captain had warned me to commit it to memory.

"Go on, then."

"Well," I continued, "the duke had been talking angrily, but I wasn't close enough to hear what he said. The first thing I heard clearly, was one of the soldiers telling the duke their plans weren't ruined yet. He said, 'They will return' and 'We'll take care of it.'"

"Sounds circumstantial. What else was said by the soldier?" asked the King.

"He said the Captain's horse was still in the stable, and no horses were missing. He said, 'They can't cross the desert on foot.'"

"Hmmmm," the King half-growled. "How did the duke reply?"

"First, he asked about the *other horses*, the ones belonging to their guests outside the city. It sounded odd to me, but I now think he was talking about the—"

"Please," interrupted the King again, "No opinions. You may only report facts in your testimony."

"Yes, Sire." I paused for a moment to think about my next words. I noticed Nathan had stopped writing. "The soldier said all the horses were accounted for. Then he told the duke not to worry, and he promised the duke '*the Captain and his guest*' wouldn't make it through the night alive."

"Did he use the exact words, 'the Captain and his guest'?"

"Yes, Sire."

"And what did the duke say?"

"He warned the soldier to make sure we *didn't*, and told him his life depended on it. The soldier's life, that is." The King's face turned grave when I added, "Then the duke said, 'If the usurper heard of my plans, we're done for.' He said *the usurper* would pay for what he stole, and for casting him into the desert. He sounded *very* angry when he said it."

"Are those the words he used *exactly*?" asked the King.

"I remember the exact words: 'If the usurper finds out my plans, we're done for'. I didn't know what 'usurper' meant yet. I thought he said 'If you *serper* finds out…' but it didn't make any sense that way."

"And how did you learn what usurper means?"

"The Captain told me, after he heard the duke's plot." The King turned to the Captain.

"Andrew, did you coach Mark in his testimony? Was he fed any words as you tried to discover what he heard?"

"I was careful, Sire. I used the outline for questioning taught to me…" he paused to throw me a sidelong glance, "*in my training*." The King nodded and turned his attention back to me.

"Was there anything else relevant to your accusation, Mark?"

"Yes—the horse with the scar. We saw a lot of trolls in the dunes on our way to TerkEtmek. The one who acted like their leader, rode a horse with a jagged scar on its…uh…rump. It was very large. I saw the same horse in the duke's stables the night I heard the soldiers talking."

"And did they know you were there? What did they say?"

"They didn't know I was there, Sire. I hid behind Yashel, in her stall. They were talking about taking the Captain's horse—they said, 'now that he's gone'. One soldier said the duke might have plans for the horse, but the other said he didn't because she was too old. Then one said something like, 'what if the Captain hears you?' and the other said Nigel should have already *met up* with the Captain and *finished him*."

The Captain sat straight up, clearly alarmed, but said nothing. The King's eyes widened, and for a moment he looked as if he'd been stabbed in the back.

"Who?" asked the King. "What name did he use?"

"Nigel, Sire. He said, '*Nigel*.'" The King's eyes questioned the Captain.

"Andrew, have you ever spoken this name in front of Mark?"

"I have not, Sire. I hadn't heard him say it until now. May I?" the Captain asked as he turned to me.

"Of course," replied the King.

"Mark, why didn't you mention this name before?"

"Didn't I? I don't know, I guess I didn't think about it. I wasn't thinking so clearly after hiding in the stable. If I'd thought hard enough on what they said, I never would have gone to see the duke. After all—they implied he knew about the plot." I remembered what the King said about only the facts. "I mean…they mentioned the duke didn't have plans for your horse." The King exchanged glances with the Captain before he spoke again.

"If there is nothing else, Mark, I will hear the Captain's accusation now." I nodded, unsure if I was meant to say anything in reply.

"When did you first suspect the duke of such a plot?" The King asked the Captain.

"Sire, to be honest, I had not trusted him since the merchant disputes began and the timber trade irregularities appeared."

"What? Why didn't you mention this, Andrew?" asked the King, obviously surprised.

"I had no accusations to bring, Sire. I spoke of my suspicions to no one."

A pause, then the King spoke, "I understand. When did your suspicions grow?"

"The troll caravan in the dunes disturbed me. After seeing how numerous and heavily armed they were, I didn't see how traders could possibly make routine trips through the dunes without entering a pact with them. Considering how close the merchants are with the duke, my suspicions of him grew. I had no suspicion of a plot against my life, however, until I was attacked in the duke's barracks. I found

Mark, and we left the city under the cover of darkness. When Mark told me what he heard from the duke, I sent him into the desert to wait for me, while I returned to speak with the duke directly. I hoped he suspected me of some wrong-doing and had illegally ordered me killed. It would have been far better than the plan I heard from him."

The Captain told the same story he'd told me in the desert: how he'd tricked the duke into thinking he was trapped, how the duke explained the plot to him, and how he escaped through the window and left the city with our donkeys. He explained how we found the ice troll and how he swore loyalty to the King, even though he was probably lying. He brought up the troll's need for water and ice, and lastly, he mentioned his own suspicions of the troll's true plans for the kingdom, and how Sphotch had seemed to confirm them. The King gave the Captain room to speak of more than the bare facts, perhaps because he valued his opinions.

The King asked the Captain about the assassin who'd tried to kill him. The Captain said he was certain he was dead, though he wasn't able to identify him. The King nodded sadly. I made a point to later find out who Nigel was; he seemed significant to them both.

Finally the King sent me to call for the troll, and to ask for a large block of ice from the icehouse to be brought for the troll to sit on. When I left the room and conveyed all this, the troll sighed and the soldiers looked suspicious. I added the King had ordered for the ice specifically, and they nodded.

The troll was brought in, and soon afterward the ice arrived. It was placed between the Captain and me. When the troll sat, the Captain and I each held a length of the rope still hanging from the troll's neck. He actually smiled to touch the slippery ice. The King spoke to him.

"Sphotch...I know of your role in the plot to murder me and my family. I know of the duke's plan to usurp the throne and rule the kingdom by force. And I know of your own plot to take the kingdom from him. It would seem you are out of friends."

Any happiness the ice brought the troll left him. He seemed to quake, and I guessed it wasn't from the cold block under him.

"I was happy to hear you've sworn your allegiance to me and my kingdom. Even so, your crimes are punishable by death. While this sentence isn't completely ruled out, I see another path for you, and I hope you'll choose it. I want you to learn what we have to teach about loyalty, and serving our kingdom. I hope you will help me bridge the gap between trolls and humans. I want our peoples to live in peace."

The troll eyed him coolly. He seemed to want to trust the King, but I don't think he was capable of it.

"To live in peace and *be ruled* by humans, you mean," Sphotch replied scornfully.

"*Not* ruled by humans. There are many people groups in my kingdom who rule themselves. As long as they are loyal to me, and extend our most sacred freedoms to all others, I don't interfere," replied the King.

"Loyal to you? What's the difference—to be ruled by one human, or ruled by many?"

"Sphotch, even I am not free to do what I want," said the King. "I'm bound by what's best for the kingdom. So in a way, *I* am ruled by many humans. I do not mind, because I see the good in it. If you saw how much you could do to help your people, I'm sure you would want to do the same. Before you get too worried about a human somewhere, to whom your people would have to answer, I will ask you this; is there a troll alive who could rule over all humans, without hating and exploiting them?"

The troll looked genuinely surprised at the King's question, though his expression quickly returned to scorn. He paused for a moment before answering. "What do you want of me?" He looked utterly defeated.

"I can see you are not ready yet to make this decision. For now, I need to know you're *capable* of honesty, and whether or not you're willing to cooperate. I want to hear the duke's plot in *your* words."

The troll spoke for a long time. The King looked somehow ancient as the duke's crimes were listed before us. The dates and places Sphotch named, matched the plot as far as we knew it. He confirmed what we knew and suspected, and even added a little the Captain hadn't yet guessed. He told details of the troll army in the desert, and the troll who led the army, whom they called the *Troll King*. He told of so many crimes the duke had committed, I began to wonder how the King had ever trusted him. Perhaps he hadn't. The duke hated the King from birth it seemed, impatiently biding his time, and always searching for a chance to steal the throne.

Even though Sphotch's story seemed true, the King was doubtful. It would be a long while before we could be certain.

When our testimonies were complete, the King ordered for the troll to be secured in the palace basement. He ordered plenty of ice to be brought to him, and whatever food he asked for. It shouldn't have surprised me when I later learned ice trolls don't cook anything they eat—not even meat. In fact, there's little else they eat beside meat, with few plants as high above the snowline as they live.

After the troll left, the King dismissed the older man taking notes. When the door was closed again, the King hung his head low and grumbled.

"What is left to do, Andrew? Not only a Ward duke has turned, but one of the *Honor Knights*? We may be entering a full scale war with the trolls. It's a dark hour for the kingdom."

So Nigel was *an Honor Knight,* I thought to myself. At least one piece of the puzzle fit. I wondered if the older man, Nathan was also a knight. I couldn't decide whether the King asking him to leave was proof he *wasn't* a knight, or proof he *was*.

"I can only think of one reference in our records sounding quite so desperate," the Captain said in a pained voice, framing his words as a question.

"Yes, it's a possibility we can't ignore." The King spoke softly. Then, as if to change the subject, he turned to me and raised his voice.

"Mark, I understand you have accepted the offer of apprenticeship within our order, the Honor Knights." I gave a surprised look, wondering what gesture or guarded comment the Captain might have used to signal my acceptance while Sphotch had been present.

"Yes, Sire," I said finally, in as serious a tone as I could muster, "I have."

"I'm sorry this news wasn't conveyed in happier circumstances. There will be time for us to celebrate your apprenticeship, I trust, in the future. For now, allow me to congratulate you; it is a great honor to be invited into our order. I'm afraid no one else will offer you congratulations, as no one else will know until such a time comes as you may become a full knight."

The King looked happy and yet weary at the same time. There was pride in his face too, though tempered by the news of the duke.

"Now please, go and rest. The Captain and I will be very busy after this news, but we will send for you soon. I don't need to remind you not to discuss this plot with your brother, or anyone else."

"No, Sire. But...if I may ask...what *can* I speak of? Is Sphotch a secret too?" The King looked at the Captain, and the Captain answered.

"No. Too many saw him when we entered the city walls. Half the palace will hear of him today, if they haven't already. If your brother asks, tell him only how I brought the troll back to stand in trial before the King, and you were along for the ride. This much is true. You can speak of our trip, and of the pools, and your healing. You can mention the duke, but don't mention any wrong-doing on his part, or any suspicions of him. You can mention the small troops of trolls we saw in the desert, but not the armed caravan, or the desert barracks. Don't speak of our journey at all, with people you don't know well."

"Then you believe us, Sire?" I asked. The fear of a death sentence still hung over my head.

"Most assuredly, I do," answered the King. "But you raise a good point. Officially, your testimonies are sealed under consideration until I launch an independent investigation, and the duke has a chance to defend himself. Until the duke refuses to appear before me, as I'm sure he'll do, you must remain in the greater palace grounds. If your brother or someone else you know well asks about this, tell them you're under quarantine after being healed of such a nasty wound." The King saw my hesitant expression, and explained further. "Yes, I know; these statements are true, but they are only a small portion of the truth. You are a very honest young man, and this goes against what you feel is right. If this were not so, you would not have been considered for apprenticeship. However, as an Honor Knight, or even as an apprentice, you are operating as an agent of this government. It is not wrong for a government to conceal information concerning war or the security of its people, even if such concealment involves deceit. The difference between this deceit and lying is this; any words you may speak in deceit are known by your mentor, and are for the purpose of protecting state secrets. They are never spoken for any personal motives of the agent telling them. Does this make sense to you?"

I understood what he had said, even if I didn't yet know if I agreed with it. I nodded slowly. My world was growing more complex. I knew I would have to be careful—*painfully* careful—about everything I said from then on.

As if the Captain read my mind, he added, "You will learn to talk slower, to consider what you say before you speak. This isn't a bad thing, it's something we should all do—whether we're guarding secrets or not."

"And now Mark," the King added, "the Captain and I have a lot of planning to do. Please use the next day or so to rest and spend some time with your brother if you like. Thank you for your service to the kingdom so far. We are better off for having you with us."

I thanked the King and quietly left. On the way to the barracks, I realized how tired I was. It was nearly noon, but I thought of nothing but sleep as I plodded toward my cot.

When I entered the barracks, it was too dark to see. Before my eyes could adjust, a dark shape rushed at me. I reached for my sword, but it wasn't there. Just before we collided, I rolled to the ground to dodge my attacker. In doing so, I tripped my brother, and he fell heavily on top of me.

"What are you trying to do to me?" he asked, surprised, but also agitated. He was excited to see me, but I could barely lift my head. Sleep would have to wait a little longer.

5.1 Rest and Preparations

David kept me awake for some time, asking every conceivable question about the trip, my scar, and the rumors he'd heard of the ice troll. What seemed so far away in my memory was only days ago. Afraid I'd blurt out something I swore to keep secret, I told him as little as I could manage. It wasn't hard; I actually fell asleep several times while talking. After the third time, David gave up and left me to rest. I slept the rest of the day and through the night. He woke me impatiently the following morning, at dawn.

"Hey, you're awake," he said, in mock surprise.

"Only because you've been kicking my cot."

"Well, it's time you woke up. Yesterday you made no sense at *all*. You only mumbled and fell asleep every time I asked you something important."

At least I hadn't told him something I shouldn't have. He nudged me with his elbow, making sure I stayed awake.

"So your scar's healed, I see. What happened? How do you feel?"

"Completely back to normal. Does my voice sound different to you?" I began to wonder if I was fully awake or not. My head was in a fog. I told him as much as I could of the long trip. When I told him specifically what had healed me, I wondered if he believed a word of it. It sounded ridiculous even as I explained it.

"What about the troll?" he asked, "I thought the Captain told you he was melting."

"At the time, I thought he *did*—but when I think about it, I was the one who said he was melting, right after I came to." David only looked more confused. "I'd fainted. When I woke, I told him the ice troll was melting. The Captain looked shocked, as if I'd guessed something important—maybe he was only shocked I was awake. As it turns out, the troll was losing weight fast enough to kill him. The trail of mud behind his cart was vomit and…from being sick all the time." I shuddered.

"Well *I* never believed he was melting," David declared.

"*Sure* you did," I teased. "Anyway, now he looks even worse—like a skeleton with skin stretched over him. He had to drink constantly to stay alive, even in the cold pit."

"Well, I promised to bring you to the Princess as soon as you woke. Hurry up and get changed."

Not wanting to re-tell more of my story than I had to, I got ready as fast as I could. I missed the Princess, but I especially wanted to see Lady Sally. After the past week I felt I understood her better, and held a new respect for her.

On our way, I asked David how his training was going.

"Fine. I started an intensive course in scouting. It's kind of like spying on other armies. It's a one-person course, just me and an officer in the army—he's not part of the Royal Guard. I have to leave the palace grounds every day to train with him. It's pretty tough training, but I like it. I've done so well, he's agreed to be my mentor. It means I had to agree to be his protege and work for him until we find a way home, and he agreed to teach me everything he knows about scouting." I eyed David suspiciously. A *scout protege?*

"What's the officer's name?" I asked.

"Oh, you've met him. He's the same lieutenant who gave us work to do, when we first arrived in Engdynlor. His name is James, but he's just *the Lieutenant* to me…Lieutenant Underhill to be official."

It seemed odd the both of us would be so busy—and neither of us working on a way home. I assumed the King had men working on it, and our jobs as proteges were a way of earning our keep. David interrupted my thoughts.

"What about you? Do you know what you'll be busy with, now that you're well?"

"Oh—I forgot to tell you. The Captain hired me as his armor bearer. I'm supposed to help him with some of his duties, and even learn stuff about the Royal Guard. I guess it will keep me busy while you're being mentored with the scouts."

"Why do you think the King is giving us so much training?" David asked.

How could I explain? I couldn't tell him *the Captain hopes to make me a knight.*

"I really couldn't say. What do *you* think?" I asked back.

"I asked the lieutenant training me, but he said he was only asked to train me, and wasn't told why. I'm afraid the King might expect us to serve in his army at some point. I begged the Princess to help me see the King right away, and somehow, she—"

"*It's not allowed*," I protested.

"I know. I asked her when Lady Sally left the room, the day you left. Schelli could tell I was worried about you, and she agreed to try. A page called me into court two days later. I thought I was *being arrested* for getting the Princess to ask for an audience—but court is just what they call the King's throne room, kind of like his office. Anyway, it was quite a meeting. He's a very...*unique* person." I remembered the first impression the King left on me, but I didn't interrupt my brother's account.

"He knows our story, how we got here, and how badly we want to get home. Most importantly, he *believes us*. I was worried he'd think we're crazy. His scholars and historians are looking for a way home, but he said it would take some time—maybe even *months*.

"He said we might as well learn something about his kingdom while we waited. If I refused, it would have been an insult—like saying nothing in his kingdom is worth learning. He said it might prove impossible for us to go home, but he was almost certain this isn't the case. Still, if it *is*, he'd like us to train and serve in his kingdom as—I don't know—soldiers or advisors or *something*. I guess we impressed him, or he feels like he owes us for freeing the Princess."

By then we'd reached the front entrance to Engdynlor, and we asked to see the Princess. The guards at the gate allowed us to pass, and a soldier led us to her quarters. The lady attendant outside her door put down a large scroll she'd been writing in, then opened the door slightly and poked her head through the doorway. She announced us formally and let us in. Apparently we were interrupting Schelli's history lecture, delivered by Lady Sally.

As soon as we entered, the Princess rushed over and hugged me. Sally smiled and greeted us at a more stately pace. She invited us to sit on a group of low sofas near the back of the room, and offered us bowls of fresh fruit and sweet rolls. I was a little embarrassed when I realized we'd nearly emptied the bowls before we'd said anything but polite greetings. Lady Sally would have to be content with slow progress on our manners.

They were both excited to see me completely healed. I had to repeat the story of the ice troll and the mud baths. When my tale was over, the Princess congratulated me on the upcoming banquet, and asked what we would wear. I gave her only a blank expression in return.

"You mean David didn't tell you yet?" she asked, kicking him lightly on the shin, and thus earning a scowl from Lady Sally. "There's a banquet tonight in the Captain's honor…for his recapturing the Winter Palace from the ice troll. You and David are listed as honored guests for rescuing me, and now, I suppose, for your help in re-capturing the troll. You'll both sit with us at the table of honor."

Part of me wondered if it wasn't a public way for the King to congratulate me on my apprenticeship, or for uncovering the plot against him, but it was probably wishful thinking.

"It's a great honor," Sally added. "You may be the youngest guests to ever receive such recognition."

"But I didn't really do much—I just did what the Captain asked."

"Trust me," said Schelli, "that's *plenty*. If everyone did what the Captain asked of them, there wouldn't be a problem left in the kingdom. Let's not forget how hard it must have been to climb into the mine pit to find the troll, after he attacked you." I was uncomfortable at hearing her say so. It *had been* difficult, but David didn't need to hear me praised any more. When no one spoke, he broke the awkward pause to tease Sally.

"How *was* the pit?" he asked me, "Did you find any *gold?*"

Sally first looked shocked, but changed her expression to a mock frown when she realized David was joking.

"Still worried about all the wasted gold, are you?" she asked.

"We saw no gold, I promise," I continued, jabbing my brother with my elbow. "We used ropes to get in and out. The Captain had to drag the troll up the side of the cliff. He's so pathetic now, too scrawny to do anyone harm. I feel sorry for him."

At hearing this, Sally's expression changed again. This time she seemed deeply concerned, and her eyes held the spark of a shared secret.

"Then you've forgiven him for the *wound* he gave you?" she asked.

I sighed. The memory of my third dunk in the mud pool flooded over me, and it nearly overwhelmed me. My hand tingled with a ghost of the sensation my fingers felt as they scraped over my neck, searching in vain for the lump of scar tissue.

"Yes," I replied, my words struggling out of my mouth, "I decided I'd held onto that pain long enough." She sent me another knowing look and smiled. David and the Princess didn't seem to notice these few words, though they conveyed volumes to me.

I told them about our trip across the desert, the Great Dunes, and the two small groups of trolls we fought.

"They attacked you?" asked David. "What did you *do?*"

Looking at the Princess, I wished I hadn't brought it up. Her face was suddenly overcome with grief. *Why is this so hard for her to hear?* I wondered.

"Well," I replied, hoping David would notice my reluctance and drop the matter, "we fought back..."

"Did they hurt you? Did they run off? Did you kill any of them?" he asked, suddenly leaning toward me, as if I might only whisper my reply. I opened my mouth to answer, but my eyes were fixed on the Princess.

"The Captain was struck in the shoulder and hurt pretty badly by the second group of trolls. I got some bruises, but nothing worse. The Captain saved my life. When two mounted trolls rode toward me to strike me down, he jumped off his horse to draw them away from me."

David didn't relent. "Did you kill any of them? Did you strike *them* down?"

"Perhaps you can tell us about your struggle another time," Lady Sally interrupted, also eyeing the Princess. "I imagine it isn't pleasant for you to talk about *just yet.*"

David was disappointed, but sensing something amiss, he finally ended his interrogation. The Princess's eyes were on the floor, avoiding me. "Are you all right?" I asked quietly, leaning toward her. When she didn't reply at first I added, "Like you said, doing everything the Captain asks isn't easy." She looked up again and tried to smile a little. Her eyes were watery, but she held back her tears. Already, I felt guilty for blaming the Captain.

"I'm fine, thank you," she replied. "My mind wandered for a moment." I returned my gaze to David and Lady Sally, and quickly changed the subject.

"We rode all night to reach the duke's mansion. I was very sick, and barely awake. I think the Captain's shoulder was injured worse than he let on. When I woke a day and a half later, I was much better, and the Captain's shoulder was better too." I turned and asked Sally, "Did the duke do this? Does he have some special medicine, or a private doctor?"

"Not quite," she replied. "The Royal families are trained in ways to make the sick well. But from what I've heard, it wasn't enough to heal your wound—only enough to let you travel to find your own healing."

I finished the tale, and we began to talk of Tume Belor: how wonderfully unique it was, and how we wished we could visit it together once again. I didn't mention it had been poisoned. Perhaps by then, the spring had already been washed clean.

Soon it was time to prepare for the banquet.

"You only have a few hours before it begins," Lady Sally explained. "You'll need to wash up and see the royal tailor. He will fit you with the proper attire."

She had an attendant show us to a washroom where I had my first hot shower in a long time. We were brought to another room where a tailor had us put on fancy clothes and made adjustments to them. He was a small, thin man who seemed constantly worried. I didn't like the way our new clothes looked, but we weren't given any choice in the matter.

The clothes were cut from a soft felt or velvet, and were very light. I thought they were too tight in some places and too loose in others, but the tailor assured me they were approaching a proper fit.

He measured and re-measured us, and had us change many times into borrowed robes while he made endless adjustments. He worked quickly, but as far as I could tell, seemed to change nothing at all. Not only did the clothes seem to fit badly when he was done, they seemed even worse than when he'd started. He seemed to be considering whether he should have us change once again when a messenger came to warn us the banquet was soon starting. I found the messenger's concept of *soon* was very different from my own.

"*All right then*," cried the tailor finally, "Back into your robes and sit down while I have some food brought to you."

"Food?" I asked.

"Before a *banquet*?" David added.

"Of course—you'll be at the *table of honor*. People will be watching you the entire evening. There are speeches to be made, and awards to be given. Etiquette precludes you from eating during any of them. Do you want to sit there smelling fine food while you're *hungry*?"

"You mean we can't even *eat*?" I asked incredulously. "Do you have any idea what I've had to eat for the past week?"

"Oh my dear," shrieked the tailor. "You've never *been* to a banquet before? Well…don't worry. We'll go over the proper etiquette right now, while you eat. What would you like?"

"What do you have?" asked David.

"Anything. The royal chefs can make whatever you want."

"I'll have some beef stew, some rolls and butter, and a *lot* of cold milk," I said. I remembered to ask for it *cold,* ever since I was served milk still warm from the cow.

"I'll have some steak on a sandwich, and some vegetable soup," added David, "with *even more* cold milk."

"How much milk should I have brought to you?" the tailor asked my brother.

"More."

"More than *what?*" the tailor asked, rising to a new level of fretfulness.

"More," David said with a hint of a smile, "than they bring for Mark." I bit my tongue to stifle a chuckle.

The tailor threw his hands up in surrender and nodded to his assistant, who then left to fetch our food. While we waited, he told us what to expect at a royal banquet. The table of honor is set at the front of a large dining hall, while the tables of distinguished guests face the table of honor. There would be speeches, awards and promotions— none of which sounded interesting to me. We would be served several courses of food, and eventually see some form of entertainment. Then the other tables would be removed and the guests would mingle. We would remain at the table of honor the entire banquet, and be introduced to many people.

When our food finally arrived, we ate it greedily. The tailor looked ill as he watched us. He told us to stop before we were full, or we wouldn't fit into our new clothes. It would be best, he warned, if we ate a little of everything served at the banquet, but not much of any one thing, "…or they'll think you're barbarians for certain." We did our best not to snicker. "Just watch the others at your table," he droned on, "and *try* to do the same. Take very small bites, and chew them slowly. Sit up straight, and never lean forward to meet your food. Remember this, and you'll do fine." His words were more hopeful than reassuring.

He took our food away and left just long enough for us to change clothes one last time. Then he rushed us down hallways and a long staircase, to the Grand Banquet Hall.

While we passed through one stone hallway with a low roof he told us, "We're actually no longer inside Engdynlor, but crossing to another building nearby."

"You mean we're underground?" David asked.

"Yes, though not by much."

I wondered how many passages the palace held, and how many of them were secret. Maybe I would find out one day as a knight. For some reason, the thought turned my mind toward home. *Our parents must think we ran away*, I thought for the thousandth time.

We climbed up a flight of stairs and came to a wide set of open doors leading to the banquet hall. We were led by soldiers in fancy clothes to the table of honor. It reached from one side of the room to the other, and was beginning to fill with honored guests. When I saw how many people would be sharing our table, I felt a little relieved. The entire room's eyes wouldn't be fixed on us after all.

We took our seats near the middle of the table, in front of tiny plaques with our names on them. Many people were milling around, engaged in quiet conversation. Our long table was still half empty. Soon Sally came in and sat to our left, toward the center of the long table. David asked where the Princess was, and she told us she would enter with the King from the back of the room, when it was time for the banquet to begin.

"The Royal Family is always *announced*," she added.

She told us a little more about the banquet. Apparently, it would last even longer than the tailor led us to expect. I noticed the Captain was sitting just a few seats away, closer to the high-backed chairs reserved for the King and Queen. He smiled and nodded toward me when I caught his eye. He was wearing a fancy breastplate of armor, polished to a shine. I noticed his clothes were different. They were a lighter material then what he usually wore, perhaps the same velvety material I was also wearing.

When everyone was seated, a man in bright clothes appeared from a small door behind the table of honor. A soldier in a fancy uniform walked beside him and blew a long bugle. All stood as the brightly-clothed man announced in a loud voice the Princess's full name and title. It seemed she had enough names for an entire family; I lost count at seven. She walked in wearing a fancy dress, far too puffy to be comfortable.

After Schelli found her seat, the Queen was announced and stepped in wearing a dress cut similar to the Princess's. She paused just in front of the announcer. The King was announced last, and he stepped in while the bugler played another little tune. The King took the Queen's arm, and they sat together. Finally, the rest at the table of honor sat, and then the other tables before us. I'd never seen such a ceremony made of sitting.

The King thanked the entire crowd for coming, and told them how glad he was to hold such a celebration. He dedicated the evening to the Princess, and spoke of his happiness to have her safely returned to him. He thanked the Captain for bringing her home, then turned to David and me, and thanked us for setting her free. My face turned red and I saw Schelli smiling broadly, looking our way. The King ended by inviting the crowd to enjoy the evening.

An attendant standing behind the King rang a little bell, and servers began to pour out from the doors along the right side of the room. They pushed carts filled with tiny pieces of food. Soon, nearly every table was set, but no one ate. I glanced from table to table and decided they were all waiting for the last table to be served. Finally, when the last cart wheeled out from the banquet hall, people began eating. It smelled delicious.

The plates were on little pedestals set between each person. Every second plate contained the same food. I watched as people sampled the foods to their right and left, and my brother and I did likewise. The dish on my right was some sort of pastry with meat inside. On my left, was a plate of tiny pies, each filled with sweet-pickled fruit.

Servers brought out course after course of fine foods. I wished I hadn't eaten so much in the tailor's room. I was careful to eat slowly, and even ate some of the few dishes I didn't like. One soup smelled like old cheese; I tried one sip and left it alone.

Finally the last course had been served: fresh berries in sweet syrup, piled over tiny cakes. When the plates were cleared, the man with the bugle played a half-dozen quick notes, and everyone stood. The King stood last, when an attendant brought a sort of half-podium and set it on the table before him. He asked everyone to sit down again and announced he would recognize those who performed notable acts of service to the kingdom.

He called on many different people. Some were from the crowd in front of us, while others were seated at the long table we shared with the Royal Family. The King called out their *act of notable service* while they walked to his podium and shook hands, and an attendant handed each person a gift. The first people to be called were apparently receiving promotions in the King's Court. Their notable act was simply "loyal and diligent service in the King's Court". Mostly they were given wall hangings and a pin, which I assumed showed their rank.

Then a captain of one of the few Navy ships was called forward and honored for rescuing a sailor who fell overboard during an unexpected storm. The King told a brief story, describing the ferocity of the storm and the captain's small chance of survival. The King rewarded his bravery with a decorative golden compass. It looked very heavy, and I wondered if it was pure gold.

I sat up at hearing the next name; it was my brother's turn to be recognized. As he walked toward the King, the King announced he was being rewarded for a daring rescue of the Princess and for aiding in setting free the Captain. The King went on about how dangerous the rescue was, and how very grateful he was to have his daughter returned safely to him. The crowd had clapped for the earlier awards, but they stood and cheered for David. He received a collapsible telescope in a gilded, wooden box set with jewels, a small dagger in a gilded scabbard, and what looked like a glass plaque. When he returned to his seat the King called for me. I knew it was coming, but when I heard my name called, suddenly I was walking through water, and my head was full of fog. I heard the King's words as if from a great distance.

"For the daring rescue of my daughter, the Princess, Mark and his brother faced a small army of trolls. Through their bravery and wit they were able to free the Princess and also the Captain of the Guard. More recently, his assistance to the Captain of the Guard helped secure and deliver into custody the criminal responsible for her kidnapping. Mark, you have my eternal gratitude for these and *other* distinguished acts performed in your service to our great kingdom."

The crowd stood and cheered again. I saw their faces as I walked around the long table. Their expressions were warm and friendly, as if it were their own son receiving the award. *Why do they look at me like this?* I barely had time to wonder.

The King enveloped my hand in his own and smiled at me warmly. He whispered another thank you to me, but I was too flustered to respond. I nodded quickly, and then the attendant was handing me gifts. I received a decorated sword in a gilded scabbard, a matching dagger, and an antique medal hanging on a ribbon loop I would later learn was awarded long ago to a soldier, for his bravery. I held them clumsily for a moment, then the medal slid out of my hand. I caught it with my left hand, and its ribbon loop slid down to my elbow. Not knowing what else to do, I turned back to the King, and with the medal still hanging around my arm at the elbow, I held the sword and dagger out toward him at arm's length and bowed low, as if to say thank you. The crowd cheered even louder for a moment, leaving me wondering if I'd imagined it. I would have simply said *thank you* if my mouth had been working at the time.

When I sat down, David asked, "What was *that* all about? Why'd they cheer for you a second time?" I only shrugged. As I did, the Captain was already being called.

"Andrew Williams, Captain of the Royal Guard and Chief Protector of the King," the King said warmly.

The Captain marched quickly around the table to stand in front of the King as his notable service was read.

"...recapturing the Winter Palace from a troll rebellion and delivering the Princess safely to her home, and for re-capturing the ice troll and delivering him into custody. For these and *other* distinguished acts, I am eternally grateful..."

The Captain approached the King and knelt in front of him. The King reached around the podium and leaned over the banquet table to take the Captain's hand, signaling him to stand, then shook it vigorously. The King whispered a moment to the Captain, who smiled and nodded. The attendant handed the Captain a heavy scroll in a finely decorated metal case. I learned later it was a very old copy of an ancient scroll chronicling the kingdom's distant past.

When the Captain returned to his seat, the King asked the crowd to stand while the tables were cleared for entertainment. The entire crowd stood but for those at the table of honor. The other tables were quickly removed by a flurry of attendants, and the chairs were lined against the two sides of the banquet hall. People stood near the seats and some sat again. Attendants came and served drinks to the crowd and to our table as well. There was a low murmur as the guests visited amongst themselves. I noticed a line of people forming at the far end of our table, to our left.

The line was not long, but it remained steady for the rest of the evening. In an orderly fashion, the guests walked along the table of honor, offering congratulations or a short piece of conversation. They were very polite, but most of them didn't speak to David or me, other than a quick "congratulations". Most did not speak to Sally at all, and I wondered if she felt sad, though she did not look it. The King was busy the rest of the evening. He smiled and shook hands with nearly everyone in the room. The Captain was almost as popular.

The few who spoke to us directly, mostly asked if we were scared at the Winter Palace. Some asked how we knew where the Princess was, to which we didn't really have an answer, since we had of course found her without even knowing who she was. Before long we found ourselves giving canned responses to those who asked us questions. We explained we'd heard her chipping through the ice, trying to escape on her own. The guests only smiled, then moved down the table to talk to others.

I hardly had time to notice, but while people sat and talked, or while they waited in line to meet the King, entertainers were doing some sort of acrobats in the center of the grand hall. They moved very slowly, and balanced on top of each other. At one point they formed a giant pyramid, which nearly reached the high ceiling above us.

By the end of the evening I was so tired, I nearly fell asleep while shaking hands. When other guests at the table of honor began to leave, we said goodbye to Lady Sally. The King and Captain were too busy with other guests for us to get near them. The Princess remained at her seat between the two of them the entire evening. As we stood and turned to leave, Sally invited us to eat breakfast with her and the Princess the next morning, in the Princess's quarters. When we accepted, she told David his instructor had already been notified not to expect him at training the next day, at the Princess's request.

We dragged our feet on the way home, showing our gifts to each other. David's telescope wasn't leather like the Captain's. It was metal and collapsed inside itself to fit inside its lavishly decorated box. The dagger he received was very much like mine, and we compared the two of them side by side. When he showed me the framed piece of glass, my eyes grew large. In the dark it looked an old weathered mirror, with specks of its reflective material missing. A dividing line ran down its center. I knew exactly what it was, and I wanted it very badly for myself.

"Do you know what this is?" I asked him.

David nodded proudly. "They're pieces of the golden mirrors from Eastward and Westward, for reflecting sunlight onto Golden Mountain. One half is from Eastward, and the other is from Westward. See? The frame has a hinge in the middle so you can set them to concentrate light onto something set in between them. Sally told me about it while you were walking up to be recognized."

My face turned red and I tasted bitter envy in my mouth. I'd received three very special gifts, but all I could think of was the mirrors given to David. I turned over the medal I'd received in my hand, noting the worn details still visible. I planned to show it to the Captain and ask him if he knew anything about it. And yet, my eyes kept wandering over to David's gilded mirrors. I thought of all the history I'd learned from Sally and the Captain about the three mountains and the mine pit, and how I wanted to *own* a piece of that history. *Why do I feel like this? I surely don't want to.* I was pulled from my thoughts when David asked me a question.

"Why did the King say 'and *other* distinguished acts' when he thanked you and the Captain?"

"I don't know *what* it means," I answered honestly. "But remember, he wasn't reading a script. Maybe he was just trying to thank everyone a little differently." Even while I said it, I suspected he'd thanked me for things he couldn't mention in public. I reasoned to myself; the plot we'd uncovered was important to the entire kingdom, and surely the King was thankful we'd reported it to him.

When we reached our barrack, I laid my gifts under my cot just as David did with his gifts. It felt odd to lay such valuable items under the simple cots, but where else could we put them? We had small shelves to hold the few changes of clothes we'd been given, but they were full. So our new gifts lay on top of the packs the silent duke had given us. I remembered him fondly—our meeting already seemed half a lifetime ago. I fell asleep thinking of home for the first time in a long while, wishing I would be there soon.

While I slept, I dreamt we'd found a way home, but I couldn't decide whether or not to take it. I was sad to think of leaving our new friends, but felt like I couldn't stay either. I woke with these thoughts on my mind. With a heavy heart, I walked with David to Schelli's quarters. I didn't share my thoughts with him, knowing he would only join me in my dark mood.

5.2 Inside Engdynlor

We arrived at the Princess's quarters and asked the lady attendant at the door to announce us. As far as I could tell, the attendant's only purpose was to see if Schelli was ready to receive guests. A moment later we were ushered in and found Sally and Schelli sitting at a table served with enough breakfast for a crowd.

Schelli ran to greet us, and congratulated us again.

"How did it feel," she asked, "to be up there in front of all those people?"

"Great," David answered enthusiastically.

"It was all right, but a little fuzzy," I said.

"*Fuzzy?*" The Princess and Sally both frowned.

"Yeah. My head felt like it was in a fog, and everything sounded...well, *fuzzy.*" The Princess laughed out loud and Sally smiled wide.

"Fuzzy is about right, then," the Princess giggled. "I felt fuzzy just *watching* you two."

"Why?" asked David, "Don't you go to banquets and ceremonies all the time?"

"Well, sometimes, but I'm never called out for an award, like the two of you were. Except for my entrance, I don't think anyone noticed me. But you two—last night the entire city was probably talking about you."

"Why would they?" I asked. "I thought you had banquets like this every year, at least."

"Yes," answered Sally, "but never have such prestigious recognitions been given to guests as young as you. You should feel very honored."

"How did you know to offer your weapons to my father?" asked Schelli.

"What do you mean—when I held them out and bowed?"

"Yes. Did the Captain tell you?"

"I don't know what you mean," I said, looking to Lady Sally for help. She only smiled. "I didn't know how to say *thank you* at such a fancy banquet, so I just held them up and bowed—you know, to say 'thank you for these.'"

I felt like I wasn't making myself understood. Sally looked as surprised as I'd felt at the banquet.

"No one told you to do it?" she asked as I shook my head. "Amazing."

"I don't get it," David finally joined in. "What's so important about the way he held up his gifts?"

"It's an old tradition," Sally explained, "though it's fallen out of use recently. When a subject receives a *weapon* as a gift from the King, he holds it up and bows to make a pledge: to use the weapon in loyal service. Perhaps it fell out of fashion since subjects who are honored with such gifts are *expected* to serve the King. But last night, the entire crowd was delighted to see Mark breathe new life into an old custom. I'm sure we'll see it again at the next award banquet."

"Hmmm. Doesn't seem like a big deal to me," David added.

"Don't worry about it," I replied in solace. "Remember, the crowd cheered when the King thanked *you* too." He frowned and turned to Lady Sally.

"I still think it meant something important when the King thanked Mark and the Captain for 'other distinguished acts'. What do *you* think that means?"

"Had he?" asked Sally, looking surprised again. "I hadn't noticed," she added in a thoughtful tone. The Princess cut in.

"Maybe it was just a little *extra* thanks. You know, because they went on a second trip together, and ended up getting the ice troll."

"It sounds about right," I said, knowing full well it had everything to do with the second trip.

"Anyway," said Schelli, "let's not let your breakfast get cold. We knew your first banquet in a fancy hall would be tiresome, so I decided to throw you another, more relaxed party—*for breakfast.*" Eagerly, she led us to her table. Just as the table of honor had been arranged, each place setting had a tiny scripted plaque with our names on them. The food was still warm.

There was far too much food for the four of us. I ate my fill of my favorite dish from the banquet: sweet berries in syrup and tiny fluffy cakes. I must have eaten a dozen of them, but I somehow found room for a small steak, two eggs, sweet bread, and several glasses of fresh fruit juice. David concentrated on the meat-filled pastries, but had plenty of room left over for fried eggs and sausages. The Princess and Sally mostly watched.

When we could eat no more, Schelli brought out two tiny boxes wrapped in bright paper and handed one to each of us. We both looked at her in surprise, but she only smiled in return. We opened them together, anxious to see what was inside them.

A small brass skeleton key fell to the ground when I opened my box upside-down. David's box also held a key, but shaped a little differently.

"What is it?" asked David.

The Princess smiled. "Why, a key, *of course.*"

"Is it a riddle?" I asked.

"No," she giggled, "it's a *key.*"

We looked at each other, dumbfounded.

"They're *door keys,*" she exclaimed. "I talked to father, and he agreed the two of you shouldn't stay in the barracks anymore." With a playful air of importance, she added, "You're important figures in the kingdom now, you know. Why, everyone for a day's travel knows your name. In a month, the *entire kingdom* will probably know who you are."

"Do we have to move out of the palace grounds?" I asked, perhaps with a little apprehension. I'd enjoyed being nearby, close to the Captain and Sally and Schelli.

"No," she giggled, "Your new rooms are *inside Engdynlor.*"

"*What?*" we asked in unison.

Sally explained, "It isn't common, but loyal servants are sometimes rewarded with rooms inside the palace."

It took me a moment to realize what she meant by *servants.* I imagined a page or an attendant in the King's Court, but it wasn't what she meant at all. Sally and the Captain always referred to the King's loyal followers as *servants to the King,* while the King called them *servants to the kingdom.* I realized Lady Sally was going on, and I was missing her explanation.

"The Captain and I both have rooms here…as well as much of the Royal Guard. The rest of the Guard and many others who work in

Engdynlor live in other quarters in the palace grounds. It's a great honor, and much more comfortable, too."

I was shocked. David was a step ahead of me.

"What's our room like?"

"Let's find out," Schelli teased.

We nodded and followed them down a long corridor, then a short hallway. Schelli had said *rooms*, I thought hopefully, as in *separate rooms*.

"Almost there," Schelli called over her shoulder. She was nearly as excited as I was. The short hall was decorated with wall hangings and paintings. Schelli stopped at the end of the hallway, and turned to face us. "Here we are. David, you're in this door, and Mark, you're in here," she said, pointing to the doors on either side of the hallway. "Now, why don't you try your keys out?"

We opened our doors and walked in. Schelli followed David and Sally stepped into my new room behind me. Instead of shelves, there was a finely carved armoire and chest of drawers. I had a full bed with a mattress instead of a cot. The blankets were smooth and thick, unlike the scratchy wool blankets I'd nearly gotten used to in the barracks. There was a window on the far side of the room from the door. Through it I could see the open courtyard in the center of the palace, boxed in on all sides.

Sally pointed to my right.

"Look, you can see the Princess's quarters from here. See the inside corner with windows on both sides? That's where we just came from. If it wasn't for the heavy curtains, you could see the breakfast table we just left."

I followed her arm and saw it.

"Ah. It looks smaller from here," I said, not really paying much attention. I looked in the chest of drawers and found the clean clothes in them to be mine, and also new clothes I hadn't seen before. The fancy clothes I wore to the banquet were cleaned and folded in another drawer. I turned to open the armoire but it was stuck.

"Try your key," Lady Sally advised. I did. It was keyed the same as the door to my room. The armoire had my armor inside, my new sword and dagger as well. The medal I'd received hung by its ribbon from a small nail. I smiled to see them again, then turned and sat on the bed.

Sally sat beside me and asked what was wrong.

"You won't miss the cold barracks, will you?"

I looked at the small woodstove at the foot of the bed, and its stovepipe chimney disappearing through the ceiling. There were three such circular stoves in the Princess's quarters, with a metal box of small pieces of firewood near each. While the Princess's stoves were tended and filled by her attendants, I wondered if I would need to fill and maintain my own. But Lady Sally was still waiting for my reply.

"No, I won't miss the barracks, not a bit. This reminds me of my room at home—my *real* home. It's not this big, or as nice, but I miss it... My parents must think we're dead."

She drew me to her and hugged me. I became immediately tense, but soon relaxed and accepted her comforting.

"I'm sure they still have hope for you. I imagine it's not easy—I've seen parents lose children, and children lose parents. Just remember you haven't really lost each other, only...temporarily *misplaced* each other. You'll be together again one day, I know." I hoped she was right. Just then, David popped through a door in the wall adjacent to the door to the hallway. I jumped to my feet, surprised.

"How did you get in *there*?" I asked.

I'd assumed the door was to a closet. When I thought about it, I realized there wasn't much sense in putting an armoire in a room with a closet.

"Come and see," David called back impatiently, then disappeared through the same door.

I followed him and found a private bathroom, complete with its own shower. There was another door on the far side of the bathroom, on the same wall of the door I'd just walked through. David pointed at it.

"My room's *right through here.*"

I knew there weren't many bathrooms in the palace. For our new rooms to share private access to one, I knew they must be for important guests. I followed David through the door into his own room. It looked just like mine, but reversed.

"Amazing," I said to the Princess, "You must have begged your dad for a week to get us rooms like *this*."

"Actually, he already planned to move you into them," she beamed. "I just didn't know about it until I asked."

"Well, thank you anyway," I replied, "They're fantastic." David thanked her also, then turned to me.

"Look out my window—you can see our barracks."

David was right. I could see the small yard where I'd trained with the Captain, and the barracks beyond them. Farther still, I recognized the palace wall, then the straight and narrow roads of Thraen Kholl. Beyond those narrow streets was another wall, surrounding the entire city. I missed home very badly just then. The feeling came and went, though I didn't understand why. I decided not to mention it to David.

We enjoyed the view from David's window, three floors over the palace grounds.

"Hey," David called, "is that a statue?"

"It's called 'glory'," Schelli replied. "Haven't you seen it?"

"No, not yet."

"Well, do you want to?" she asked. "We can go now if you want."

"Why not?" he replied. As he headed through the door, he turned back to me and asked, "Aren't you coming?"

"I've already seen it. You go ahead, I'm going to relax for now. I hardly slept last night."

David and Schelli were off. Sally went to leave also, but I held her back.

"Sally? Could you tell me something?"

"Certainly, dear. What is it?"

I paused for a moment while I tried to think of the best way to begin.

"Yesterday morning, when David kept asking me about the trolls.... Schelli looked very upset."

"Yes, that's right," she replied in a guarded tone.

"It made me wish I hadn't mentioned them at all. The Princess looked as if I'd killed her best friend."

"Yes. There's a reason for that. Suppose you follow me down to my room, and I'll tell you about it over tea."

"All right," I accepted, somewhat concerned with her suddenly grave demeanor.

After my surprise at the plainness of the Captain's room, I was a little curious what Lady Sally's quarters might look like.

"Let me leave a note for David," I said as I searched the little drawer in the nightstand.

I found a small cup, a stack of small papers, quill pen, and a small book. I wondered about the book, but decided to leave it for later. I took the pen and a sheet of paper and wrote *waiting for you at Lady Sally's room* on it. I left the note on David's bed.

We walked toward the Princess's quarters and down two flights of stairs before reaching the door to her room. As she welcomed me in, I was surprised by the marked change in atmosphere.

Upon entering her room, I noticed the morning's chill seemed to leave. The single window was large, and encased in dark curtains drawn back, and a dark lace, which seemed to color the light shining through it. The walls were not brick or stone, as they were in some parts of the palace, but rich wood panels, and in places, smooth plaster painted in dark browns and reds. The upholstered furniture seemed overstuffed, and was covered with fabric of similar colors. Sally's room was much smaller than the Princess's quarters, and though it didn't feel crowded, it contained not a few pieces of furniture: a high bed, a large bookcase, a small sofa, an armoire, several soft chairs, a secretary's desk, and a low wooden table. There was a tall, round woodstove at the foot of her bed. Fancy scrolls of cast iron crept from every inch of its sides. There was a door in the wall to my right; I assumed it led to a private bathroom. The room couldn't be more unlike the sterile room the Captain kept.

Lady Sally lifted a copper teakettle from the woodstove, and poured hot water into a ceramic teapot. She filled a tiny metal ball with curled tea leaves, then dropped it into the teapot and placed it on a trivet on the low table. I sat at one of the pillowed chairs near the table. As she sat across from me, she told me the story of Schelli's first close friend.

Nearly a decade ago, an old troll woman had worked in Engdynlor as a housekeeper. The Princess was just old enough for Lady Sally to have begun introducing her to the subjects she would soon study, and there were still loyal trolls in Thraen Kholl. The troll woman had a young daughter, just older than the Princess, and they became fast friends. Their friendship was unlikely, though not unexpected. Resentment toward the trolls had been building over decades of increasing skirmishes, called the Troll Battles. These unprovoked attacks were ill-organized, but effective, and had left many scars in the kingdom, both physically and emotionally. Nearly every human knew someone who had been harmed by a troll, or lost a loved one to the trolls' raids and attacks.

The King offered the woman a job cleaning a portion of Engdynlor's many rooms when she had been declared a widow. Her husband had run off to join the troll rebels, and no more was ever heard of him. When she was tormented by her human neighbors around Thraen Kholl, the King eventually had her moved into Engdynlor. He meant to show an example of trust, and also of trolls and humans living together peacefully, but his plan backfired. Soon the others in the city grew jealous of the cleaning woman. The King eventually had to ask her to leave the city for her own safety, and provided her with a generous severance. She loved the King and was loyal to him, and she understood why he asked this of her. During her last years, she'd been afraid of leaving the palace at all.

The King offered the old cleaning woman an escort of his most loyal soldiers, to carry her and her daughter elsewhere in the kingdom. She politely refused, as she didn't trust even the King's soldiers.

One evening after playing, Princess Schelli's young friend told her she and her mother would leave the palace in the morning—for good. Schelli thought she was only teasing, but when she woke the next morning, she began to worry her friend had spoken the truth. She ran to the room where the old housekeeper and her daughter slept, but found it empty. She fled the palace grounds to search the streets of Thraen Kholl. The old woman and her daughter had left early in the morning to avoid being seen. They'd already reached the streets of the city when the Princess found them.

Just outside the palace walls, a group of hecklers gathered and threw garbage at the housekeeper and her daughter. The old troll began to wheeze, which might have sounded like a mean-spirited growl to her tormenters. They began throwing sticks at her. She dropped their meager belongings and covered her daughter in her arms, and her breathing grew more labored. When Schelli ran through the gates in the palace wall, she came upon this scene. She was livid. Palace Guards watched idly from their posts at the gate, unconcerned. She screamed to the guards, who finally stopped the ruckus. The old woman was right; even some of the King's soldiers didn't care for her safety.

At this point in the tale, Lady Sally quietly stood and walked to her cupboard. I thought it an odd place to stop, as she was not one for dramatic pauses. She selected a pair of teacups, and set them on the table before me. She didn't yet return to her seat, but stood over it, facing away from me for a moment. Still, she said nothing.

"What happened to the old lady and her daughter?" I finally asked.

"For the old troll woman, Schelli's screams didn't come soon enough. By the time the soldiers stopped the ruckus, the old troll woman was dead. A stone thrown by one of the hecklers had caught her in the temple. Blood trickled down her face and stained her daughter's clothes."

The tea had steeped. Lady Sally poured it into the small cups before us. She pulled lumps of sugar from a small jar—they looked like rock candy—and dropped them into the teacups. I said nothing.

"When the soldiers saw this," she went on, "they rushed Schelli back to the palace, but not before she heard a snide remark from the cruelest of the gate soldiers."

"What did he say?" I asked. She wore a distasteful look on her face as she spoke of the soldier.

"He said, 'That ought to teach her a troll's rightful place: six feet under, and without a coffin.' The Princess leapt at him, enraged. She learned his name from the other soldiers and reported him to the King. He and the other soldiers who had stood by were charged with dereliction of duty. When they were released, they were banished from ever returning to Thraen Kholl."

"What happened to the daughter? Did she live?" I asked. Lady Sally's expression turned warm.

"Yes—she wasn't harmed at all—at least not physically. The next day the young girl was taken by the Captain himself to a place where a peaceful band of trolls lived, at the far edge of the desert, where the land isn't useful enough to hold any real value. Sadly, we've never heard of her since."

"What about the people who killed the old woman?" I asked. "Were they arrested too?"

"And which of them would you say is guilty of murder?" she asked, eyes full of frustration. "The soldiers who ignored the incident? The indigent teenagers who threw garbage at her? The adults among them who threw sticks? Or the one person in the mob who threw the stone that struck her temple?"

"Well," I began, startled by her question, "I guess...*all of them.*"

"But they didn't *all* mean to kill her—maybe none of them did. Most of them only wanted to humiliate her."

I struggled with the idea. *Someone had to be responsible,* I thought. Sally saw the irritation in my brow and nodded.

"It is hard to judge against a mob," she said. "They're all guilty, but of what? Nonetheless, they *were* punished, though the King never found which of them had thrown the stone. Perhaps no one had; she could have tripped and hit her temple on a loose cobblestone."

We sat and sipped our tea in silence. Only when I'd finished mine did Lady Sally speak again.

"Since then, Schelli has never seen a troll who didn't remind her of her young friend. This is why it was particularly hard for her when trolls took over the Winter Palace. She couldn't stop herself from trying to make friends with the guards posted at her door. Every time they ignored her, or growled for her to stop talking, it affected her."

"She told you this?" I asked, upset by her words.

"Yes—the first night after you and David freed her. I'd taken her to the place where one of her troll guards was imprisoned by the Captain and his men. She'd talked to him every night he was assigned to guard her room. She felt like she'd begun to teach him trolls and humans don't need to be enemies. Though she insisted, I knew it was a bad idea. When we found him, he wouldn't even look at her."

"Oh, no," I said, remembering the Princess's expression when we'd first met. "Now I understand how she acted when we freed her."

"What of it?" Sally asked, leaning forward.

"When she first jumped through the hole we'd chipped in the floor of her room, she looked back toward her sleeping guard, as if she were undecided about something and—well, *regretful.*"

"Yes," said Sally, "I suppose she *did* feel regret. It hurt her a great deal to leave him locked in the Winter Palace."

"What's happened to him by now?"

"We don't know for certain. The Captain assumed other trolls would enter the palace and free the ones he left imprisoned. The duke's reinforcements might not have been sent early enough to prevent it."

I knew what Lady Sally didn't. The duke certainly had *not* sent reinforcements—unless they were trolls sent to keep the Winter Palace from falling back under the King's control. I shuddered to think of the Princess's expression from the previous day, when David kept asking if I'd killed any trolls.

My mind turned back to Sally's story. I felt a powerful anger rise in me, to think the Princess should have to witness such a thing—and for such tragedy to fall on those she loved. One killed, the other orphaned and sent alone to a strange land—I knew the pain it must have given Schelli to see it.

"How can someone as kind as the Princess suffer so much? And the few innocent trolls—they received the punishment due to their warring relatives, didn't they?"

"I'm afraid so," Sally replied. "The kindest among us are often the ones who suffer the most. While they are undeserving, they're most capable of bearing it. And whatever brings suffering to the kind, may pass unnoticed in the hearts of the calloused. The Princess is the best in all of us, in so many ways. *She* is why the King has so much hope for the future of humans and trolls. He sees it's possible for humans to treat trolls as equals, to respect them, and to befriend them. Such a large heart for such a young girl…"

Sally broke off in mid-sentence, her voice cracking. She turned away from me for a moment. Not knowing what to say, I fought to remain silent, instead of saying the wrong thing in such a quiet moment.

When I broke the silence, I told her, "When I rode with the Captain into the desert, I understood so little about your commitment to the Princess and the King, and of Schelli's ability to forgive even the trolls who captured her. The silent duke and his hill troll, the Captain and his…willingness to serve and to…teach—".

I bit my tongue. *I'd nearly mentioned my apprenticeship.* I knew I must think more and talk less, as the Captain had warned.

I thought back to the Captain's words, and for the first time, I felt like I finally understood why the duke had learned to hate so *furiously*. The Captain had spelled it out for me on our long trip home, but it hadn't sunk in past my mind. Suddenly, I could imagine the duke, raised on his mother's hatred and lies as if they were food. What chance did he stand to choose what's right? He and the ice troll were the same, and the silent duke was their opposite. He understood hatred, and the small likelihood it offers its victims to do what is right. Even so, he was still willing to sacrifice his possessions, and his very safety, so the hill troll could know what it's like to be treated by humans as an equal. I'd thought the silent duke was merely irrational, or reckless. I'd assumed he knew nothing. When I'd warned him the troll living in his manor might hurt him, or even kill him, his only response scrawled by his quivering hand was:

What if? Old man!

Unexpectedly, I realized I was finally growing to understand him. *What I could have learned from him,* I thought.

Sally turned to face me again, and refilled both our teacups. She leaned toward me and asked expectedly, "But now you see? You understand?"

"*Yes*," I woke from my thoughts and turned toward Lady Sally. "And it feels…*horrible*—horrible and wonderful at once. Why does something so awful also feel so…*inspiring?*" It was exhausting to finally put these thoughts together. I looked up to Sally, who stood and walked over to me with a tear rolling down from one eye.

"I'm so *proud* of you," she said.

Proud? I thought, *She hardly knows me.* But looking into her eyes, I imagined the comfortable embrace of a mother holding her child. I realized Lady Sally—who'd never married and never had a child of her own—was a mother to many. She'd cared deeply for, and taught and trained countless young minds. *Can I really read so much from a single look?* I wondered. For this moment, time seemed to trickle by, and I swore I could see straight into her soul. The conversation we shared in her room over tea is burned into my memory, just as surely as if it had been carved in stone.

Just then, there was a knock at the door. Schelli and David entered without waiting for a response. They paused uncomfortably at finding Sally standing over me in silence.

"We…just got back from seeing the statue…" David said, his voice trailing off.

"We're hungry and going to lunch," Schelli followed, sounding nearly as awkward. "Would you like to come with us?"

"We'd love to," Sally said, smiling. "We just came down for a cup of tea."

David and Schelli looked past us to the teacups on the table—both filled to the brim and seemingly untouched. Sally turned back to me and smiled.

"Well, we've had our fill of tea, I suppose," she said with a hint of laughter in her eyes.

5.3 Two Tables

The awkwardness of the moment had lifted by the time we reached the Princess's room. As we entered, we were surprised to find the Captain inside, looking out the windows. Without hesitation, Schelli asked if she could help him in any way.

He bowed his head slightly as he replied, "Not at all, your highness. I'm only checking your room and windows as a routine precaution. We must keep Engdynlor safe for you and your family. How have you been while I was away?"

"Just fine, Captain. I was glad to see you and Mark return safely. Congratulations on your honors at the banquet last night."

"Thank you, your Highness." Schelli seemed to bristle at the second time he called her *highness*.

"Andrew, you know me too well to call me *highness*, at least while we're not in a banquet or the King's Court."

"Forgive me, Schelli. Formalities do get in the way, don't they?" He patted her shoulder and turned to the rest of us.

"I take it you enjoyed the banquet last night?"

"*Immensely*," David exclaimed. I smiled and nodded, unsure how I would talk to the Captain while surrounded by others who didn't know the secrets we shared.

"Schelli," the Captain went on, "I wondered if I might steal Mark from you for a while. I need to talk with him about a short trip I might be taking soon. He's agreed to be my armor bearer, you know."

"Oh—not far, I hope?" she pried.

"Just preliminary plans for now," he smiled in reply. It was clear he wouldn't offer more details.

"Well, don't keep him all day, please," Schelli said politely. "We were just about to eat lunch." The Captain moved toward the door. As he answered over his shoulder, I followed.

"I'll send him back as soon as I can." As we walked down the hallway, I felt the need to defend myself for being hard to locate.

"I thought you and the King would be busy for a while, so I didn't bother checking in…"

"You did exactly as the King suggested. I won't keep you long if I can help it. Hopefully you'll be able to rejoin your group for lunch. You've come to know Lady Sally and the Princess well, it seems?"

"Oh yes. The Princess is very nice. She wanted to give us a fancy breakfast to celebrate our part in the banquet. And Lady Sally is kind and wise. She's always telling me about things like service and forgiveness."

"Oh?" he raised an eyebrow. "Then she is wise *indeed*."

As we neared his quarters, the Captain's mood became somber, though I couldn't guess why. I had questions for him, but decided to wait until we could talk freely. The troll, our testimonies, and what the traitorous duke might do next all weighed on my mind, though surely not nearly as heavily as on the Captain's.

As we walked through the Captain's door, I noticed a large wooden table I hadn't seen before. It looked odd sitting next to his small desk, and gave the room a crowded atmosphere. I thought I noticed something else new; an armoire I couldn't remember seeing before. The Captain walked to it and unlocked it with a small key. The keyhole wasn't where I'd expected it, but hidden in the intricate carvings of one door.

He pulled maps and other papers from the armoire, before closing and locking it once again. He spread the largest of these across the new table, and stood back to allow me to inspect it closely. It was a map of the entire kingdom, showing water on all sides. As I'd come to expect from my attempts to learn where we were, there were vast empty areas on the eastern end of the island. I recognized the jungle where we first arrived. I saw the silent duke's manor, the swamp, and the grassy hills preceding Otlak Plain. I saw Golden Mountain, as well as Eastward and Westward and the other mountains in the range dividing the island into the eastern and western halves. To me, these halves were still divided by memories I felt were real, and those recollections from my hazy first week in Terreldor. For the first time, I saw how all these parts fit into the lonely continent of Terreldor. I saw the long desert Enthicia, TerkEtmek, the freshly inked troll camp in the Great Dunes, the Desert Trail, the oasis at Tume Belor, and Thraen Kholl, all clearly marked. It surprised me to learn all the places I'd visited added together made up far less than half the kingdom.

The map showed a thick forest encroaching on Thraen Kholl from three sides. There appeared to be cities and villages along roads in each direction. After the Desert Trail passed TerkEtmek, it turned west and eventually led out of the desert. The road looked like it eventually met up with a road leading from Engdynlor, curving west and south along Terrezia Plain.

"Is this the first time you've seen a map of the entire kingdom?" asked the Captain.

"Yes. I didn't know there was so much I hadn't seen—"

"Well, you've seen the Eastern Coast, *both sides* of Golden Mountain, Enthicia, and every corner of Thraen Kholl. It's no small portion of the kingdom," the Captain said, pointing to parts of the map.

"What's this here?" I interjected. "And here? Are these bays? And what's this, an island chain?"

"*This* is Terrezia—a plain between the *forests* and *shore* of the west coast," he said, pointing to their locations. "*This* is the North Forest, where I was born. That *is* a bay, with a small settlement behind it. Both the bay and its settlement are blocked off from the rest of the kingdom by difficult mountains and barren land. This *here* is Oyster Bay, with its large city wrapped around it. This *island chain* as you called it, is the *Broken Coast*. It is mostly a collection of rocks tall enough to rise out of the ocean, perhaps a mile from shore. They follow the coast for the distance of a whole day's sail. Many smaller rocks of the Broken Coast chain are large enough to hold dirt and grow trees and plants. One or two are very long, and even wide enough to hold small forests." He paused and looked at me to see if I would blurt out further questions. When I did not, he continued.

"We know the trolls built a settlement and are gathering *here*," he said, pointing to the fresh ink in the desert. "We also saw them traveling past TerkEtmek, probably to the forests southwest of the desert. We must assume they've been gathering at the far end of Enthicia as well. The larger trading guilds own a lot of land *here*," he said, pointing to the forests he'd just described, "so we'll probably meet resistance there as well. We can expect attacks from the desert and from the forests and plain southwest of Thraen Kholl—"

I interrupted the Captain again. I was far too excited about finally getting a complete picture of the kingdom to notice how rudely I was acting.

"This looks like there are roads through the forest southwest of Thraen Kholl, leading to the far side of the desert. Why didn't we take this path to TerkEtmek?"

"Firstly," he replied in a dry tone, "this is the best maintained and most travelled road in the kingdom. Most of the food you've eaten has travelled on this road, and a good deal of the guilds' trade is made possible by it. However, it's a much longer path to TerkEtmek. The Vuori Mountains make the Desert Trail the shorter route; it's why we took it. Even though it's the longer way around, we must assume some rebels will use it to attack us from the southwest. For all we know, Terrezia Plain is full of rebels. The King has already sent scouts to investigate."

I thought of David. *Would his mentor be sent? Had he already left?* "What about to the north?" I asked. "Could there be rebels there, too?"

"I'm sure the scouts are searching for rebels there also, but I'm just as sure they'll find none. The Harrington family owns a lot of land up north, and they hold a lot of influence there as well. They would never side with a Ward or move against the King."

He hadn't answered my real question. Frustrated, I finally asked him plainly.

"What about my brother? Will his mentor be sent away? Will David be sent with him?"

The Captain replied first with a heavy sigh. "I don't know, Mark. The King hasn't spoken to me about this. The investigation prevents him from confiding much in me until my name is cleared. I'm afraid it *is* a possibility."

My mind raced as I pressed him further, "Which is? His mentor might be sent, or David might be sent too? Would they go to the north, where it's safe, or to the south where the rebels are?"

"I don't know. I wish I had better answers for you."

The Captain remained silent, waiting patiently. I knew I had interrupted him several times already, but more importantly, I also understood he didn't have the information I wanted.

I was afraid for David. In fact, I was horrified. I pushed back the fear, pressed it deep into the back of my mind. I had no way of knowing it would resurface just a few hours later. I decided to wait until he was finished with whatever he meant to tell me, no matter how long he took in doing so. When he turned back to the map but remained silent, I gave up.

"Captain, why did you bring me here? Is there something you want from me?"

"I guess you could put it that way. First, we haven't spoken of your training for a while, and we might have little time for such things after the investigation. Part of being an apprentice is actually working with your mentor. There are a lot of things you can learn from a man by working with him. More urgently, I wanted to show you this map. It will be marked with many plans once the King's investigation is over. I wanted to make sure you were familiar with it before this happens. I also wanted to give you some idea of what might happen once those loyal to the King go to war against the duke and his rebels."

The Captain's words shook me. Of course I knew there might be war. But hearing it said so emphatically, after the banquet and after our relaxed breakfast with Schelli and Sally, was like a bucket of cold water thrown onto an unsuspecting slumberer. Inwardly, I scolded myself for being idyllic, while the kingdom around me was hurtling into war. I pulled myself from my thoughts; the Captain was still speaking.

"There's a good chance there will be fighting on two fronts. One will be in between Thraen Kholl and the desert, or in the desert this side of TerkEtmek. The other battlefront would be somewhere along this road, through the farmland of Terrezia Plain. The duke's armies could steal a lot of supplies and wreak havoc, tearing through the farm villages there. We will most likely send armies in both directions."

"How many armies are there?"

"If the King raises his full armies, there will be three. Remember the conversation we had on our way out into the desert? I told you in times of war, I command the King's armies. If I am cleared in the King's investigation and we go to war, I will command his three armies, and the Navy, should it be needed. It's not a role I look forward to." The Captain paused for a moment, his thoughts weighing heavily on his mood. "Now, putting aside what *might* take place, I hoped we might continue your training."

I nodded at him, and he began to quiz me on some of the things he'd shared with me only a few days ago. As I answered, each of my answers prompted more questions in my mind.

"Sally—I mean *Lady* Sally," I corrected myself, "told me the kindest people often suffer the most, because they can bear it. How is this fair?" The Captain showed a curious grin.

"Did she now?" he asked, feigning surprise. "Well, she is right to say so. And the answer to your question is: it's not fair at all. Now can you think of reasons why the kind might suffer more than others?"

"Do you mean they might somehow deserve it?"

"No, of course not. Other reasons—how might a kind person and an unkind person react to the same things?"

"Lady Sally thinks a kind person can *tolerate* more suffering than others. Like the silent duke…he allowed the hill troll to steal from him again and again. Anyone else would have set a trap, or fought off the troll, or at least protected himself."

"Right," said the Captain. "Part of self-preservation is to isolate yourself from those who would do you harm. Sometimes this is your duty, but it also may fall to you to endure suffering. It's also true, a kind man may choose to put himself at risk more often—for a good cause."

"The same goes for a kind woman," I replied, "like Lady Sally—or a kind girl, like the Princess." The Captain was taken back when I mentioned Schelli. His manner changed, though I couldn't read if it were anger, or something else.

"How do you think the Princess has suffered?" he asked cautiously. "Other than the time she spent imprisoned in the Winter Palace, of course."

I was surprised he didn't already know the story Lady Sally just told me. I bit my tongue to keep from smiling; I was about to teach the Captain.

"I don't think it was her time locked away that bothered her so much. I think it was after we freed her."

I saw doubt in his eyes. I went on to describe the guard she tried to befriend, and what Sally told me of how it must have felt to her, leaving him locked in the Winter Palace. The Captain looked thoughtful, his eyes lost in focus on some private thought. I went on.

"And she suffered long before this, when her friend's mother was killed. You know, the troll woman who cleaned in the palace."

"Yes," replied the Captain, his face turning grim. "I'd hoped she was too young to remember. It was a delusion to think the Princess could forget someone else's pain, seen so close."

"She might have been young, but I guess it left a deep impression. David asked if we ran into any trolls in the desert in front of the Princess. He asked if we killed any. When he did, the Princess looked like she might cry."

The Captain's expression turned hard. "And your answer was?" he asked slowly.

"I dodged his questions. Lady Sally helped. Then this morning I asked Sally—I mean *Lady Sally*—why the Princess was so upset. She told me about the troll woman and her daughter. Lady Sally thinks no one is ready to treat trolls as equals as well as the Princess."

"Perhaps no one but the King. It's a heavy burden to carry—to know where the people should be led, but are unwilling to follow."

I had no idea what he meant by this, so I asked him.

"The King desires to see all humans treat trolls as equals, and all trolls to treat humans in the same way. Few are willing to follow in his example. Too many humans carry the pain of loved ones lost in the troll battles. Or even worse—to have lost family members to the murderous hordes who attack the farmers to steal their crops and cattle."

The Captain saw surprise in me.

"It's not all one-sided. Every adult troll is old enough to remember hatred and disrespect received from humans. It's never been easy between trolls and humans, and I expect it will get much worse."

"Why?"

"*The coming war*, of course." I shivered slightly, to hear him mention it again. "The trolls may have been disorganized, but they've attacked peaceful farming villages for generations. Do you think the duke will hold them back once he's organized and trained them? He'll try to use trolls' and humans' hatred to feed his war, to divide our kingdom further apart than it has ever been. In this goal at least, I'm afraid we've already lost. Humans and trolls are sure to hate each other more, for all the duke's treachery."

We talked for quite a while, about trolls and humans, and many other things. When our conversation fell silent he began to doodle on a small piece of paper.

"Remember on our way back from the mineral pool, when I began to tell you of the Table of False Reflections?" I nodded. "Would you like to see it? And the other tables as well?"

I'd nearly forgotten about them. I nodded again as I wondered what they might look like. Were they hidden in a secret room? Did he have a smaller version of the table hidden in in the armoire, made of gold and jewels perhaps? I looked around the room, wondering where the table might be.

"Well?" said the Captain, "*Here it is.*"

What's he talking about? I wondered. He slapped his hand on the large wooden table in front of us, mostly covered by the map. *Of course, I thought. The secret must be hidden in some detailed inlay on the tabletop. This is surely why he had this huge table brought into his room—and why he covered it so quickly.* I moved the map and other papers aside, trying to discover the table's secret—but I found none.

"What are you doing?" asked the Captain, "I thought you wanted to see the tables."

Finally, I realized—he wasn't pointing out the *tabletop*, he'd clapped his hand down on the paper he'd been scribbling on as we talked. Then I saw he *hadn't* been scribbling—he'd been *writing*. He slid the sheet of paper back in front of me. I stared at it, not knowing how to react.

In disappointment, I realized the tables he'd been talking about were only tables of words, written in rows and columns. They were not some magical or mysterious tables made of wood, stone or gold. The first table lay before me. It was covered with the flowing print of the Captain's hand. I scanned it quickly, but most of it made little sense to me. *Perhaps it's encoded,* I hoped silently.

Table of False Reflections
Worthy and Honorable Characteristics, and their Pale Imitations

Boldness: Stand against strong opposition for what is right	**Rebellion**: Stand against what is right for your own preferences
Freedom: Glorious, unnatural & precarious state where citizens are free do right w/o gov't interference	**License to Wrong:** Abuse of freedom to wrong, exploiting gov't restraint from defining morals
Love: Consistently & reliably choosing to provide for another, promoting every facet of their lives; desiring strong, healthy relationship	**Lust**: Need to have selfish desires filled by another, regardless of the other's needs
Compassion: a. Allowing/ providing what's best for others at own expense. b. showing mercy out of love. c. willing sacrifice to create chance for others to choose right	(Negative) **Weakness:** Lack of ability to make hard decisions or to show strength (Deceitful) **Feigned Compassion:** deceitful by intent & practice; leads to distrust
Submission: Understanding & operating in your position in chain of authority	(Negative) **Timidity**: lack of boldness & strength (Deceitful) **Feigned Submission**: submit in words & public actions only: leads to disloyalty & treachery
Selflessness: putting others & their needs above yourself & your own needs	(Negative) to disguise selflessness as a **weakness** (Deceitful) **false selflessness**: hidden pride, leads to selfishness
Leadership: (servitude) serve those who follow you, imbue them with your values & give them opportunity to choose to follow. Preferable to supervision, which teaches nothing	**Manipulation**: motivate others to do your will through fear, greed & other wrong or hurtful desires
Conviction: desire to cease wrongful conduct: results in true behavioral change	**Guilt**: causes shame, does not foster change, leads to separation or loss of relationship

Humility: accurately understanding yourself & your abilities	(Negative) **Insecurity**: Self-doubt, often combined with a crippling fear of failure (Deceitful) **False Humility** (a type of pride)
Strength: the degree to which you reliably oppose wrong & stand for what is right	**Anger, bullying, forcefulness** all used to assert your will without regarding how it affects others
Forgiveness: freeing someone from the wrong they did to you; choosing not to recall the pain or damage caused. Dismisses retribution, not punishment	(Negative) **Weakness**: lack of resolve or ability to take revenge (Deceitful) **Feigned Forgiveness** leads to hidden unforgiveness
Loyalty: Integrity in relationships, duty, & commitments: prevents betrayal	**Unreliability**: Reduces relationships to brief alliances motivated by greed, masked by deceit & ripe for betrayal
Wisdom: Degree experience, knowledge, & insight used to make decisions. Joined to maturity & humility. Demonstrated by choices & actions, not professions or claims	**Knowledge**: Result of learning. Without wisdom, knowledge cannot lead to wise action. Alone it leads to pride; doesn't prevent foolishness
Peace: Contentedness, lack of worry or stress: does not infer a lack of productiveness	**Lethargy**: lack of productivity or meaningful action. Often joined to lack in boldness, strength, & concern. Exposed to manipulation
Patience: Self-discipline over whims & fleeting desire	**Stubbornness**: Willingness to bide time until easier to assert will over others. Reflects selfish desire
Honesty: Integrity displayed in words & actions. Fulfilling commitments & duties	**Well-planned Deception**: Practiced deceit, hard to discern. Prevents loyalty & reliability

The Captain said nothing, so I turned my gaze back to the list and read it through—twice. The Captain had already taught me about many of the items in the table. My expectation of a great revelation fully dissolved, and the Captain saw it in my eyes.

"Not exactly what you were expecting?" he asked. I could only tell him the truth.

"I thought they were... *real* tables, made of stone or expensive wood or precious metal. I thought some kind of illusion would make things look like they were reflecting...you know, *false reflections*. I thought these tables would be hidden in a secret room only knights knew of."

The Captain laughed loudly. When he saw my face redden, he stopped abruptly.

"I'm sorry," he said, still smiling, "I didn't mean to laugh at you. I just never thought—I never meant to make the tables seem *mysterious*. Looking back, I can see how you might have drawn such conclusions. It's of the utmost importance we should *not* keep them secret. We will share them with anyone who's willing to be taught. Remember, one of the roles of the Honor Knights is to teach others all the values needed for the New Rule to be ushered in."

It made sense, after discovering what kind of tables they were, and yet, I couldn't help feeling disappointed. The Captain seemed to read my thoughts.

"Trust me—in the long run, these written tables will have a greater effect on your life than secret rooms or fancy furniture."

"I'm sure you're right, sir," I said, though not convincingly. I looked at the list again and asked, "Why do some rows have *two* opposites?"

"Ah—an important distinction to make. Firstly, they are *not* opposites. The first column contains valuable characteristics we all need in order to grow. The second column contains a pale imitation of each characteristic. Each good quality is mimicked by a *false reflection*— something that looks the same on the surface, but is drastically different beneath."

"Who made the imitations?" I asked.

"Why, I don't think they needed inventing. If left to our own vices, we would all tend to exhibit the false versions of these qualities. They are far easier to show because they come so *naturally* to us. We must work to train ourselves in the *true* characteristics of maturity."

You still *haven't answered my question*, I thought. "Why do some of them have two *imitations* then?

"Oh, yes. Some of the positive traits, like *compassion*, are not only imitated; they are often distorted so they appear to some as weaknesses. Compassion is sometimes faked, or *feigned*, by someone who *pretends* to be compassionate. Other times, an immature man may fool himself into believing acts of compassion are instead acts of weakness. This deception couldn't be further from the truth. It takes true strength to act compassionately. Believing otherwise is a sign of immaturity."

"Oh, I see—like submission; someone might *fake* submission but still act rebelliously, while someone else might say submission is for the weak-willed."

"*That's right*," the Captain happily replied. "I think an understanding of this table is growing quickly in you."

Glad to hear this unexpected praise, I asked why some of the characteristics on the table didn't match their definitions.

The Captain answered, "Remember, these definitions of these words are *true*. They are very old, and haven't been altered by society's incorrect or abusive use of the words."

We talked a while longer, until the Captain thought I had a basic understanding of each of the characteristics.

"Now *here* is another table altogether," said the Captain, sliding a second sheet of paper over the first. The Captain went on as I studied it, still disappointed, but with a little curiosity left in me.

"Some of the desirable traits are the same, but the negative traits matched to each one are *opposites* instead of veiled imitations. Just as the *false reflections* table is useful to recognize when a good trait is merely imitated, this table is also useful. When we find ourselves acting out the traits in the second column, we use this table to find the positive trait required to *replace* our actions. It's easier to *replace* a trait in our actions than to simply *remove* it." With this in mind, I read through the second table.

Table of Opposites

Honorable Characteristics and their Opposites
-a quality's false reflection often leads to its opposite-

Humility: accurately understanding yourself and your abilities	**Pride:** traits stemming from the deep-rooted (and often hidden) belief in every man that he is better than others
Compassion: a. showing mercy out of love. b. sacrificing to create opportunities for others to choose what is right	**Judgment:** desiring Justice over mercy for others; desiring to see others punished **Indifference:** disdain or lack of care for others, holding no value for their lives or growth.
Wisdom: Degree experience, knowledge, & insight used to make decisions. Joined to maturity & humility. Demonstrated by choices & actions, not professions or claims	**Foolishness or Recklessness:** decisions or actions utterly lacking useful thought, knowledge, and values. Disregards consequences and scorns reflection and forethought
Love: Consistently & reliably choosing to provide for another, promoting every facet of their lives; desiring strong relationship	**Hatred or Indifference:** counting as irrelevant, selfishly discounting inherent value of, desiring destruction of a person or group
Forgiveness: freeing someone from the wrong they did to you; choosing not to recall the pain or damage caused. Dismisses retribution, not punishment	**Judgment:** holding someone responsible for wrongdoing, enacting punishment or retribution
Self-forgiveness: willingness to receive forgiveness for your wrongs, to release guilt for your actions following Conviction	**Self-condemnation:** inability to release guilt, usually from a lack of Conviction. Imitates piety or duty, fosters no change

Loyalty: Integrity in relationships, duty, and commitments: prevents betrayal	**Dissention and Betrayal:** sown in distrust and selfishness, inability or refusal to recognize authority
Generosity and selflessness: Sharing coupled with Contentedness, or the peace accompanying having enough	**Greed and Poverty:** perception of not having enough, regardless of possessions or lack thereof. Constant desire for More, irrespective of reality
Peace: contentedness, lack of worry or stress: does not infer a lack of productivity	**Restlessness or Discontentedness:** mental or emotional state of dissatisfied unrest. Married to anxiety and stress
Submission: understanding and operating in your position in a chain of authority	**Rebellion:** refusing to recognize your position in a chain of authority; feigns ambition, robs peace, prevents contentedness
Conviction: desire to cease wrongful conduct: results in true behavioral change	**Arrogance:** Refusal to or unwillingness to recognize the need to change, rebellion combined with resolve

I read through the table twice. The Captain's explanation sounded simple enough, but I was confused nonetheless. The new table held some of the same characteristics as the False Reflections table, and this didn't help. I compared the rows for each characteristic listed in both tables. I glanced back and forth between them, trying to understand their differences. When I came to *Submission* and *Timidity* in the False Reflections Table, I objected.

"I thought *Submission* was the opposite of *Timidity*, not Rebellion."

"Remember to keep track of which table you're looking at," the Captain began with a smile. He pointed back to the Table of False Reflections and said, "Submission and Timidity are *here*. The false reflection of an attribute may or may not be its opposite, and in this case, it is not. But look at these," he went on, pointing to a row in each table at once. "Humility is imitated with False Humility, which is a *form* of pride. And Pride is the opposite of Humility."

"Well…I guess," I offered, reluctantly. My mind was still having trouble comprehending the differences between the two tables. It seemed simple for a moment—then one row seemed out of place and sent my mind back to reciting the Captain's descriptions again.

"What about Compassion?" I asked. "Its false reflection is Weakness, but its opposite is Judgment and Justice. Isn't it right to want justice? How can Compassion be good if its opposite is good also."

"I'm glad you caught that one," the Captain said. "Compassion and Judgment are an unusual pair. You would expect the opposite of something good to be bad, but in reality, sometimes it's right to show compassion, and sometimes it's right to deliver judgment or justice."

"*What?*" I asked incredulously. What kind of sense does that make?"

"None whatsoever—yet. But you will learn. Don't be troubled when you don't agree with parts of these tables. In time, you will see understanding comes after *many* questions—and this holds true for more in life than these tables. But to tell you all your disagreements are merely a lack of understanding isn't the response you were looking for; I know this. If you trust me, have faith I have long ago asked the same questions you are now asking. You *will* understand—but only if you *keep asking*."

I don't know what expression fell over my face at hearing the Captain's response, but it evoked a curious reaction from him.

"All right, then, let me give you something to think about. Was it right for the Princess to try to befriend the trolls who guarded her in the Winter Palace?"

"Yes...I think so. I can't read her mind, but it *seems* right." The Captain drew his face back in mock surprise, though the look in his eye remained warm.

"You deserve bonus points for your answer. Both for not being certain—because it's usually difficult or even impossible to know—*and* for saying you can't read her mind. If you miss this point, and assume you know another's thoughts—a whole host of problems beset you." He paused to let his words sink in before he began again.

"Now what about the King? When he passes judgment on a murderer and deals him justice, is that right or wrong?" I applied the same two points to this question.

"Well, I *can't be sure*," I replied in an exaggerated tone, "but if I could *read his mind*, I would say yes."

"So you see my point," the Captain chuckled. "And by the way, congratulations on sidestepping the treason charge in your response. Getting back to your question, *do you* understand now?"

"Well, yes and no," I objected. "When is it right to show compassion, and when is it right to give judgment?"

"When you can answer that, you'll be a wise man indeed. In the meanwhile, it's important to remember: we've sworn our loyalty to the King. This means we accept his decisions, including those on compassion—showing mercy and grace—and also those where he deals out justice."

"*Oh, great,*" I said, remembering the warning we'd received about falsely accusing a member of the Royal Family. "What if we find *ourselves* under the King's judgment? Suppose he doesn't believe our testimonies about the duke," I spoke hurriedly, my voice rising. "He could sentence us *to death*."

"Yes," he replied dryly, "he could."

"And we're supposed to accept that?" I asked, beginning to panic. "What if the King's investigators sided with the duke? What if they lie?"

"Mark, calm down. Remember the King is wise and just, and he is also full of grace and compassion—"

"But he can choose to punish or use compassion whenever he feels like it." I grew even louder, nearly shouting. "What good does it do us if he *can* choose compassion, but he's just as likely *not to*?" The Captain held his hand out, as if he could cover my words with a lid, or calm me with a simple hand gesture.

"The King loves his kingdom, and every one of its citizens. He wants what's best, not only for his kingdom, but for each of us as well. We have to trust him in this."

"But *they're not always the same*. What happens when whatever's best for the kingdom is dangerous for me?"

I knew my voice had grown louder, but I didn't care. I couldn't have suspected it then, but the anger growing within me would not be quenched for a long time to come—not completely anyway.

"Are you thinking of our trip through the desert," he asked, "or our hike through Abaddon?"

"*Yes*," I exclaimed, then continued in a much less certain tone, "well, no…maybe not."

Inwardly, I fought against the point he made. Those trips might have been dangerous, but I couldn't question how they'd both helped me—one by design, and the other by happenstance. Still, I felt desperate to disprove his logic.

"Then what about battles and wars?" I demanded, my voice loud and defiant again. "What about the people who die defending the kingdom?"

For a moment the Captain's face turned to stone. When he replied, his tone had dropped a full octave, and there was a terrible violence in his voice.

"Do you think nothing could be worse than death? What of the men whose wives and children were slain by the marauding troll hordes, but were themselves spared? Would it be a consolation to them, had the King—*for their own safety*—excused them from the battles against the trolls who killed their families? Show me a man who would *prefer this*, and I will relieve him of his cause for joy."

His appearance changed so much, it left me shaken. He spoke from some deep pain, and I dared not ask him about it. After a few breaths, he spoke again, much more calmly.

"But I've distracted myself. There were men—even some who fought under me—who bravely faced the troll hordes threatening their families, *lost their families*, and by some chance of fate, lived. And they *still* choose to serve the King, and saw the good in their service. *This is what duty is*—to serve a great cause, knowing it may cause you great harm. It's not so different from compassion after all, is it?"

I could only bring myself to nod. I don't know how long it took, but the awkward silence hovering over us eventually lifted. We discussed the tables at length and found examples of them around us. We talked about the desert duke, and why he held so much hate toward the King. He'd pretended to submit and love the King all his life, and hid his true feelings of hate, unforgiveness, rebellion, dissention, selfishness and pride. He hit nearly every negative quality on the *wrong* side of the tables. The King on the other hand—the Captain assured me—was dedicated to representing the qualities in the first column of the tables. I tried to call to mind other examples of the *wrong half*, and was surprised at what memories I found: those foggy days when I'd first found myself in Terreldor, halfway across the kingdom. I began to believe those memories served a purpose, whether or not I could rely on them.

The tiny villagers and the near-collapse of their society still seemed melodramatic to me, though their story had a sensible warning within it. The plains trolls the antelope prince had told us of were reckless fools; the mining trolls and merchants were filled with greed.

I much preferred concentrating on the "good half" of the tables. I'd seen many of them demonstrated by the Captain. I already knew Sally had shown me selflessness and loyalty, but I knew she held a deep measure of wisdom also. The Princess effortlessly displayed forgiveness and compassion. The antelope prince showed a strong loyalty to his father's promise. The silent duke was the perfect model for compassion, generosity, and selflessness. The story of tiny villagers, at its end, provided me another example of forgiveness.

I mentioned these to the Captain.

"This is a good sign; you've been given the opportunity to find true wisdom. Many examples of these time-honored lessons will fall into your life. It's up to us to learn the lessons they might teach us. Whether or not you become wise from them is for you to choose, but you've clearly begun on this path already."

I was proud to hear his compliment…but the Captain was talking again, and his voice fell deeper and more somber. Just having paid me a sincere compliment, he countered with a warning. After I listed for him each bad example I'd noticed in the past weeks, he cautioned me against hastily labeling people with the characteristics on the *wrong half* of the tables, lest I fall into the same half myself, by judging them.

"The motives of others are not for us to judge," he explained. "We can see their actions and know if they are right or wrong, but we can only guess at their motives."

Something in his tone stung me. Why was he being so harsh? I was excited to see the tables and to begin to understand them. Did he hate to see me happy about doing something right for a change? Only then did I notice it was getting difficult to read the Captain's writing. It wasn't yet dark, but the Captain's quarters didn't have a view of the afternoon sun, and the lamp at his desk was dim. What he'd intended to be a short meeting had taken the whole day.

"I think it's probably getting close to dinner," I told him.

As if on cue, a low rumbling came from the Captain's belly. He gave a wide smile and told me he would most likely see me the next day. I only nodded as I left, still hoping to hide my anger from him.

Why does he always have to point out my mistakes? I thought to myself. *That's the job of a mentor,* I argued. *I don't care, I still don't like it.* Wondering if arguing with myself might be considered a sign of insanity, I pushed these thoughts aside.

I was in a foul mood by the time I reached our new rooms. The anger stirred in me by the Captain's advice to simply *trust the King* grew with my every step.

I don't have a wife or children to protect. I thought. *What if I die? Are* trust *and* duty *opposites? How do I trust the King not to get me killed if my duty is to go to battle?*

I found David in his room getting ready for dinner. As hungry as I was, I hoped the Princess had invited us to eat with her. Her table was always full of something delicious, and usually had several choices. After skipping lunch, I intended to make up for it by stuffing myself at dinner. My hopes went unanswered when David told me there was no such invitation; Schelli was eating with her parents in the King's private quarters. This meant the King had enough free time to eat with Schelli and the Queen, which hadn't happened many times since we'd arrived.

Great, I thought to myself, *what else can go wrong?* As if on cue, David told me what Eb—Engdynlor's chief cook—had in store for us: cabbage soup.

When we weren't eating with Schelli and Sally, we ate with Eb and the rest of the kitchen staff. It was often a plain dish with little variety, and this night was no exception. I had to choose between going hungry for another hour or two while waiting for the *royal leftovers,* and eating a meal I disliked. I chose the soup and hoped I would find some nice rolls to go with it.

David knew my dislike for the soup, and teased me all the way to the kitchen. We began to argue, and by the time we reached the kitchen, my mood had grown even worse.

"What, no smiles for your favorite dish?" Eb asked as we walked in.

A glimmer of hope flickered in me as I wondered if David had only played a cruel joke on me. Then I saw the mocking smile on Eb's face, and smelled the pot of cabbage soup behind him. I glared at him but gave no other response.

The kitchen staff seemed happier than usual. I was sure they were mocking me and my hate for the soup. There was no bread other than the stale rolls to be thrown to the birds in the morning. I took three of them and set them beside my dish, wishing someone would warn me not to eat them; I was more than ready to complain of our meal. I dunked one in my bowl angrily, splashing soup onto my shirt. Someone snickered, surely at me.

Old Eb asked us to tell them about our home again, but I knew our stories would be met with his doubtful looks and questions. Some of them felt as if we were trying to call the King less important by suggesting there was a land outside his kingdom.

I felt overlooked, eating there with the kitchen staff. After all I'd been through, I felt like I deserved better. Surely, my wound, the long days in a sickbed, the trek through the desert, and warning the King of the plot against him should count for *something*.

My mind wandered until I found it replaying a bad memory. A few years before, I'd spent a long while in another sickbed—a memory I'd tried hard to forget. I forced it from my head, but still lingered on sour thoughts. I remembered bits of conversations with the people I'd met in the kingdom: the Captain—who was eating a fine meal with the King no doubt, the Princess, Sally, and the silent duke. I thought of the ice troll and the hill troll also. The antelope prince's words came to mind, and something my father once said to me, which had angered me very much at the time. Eventually, the Captain's words returned to me, the things he'd said just before I left his room. Each memory crowded into my head, and all of them seemed to ask too much of me.

I realized the kitchen staff was looking at us expectantly, waiting for a story. *Is this all we are to them,* I thought, *cheap entertainment while they eat their soup?*

"Again, old Eb?" David asked. "I think we've told you everything there is to tell of our world."

"I know a story we never told you," I said slowly, without looking up from my bowl.

I felt David's eyes on me, though he remained silent.

"We told you about our technology: how we can communicate between cities and across oceans, how we can ride on planes flying high in the air—and how each adult can drive their own carts faster than you can imagine. Yes, you *ooh'd* and *ah'd* about that, but we didn't tell you about the harm they may cause."

"*Don't*," David quietly insisted.

He knew the mood I'd fallen into, and he knew what I was going to say next. I ignored him. The room fell silent.

"We didn't tell you what happens when our carts–without–horses *collide*. Nearly every adult has their own cart—there are *millions* of cars where we come from. You might drive past thousands of them every day on your way to work. Our cars drive past each other at speeds three or four times faster than your best horses. If just one car drives onto the wrong side of the road, a lot of cars will be wrecked."

"You mean these *cars*—they *hit* each other?" asked the headwaiter.

"Why are you telling us this?" asked Eb, plainly irritated.

"*You* wanted to know all about our home," I answered, accusingly. "You didn't want to hear only the good stuff, did you? Imagine the damage caused by two cars hitting each other head-on, at top speed. Cars get rolled over or thrown into the air. They are crushed into twisted piles of metal and plastic. Sometimes they even catch on fire and burn or explode."

"What happens to the people in them?" asked the headwaiter, wide-eyed.

David squeezed my shoulder, as if he could hold the words inside me. I shook him off.

"*They wanted to know.* Why should I hide it?"

Eb looked skeptical, but kept silent. The others in the room turned their gaze from us when I raised my voice high enough to embarrass them.

"The people inside are *killed*—but not *all* of them. Sometimes half the people in the car die immediately, some make it out with only bruises, and others die slowly, waiting for help."

My voice grew even louder as I spoke, and though they seemed to listen, they continued to avoid my eyes.

"I know this because I lived through one of these accidents—I was the *only* one who lived through it. Some people called me *lucky*. My best friend's parents were the ones who died first. My friend was the one *lucky* enough to die waiting for help."

My voice rose to a shout as tears tried to fight their way from my eyes. I knew better—I even knew I risked disturbing the Royal Family, eating in their private dining room, not far from the kitchen.

"I held his hand as he died—or *tried* to. He couldn't move his arms because they were trapped under a bent seat. He looked at me and asked if he would be all right. I told him he would be fine. I knew it was a lie. *He* knew it was a lie." When I could talk again, I added in a whisper, "His eyes were pure fear. I would've told him anything."

I closed my eyes and the memory, which had too often haunted my dreams, returned to me. Once again I saw his tortured body turn toward me, and ask if he would live. With tears streaming down my face, I went on.

"I was trapped worse than the rest. The rescue workers had to cut the car apart to get me out, but only *after* they removed the bodies."

I tried to tell them how I watched as they cut apart the seat pinning my friend in place. I wanted to describe how gently they lifted his body out of the car, only to put him in a *plastic bag* on the ground, not ten feet from me. I tried to tell them how my back was broken, and how I had to lie in bed for nearly a year while I recovered from two surgeries. I tried to tell them about that year, lying in bed alone with my thoughts, but I didn't. As the memories flooded back to me, I only sat and cried.

I felt a reassuring hand on my back. I turned to David to glare at him as I shrugged his hand off me, but the hand would not be shrugged off. David's eyes were focused on someone behind me. The others hadn't been dodging my gaze, I realized; they'd been staring at the same person.

I turned around and was shocked to see the King and Queen, standing behind me, and wearing somber looks.

5.4 Queen's Wisdom

I put my head in my hands and tried to wipe away my tears. I wondered what embarrassment I might bring on myself next. I heard the King's words spoken softly over me.

"Remember Mark, you can only be healed of those things of which you *are ready* to be healed."

The kitchen staff quietly stood. They politely backed out of the kitchen, bowing slightly as they left. The King and Queen walked slowly around the table and sat across from me.

David, probably not knowing what else to do, offered quietly, "I told him he should *forget* about it. Holding onto these memories isn't good for him."

Then the Queen quietly answered, "No, David. Believing a lie can be harmful, but ignoring a lie you believe only *ensures* it will continue to do harm."

I wondered what lie she was talking about. Once again, a half-memory returned to my mind. *We all invent lies to explain things in this life. The challenge set before us is to uncover them, and to see the truth we've let them conceal.* Who'd said these words to me—the Captain?

"Mark," the Queen went on, "you've believed a lie all this time. You've believed it was *your* fault your friend died, didn't you? *So badly,* you wanted forgiveness from your friend, though he was the one person who could never give it."

An emotion I didn't understand, one I'd never felt before, rushed through me. In my mind I knew his death wasn't my fault, but my heart somehow agreed with her. It felt as if the Queen's suggestion fit with everything I'd ever known to be true, as if it somehow connected two truths I'd never before thought to put together. "You don't need his forgiveness," she went on. "You need forgiveness from *yourself.*

You need to release this lie." Then she turned to the King and added, "Wade dear, tell him."

The King added, "When the troll attacked you, he left a scar on your neck. But this lie you told yourself—it put a scar on your heart, far more painful than the troll's work. Recognize this lie for what it is, and only then can the scar on your heart be healed." There was a moment of silence, and then the Queen spoke again.

"This type of scar is brought out by new pain."

I remembered how I felt earlier when the Captain told me the scouts would be sent, and how I'd feared for David's life. Then, getting angry at the Captain, I wondered, *Why am I acting like this?* The Queen spoke again.

"The old wounds show through when you feel new pain. Instead of leaving the old wound open again, let love heal your new pain, and the old wound too."

My crying had stopped. I thought of replying, but she wasn't done speaking yet.

"You need love to get past this. Your strongest relationships can carry you through the pain of uncertainty."

How could she guess what was bothering me? I felt weak; I wished they would leave me alone. And then, a thought coalesced in my mind and I knew; it was the same feeling, all over again. I was afraid I would lose my brother.

"I don't want him to die. I don't want David to go," I said, my cracking voice sounding strange to my ears. It couldn't have made sense to my brother. His eyes probably opened wide, but I wasn't watching. My head was still on the table, buried in my arms.

"Let your love for your brother carry you through the pain of uncertainty. Look at him. You are very close, the two of you. Such a relationship should bring you strength, not hurt."

Her words made no sense to me. *Maybe they will later*, I thought. I knew how much my brother meant to me. I found I even cared for the King and the Queen. *It makes no sense*, my thoughts argued, *I hardly know them*. Somehow, I believed the King truly cared for me. His hand on my shoulder had felt like my father standing over me, as if he was standing there, waiting to help. Just then he reached across the table and put his hand on my shoulder once again, and turned from his wife to speak to me.

"Be careful with emotions coming from an old wound; they are strong indeed. Emotions are meant to be a gift to us, not a burden. At times we enjoy them, at others—we learn from them; sometimes we are tempted by them, and at yet other times, we draw the *strength of resolve* from them."

When he said the word *resolve*, I remembered taking the knife from the Captain's hand, and the certainty I found in knowing I could never hurt him again. The thought flew through my mind in a flash, while I struggled to focus on what the King was saying.

"We experience fuller lives because we have emotions. If we don't learn to control them, however, they will surely control us. This doesn't mean we can stop ourselves from *feeling* emotions. Instead, we're *responsible* for reining them in." He saw his meaning was lost to me. He cleared his throat and spoke again, perhaps a little lower than before.

"You see, we can stop ourselves from *making a decision* based on emotion. We all lose control of our emotions at one time or another, but it's important to realize even so, it's a *choice* we make. It isn't beyond our abilities to keep them from deciding for us." Then he paused, and looked directly into my eyes, and became still as stone, perhaps wondering whether he should go on.

"Emotions cannot be denied; for you to attempt to deny them is to lie to yourself. A wise man or a child can both be measured by their emotions. For he who merely *thinks* he's wise, he will hide his emotions and imitate those of others, in order to feign maturity."

I'd begun to understand him when he spoke of reining in our emotions, but the rest of his words were wasted on me. I would remember them later and play them over in my mind until they made sense. David was looking at me with deep concern on his face. The King and Queen looked as if my pain hurt them as well. What could I do? With no other idea in mind, I apologized for disturbing them.

"There's no apology necessary for needing help—or for *asking for it*." The King's eyes twinkled as he spoke the word *asking*. I realized I hadn't asked for any help, and wondered if this was his point.

"You've got a lot of thinking to do, I see," said the Queen, smiling warmly. "Why don't you get some rest for now?"

I could only nod and mumble a weak *thank you Sire, my Lady* as I left the kitchen. David followed wordlessly behind me. On the way to our room, my mind was filled with random thoughts. *My lady—is that the right way to address a queen?*

We didn't talk on our way, but David put his arm on my shoulder as if to say, *I'm here to help*. He couldn't have understood what I was afraid of. I was torn; I couldn't tell him anything without mention of the duke and his conspiracy. I wondered what he imagined I was talking about when I told the King and Queen I was afraid for him.

After David and I were ready for bed, and talking in my room, there was a knock at the door. David answered, and opened the door for the Captain. He handed David a sack, and asked if I would meet him for a late dinner. His eyes seemed to tell me he knew of my outburst, and our visit from the King and Queen. David only nodded toward me, and I threw on an extra shirt and slid a pair of leather moccasins over my feet.

As the Captain and I walked to his quarters, I asked him what was in the sack for David. "Just some fresh bread. Eb guessed neither of you had eaten much."

He said nothing else while we walked. I tried to guess why he had come to talk to me. Did I breach some code of conduct? Would I lose my apprenticeship and my chance to become a knight?

When we got to his quarters I saw there was food laid on the long table where we'd met, hardly an hour ago. He motioned for me to take a seat and invited me to help myself. He sat across the table from me, folded his hands behind his head and swung his feet up onto an empty chair.

"The King spoke to me just before I came for you. And...I spoke with Eb. You've had a long day, I gather."

"Yes sir," I blurted between mouthfuls of stew. The Captain looked at me for a moment as if studying my face. I was exhausted of all the emotions I'd shown earlier. I must have seemed almost happy, compared to how I'd acted when I'd seen him last.

"I knew there was *something* bothering you when you left, some other wound you carried. I didn't imagine it as horrifying as the things you told Eb." The Captain leaned forward and opened his mouth as if he were about to speak, but only paused, holding his breath. Nervously, I reached for the glass of milk before me and gulped. *Bleah*—it was warm.

The Captain sighed and leaned back in his chair.

"I won't press you for details. You'll bring it up again when you're ready. I *did*, however, want to tell you tonight how sorry I was to hear your friend's story. I've seen too many good men die in battle. We may not have your land's technology, but death in battle has its own horrors."

I paused for a second, my mouth ready to close on a spoonful of stew. I expected he might tell me he was sorry I had to see something so horrible, or sympathize with me as a victim of the accident. Just then, I realized in all the time after the accident, I'd considered *myself* more of a victim than my friend, though *I* had *lived*. I hid from the thought and pushed it from my mind.

The Captain remained silent. My mind raced to imagine what he was going to say.

Why isn't he talking? Surely he came to me for a reason, to tell me more than he's sorry for my friend. Am I being dismissed from my apprenticeship? Is he thinking of a polite way to tell me? Why'd I act like such a baby, interrupting the King's dinner?

I remembered the King saying I was responsible for controlling my emotions, so it was plain the Captain would say I *chose* to act in this way.

Finally, I could take the suspense no longer.

"*I don't know why I did it*," I blurted. "I didn't *want* to yell like that. I...I couldn't help myself." In the brief silence, I could hear my pulse quicken, loud in my ears. Surely my face was red. My throat felt tight and strained, like I swallowed too much dry chicken.

The Captain leaned forward and put his hand on my shoulder, just as the King had. If he'd wondered before, he knew for certain I was shaking.

"Maybe it was time for someone *else* to help you. It's true you choose your actions, but you should know sometimes it takes outside help—though I don't think this is what you meant by *help*."

Why does he always talk so cryptically? I wondered. I played his words over again in my mind, trying to guess his meaning.

"Tell me this," he said, his voice and demeanor becoming more relaxed. "When you feel this helpless, what keeps you from asking for help?"

"I didn't want anyone to—" I started, but then realized the Captain was using his *quiz voice*; he was testing me. I thought about it for a moment and answered honestly. "Pride."

"Exactly," he chuckled. Apparently he hadn't expected such a frank answer. "*Pride* kept you from talking to me about it. But I'm your *mentor*. If I am to help you mature enough to become an Honor Knight, I need to know these things so I can help you through them. You won't offend me or make me think less of you if you tell me how you feel. Not even if you feel angry with me, or offended by me—not even if you have doubts about what I've told you, or assignments I've given you. I only require you tell me these things in private, and in a respectful manner. Then, I will always try to help you."

"Do you mean…I'm still going to be your apprentice?" I asked.

"*Of course.* You've caused no harm tonight. You've told no lies, betrayed no oaths. Sure, you interrupted the King and Queen's dinner, but they were happy to help you. They spoke to me only from true concern for you. This is why I called you here. Well, this, *and* I realized you hadn't really eaten since breakfast," he said, waving his hand at the empty plate in front of me, "though it would seem you haven't eaten *for days.*"

I was relieved. I relaxed noticeably, and chortled to think how worried I'd become over the Captain visiting me. Then questions began to flood into my head.

"How did the Queen know what was bothering me? Can she—" I hesitated to say it aloud. "Can she *really* read my mind?"

"No," answered the Captain, smiling. "She saw you were hurting. She knows the signs. It may come as a surprise to you, but many people who live through an event like yours react in the same way. Blaming yourself, burying the pain, then seeing the old wound open fresh at a time of stress…these are common symptoms of losing someone close to you. We might not have *cart accidents* like people do in your world, but people lose loved ones here, just as they do anywhere else. You might say your reaction was normal, or at least *expected.*" Then he smiled, and added, "Perhaps you were even louder than you guessed, and she heard most of your story all the way from the kitchen."

I smiled, but was still surprised at hearing his explanation, though it sounded reasonable. I'd thought I was unique in my pain, and this had somehow made me feel alone. I remembered the Captain had lost his father, when he was even younger than me. I still wondered if he had lost family members in the troll battles and raids. I shook my head, bringing my thoughts to the present.

"It's worse than you know," I admitted, "I've been feeling angry— at you, and the King, also. It started this morning, when you warned me about judging others."

The Captain's eyes opened a little wider.

"I know, I know—there's no reason for it. I just felt…*angry*. Even before, I was jealous of David's mirrors, the ones from the King. *I still am.* Ever since I heard the story of the old mine I wanted to know more about its history—and now David owns part of that history. I'm all over the bad halves of the tables. Jealously, greed, rebellion, anger…I thought I was done with all that."

"*Done?*" chuckled the Captain. "Did you think you were dead—or merely perfect?"

It was my turn to open my eyes wide. *Did he really say that?*

"I didn't show the tables to you so you would never step into their *bad halves*, as you called them. I showed them to you so you'd know where you still need to grow—so you can continue to mature. I find myself on the *bad half*, even *today*. Do you think I don't have immature thoughts all the time, and I don't have to make a deliberate choice not to walk in them?"

My brow fell from surprise to skepticism.

"I'll tell you a story," he went on. "Maybe it will convince you." He shifted in his seat and his eyes focused on a far-away memory.

"A few years ago an old friend of mine died. He was a kind old man who had done much to help me over the years. I called him *Uncle*, we were so close. A few years before he died, he asked if I had a small knife he could borrow, to cut away some vines growing up the stone walls, and into the roof, of his small home. He needed a knife small enough for his tired hands to control. I was leaving the next day on an errand for the King, or I would have done the work myself. I knew I had one knife small enough…but it was one I didn't want to lend."

The Captain's glance dropped to my belt buckle. I ran my thumb behind the buckle and felt the knife I took from the Captain in the desert.

"You know I received the knife the same way you did. I imagined my friend's feeble hands slipping off the vines again and again, and my knife striking the stone wall of his home. So when my friend asked me if I had such a knife, I lied."

"*You didn't,*" I burst out, hardly aware I'd spoken aloud.

"Yes, I did. Even worse, I knew I broke the Knight's Code. All night long I tossed and turned. Sleep didn't find me all night, though I was desperate for it. I couldn't imagine lending my apprentice knife to my old friend, and yet I couldn't imagine letting my lie stand with him."

"What did you do?" I asked, leaning forward as if I could hear his reply sooner by doing so.

"I woke him early the next morning, before I left town. I explained how I'd lied to him, how I *did* have a small knife he could use. Of course, he was shocked when I told him this. 'Why would you lie to me?' he asked, plainly hurt. 'You could have simply told me it was valuable, and you didn't want to lend it to me.' I told him the knife wasn't costly, but instead a gift from an old friend. Then he was adamant; he refused to borrow it. 'I'll ruin it, cutting against the stones in my wall.' He didn't want to cause me pain any more than I wanted to hurt him."

"What did you do?" I asked again.

"I explained to him I knew it was part of the road laid before me, and he had an opportunity to help me. I asked him not to refuse to play his part in an important lesson for me. I looked him in the eye and told him his friendship was more important than anything I owned, and I left the knife lying at his feet."

"What happened?"

"When I returned from my errand, my old friend returned the knife to me."

"But was it hurt? Did he ruin it?"

"See for yourself," the Captain answered. I loosened the buckle of my belt and bent back the little piece of wire holding the knife in its place. I looked at it more closely than before. The entire knife was one piece of steel, the blade and handle together. Both sides of the blade were sharp, and met at a point. When I looked closely, I could see one side of the blade had been sharpened more, the edge on one side was closer to the centerline than the other. There was a deep nick on the same side of the blade.

"He did this?" I asked, fingering the blade's imperfection.

"When he returned the blade it was very dull and had several deep nicks. I was able to grind them all out but one. Even so, I distorted the shape of the blade, dressing it. I always had a reminder of this lesson. Now *you* will carry this lesson with you, wherever you go."

"Was it hard to do—to go and tell the old man you lied?"

"Not as hard as it would've been to let my lie stand with him. There's no shame in your actions when you are led by conviction. Conviction compelled me to confess to my old friend, not to hide the lie. Once I started the short walk to his home, it became easier still. Remember, when we go against a wrongful desire, the very act of doing so breaks the strength of our desire until we can defeat it. In time, we make a habit of the correct action. I still have the same desires, but they don't influence me as they once did. After the knife incident, our friendship was stronger for the experience."

Could the Captain be just as selfish as I was? Or at least, could we have the same desires to *act* selfishly?

"If I always want to act selfishly," I asked, very much wanting to keep my question hypothetical, "but I always resist and act generously, does it mean I'm selfish, or generous?"

"Generous," replied the Captain, his certainty surprising me. "*We are defined by our actions, not our desires. Only for the feeble are they the same.'* This is a LifeGrowth my mentor taught me when I was young. Do you know what it means?"

His tone had shifted again: his *quizzing voice.* I paused for a second, though I thought I already knew the answer.

"If you are feeble, you will always do as you desire…and your actions and desires are the same." It felt too easy; *surely I missed something.* "*That can't be right*—this would only be true if *all people* want to do what's wrong…"

"Oh," the Captain said with a teasing smile, "did you think you were the only one? *Of course* we all have wrong desires; it's part of being human."

I smiled, then I chuckled. It wasn't funny, not really, but something about it felt terribly right. I felt a sort of relief inside me, as if I set down a burden I'd been carrying for a long time. The Captain only smiled, with a knowing look in his eye.

I thought again about my jealousy over the old mirrors. I imagined not wanting them anymore, and I *wanted* to feel this way, though I clearly didn't yet. As surely as if he read my mind, the Captain spoke on what I'd been thinking.

"Don't wait until you no longer *feel* selfish or jealous. It's enough to starve the feeling; don't feed it with your actions."

He stopped, as if to let the thought sink in, and I shivered again. When it seemed like he read my mind, it made me uneasy, though I realized it shouldn't be difficult. Why shouldn't his point become clear in my mind as he built his way up to it?

I turned to him once again and asked, "When will I stop *feeling* jealous?"

"That, my young friend, can take a *lifetime.* I still feel it myself—though not as often or as strong as before. Remind yourself often: if you expect change and desire it, you will continue to grow. You will see such changes many times throughout your life. This *relearning* is a concept I've begun to show to you. We have a special name for it; we call it *LifeGrowth*.   You will come to know it well, and to teach it to others."

When I thought he would finally bid me goodnight, he added, "If you think you can stay awake, I have one more story for you tonight.   I think you are now ready to hear it."

If I had any doubts I could stay awake, he'd talked me out of it.   I nodded vigorously.

5.5 The Third Table

It was late and my belly was full. The room was dim, lit only by the oil lantern in the chandelier above us. The Captain spoke in hushed tones, his voice hardly more than a whisper. If I wasn't so eager to hear his tale, I would have been asleep in minutes.

"This is a story of *fathers and responsibility*, and of *orphans and second childhoods*. It is a story of maturity.

"I told you how my mentor found me. I was young and fatherless, drifting and rebellious. I was poisoned by hatred and unforgiveness. I was about your age: past the point when apprentices are usually chosen by their proteges. I was at the age when most boys choose to become men, or to stay children for life, and I was *not* headed down the path to manhood."

I realized my expression must have shown surprise when the Captain nodded his head and smiled. I didn't expect he considered me already past the point when boys choose to be *men*.

"Are boys my age considered *men* in some parts of the kingdom?" I asked in a cautious voice.

"No." He smiled, before he continued, "But there's an age at which boys run the risk of being trapped in childhood if they aren't trusted with responsibility. It isn't always the case, but the two often go together.

"The jobs I'd been drifting between required little responsibility. When my father died, I had no time for learning. I took whatever jobs I could find, jobs I knew would pay immediately, without schooling or apprenticeship. Between the poor jobs, the death of my father, and my blaming the King for his death, I had unknowingly chosen a dark path. Notice I said it was my *choice*; it wasn't forced on me by my situation. When young adults choose this path, they enter a second childhood, one with no parents, and where no one can teach them. They may mature physically and even intellectually, but not in any other way. They can never become a good mentor because they cannot pass on what they never learned. This is what I call having the heart of an orphan. It may last fifteen years, or more. Sadly, for some it never ends. They cannot truly mature from this point, unless they once again become a learning child. They must have the heart of a trusted son.

"When my mentor befriended me and gained my trust, I began to return his kindness with hard work. Only then was he able to teach me an important lesson." He wrinkled his brow when I opened his mouth to interject. "No, *not* my first LifeGrowth—though it was soon coming." He paused, and continued only when it seemed I wouldn't interrupt. "He taught me a skill, something I could be good at. I learned to enjoy hard work for the first time in my life. It was only a minor task, but I *was* good at it."

"What was it?" I took him by surprise, not foretelling my interruption with my expression.

"Making horseshoes. Even then, I knew it wasn't much, but I liked making them because I knew I was good at it. Then he taught me another task I could succeed at. I didn't have to win a contest, or call myself better than others, but once again, I knew I was good at it, and this was enough to enjoy it.

"After repeating this process several times, I began to learn the *skill of succeeding*. Most people don't realize *succeeding* is a skill, but it *is*. It can be applied to any challenge. Now mind you, it doesn't guaranty success; it's a *prerequisite*. It was an important lesson, one I badly needed to learn. Before I did, I hated my work, and so I could never succeed at it.

"For the first time in my life, I worked hard for my pay. For a short while before, my mother and I had drawn money from the King's public funds. It wasn't much, but I never valued it because I knew I hadn't earned it. I might have expected it, or even convinced myself I *deserved* it, but I was never *grateful* for it.

"I no longer acted like an angry child, and yet my heart was still rooted in childishness. As much as I liked my mentor, I still couldn't commit to any long-term plan of his. I wasn't allowing what my mentor taught me to truly affect me."

"Didn't you?" I interrupted. "You were a hard worker and you earned your way—isn't this important?"

"It is, but it was only a tiny step in the right direction. If I was really going to learn from my mentor—learn the deep things he wanted to teach me—I needed to take some of his priorities as my own. I needed to be concerned with the things *he* was concerned with. I saw what kind of man he was, and I even wanted to be like him, but not to the point of acting on the desire.

"One night when I'd completed a difficult project, he invited me to stay a few minutes; there was something he wanted to tell me. Curious, I accepted. As soon as I sat on an empty bench, he told me he had nothing else he could teach me. I objected. I told him I wasn't half the man he was, and there was plenty he had left to teach. I was confused then when he agreed. He told me, 'I didn't say I had no more to teach. I said I have no more I can teach *you*.'

"As you can imagine, I was infuriated. I stood to leave. He sat me down and told me, 'There are some things you've been unwilling to learn from me. Until you are willing to change in these areas, there is nothing more I can teach you.' I knew the areas he spoke of; it wasn't the first time he'd mentioned them. Then he gave me an ultimatum.

"'Take the night and think it over,' he told me, 'And tomorrow, if you are willing to change—if you are willing to learn how to turn your back on rebellion and unforgiveness—then come to work early. If you are unwilling, then your apprenticeship is over. You have learned some fine blacksmithing skills, and you would make a fine blacksmith's assistant, or even a soldier—but not an officer. To lead men, you need more than skill. I will recommend you for either position: smithy's assistant, or soldier. If these are not enough for you, if you are willing to grow, then I'll expect you here early in the morning.'

"I was so mad, I could hardly keep my mouth closed as he stood to show me the door. I stormed out of the shop, steaming all the way to my room. I started making plans for what I would do the next day. I knew I wouldn't accept his offer, or his recommendations. I was determined to make my own path. But when I fell asleep my plans were suddenly not so fixed."

"Why not?" I interrupted. "Did you have a dream that changed your mind?"

"Indeed I did," the Captain replied. "In my dream, I saw myself five years down the road, then fifteen, then *forty-five* years down the road. I had continued to distrust and mistreat people close to me, and so I eventually drove them all away. Continuing in rebellion cost me all hope of healthy relationships. In my dream, I saw the ill effects my choices had on my life. I became a bitter old man who hated everyone, who hated *life*. Finally, alone and in misery, I took my own life. *That*," the Captain said emphatically, "was the very end of the road I had chosen."

"What did you do?" I asked. I would've had the answer if I'd taken a moment to think about it.

"I was waiting at my mentor's door at the break of dawn. The following day, he told me of the Honor Knights and invited me to begin my apprenticeship in the order. I had chosen the road to true maturity, and I've continued to choose it, as often as I knew how."

The Captain smiled, and let out a long sigh as he looked at me. I was leaning my head on my hands, with my elbows on the table. He pulled my hands out from under my chin in a flash, and my head plopped onto the table.

"It looks like you're about to choose the *road to bed* for the night," he said, with a laugh. With his story over, I realized how tired I really was. I had been struggling to stay awake.

"Enjoy your day off tomorrow," he told me.

"Why? What's tomorrow?"

"Did you forget? It's Saturday." I nodded. "Well then," he said, "I advise you use it to sleep in."

He patted me on the back as I headed for the door. As I was about to leave he spoke again.

"Mark—just so you know: I didn't tell you this story because you are in danger of choosing the wrong road. You are certainly on the road to maturity. I only wanted you to have a better understanding of what the road is, from *my* point of view, when *I* chose it. And, you should know we must *continue* to choose this road many times, if we are to grow."

I nodded sleepily, and he handed me a small, torn piece of paper. I hardly remember looking at it then, but I studied this table the following day, and I've studied it for many years since. Written on the scrap of paper, were the rows and columns of the third table.

Table of Maturity

Worthy & Honorable Characteristics, & Childish Behaviors they Replace

Mature Characteristics	Childish Characteristics
Helping others advance, selflessness	Comparing others to self out of jealousy
Compassion, willing to sacrifice to give others the opportunity to choose right	Passing judgment, anger and hatred
Contentedness, joy, willing to suffer for good	Fits of anger or self-pity when selfish desires aren't fulfilled
Patience & Longsuffering (contentedness, happiness, & elation proportion; willing to bear hardships for a cause)	Focus fixed on short-term gain, impatience, expecting constant elation or entertainment
Service, and giving	Self-centeredness, inability to see beyond Self, Taking
Leadership: Allows room to grow & choose. Leads to loyalty. Gives away authority, trains others to take place. Gardener leader.	Controls others through fear, leads to resentment and disloyalty. Holds onto control. Watchmaker leader. Imparts nothing.
Humility, giving attention to others	Pride, bragging, needing attention of others
Learning priorities from father/ mentor	Rebellion: Orphanhood, no relationships or responsibilities
Controlling emotions enough to make responsible choices	Letting emotions and desires control you
Teaching path of maturity to others; giving it away	Never learning path to begin with; holds others back from finding path through negative example
Conviction, learning shortcomings and changing	Guilt, shame, shortcomings grow to insecurity, never grow past them

I *did* sleep in, and not because the Captain recommended it. As I slept, I dreamt. My dreams were vivid and long, but there was only one I remembered with any clarity. In it, I was walking along a path on a hilly plain, dotted with mature oak and beech trees. It was a sunny day, and I remember hearing birds chirping. The path led to a cliff's edge, then turned, and led me along the cliff's edge for a long way. The sky grew gray and a strong wind picked up. Farther down the road, I could see a disturbance in the wind, out past the cliff's edge.

Only then did I bother to look in this direction. What I saw made me tremble; there was *nothing* beyond the cliff. By nothing, I don't mean the bottom of the cliff was too far away to see, or even there was air, or clouds floating in the sky. There was literally *nothing* there. It looked gray, but not like a fog. In my dream I somehow knew the gray wasn't even there; it was just...*nothingness*—and it was frightening.

I continued on the path, not daring to walk close to the cliff's edge. I found the disturbance in the wind I saw earlier was a tornado, floating past the cliff, out in the midst of *the nothing*. Near the tornado, the path forked in two directions. One led away from the cliff to the sunny plains, where all was green and peaceful. The other led across a kind of broken stone bridge leading directly into the tornado. I looked down the second path, wondering who would ever choose it.

The bridge began to crumble. Bit by bit, blocks of hewn stone fell in shattered pieces from the far edge, and were swallowed by the tornado. It was whipping around madly, carrying the dust of the mortar and stone its violent winds destroyed. Bits of the bridge calved off even further, and I felt an anxious urge to cross it and enter the maelstrom. I still feared it, even more so with my sudden urge to enter it. I began to see shapes in the wind and dust. They began to materialize into something familiar, though I couldn't tell what.

Another dozen stone blocks were torn from the bridge and crushed. I turned and ran down the path to the meadow. I felt safer as I ran, but it didn't last long. The ground opened in front of me, turning into the same cliff I'd left behind. I woke in a panic, rebelling against the irony of the path I chose.

Lying quietly in bed, I heard a windstorm blowing outside my window. Thinking the wind had woken me, I rose to close the shutters outside the window. I realized the wind hadn't woken me; there was someone knocking at my door. When I opened it, I found a messenger standing with an envelope in his hand. He delivered it to me, turned around and knocked on David's door. When David received his own, the messenger left us standing in the hall, curiously opening our envelopes. David read his aloud; they were both the same.

"'To David and Mark; Princess Schelli requests your presence in taking lunch today. Please come to the central courtyard upon receiving this card.'"

"I guess she means *now*," I replied with a yawn. "Wait…it isn't lunchtime *yet*, is it?"

5.6 Called by the Princess, Called by the King

The windstorm carried an electrical storm on its tail. We heard its thunderclaps through the thick walls of Engdynlor on our way through its halls. As we approached the entrance to the uncovered courtyard at the palace's center, we saw rain pounding the garden. We hesitated before stepping out into it.

"They won't be *out there*," David said. "Let's walk around to the other entrances to the courtyard. We'll probably find them waiting for us."

He was right. We found them at the next entrance, the one closest to Schelli's quarters. Lady Sally held two large baskets, and Schelli was carrying a blanket.

"You're *here*," exclaimed the Princess. She continued in a disappointed tone, "It looks like we'll be dining indoors."

We talked and joked with each other as David and I carried the baskets up to Schelli's quarters. All were in good spirits as we approached her room. She was laughing as we rounded the corner of the hall, but fell immediately silent when she saw someone standing at her door.

Schelli asked us to wait where we stood while she spoke with the young man. She walked hurriedly toward him. We looked to Sally for an explanation, but she had little to tell us.

"He's a page: a messenger from the King," she said. "Do you recognize his uniform?"

As best I could tell, he was dressed the same as the messenger who had delivered my summons to testify before the King. Schelli finished speaking with him and approached us with a curious look on her face.

"What was his message?" asked David.

"I don't know. He will deliver it only to Mark."

I was shocked, but not as much as David was. I didn't know what to say.

"Is it urgent?" I asked.

"If it wasn't, my father would have sent a page."

David jabbed me with his elbow and added, "You better go see what it is."

As I walked to the messenger, I wondered what could be so urgent. I guessed the King might want more details about my testimony. Beyond this, I had no idea.

"Do you have a message for me?" I asked the messenger.

"Are you Mark Adams?" I nodded, prompting him to say, "You must come with me at once; the King has requested an audience with you."

"Do you know what it's about?" I asked as I followed him past the others.

"I've been told nothing else," he said, his tone suggesting it was a common response he used.

He walked swiftly, and I felt obliged to keep up. I barely had time to turn my head as we rounded the corner in the hall. David and Schelli looked somber. Perhaps the Captain was wrong. Maybe I *had* offended the King when I interrupted his meal the previous night.

As we walked down the hall and a long stairway toward the King's Court, I tried to imagine what the King would ask me. I thought of the remark I made at the beginning of my ride across the desert. The Captain had reacted nearly violently when I'd suggested it was a stupid idea to send me to a mud pool for healing. Perhaps he *had* considered it some form of treason. I remembered the Captain's surprise at the amount of time we spent with the Princess—maybe the King would reprimand me for it. I wondered if I'd broken some rules of etiquette I'd never heard of. Any of these might be true, but none of them were urgent.

Finally, the messenger led me past the entrance to the King's Court, to a hallway just beyond it. We were headed to the same room where Sally had led me, when she found how ugly my scar had grown. If I remembered correctly, it was called the King's Council Chamber.

When we arrived, there was a guard at the door. He drummed out a short rhythm on the door, and I tried to remember if it was the same as the last time I'd been there. The door opened, and another guard came out. The first guard led me into the room as the door was closed behind us. The messenger remained outside the chamber.

The King sat at a table with maps and papers spread across it, the Captain beside him. There were others in the room: a young scribe seated at the table, and two older men standing behind the King. I suspected the older men were knights or generals, or possibly both.

The guard remained at the door while I walked to the nearest end of the table. The King sat at the far end. When he noticed me, he waved me over to him, and said distractedly, "Good. One of them found you."

Did he need to send more than one messenger? I wondered.

"Have a seat if you're tired," the King added.

I looked around. The two older men were standing, and they *looked* tired. I remained standing.

"Thank you, Sire. What can I do for you?"

The King sighed as he laid a pointing stick on the table. He looked directly at me, as if forgetting all the maps and plans spread before him. For just a moment, he peered into my eyes and said nothing. There was no question; he had given me his full attention for the time being.

"Mark, my official investigation is over. I received messages from my agents. The duke has confirmed the charges against him."

"He *did?*" I blurted out without thinking, "*Already?*" If anything, I was sure the King didn't call to answer *my* questions. *Of course,* I thought immediately, answering my own question, *otherwise the Captain would not be going over plans with him at the table.*

The King chuckled at my response, but managed to keep a weary face as he did.

"Yes, he did. It's been three and a half days since you returned. My messengers brought homing pigeons with them and I've already received two messages by bird. Those messages told us the duke's soldiers attacked and killed my first messenger. My second messenger watched from a distance, and sent his birds unseen. The duke came outside the city walls and spat on the body of my first messenger. *The duke...*" He turned to the Captain and muttered, "Andrew, how long will it take before I stop calling him that?"

I didn't know what to say. Who would spit on a dead body? The thought of it made me cringe.

The King went on, "Well, he's no longer a duke. He's now an enemy to the kingdom. I think history will call him *Neil the Traitor.* It seems he's rallied the trolls and several of the larger trade guilds to fight with him. The troll city you saw in the desert is growing; the last homing pigeon told us as much. It won't be long before they're on the move."

"What can I do?" I asked. I was curious to know this, but I still didn't understand why he sent for me.

The King was thrown off by my question. "Eh? Why, *nothing*. Well, nothing *right now*, anyway. No, I called for you to tell you my investigation is closed and your testimony, as well as the testimony of the Captain—scratch that—the *Commander*, has been entered into court record, confirmed as truthful and accurate. It is a sad occasion for the kingdom, but still, I owe you an official notice of gratitude for your part in bringing this news to me. You don't hold any formal position in the military, so it is customary for me to make my appreciation publicly known. This is no cause for celebration, due to the dire circumstances involved. Whether this is eventually labeled as quieting a rebellion or not, in truth we shall soon be at *war* with…*the Traitor* and his rebels.

I remember feeling excited to hear the King would publicly thank me, but also guilty for taking pleasure in such a dark time. I wondered what exactly a *public thanking* from the King meant. I tried to hide my excitement, but was unsuccessful. I remembered the Captain's words about not being the only one with selfish desires, and relaxed a little.

The King, seeing my emotions, smiled and continued, "It's all right, Mark. It's not a happy occasion, but it doesn't fall on your shoulders to carry the grief of the kingdom. Go ahead and be proud of your part in uncovering this plot—it's no small matter. It's tradition for me to grant you a gift of your choosing, and I am happy to do so. So name your gift. Within reason, I will grant it."

Immediately I thought of the hinged mirrors from Eastward and Westward David had received. I pushed the thought out of my mind thinking, *now is not the time.*

"Sire, it was enough to help you, and the kingdom."

"Come now, it isn't right for you not to be rewarded. You *must* choose something. As humble and noble as you'd like to be, you *will* be rewarded."

"I won't trouble you with any request just now then, Sire. I know you have more important things to concern yourself with." I was proud of my reply, though the mirrors still hung in my thoughts, taunting me.

"Very well. Just make your request known to the Captain—make that the Commander. As busy as he'll be, I'm certain you'll be seeing a lot of him."

I looked up at the Captain and mouthed, *Commander?* He turned and nodded.

"Not at all a welcome promotion," he responded. "It's one I hoped to never receive."

"And *this*," said the King, "is partly why you're the best man for the job. The kingdom hasn't needed to raise our three armies for centuries. No matter how swiftly this may be resolved, I fear there will be terrible loss. Nothing good can come from this."

The Captain—I still thought of him as *the Captain*—added, "We can always hope, Sire."

"Yes, the *prophecy*. Of all of us, I should expect, *you* will not hang our hopes on this. If this can be resolved diplomatically, it must be. For the sake of all the lives in the kingdom, *I hope* this rebellion has nothing to do with the prophecy."

"Of course, Sire. If there is any way out, any middle ground our kingdom could survive, I will find it."

"I know you will," the King said quietly.

The prophecy? I wondered. I made a mental note to ask the Captain about it later.

"Mark, I will send for you soon," said the Captain. "We need to discuss your role as my assistant." I looked up with my question written plainly on my face.

He went on, "A commander has no hired armor bearer. Generals and commanders have a junior ranking officer to assist them with this duty, and others."

I didn't want to start a lengthy discussion while he and the King were so busy, so I only nodded. When neither of them spoke to me I took a step back. When their attention returned to the maps and papers before them, I took it as my cue to leave. Halfway across the room I heard the Captain call after me.

"*Mark*—just to let you know—the announcements have already been made. There are no secrets concerning the coming battles, the raising of armies, or the Traitor's denouncement. This news is going by fast riders all over the kingdom tonight."

I nodded back to him. When he turned back to the King, I turned again to leave.

The guards on both sides of the door played the same knock-and-switch trick as I left the Council Chamber. I wandered back to the barrack where David and I had stayed, my head full of everything but where I was headed. When I arrived, I realized there was nothing there for me. The barracks were quiet; I went inside anyway.

Our cots were bare and lonesome. The shelves where we'd kept our clothes were empty. Without so much as a thought, I folded my cot and moved to lean it against the nearest wall. Something caught at the legs of the cot. I moved it aside and found my backpack, the very one the silent duke had given me.

I wondered what had happened to the old man. I hoped the hill troll never returned to his manor, though I knew it would sadden the duke. A schizophrenic wave tumbled over me as I remembered those first days on the island. I'd felt so confused and alone, I felt half-mad recalling it. *Could it really have happened as I remember?*

Standing in the empty barrack I was absolutely certain I wasn't hallucinating or in a dream. Still, I felt unsure about my memories of those first few days. I had no way to explain talking animals or tiny humans, and it bothered me. I wasn't comfortable not knowing the *why* or *how*. I wanted to believe they were each separate dreams I'd had in the nights after we'd arrived, but somehow felt I might never be sure.

I went through the items in the pack: an old piece of waxy paper once wrapped around bread we'd eaten long ago, a small wool blanket, some rope, a canteen, and...the giant catfish tooth. I'd all but forgotten it. I realized I had no memory of the Captain returning it after he'd taken it and left us alone with the Princess, in the tunnels under the Winter Palace. I was glad to find it; it helped me trust my memories of our first days in Terreldor. I folded David's cot, collecting his pack as well. I slung a pack over each shoulder and left for the palace. I held the giant tooth and turned it over and over in my hands. I knew there would be much to do soon, though I had no idea what the Captain's plans were for me.

My mind was focused on the coming war, and what it would mean to everyone I knew. My mind seemed too full of important matters, and I resolved to forget them for the moment. Still inspecting the oversized tooth, I tried to remember the hill troll at the duke's manor, Otlak Plain and antelopes, the tiny villagers, and everything we saw on the back of Golden Mountain.

Soon I was nearing the Princess's door. Before I could ask the door attendant to announce me, she told me the Princess requested I stop to visit her. Without waiting for an answer, she popped through the door, then opened it wide for me.

David, Schelli and Sally were sitting down at a table, apparently finished with lunch. Only then I realized how hungry I was. They pelted me with questions.

"*All the soldiers are gathering.*"

"What did my father want with you?"

"*Do you know what's going on?*"

I grabbed a piece of chicken and bit into it. "*All right,*" I said with my mouth full, "I'll tell you everything, but can I get a bite to eat first?" I was done with a drumstick before they could answer. Greedily, I reached for David's milk, then paused. "Cold?"

David smiled wryly. "Cooled from the same ice brought for the ice troll," he answered. I gulped it down and reached for a roll.

"The King is gathering the soldiers and raising the three armies," I began, my mouth still full. Schelli's eyes opened wide and Sally gasped aloud. David looked at both of them, wondering what it meant.

"Why? What is so terrible, he needs all three?" asked Schelli.

"You don't know yet?" I got blank stares from all of them. "I guess the news is still being spread. The Duke of Enthicia has been denounced, and the King has labeled him a traitor. He's leading an army of trolls and rebel merchants to try to steal the throne. He was even behind the trolls who took over the Winter Palace, who planned to kill the King there."

"*Impossible,*" said Schelli, then added, "*Why?*"

"*Sweet mercy!*" exclaimed Sally, her voice shrill.

David just looked at me, doubting. "Why did he send for you—why not the Princess?"

"Oh." I'd nearly forgotten. "I stumbled across the duke's—I mean *the Traitor's*—plot first. He was trying to kill me and the Captain…who's a commander now, by the way. The Captain figured out he was planning to take over the throne."

Sally's face had turned white. Schelli asked, "Can…can I go see my father?" I didn't say anything until I noticed her staring at me. I realized she was asking *me*.

"What? How would *I* know? He's busy making plans with the Captain…I mean the *Commander*, and some other men."

Schelli looked disappointed. I realized she was really asking if the King was busy. Unsure of what to do, I put my hand on her shoulder.

"I'm sorry, Princess. It seems like everything is happening at once. I guess the plans they make in the next few hours will make a big difference for the kingdom." She nodded, but her gaze dropped to her feet, and she said nothing in reply.

Somehow I knew Sally's love for the kingdom was deeper than someone our age could understand. For Schelli, the kingdom was like part of her family. David looked disturbed, but I knew it didn't affect us as it did the others.

"What else did he tell you, dear?" asked Lady Sally, still pale, and clearly shaken.

"Well," I started, "he had to tell me because there's a tradition... I'm not in the army, so he has to thank me for helping bring the news to him...you know, of the *plot*."

The Princess said, "An *Official Note of Gratitude*. There'll be a public notice." Finally, the hint of a smile crept back in her face. "People really *will* know your name throughout the kingdom *now*." She paused, and her smile vanished. "I can't believe the duke would commit *treason*. I can't believe my father *believed* you. Wait a second—he wouldn't have listened to you unless you had two more witnesses...*the troll! That's* why you brought him back. To stand trial *indeed*, it was the *duke's* trial—*you knew all along*."

How could she be angry with me? I met her glare and replied in an even tone, "Like you said, sometimes doing all the Captain asks is doing a lot. He swore me to secrecy." I looked to David; soon he would be the most affected by my news. He didn't know about the law of three witnesses, and so he had no idea what Schelli was talking about.

Lady Sally mumbled absentmindedly, "Yes...three witnesses to bring an accusation against any member of the Royal Families, even a Ward."

If David looked betrayed before, his expression doubled at hearing how much I'd hidden. None of their reactions were as I'd expected. I'd done my best to be loyal and honest, but all those close to me acted as if I'd betrayed them.

"What *should* I have done?" I asked them, "Disobeyed the Captain and the King, betrayed them both just so you could know a few days early?"

I watched their faces turn from anger to something else. Maybe they *didn't* blame me.

I went on, "Look—it was no picnic for me. I felt awful, not able to tell you three—especially you, David." I saw his face relax a little. *Ah, I thought, he wanted recognition.* He only needed to know I wanted to tell him most.

I decided at that moment our emotions are too complex for our own good. Even so, I understood they account for much of who we are. *As far as we grow in life,* I thought—the fact I was only fifteen notwithstanding—*our emotions drive us to impossible ends. If a man lives to be a hundred, can he truly outgrow something as childish as petty jealousy? Will I ever see someone get what I want, and feel happy for them?* I wanted to bind up my emotions in a jar and keep them locked away forever. That's *how I'll grow mature,* I thought.

I thought these things as Sally gathered the three of us into a crushing embrace.

"If this is the worst we go through in the war to come," she said, "we'll be blessed indeed."

Caught in the tight grip of her arms, I felt my face flush red. I remembered the words the King had spoken to me. *He who merely thinks he's wise, he will hide his emotions...* How could I have forgotten so soon? I felt I understood a little more of what he said, and I knew it to be right.

"Sally is right," the Princess added, upon our release from Sally's arms. Her expression was sternly fixed on David and me. "Big changes are coming, and we need to be a little less worried about our own feelings. Now tell us what happened, Mark, and everything you know about the coming war."

"It all started when I couldn't fall asleep on our last night at the duke's—I mean *the Traitor's* mansion. I walked outside to see Yashel..."

"Who?" interrupted David.

"*Yashel.*"

"Who's that?" asked Schelli.

"My *horse.*" I could tell I would be a long time in telling my story. I took a deep breath and sighed. *All the better.* I had to think ahead and make sure I didn't mention the Honor Knights. I was relieved it was the only secret I had left to keep.

I told them the entire story of the Traitor's plot, and how we brought the ice troll out of the pit. I left out the part of the poisoned oasis so I didn't need to tell them of the secret room behind the waterfall—I expected the Captain still wanted this to remain a secret.

When I was finished, the three of them sat silent. I used the time to grab more food. Sally interrupted just before I finished a pumpernickel roll.

"What about the coming war? What's to happen now?"

"I really don't know," I replied. "They only told me they expected the Traitor to start moving his troops soon. They said the armies would be raised and the Captain was promoted to commander. Oh, and since a commander doesn't get an armor bearer, I have to be his…*military assistant*, I think."

"*Really?*" Sally asked, plainly surprised.

"I think so. Why?"

"Oh, it's nothing. It's just…well, it's an important position."

"It is? I think I just have to run errands for the Captain."

"Well yes, you would," Sally went on, "but it's a position that…well, it may be different for Generals. We haven't had a commander for so long, I just don't know…"

"Why hasn't there been a commander?" asked David.

"A *commander* commands all three armies and the navy. In peacetime—like the peacetime we've had for so long now—we have only one army, and it's a small one. We only have a commander when the other armies are raised—for *war*."

"But what about the assistant?" David pried. "What were you going to say?"

"Well, it's an officer's position. You know…*higher than a sergeant*. It's no small matter. It means Mark has joined the army—or he's been drafted."

I interrupted quickly. "The Captain didn't say anything about *drafting me*. He only told me I was *supposed* to be his assistant. I'll talk to him about it later, I guess."

"What else do you know?" asked Schelli.

"That's about it. The trolls from the new barracks in the desert are expected to be on the move soon. I guess the announcement going out means the three armies will enlist people. Are they volunteers? Are they drafted?" I looked to Sally.

"It depends. I certainly hope they're volunteers, but it depends entirely on how many men the King and the Commander think they need. It depends on their battle plans and how many trolls and men they think they'll face. If the King can help it, he will use mostly volunteer militias, rather than fulltime recruits."

"What will you do, David?" I asked.

"What do you mean?"

"In the coming war—your mentor's in the scouts, so he'll be assigned *somewhere*. Will you stay here?"

"How do you know he'll be sent?" he asked defensively. "He's just as likely to stay here."

"It's *not* just as likely," said Sally. "I'm afraid Mark is right. If all three armies are to be raised, the only military to stay behind will be the first army; they protect Thraen Kholl and the palace. There'll be far more use for scouts in the two armies going to meet the enemy."

"*It's not true*," David objected. "They'll need scouts to make sure armies aren't sneaking up on the palace."

He sounded uncertain even as he said it. When no one responded, he stood up and paced angrily around the room. When he could hold his tongue no more, he stopped short and stomped his foot.

"Well, enough waiting," he said. "I'm going to find the scouts and see what's going on." He started for the door.

"David, *wait*," Schelli called after him. He didn't turn back. I ran across the room and caught him by the arm.

He spun around to face me. He wasn't *angry* with me, but he certainly expected I had something important to say after jerking him back through the doorway. I realized I had only meant to keep him from leaving; I had nothing to say.

"Be careful...and *be wise*," The words sounded odd even as I said them. I squeezed him briefly around the shoulders, and he was out the door. I stood in the doorway, watching him disappear down the hall. As he did, I saw a messenger quickly approaching, his eyes locked on me. I heard Schelli's voice as if it were a thousand miles away.

"Sally, what's going on? Why are they leaving?"

Then, clearer, I heard Sally's reply. "Princess," she said in a somber tone, "let them be. The kingdom is falling into war. By tomorrow, your young friends may both be in the army and on their way to meet the enemy. And what's worse: the King's armies may even *need* them before we're through."

5.7 Battle Plans

I had no chance to say goodbye to the Princess or Sally before I left. The messenger sent me directly to the Captain's quarters, insisting *he* would explain why I needed to leave so quickly. *You could tell me first*, I thought, frustrated with the messenger.

All the way to the Captain's quarters, I wondered about my brother and the scouts—and about being a military assistant. *Would it really make me an officer?* And then, almost surprising myself, I thought, *Do I even* want *that?*

When I came to the Captain's room, there was a young guard standing at his door. When I gave him my name, he let me in. The Captain was sitting at the same wooden table where we'd sat the previous day. I was embarrassed to remember what I'd thought the last time I'd sat there, expecting to see golden mirrored tables set with fine jewels.

The table was still full of maps and long paper lists—almost as cluttered as the table in the King's Council Chamber.

"Mark," he said excitedly, "come sit down." He pushed the chair beside him away from the table with his foot. When I sat, he turned back to his papers and said, "Well, what do you think?"

"Captain? I mean...*Commander?*"

"A little difficult to call me by a new name, is it?"

"Sorry. And hard to remember to call the duke a traitor."

"I know," he answered, "but it's important for those who hear us to make these distinctions." He smiled. "When we're alone, feel free to call me Captain; it makes no difference to me. Now...what do you think of the battle plan so far?"

I looked at the map of the kingdom and noticed the broad strokes of arrows indicating troop movements with numbers and letters beside them. I studied it for a minute, guessing what each mark meant.

"It looks like…the first army stays outside Thraen Kholl and patrols the surrounding area…the second army heads out to the desert, to the troll city and TerkEtmek…and the third army heads for the west coast, along Terrezia Plain. And…are these *scouts*? They go north into Harringtonwood and the North Forest. More scouts go ahead of the second army into the desert, to the troll city and also to TerkEtmek. And still *others* go ahead of the third army, into the road along Terrezia Plain, all the way around the Vuori Mountains and forest, to the south end of the desert where they meet up with the scouts at TerkEtmek. Is this the entire battle plan?"

The Captain raised an eyebrow and looked sideways at me. "No, but it's an important start. How did you know the meaning of all the symbols?"

"I didn't. But look, these arrows are the biggest, and there are three of them, just like the armies. All these *S's* have little *a's* on their arrows, and everything else has little *b's* or *c's* or other letters, so the *S's* probably move out first. It makes sense scouts would go first, to tell the armies what to expect. The big arrows have little *b's* near them. They must go out second, so they're probably the second and third armies."

"Hhhmm. I thought I would need to explain a *little* more of this. What else can you guess?"

I studied the map further. A lot of the lettered arrows had little numbers near them; they had to signify *something*.

"Well, scouts have *a's* and go out first, then the second and third armies have *b's*, until they reach their first stop. After that, there are several arrows for both armies, labeled with *c's*. Does that mean they split up? Or maybe they choose *c1* or *c2* according to what they find…or what the scouts find? The second and third armies have two *c* choices, and then, from those points, even more *d's*. I have no idea whether the different choices mean the armies split, or if they choose one option over the others."

"And neither do I", said the Captain. I thought he was teasing me until he continued. "Either could happen; they *could* split, or they could choose one option over the others. You are correct; it depends on what the scouts report and what the armies find for themselves. Was it really so easy to guess? I shouldn't be surprised; we didn't attempt to obscure our plans in code."

"We? Does that mean you and the King are done for now?" I asked.

"Just for now. We've been working on these plans since you and I returned from the desert with Sphotch. We worked separately until the investigation was over, but together as soon as I was cleared."

"*Really?* Do the scouts go out tomorrow?"

"Oh, no," replied the Captain, thrown by my question. "They were sent out immediately—nearly four days ago. Scouts have already reported back from Tume Belor and Harringtonwood. Others should be reporting back by the time our armies get out as far as the oasis and Terrezia Plain."

I sighed inwardly to hear the news. If the scouts were already sent out days ago, David missed it. Then it hit me. This was why David's mentor gave him time off from his duties. *Of course*—the King said he needed to conduct his *own investigation* to confirm our testimony...who else would he send but his scouts? He used a different word...*agents of mine*, I think, but they could've been scouts just the same.

I turned back to the Captain. "When do the armies leave?"

"Tomorrow."

"*How?*" I asked doubtfully. "Can two new armies be raised in a day?"

"No, but the King had to make plans in case his investigation showed we were telling the truth. Many of the Royal Guard and officers of the First Army were warned the three full armies may need to be raised. They were organized into the chain of command of the three armies. We only need to finish recruiting the privates, some sergeants, and very few officers."

This didn't seem like such a trivial need to me, and I thought briefly of interrupting him to say so.

"Also," the Captain went on, "the third army will expect to recruit more troops as they go through the farm villages along Terrezia Plain. The scouts headed north are recruiting men to join the second *and* third armies. They will also recruit many to join the dwindled First Army near Thraen Kholl. This brings me to my next point. I need a military assistant, and you never gave me your answer."

I fidgeted in my chair before I caught myself. Fidgeting didn't seem like knightly behavior to me.

"Don't you need an officer?" I asked in barely-masked enthusiasm.

"I *need* someone I can trust, and someone who's available. All the junior officers I trust enough for the position are badly needed in the chains of command for the three growing armies. I trust *you*, and you aren't able to lead soldiers into battle."

"Well," I replied, "when you put it that way…"

"You shouldn't be offended. It should be no surprise to you, I wouldn't assign you to lead a troop of recruits into battle."

"No, Captain, I wasn't being sarcastic. I was afraid you were expecting me to be as qualified as an officer." I couldn't imagine leading a troop of grown men on a hike, let alone into battle. Who would follow me? And what could I have to offer them as a leader?

"Well, know this then; this role will stretch you further than you like…and I *do* expect you to be as qualified as an officer, just not yet as a leader of men. You'll find yourself doing things you didn't know you were capable of."

I wasn't sure I liked what he was suggesting. The Captain looked as if he expected me to say something. Shortly thereafter he added, "Well? Will you accept the position?"

"Oh! Well…what does a military assistant do?"

"Usually, an assistant would help me plan battles and perform all the tasks I won't have time for. The tasks will be many—I'll be very busy now that the Second and Third are moving out. As for the battle planning, you don't have the required training, so I'll have other officers assist me in this role. You'll be responsible for keeping track of my maps, battle plans and assignments, and for keeping them secure."

I wondered briefly how I might be expected to keep maps secure.

"When I said I needed someone whom I can trust, I wasn't being facetious. Some of the battle plans and contingencies will be extremely secret, known only to myself, and at times, the King. I may also have need of a messenger, to carry documents or messages between myself and others in the chain of command."

The Captain paused just long enough for my mind to catch up with him. It was a lot of information, and I felt like I should be taking notes. I remembered he was only describing the position so I could choose to take it or not. I began to wonder if I really had a choice.

"Now let me warn you about the information you'll have access to," he continued. "There are times when men are sent into very risky battles, even times when a mission is so dangerous *and* important, the soldiers sent out may not survive. This is part of what makes war so horrific; these missions have to be planned…and I must send men on missions I know they won't likely survive. Is this something you can live with? Would you carry instructions to the men who may die carrying them out?"

I couldn't imagine the Captain ordering men to go on a mission he knew would kill them. I supposed if trolls were coming to kill an entire village of innocent people, and there weren't enough soldiers there, the Captain would have to send as many soldiers as he could spare, even if they might all die.

"I—I think so, Captain."

"You have to be sure. Would you be tempted to change *any* order before you delivered it? Or would you deliberately *not* deliver it? If you disagreed with my decision to send such a mission, would you even *hesitate* to deliver it?"

I thought about it carefully. Any such mission must hold many lives in the balance, either way. If I changed it or threw it away, then *I* would be responsible for the deaths it caused. To think of it scared me, and I told him so.

"You're exactly right; I'm glad you came to this conclusion yourself. So then you accept?"

"Yes, I do." I thought further for a moment, and added, "Did I really have a choice?" He smiled back at me.

"You did until you refused—then I would have drafted you. This way I know you'll do a better job." His answer stung. Just then, I remembered something he'd said while we were on the run from the traitorous duke, approaching the Spill Hills.

A difficult time can mean oaths and obligations make your choices for you. There may be little room for error.

I guessed the Captain would soon have less room for error than ever. Perhaps he had *no choice* but to draft me. If he hurt the feelings of others in making all the decisions his role demanded, I could only imagine what it might do to his *own* feelings. *What would it feel like to send men to certain death, even for a mission to save many more lives?* I shuddered again to think of it.

"Then it's settled," the Captain said. I pulled myself from my thoughts and looked back to him. He asked me, "Do you have any questions?"

"Will we leave tomorrow?"

"No. I need more information before I know where I'll be needed most."

"Information from who?"

"From *whom*," he corrected. "From the scouts, from the Second and Third, or from homing pigeons any of them carry."

"Who was Nigel? Was he an Honor Knight?"

"*What?*" I'd obviously touched a subject he hadn't anticipated. I read in his eyes; he'd let his guard down, and already given me the confirmation I'd hoped he would. "I was only asking for questions on your new position. Besides, you know I can't answer such a question—you can't know who the other knights are, and I can't narrow the list down for you." He paused for effect, but I felt no guilt for asking. Nigel was certainly someone involved in the plot to usurp the throne. "I can tell you this," the Captain added in a conciliatory tone, "Nigel was the person sent to kill me in TerkEtmek."

"What is this *prophecy* you and the King mentioned?" I hoped to catch him off guard again, more than I hoped for a complete answer.

"Well...yes, that's a hard one. I'm not sure how much of this I can tell you." He seemed at a loss.

"Because the King won't allow it?" I asked, somewhat surprised.

"No, he trusts my judgment in this matter completely." He squinted one eye and rubbed his temple as if he had a headache.

"There are old records from the Harrington family," he finally began. "Some were recorded so long ago, we know nothing about their origins—not even exactly *how old* they are. We know these to be the oldest records we have.

"They're like pages from long-lost books. Some of these pages are...well, not completely trusted. Some describe the kingdom as it was long ago, and some describe characteristics on the tables I've shown you. Other pages tell of the New Rule and what it should be like. Still others seem to talk of the future: sort of a future history."

The last part of his answer made no sense to me whatsoever. How could the future be history?

"What do you mean?"

"They're written like pages from history books, but many items they mention seem...well, they sound like they're talking about the future. Some of them describe, *in detail,* events well known to occur since they were found. Those who know of them have very different ideas on what they might mean. Some think they foretell the future, and others think they are an ancient history *coinciding* with recent events, purely by chance. Still others believe them to be a hoax. I know one thing for certain about them: all the kings in the Harrington line have considered them as *possible* prophecies, and have given each of them careful consideration.

"One page describing the ushering in of the New Rule, tells of a horrible battle beforehand, which will rob the world of those who are unable to accept the New Rule. Mind you—it repeatedly states the war is unavoidable by those who defend the kingdom, and is in no way fought for the *purpose* of removing *anyone*. The events leading up to this battle are very similar to the events unfolding in the kingdom today."

Now *that* sounded interesting. I wondered if such a thing were possible.

"Do you think it's true?" I asked. "Do you think this is the war in the...*prophecies?*" It felt strange to call them prophecies, when I so strongly doubted the term was accurate.

"I would be derelict in my duties to assume so. This is basically the warning you heard the King give me; if I assume this *is* the battle the page speaks of, I wouldn't look for a peaceful solution, or consider negotiating a conditional surrender. If I believed this was the *Last War* in the prophecies, I would believe all our enemies need to die in battle with us."

I saw immediately how disastrous holding this belief would be.

"This could only come," the Captain continued, "at a huge cost of lives on both sides. Worse yet, losing most of the trolls might mean the extinction of their entire species. If the New Rule is about anything, it certainly isn't *genocide*. It's about the folding in of *all* peoples, into a peaceful kingdom capable of fair self-government. I must look for a path to preserve our King's rule as the highest priority, and secondly, a path minimizing loss of life. In the long run, I'm certain these goals are the same."

I thought about what he said. In the long run, would preserving the King's throne mean fewer deaths? I let the thought pass, reminded of something he'd just told me.

"You said the events in the prophecy look like the events we're seeing now. How so?"

"I hesitate to tell you." For a short second I thought he was joking. He wasn't.

"Why?" He must have known I wouldn't be satisfied with so short an answer.

"First of all, you may be convinced the prophecy is legitimate, which would affect your ability to perform your duties—"

"*No it wouldn't*," I interrupted angrily. I paused to keep my tone in check. "I'm pretty skeptical...certainly enough to doubt someone could predict the future."

"How can you say that? You have no idea how convincing the evidence is."

I thought for a moment. "It's only *theoretically* possible there could be proof so convincing, I couldn't help but believe it."

"In this case," he replied with a smile, "the proof fits your theory." Then, in an instant, his smile left and his voice grew somber. "This page has only been seen by a small handful of people, most of them knights. I've never heard of an apprentice knight who had access to this information."

"Well," I argued, "have you ever known an apprentice who was an assistant to the Commander over what *might be* the *last war*?"

The Captain pursed his lips and his eyes focused on the air in front of him.

"I'll concede you have a point," he said reluctantly. "Know this though: what I'm about to tell you is one of the closer guarded secrets of the kingdom." I couldn't help but to interrupt at hearing that.

"*Really?* Why?" When he didn't respond, I tried to feign patience as I waited for him to begin.

"Well, for one, it sows a seed of distrust in the Royal Families. It also could lead to people believing the trolls should be wiped out. At the moment, the trolls represent the largest share of our enemies. We will not excuse the hatred some humans have for trolls. To share this with the entire kingdom would certainly breed more hatred toward them."

Wanting very badly to hear what he might say next, I kept silent while the Captain paused yet again.

"The prophecy tells of a traitor from one of the Royal Families. He leads the rebellion and starts the *Fast War* or the *Final War*. Some believe it's called the *Final War* since the New Rule is issued afterward and the need for war should—in theory—be gone. It also tells of a young outsider who helps uncover the plot. Since you and your brother arrived, there's been a lot of talk about this page among the knights. We've never had someone who fit the description of a *young outsider* as well as you and your brother."

At this, I couldn't help but to interrupt.

"What about the Royal Guard back on Golden Mountain? They said there was a prophecy about me having special dreams. Were they talking about one of these pages?"

"Yes and no. Very few have access to the page I'm telling you about. The story of a young outsider who dreams true dreams survived through legend. The men you remember speaking had no knowledge of any pages in the King's records concerning such things, only *legends* of prophecies and dreams."

At first I thought the Captain had unintentionally told me there were no other Honor Knights in the Royal Guard. Disappointedly, I realized any knights present would have known to keep their mouths shut. His eye twinkled the hint of a smile before he began speaking again. Were my thoughts so easy for him to read?

"Now, back to the Final War page," he started. "It also describes your involvement—sorry, I mean the *young outsider's* involvement—with the tiny people you said you met on the other side of the kingdom. Even your injury—there is something described in the Final War page that could be interpreted as the injury you received from the ice troll."

"I see what you mean," I replied. "It's hard *not to* suspect it's real. How could it predict all those things about me? Is there anything it lists about the 'young outsider' that *doesn't* fit me?"

"I would say so, yes. Depending on how you view the events described in the prophecy, they might look like things you've done, and they might not."

I tried to imagine such an event, but thought of nothing. Either the prophecy described something I'd done, or it didn't. I asked the Captain how it could be otherwise.

"Well, take your scar for instance. The prophecy says the young outsider receives a scar from the enemy, and cannot easily be healed. Then later, it states the young outsider is never wounded by the enemy at all. They can't *both* be true…"

"What if there are *two* young outsiders?" I asked, "There might be one who is injured, and one who isn't. Hey, David would like that—it's like a guarantee he'll never be hurt."

"You see?" the Captain replied with a smile. "It depends on how you look at it—and it gets even *more* complex. There is mention of the outsider healing the scarred land, bringing her people back together, and leading an oppressed people out of bondage. But the order of these events seems backwards, as if the outsider grows younger as time passes."

Any explanation I thought of seemed too contrived to consider. The Captain's strange tale no longer seemed intriguing to me.

"It doesn't sound so convincing to me," I said, breaking the brief silence. The Captain eyed me with mock suspicion, then changed his expression and went on speaking.

"It gets even less convincing. The prophecy says the Final War will come at a time when there is a peace treaty between the kingdom and her enemy. There is no such treaty, and there never has been. Then the prophecy tells how the enemy used lies and dissention to buy allies to fight against the King—and this fighting takes place while the enemy remains true to the peace treaty. If all this were not enough to cast doubt, it goes on to list specific west coast cities rebelling against the King. Just before you came to my quarters, we received two homing pigeons from scouts who reached two of those cities. They found only loyal citizens who pledged their continued allegiance to the King. This is all evidence against the prophecy, or at least evidence the prophecy speaks about some other war."

"What else does the prophecy predict?" I asked. "What other things *haven't* happened yet?"

"There are plenty. The traitor is in turn betrayed by his allies. There are vague descriptions of significant acts played out by the Navy, and others involving the knights, and forming peace with the trolls."

"Betrayed by his allies—really? Is this why you thought the trolls would eventually turn on the duke—because the prophecy *says* they will?"

"No, no," he replied, wrinkling his brow. "As I said, I can't assume the prophecies are real. To command the King's armies I need to remain objective." I didn't mention he wasn't yet a commander when we'd had the conversation about the trolls turning on the duke. I suspected the Captain *did* believe the prophecy was true, but couldn't admit it, not even to himself. I changed the subject.

"What's the prophecy say about the Navy?"

"Like I said, it's very vague. Some significant act depends upon the Navy delivering someone to a specific place at a specific time. It seems unlikely, since the Navy has only a few boats, and serves only two purposes—neither of them diplomatic."

The Captain saw the question in my eyes before I could interrupt him.

"One purpose is scientific: to map the coast and research the land under the ocean—I told you this once. The Navy measures the depths of the oceans. Their few ships have always found it gets deeper the farther from land they sail. Their other purpose is to deliver messages or supplies to far away locations near the coast. Mostly they run between Portsmouth and Oyster Bay, since there are no roads to Portsmouth." The Captain screwed his expression into a thoughtful look.

"However, delivering quick messages does have military value. The Navy is sure to come in handy if the war lasts very long. Homing pigeons *fly home* to Thraen Kholl, but they can't deliver messages to a moving army. Still, the prophecy is specific about the Navy carrying *people*, not information. Those people are needed for some event to take place. Maybe the Navy could deliver the King to sign a peace treaty. The truth is, *I don't know*."

"It sounds like you've spent a lot of time trying to figure it out," I said. By then, I was nearly certain he believed the prophecy. If he noticed I was teasing, he didn't show it.

"Yes, we all have—I mean the knighthood, of course. The Final War page and their notes are required reading for Honor Knights as part of our training."

"What notes? Are they guesses at interpretations?"

"Some would say they are."

We talked of the Final War prophecy and the coming war late into the night. The Captain ordered food brought to us. After we ate, we talked about what I would need to do as his assistant. It sounded like I would be doing almost *everything* for him, but surely he would be even busier. Finally, he dismissed me and wished me a good night's sleep. As I left, I turned back to see him bent over the maps and lists on his table. It was the second night in a row the Captain taught me more than I thought my head could hold. I thought about the previous night and how far away it already seemed. As I turned at the end of the hall I remembered the Third Table—*I'd never even brought it up*. I'd scarcely taken the time to look at it. I pulled it out and read it once more as I walked to my room. I sighed as I thought it might be my last night to enjoy a soft bed—a cruel irony after just receiving my lush room in the palace the day before. I'd surely be sleeping in a cot before long, wherever the Captain would be stationed during the war.

When I opened the door to my room, I found my brother there, asleep. He'd left a candle lit, and I could see him clearly, lying fully dressed on top of my still-made bed. I stood at the edge of my bed and rocked his shoulder. He sat up groggily.

"How long did you plan to stay out," he asked, "all night?"

"I lost track of time. It seems like I'm going to be pretty busy as the Captain's assistant. I'll even need to travel with him, wherever he goes during the war."

I knew this would bother David. His mentor had surely been called away, and David would be left behind at the palace. At least I'd know he'd be safe.

"Well, at least I'll know you'll be safe," David said. I spun my neck around and stared at him.

"*What do you mean?*" I snapped.

"*You'll* be with the Commander. They'll make sure he's safe no matter where he goes, since he commands all three armies. You'll probably be sleeping in a nice, comfy bed for most of the war."

"Why? Don't you think he'll be called away?"

"Sure, once in a while," David said, "But how do you think he'll command three armies unless he stays somewhere safe, somewhere in between them all? He'll be here, in the palace." How did David know all this? I stared him hard in the eye.

"Who told you this?"

"My mentor left me a note with a new officer in the Second Army. He recognized me from the Winter Palace—he was one of the prisoners there. The message says I'm to meet with the Second out in the desert—*tomorrow*. The scouts are spread thin with all the information the Commander and Generals need. I'll be going on *real missions*," he added, clearly excited.

I felt like the bottom of the room fell from under me. The security of thinking David would be safely left behind was too fresh for me to lose it. I realized David probably felt the same way when I'd left with the Captain, just over a week ago. *Could it really be so short a time since then?* I wondered.

While I'd been walking back to my room, I'd felt like I couldn't stay awake another minute, but learning David was leaving the next day shook off all my sleepiness. We sat and talked for a very long time. I warned him of all the dangers in the desert I'd seen and heard of. When he got up to leave, I started emptying my pockets to get ready for bed. My hand closed on the catfish tooth, still in my pocket. I held it out to David, who smiled at seeing it.

"It seems so long ago," he said. I handed it to him.

"Take it. Maybe you'll need to chip through some ice where you're going." He smiled again—he wasn't likely to see any ice in the desert. He thanked me and we embraced.

"If I don't see you tomorrow, *keep safe,* and *be wise.* And keep the Commander from doing anything crazy," he said with a smile. This has been forever burned in my mind as the moment the words *keep safe, be wise* somehow become our unofficial motto. It's something we've said to each other when we've parted ever since, and it all began with those clumsy words tripping out of my mouth, early in the morning as David left Schelli's quarters in a fit.

"I'll see what I can do," I replied. He left, and I tried not to imagine what the next day might hold. I fell asleep in my clothes, and slept like the dead. My future had seemed uncertain since I'd arrived in this strange land, but never more than the night before the kingdom fell headlong into war. It was a war fated to change Terreldor forever.

Continue the adventure in *Terreldor at War*
Available at Amazon as Trade Paperback and Kindle eBook

The Kingdom of Terreldor has fallen into war, and Mark must choose the path to self-preservation, or follow his mentor to battle a great evil. He will learn the lasting scars of war are not always wrought on the battlefield.

Mark and his brother are unlikely visitors in Terreldor, ever in search of a way home. The course they choose will shape not only the world they leave behind, but also their destiny, and the men they will become.

ISBN: 0615734448 (tpo.)   Terreldor Press
www.Terreldor.com

Epilogue

I am Andrew, the eldest son of the man who recorded this story. I truly don't know whether to say *recorded* or *invented*. Did my father mean for this to be taken literally? Did he name me after his childhood mentor, or give my name to a character he created?

I can easily imagine my father conceiving this story as a way to teach his life-lessons to those he would never meet—but why all the detail? He'd never before shown an interest in writing. When I first encouraged him to compose a book of his memoirs, he was very resistant. That was five years ago. How did he turn from reluctant chronicler to hopeful novelist? I asked the same questions of my cousin—the elder daughter of my uncle David—and told her of the manuscript I'd found. She was shocked.

After her father died, she found notes for a book he was planning to write, though apparently never did. Just as my father, he'd never shown any interest in writing as far as anyone knew. The most amazing part was, my uncle's earliest notes matched my father's story in nearly every detail. When had they conspired to invent such a tale? Why hadn't they told anyone in all their many years? Could it be they both wrote of events they believed took place? This is doubtful to even the most imaginative mind.

My father has been gone for two years now. He'd never mentioned anything like these stories while he was alive. Certainly, the *Three Tables* were as recognizable to me as our family name. I'd seen many versions of them growing up. The tables in this story most resemble the last ones he'd shown me, after I had children of my own. The earliest tables I saw were child-like in their simplicity. He taught them to me and my siblings as soon as he hoped we might understand them. He even taught them to my *own* children when he found I'd passed on the same lessons, without drawing them into actual tables.

My father was somewhat stubborn—or maybe I should say *passionate*—about arranging these lessons into tables. He claimed these tables made a world of difference in his own life. They certainly made a difference in the lives of our families. My brothers, my sister and I grew up in a happy, loving home. My father claimed it came from the values he installed in us, beginning when we were so young. As each of us met with our own various forms of success, again he claimed our upbringing—including the many lessons he left scattered throughout this tale—played a large part in our accomplishments, and in our maturity. My cousins each tell a similar story of their upbringing.

So perhaps this story *is* real—at least it was real enough to affect my entire family. And if it's a confabulation, a shared delusion by two aged minds, it may still be real enough to affect you.

Notable Characters

Right and Honorable King of Terreldor: Wade Harrington
Princess: Schelli Harrington
Princess's Steward: Lady Sally
Captain of the Guard: Andrew Williams
Lieutenant of the Scouts: James Underhill
Duke & Hon. Protector of Enthicia: Cornelius Neil Ward III
Protagonist: Mark Adams
Mark's brother: David Adams

<u>Adventures in Terreldor</u>
Journey to Terreldor
Terreldor at War
The Long Path Home
availability and details at http://Terreldor.com

Excerpts from C. M. Hibbard's online reviews on iTunes, Kindle, Nook, & Smashwords

"[Hibbard] takes the reader on a thrilling ride...a journey of suspense and adventure." *-Susan Mahoney*

"An original idea and thought-provoking story." *-J. D. Howard*

"A gripping read." *-Sandra Hicks*

"Amazing insight." *-Parul, Amazon user*

"Interesting story with unexpected turns...beautifully written." *-Nook user*

"I would love to see more books by Hibbard." *-Maya, Amazon user*

"So much meaning it leaves you asking what's important in life." *-DebbieS, Amazon user*

"A must read." *-Larry B. Gray*   "Amazing!" *-Odetta, Amazon user*

"Leaves you wanting more!" *-Diskson Magombedze*

"Excellent, meaningful book." *-MinisterAsh, iTunes user*

--------------------------**Tear along lines**--------------------------

http://Terreldor.net Adventures in Terreldor
http://Terreldor.net Adventures in Terreldor
http://Terreldor.net Adventures in Terreldor
http://Terreldor.net Adventures in Terreldor
http://Terreldor.net Adventures in Terreldor
http://Terreldor.net Adventures in Terreldor
http://Terreldor.net Adventures in Terreldor
http://Terreldor.net Adventures in Terreldor
http://Terreldor.net Adventures in Terreldor
http://Terreldor.net Adventures in Terreldor
http://Terreldor.net Adventures in Terreldor
http://Terreldor.net Adventures in Terreldor
http://Terreldor.net Adventures in Terreldor
http://Terreldor.net Adventures in Terreldor
http://Terreldor.net Adventures in Terreldor
http://Terreldor.net Adventures in Terreldor
http://Terreldor.net Adventures in Terreldor
http://Terreldor.net Adventures in Terreldor
http://Terreldor.net Adventures in Terreldor
http://Terreldor.net Adventures in Terreldor

A Word on the Typesetting

I had *Journey to Terreldor* set in 12 point Garamond and printed on cream paper—both deliberate choices with the reader and environment in mind. By far, the easier of the two choices was the paper.

The most hazardous chemicals used in the manufacture of paper are the chlorine compounds used in the process of bleaching it white. Cream paper is not only easier on eyes with its utter lack of glare, it's easier on the environment.

Garamond is considered among the most legible of all typefaces, but it is also heralded as one of the most *green* of the major fonts in terms of ink usage. With such a highly readable font, a 12 point typesetting is effortless to read.

A Brief History of the Garamond Type

The name Garamond describes a collection of humanist serifed typefaces named after the letterpress punch-cutter Claude Garamond (1480–1561), though it is clearly a misattribution. Sixty years after Garamond died, Jean Jannon issued a typeset in France with several similarities to C. Garamond's, though it was unquestionably a new work with undeniable intrinsic value. It is *this* typeset today's Garamond fonts most resemble.

The French government raided Jannon's office and stole his new typefaces, which were then forgotten for two full decades. When they were next uncovered, they were chosen by the Royal Printing Office as their standard type. Eventually this office evolved into the French National Printing Office, which officially adopted Jannon's type in 1825, erroneously crediting it to Garamond.

New Garamond fonts have poured in throughout the 1900s, predominantly based on the original work by Jannon—even the so-called Garamond-revival fonts. Typographical scholar and journalist Beatrice Warde famously corrected the misnomer in 1925, but by then, the nomenclature had already become permanent.

An inordinate number of popular book titles published this century have chosen Garamond, but its usage isn't limited to the literary world. Its extreme popularity has crept into nearly every corner of modern life.

When Apple launched the Macintosh in 1984, it developed a proprietary version of Garamond for its introduction. This Garamond dominated Apple's marketing and became a major part of their brand recognition for nearly two decades.

Nintendo chose italic Garamond in 1985 to describe the versions on their 1985 game consoles. Fifteen years later, Nintendo named a character Garamond—a successful author—in their RPG video game *Super Paper Mario*.

Though using a common font for a corporate logo can restrict trademark laws and protections, Abercrombie & Fitch chose a Garamond typeface for their famous logo, which is why it looks so familiar to you as it is printed on this page.

The same can be said for Neutrogena, who has proudly imprinted their Garamond logo on their famous bars of soap for decades, as well as their other products and accompanying packaging.

As the Garamond typeset approaches its 400th birthday—by Jannon's date of publication, not C. Garamond's—it seems there is no sign of slowing for this classic font. It may well be just as popular in another 400 years.

Apple and Macintosh are registered trademarks of Apple, Inc.
'Super Mario', 'Super Paper Mario' and 'Nintendo' are registered trademarks of Nintendo Co., Ltd.
Abercrombie & Fitch is a registered trademark of Abercrombie & Fitch Company
Neutrogena is a registered trademark of Johnson & Johnson Inc.